D1246693

HARVESTING
BALLADS

HARVESTING BALLADS

PHILIP KIMBALL

E. P. DUTTON, INC.   NEW YORK

Songs by Steven Kimball

"Isadora Whitehands Learns Who She Isn't" originally appeared in
New Mexico Humanities Review;
"Soft Shooting" originally appeared in *Green Mountain Review.*

Indian verses are from:

Walk in Your Soul by Jack Frederick and Anna Gritts Kilpatrick used
by permission of Southern Methodist University Press.

*Published in the United States by
E. P. Dutton Inc., 2 Park Avenue, New York, N. Y. 10016*

*Library of Congress Cataloging in Publication Data
Kimball, Philip.
Harvesting ballads.
I. Title.*
PS3561.I4165H3   1984   813'.54   83-27485
ISBN 0-525-24228-7

*Published simultaneously in Canada by
Fitzhenry & Whiteside Limited, Toronto*

COBE

10 9 8 7 6 5 4 3 2 1

First Edition

To Mama and Daddy, all the family,
wherever deposited in the slip of time.
For the lessons of this life,
discipline and inward calm.

HARVESTING
BALLADS

Soft Shooting

Shooting snooker and pissing in the shuffleboard machine. Seemed to be bout the only things to do in Buffalo Gap. The wind howling, hot dusty night and stars, roiled the South Dakota shortgrass prairie hills. A wind-eaten, wood-frame tavern out south of town on Highway 85. Yellow wind-tossed light on a splintered creosoted telephone pole, the gravel drive swirling up dust. A few pickups, cattle sideboards, an old blue-green GMC ton-and-a-half with a jag of wheat, scoop shovel sticking out the northwest corner of the bed. A John Deere tractor. The screen door of the place kicked out at the bottom, the front window neon *beer and wine. Open.*

Inside the air is yellow brown dust-hung smoke, vibrating, pulses beer sign lights, watch fobs turning red blue green blobs of oil and clocks. Falstaff, Miller, Bud. The jukebox plays some Kitty Wells. A long wooden bar the entire length of the building, brass rail, gray wooden stools. A nine-point buckhead glass-eyed on the wall. *We made a deal with the banker. We won't cash checks if he don't sell beer.* Fly-speckled. Uneven board floors, kernels of grain in the cracks, trod dustworn from door to bar, around the shuffleboard at the south end and the snooker table to the north. Lots of loud laughing, pounding beer glasses on the bar. Just plain ol whiskey. Cowboy boots, hightop shoes, old Levi's, Big Smith bib overalls, khaki sleeveless army shirts, discolored T-shirts on muscle dark sun harvest brown.

Snooker balls clicked thudding pocket drop and the jangling electric digit counters flash neon numbers from the shuffleboard machine. The old farmer zippered his pants, slobbering a grin, two or three brown teeth nubs, and wobbled straight-legged prostate to the door. Amber yellow foamy puddle uric across the floor around the leg of the machine. For the life of me I don't know how he kept from shorting the damn thing out and electrocuting himself.

Hank and I sat down, ordered a couple of beers. The short stubby-fingered woman behind the bar plunked down the bottles. We pull them empty.

"How's the wheat harvest looking around here?"

She washes a few glasses. "Well. I don't reckon it's gonna be the best we've ever seen. Hasn't rained in six weeks, and it's been over a hundred and four the last ten days. If you fellers is looking for wheat to cut, you might as well come back next year. A crew stopped by this morning heading back south. Say it's just as bad on up north."

"Is that right."

We ordered up another round, turned on the stools to watch the snooker game for a while. A young kid and an old guy. Pretty fair shooters. I look over to Hank and he kind of smiles.

You see, Hank taught me to shoot snooker when I was in high school back in Alva, Oklahoma. He's been working for my dad ever since I was born, and one day when I was a senior, I'd just been named to the '58 All-State football team, so was feeling pretty good, and Hank says he figgered it was time for me to learn to do something useful. Meet me out back behind the shop at noontime and I'll learn you what they don't teach in school.

Now I'd never cut class before, in fact was a pretty good student. Salutatorian of the class. Would've been valedictorian if it wasn't for Sondra taking all them English courses. Anyway, I sneak out behind the shop after Algebra 3 and hop in the old red Dodge pickup with Hank and we head for the Downtown Recreation Center. Man, I'm really feeling tough when we swagger into the place. Old Dodson behind the bar calls out hey is that man 18, Hank says hell yes, and we all laugh cause you see my football number was 18. Hank hands me a beer and racks up the balls.

"Now the secret of snooker is soft shooting."

So anyway, Hank kind of smiles at me and motions with his head toward the snooker game. I sidle up to the table. The felt is worn white at the foot spot, but no tears, table roll not too bad for Buffalo Gap. The kid racks them up at the north end. The old man studies the table, slowly chalking his cue. Nineteen-ounce. Picks up the cueball and places it in the *D* at the south end. Sights down his stick, moves the cueball to his right a sixteenth, glances over at me. A nice smooth stroke, a couple of times, then cues the ball feather-soft just below the apex of the rack, spreading the northwest vertex ball slowly rolling plop into the corner pocket. The cueball good shape on the 7. He sinks it. Spots it. Keeps on shooting. A red ball then the 7, scores 65 points before he has to take a long green shot at the 4-ball. Misses badly, looks at me again. "The ol eyes ain't what they used to be. Sometimes those balls get to shimmering, look big as watermelons, other times like damn bird shot."

I nod a smile. Hank brings another beer. The kid runs the rest of the red balls, alternating mostly the 5 and the 6-ball, misses the 2, but leaves the old man snookered behind the 4 about midtable with the 2-ball behind the 3 in the southwest corner.

The old man surveys the situation, chalks his cue. Banks off the east side rail, the head rail at the corner, a fraction between the 2 and the 3, kissing the 2 in the pocket pretty as you please. The cueball comes off the west side rail and rolls to a stop with an easy cut on the 3. I nod again. The game's over, the old man runs the rest of the balls to the 7, which he misses, glances at me grinning, the kid sinks it, the score 85 to 39.

Hank nudges me, the old man looking, I knew what was coming. And dammit, didn't really want to do it. But Hank urging me on, and besides didn't have all that much to do in the morning, and it didn't look much like we'd be getting any cutting soon. If the old man was sucker enough, might as well pick up a little change.

The kid racked them up again. The old man circled the table.

"My young friend here is had enough. Either of you interested in shooting a game or two?"

Hank says naw.

"How about you, Butch?"

Makes me a little mad. Be glad to take the bastard's money. Talking about my hair. Normally long and curly, blond, especially after being out in the sun all harvest, but got it all burned off down by Gordon.

Gordon, Nebraska. Population 2,060. A thousand white people, a thousand Sioux. And sixty dogs. We'd pulled in from Alliance, but it was still too green to combine, so we park our rigs on a vacant lot right next to the sale barn, right on the railroad tracks in the Indian part of town. Not much to do. Go down ever day to the state Department of Labor to see if we could find anybody whose wheat was ready, and that was about it. Read. Walk around town, through the sand-blown houses of Indian territory. People stolid quiet on their porches. In the streets at night, war whoops and call.

I'd shoot snooker down at the Alamo Bar. Or just sit around in the shade of the tarp, strung from the old International Harvester to a telephone pole, playing my steel-bodied guitar and singing.

Actually, spent my eighteenth birthday in Gordon. Hank and I had strawberry malts down at the Frigid Queen. Called Dad. Back home holding down the fort. My mother died in California when I was born.

I had to register for the draft some kind of way. Found out the closest draft board was in Rushville, so that night I get my towel and soap, hadn't had a bath in two or three weeks, and snuck over to the cattle pens, found an empty stall, hung my shorts and towel over the fence post and slipped into the water tank. Next day I head for Rushville and register. When it came time for the man to fill in the question about race, he looks at me. "You are white, aren't you?"

I guess I was pretty tanned. But seems like he could tell from my hair.

Which is what I was telling you about, how I got it all burned off.

After about three weeks of waiting around, I'm about going crazy. I can't take it doing nothing. Tinker with the combine and

4

truck, but there's only so much tuning you can do. Playing the guitar helps a little, but not sixteen hours a day. I like shooting snooker too. Only been at it six or seven months, but after about the first week, I haven't been beaten. Still I only like it if there's some sucker to be hustled that thinks he's tough shit. I just can't play for the fun of it.

But like I was saying, we finally got some cutting, together with this other crew. We had our beat-up International and they had a brand spanking new Gleaner Baldwin. Seems this guy, Ray Henry I believe his name was, had worked the harvest all his life for other people, mostly with the Wiley outfit from Texas. Twelve combines, twelve ton-and-a-halfs, five pickups with 20-foot house trailers, three cooks, crew of about thirty. Man, when they pull onto the highway the convoy stretches for over a mile down the road. And on a good day they can clean out two sections of wheat. Well, Ray Henry finally saved enough money for a down payment on his own machine and this was his first year on his own. Sort of down on his luck though. The worst harvest in recent memory, and him having to make installments on the Gleaner and the truck. And we get this job together, cause the farmer wants to get it in quick before the sun burns it up. Had turned hot and dry you see.

So we pull in, and I mean to tell you it is hot. Must have been 107 in the shade by eleven o'clock, and of course out on the combine there wasn't much shade. A nice gentle southern breeze. Just enough to blow all the dust and chaff and engine heat over on you when you're heading north. I mean the metal is so damn hot you can't touch it. Take your hand off the steering wheel for a second it almost blisters when you put it back. Wind ripples white heat. Hot. Rolling countryside as far as you can see in wheat. White blue sky. The sun so hot you can't even see it.

I'm in a trance. Following Ray Henry's Baldwin about two hundred yards back. Shimmering silver reverberates trembling white blue radiation. Numb pain. Should stop. Get out of this sun. I don't. Can do it.

Each round we unload on the go. I give the signal to Hank in the truck. He pulls up alongside the combine, hanging out the door standing on the running board leaning looking over the cab, easing in up close to me, sighting the truck fender and the combine header barge. We're rolling, gaining and failing over terraces tipping side to side, five miles an hour, chewing up a 14-foot-wide swath of 30-bushel wheat. Hank's got it now. I trip the lever with my heel and the unloading auger kicks in, bursting chaff at the spout, dumping grain into the truck bed. We're rating each other trailing wheat berries, beard bits, weed seed and dust on the wind. Till the bin's empty. Hank signals want-a-break. I shake my head and he peels off out across the white hot dust and stubble yellow blown.

I jump up a rabbit. She springs along in front of the sickle bar. The sickle guards race mesmerizing seeder rows, reelslats slapping wheatstocks down into the auger, bunching to the center flashing cylinder fingers grab it in. The cottontail zagging on back and forth in front of it all, a hundred yards, go girl get it. Until she tires of it and veers off into the uncut wheat. I laugh weakly. And the heat.

Finally the truck is too full to unload on the go. Have to stop. I'm weak and dizzy, mouth clammy sticky thick, almost slip off the ladder getting down. Feel like I need to piss, but the dick's shriveled, dull ache at the base, bladder, burning urethra dark brown single drop. Need to get out of this sun. Drink as much water as I can. Hank leans over the sideboard. "Want me to take her a round or two?"

"Naw."

Pull myself back up, put her in gear and take off. Hank heads for the elevator. I fix on Ray Henry's Gleaner in front of me, disintegrating now and then, silver, orange blobs oscillating incandescent mirage water silver blue.

Damn. Like to lie down. Somewhere. Cool.

We fill up Ray's truck, his 13-year-old kid driving. Hank gets back from the elevator. Pulls up alongside the Gleaner. Ray signals stop. Jumps down and Hank climbs up to take over. I unload on the go, Ray Henry driving the truck now. Can't cut wheat like me, Ray.

Yeah. Ray a little down on his luck. First day in the field with his new Baldwin back in Carmen, Oklahoma, his boy forgot about the unloading auger spout, took her a little too close to a telephone pole, ripped the whole damn side off the grain bin. Got her baling-wired together, and the next day the kid forgot that the clutch locks when you set the handbrake. And broke the damn lock off trying to engage the clutch. Yeah, Ray. Heat a little too much for you.

Heat. Engine throbbing, cylinder hiss and moan. Dust prisms

the sun drifting from the Gleaner's straw-walker in front of me. Silver orange. Sun. Orange heat. Distorting an orange ball to fire in the sun. Growing, bleaching color, all color gone, just an orange ball of fire growing on the side of the Gleaner Baldwin. Then it falls. Disappears in the stubble. Reappears orange. Growling closer. Fire. That is. A. God. Damn.

FIRE!

I stop. Real jolt of adrenalin. There's a three-foot circle of fire in the wheat right in front of my header barge. Look around. Alone. The highest point in the field. Sloping south yellow stubble, green sunflower fence row and the next field. Niobrara River basin meandering beyond it. No one. North, white long-bearded heads of uncut wheat ebb and flow. Half-mile to the fields across the road. Grain elevator on the horizon. Hank's up ahead disappearing over the next hill. Probably singing one of those goddam cowboy songs his friend wrote, like he always does, not paying attention. Black smoke swirls up around my combine. Four-foot fire circle. I'd better do something. Quick.

I grab my shirt from the railing, leap to the ground, four-foot fire isn't much. Can beat it out. It's five foot now, the melted handbrake housing on the ground in the middle of it. Ray set the brake, the clutch lock still broken. Hank didn't realize and drove off with the handbrake set.

Wind whips sudden flames in my face. And I thought the sun was hot, start pounding the fire with the shirt. Excitement. Joy. I can do it. One half out, I leap to the other side of the circle, beat it out. But the first half starting up again, seven foot. I jump back over, wind churning up the flames straight for the uncut wheat, the combine. Heat keeps driving me back.

Fire! I gotta save the machine. Fly up the ladder, throw her into high gear, she shudders shakes moans, doesn't move. Reelslats batting flames, black smoke, hell of a time for a breakdown goddam nervous bustdown of some kind. God damn, the grain bin two-thirds full eighteen hundred pounds of wheat. The belt drive can't cope in high. Too heavy, the belt from the engine slipping and whining on the drive pulley, I shift to second and the combine jumps off leaping fire. I'm standing on the platform hanging on the steering wheel bouncing down the hill yelling and waving like a wild man.

7

Finally catch Hank on the Gleaner at the truck in the west end of the field. Sure enough singing. Point back east at the boiling black cloud, point down at the handbrake shoe missing from Ray's combine. A look of panic in the truck cab, Ray leaping out, dashing up the ladder, almost pushes Hank off the platform, yells follow me, and something about no insurance. Dumping wheat on the ground to get rid of ballast as he heads the Gleaner back east into the fire. Hank motions with his head. "You go on. I'm gonna get our rigs out of the field."

I haul ass off running after Ray, shirt flapping in my hand, bout to break my knees on uneven earth beneath the stubble, heading for the high ground. The sky is turning black.

What the Sam Hill am I doing this for?

The fire is plenty big. About an acre burned off already. Ten, twelve-foot flames cracking and popping air superheated convection wind. Nasal passages and lungs searing hot. Ray gone plumb crazy seems to me, got the header in the dirt wide open, thrashing fire. Man, the wheatstocks piled up on the cylinder housing are burning, fire spewing from the straw-walker, belching from the grain bin, licking around him standing up there on the Gleaner Baldwin spread-legged, left hand spinning the steering knob, the right on the variable speed, dust smoke and fire, his eyes are bugging out crazy.

I start running after him, beating out little fires with my shirt. He plows through the flames spreading smoke dust and burning straw out the ass-end. I'm highstepping firedancing flamejumping, my black canvas cross-country shoes soaking in the heat, hot foot like you've never seen whooping and hollering and damn if I'm not laughing like a crazy man myself.

Stop to catch your breath where you think the fire's out and a loud pop behind you, jump around and a single two-foot yellow flame cracking up your ass. Whop it once, another crack behind, whop. The whole horizon on fire cresting the hill, crack whop, Ray and his combine some insane insect breathing flames.

I take out running after them again across the fiery blackened wilderness.

What happened to Hank?

North, ten, fifteen acres black smoldering blue, crescent of fire almost to the road, the next field, out of control. The elevator on the horizon, the entire state of Nebraska to the north, gone. The Dakotas. Clear to the Canadian tundra, what could stop it.

Lean back. Alone. Crack. Whop whop. Out of my hands. Pace yourself. To chase this lunatic all the way to Saskatoon.

Fire along the fence row. Jump the road anytime now. Here comes Hank. Some others. In pickups, cars. The neighbors to help. An old Poppin' Johnny bounces over the field to the fence to plow a fire line, the man driving reaches back to sink the shears pulls the rope. Just rope. The plow jarred off back at the gate coming into the field. Everybody laughing now but Ray. Fire in the ditch will jump. But we're caught up laughing anyhow.

The wind changes suddenly. Folding flames back, consuming themselves. And quicker than it started. It was out.

Before the Gordon Volunteer Fire Department got there in the 1946 fire truck. And nothing to squirt. But each other. Good thing it didn't last longer than fifteen minutes, it would have killed me.

Back at the truck I find out it lasted two and a half hours. Hank hands me a Grain Belt beer. I wipe my brow, run my hand through my. Stubble. Briar. Singed stench stick brittle burned. Head and face, eyebrows. Gone.

"How bout you, Butch? Want to shoot a friendly game?"

"I reckon I got time for a game or two. But I only learned to play bout eight months ago."

"Well, son, we'll see how she goes. You lag first."

I roll a few cues on the tabletop. Mighty crooked some of them. Find a good one, but only 17-ounce. A little light for my taste. Hold it in my right, chalk the tip with my left. A few people along the bar turn to watch. A little uneasy. I toss the cueball up and down in my right hand, put it down at the balk line. Left hand bridge, intentionally stroking too hard up and back bouncing three feet off the head rail. I smile. The old man breaks. Doesn't sink anything, leaves me a good easy run of six or seven balls, but I miss the third one on purpose. He sinks a couple, misses. Neither of us doing real well. Finally I run the last four balls and win by two points.

"Rack em up."

He wins the second and the third games. "How bout making it a little more interesting, Butch?"

Got him right where I want him. "Whatcha mean?"

"Putting a little side bet down."

A couple of harvest hands amble over from the bar, pull up stools around the table. I scratch my head. "I don't usually play for money. How much you have in mind, ol man?"

"Oh, couple a dollars a game. Just to make it interesting."

"I guess I can afford that."

Get our money out. He's got a pretty big wad. Sudden excitement. But should I take it from an old man. Guess he's kind of asking for it.

"Your break, Butch."

More people watching. Makes me a little bit nervous. Get another beer. Look at Hank. Nothing. I break, put one in the northeast corner, but miss an easy shot on the 5. Nervous. But doesn't matter. The old man goes on to win the game by three, just the way I wanted. I win the next two. Then let him win five straight, each game getting better, fancier shots. In the ninth game I'm leading by twenty with the 4, 5, 6 and 7-balls left. The old man's snookered. About six inches away in front of the east side pocket, lined up north to south, the cueball, the 6 and the 4, with the 5 blocking the pocket right on the lip. Shakes his head, chalks his cue, circles the table rapidly a few times looking here and there at the angles, stops on the east side. He cues a little high left english, almost straight across the table. Hits the west side rail just north of the side pocket, caroms east-southeast back across. Kisses the 4 hard on the southwest, drives it off the east side rail, just south of the pocket, past the 5 back across. Slow easy roll to the west side pocket, hesitating, drop, plop, a burst of clapping, pounding on the bar. I smile weakly. "Hell of a shot, ol man."

He nods, quickly sinks the 5 and 6, just five points down now, long green on the 7, but an easy, almost straight-in shot. Chalks his cue. Leans over the table. Misses the shot. The crowd groans, he rubs his eyes looking at the lights above the table. "Damn."

I put it in. "Rack."

"Naw, Butch. I've had enough. The old eyes, you know."

"You gotta give a feller a chance to win back his money, ol man. I'm six bucks down."

Rubs the eyes. "Well, maybe a few more."

"How bout making it ten bucks a game this time?"

Pause. Shrugs resigned. "Sure thing, Butch."

Lots of people around the table. Cigarette, cigar smoke. Ten-gallon hats, Caterpillar, straw. Leather burned cheeks and noses, pale forehead harvest dust creases wrinkled smiles and toothless grins around tobacco stains. The air close, loud. I lean over to break, sight down the long tapering cue leather tip white stained blue, left hand first finger hooked to thumb blue chalk, the cue gliding back and through feeling smooth, feeling good, so much noise. Balk line *D*. Yellow green brown, middle spot blue 5, foot spot 6 pink rack red in front of the black 7. Balls reflecting the hooded lights, glowing table felt, green worn rails, shadows, dark grain wood, cigarette burns, faces. Noise. The old man standing at the foot, leaning on his cue, both hands, right above left, holding near the tip, smiles down. At me. I can do it ten dollars a game. Better do it. Only thirty dollars between us. Hank. Where's Hank.

Bad break. The old man cleans up, I'm hopelessly behind after the first inning. Not bad for tired eyes. Hank at the bar. I run the rest of the table, too late, ten dollars a game, but feeling better. Ready to get him now. Crowd friendly to me, on my side. Crowds always love. The underdog?

I win the next game. And the next. Easily. He's too old to keep up, and my big surprise still to come. Win the next. Okay. Ease up a little. Lose. And again. Win. And lose three in a row. Twenty-six bucks down. Time to raise the . . .

"Sorry, Butch, but I gotta go. Practice a little and maybe I can give you another chance sometime."

"Come on, ol man. I'm just getting warmed up. I mean you're the one wanted to play in the first place. We'll make it thirty dollars a game."

"Naw. I'm too old for this kind of carrying on. I just wanted a friendly game, didn't know you was such a hotshot, Butch. You take the game too serious."

Everybody gone quiet. Watching a. "Okay, tell you what, ol man. We'll make it fifty a game. And I'll shoot left-handed."

Pause. The old man strokes the chin whiskers, leaning on his cue. Slowly smiles. "Make that two-fifty, Butch." Silence sudden rushing whistles, laughter, shuffling feet on the board floors. "And

I couldn't have you shooting left-handed. What would people think? Besides. Your left hand might be wet from those beer bottles you been picking up with it."

My asshole drops to the floor. He knows. Panic flutters my rib cage. I am. Left-handed. I've been hustled. Bad eyes. Look for Hank. Everybody looking at me. Can't back out now. Can't quit. Can't let an old man beat me. But. He is old. I can shoot almost as good right. Two hundred fifty dollars. Don't have two hundred fifty. Other than operating money. Have to win the first game. Can't back out, hasn't shown me anything much. Let him win most of the games. A few lucky shots. Two-fifty.

Hank pushes through the crowd. "Come on. We gotta be going. Gotta pull on north tomorrow early."

Everybody waiting, watching. Sweat fills my eyesockets. The small of the back. About to explode. Run for the door. But can't. I can do it, let me do it, Hank. "You go on, Hank. I gotta teach this old man a lesson in how to shoot snooker."

Hank looks hard at me. Can't read what he's thinking. Looks at the old man. Back at me. Remembering something. Smiles. Slowly reaches in his pocket, pulls out the keys to the Dodge and hands them to me. "Okay. I'll hitch on back to camp."

The young kid that was playing before. "I'll take you back, sir."

The prairie wind billows dust through the door as they leave. Me alone in the middle of. Throat dry. Can't even afford another beer. Maybe I.

"Let's lag again for break, Butch."

"Sh. Sure."

I push through to the wall for some talc. Hands nervous wet. Rub down my cue, chalk the tip. Steady now. Two hundred and fifty. More talc. Look at the wall, the rack of cues. Out through the window, the highway curving off shining asphalt blue. Wind roughs the buffalo grass, brome, grama grass receding brown Dakota steppes and night.

Take a deep breath and go back to the table. My lag rolls to a stop an inch away from the head rail. Not too bad. Shouts, that a way, Butch, go get him now. Side bets. Didn't know there were so many people in Buffalo Gap. The old man steps up. The cueball doesn't even seem to change speed. Up and back, stops dead a quarter of an inch from the rail. Eyes. My ass. He sinks two red balls on the break, then the 7. Spots it, sinks another red ball, the 7 again, a red ball. But no shot on the 7 this time, the 5 his shot. Pretty thin cut, but still. He misses. Maybe his eyes are. "What's the matter, ol man? Light hurt your eyes? You might as well start counting out the two-fifty now."

"Butch. You're a good shooter. But you don't know nothing."

I need to piss all of a sudden. Damn beers. I've got him. Wasn't putting on about his eyes. Didn't leave me much, but. "Be back in a second."

Make my way to the head, feeling good. Just win the first game and the pressure's off. Pine board walls, initials, penciled, carved, piss and shit permeate the nostrils, *you cant shit here your assholes in Washington. Meet me six o'clock. Suck big dick. Indian Pussy 301-7084.* Yellow black streaked blue plastic screen soaked cigarette butts trickling nicotine brown. Speckled mirror broken. Tin boxes for the prevention of disease only. Special lubricating. Twenty-five cents. Pleasure bladder draining. Two hundred and fifty.

"Is the game over yet, buddy?" Stall door, cowboy boots, dungarees bunched around the ankles.

"What?"

"Has the ol man wiped the kid's ass yet?"

"Not yet. What makes you so sure he's gonna beat the kid?"

"Don't you know who that is?"

"Can't say that I do."

"That's Sapulpa Slim."

Pause. "So?"

"Saw him win four hundred bucks off a feller just the other night over to Camp Crook. Some a the best snooker I ever seen. Suckered that boy right in, give him the same horseshit bout his eyes, then let him have it good."

"Oh yeah?"

"They say he owns a pool hall down in Oklahoma. Won it too. Came into town one day with nothing but his stick in a leather case. Started shooting snooker. Taking on all comers, just barely beating ever body. Shot four days straight. Ever pool shark in Oklahoma and southeastern Kansas hearing about it, coming to knock him off and leaving town broke. Greyhound bus station full of down-in-the-mouth punks trying to hustle their way back home.

"Well, the owner of the place decided it was time to put a stop to it. Screwed together his cue, and they started shooting for a thousand dollars a game. The old man been up going on ninety-six hours. The owner won the break and ran six straight games before the old man even got to shoot. Down to his last thousand.

"By this time the news of the game had spread from the Dakotas to Texas, the Rockies to the Mississippi, and the pool hall jammed full, people standing on the bar, sitting in the rafters, money flying ever which way in the side bets. Ever kind a flimflam card shark pickpocket and whore in seven states gathering to get part of the action. Couple a beer trucks a day to keep the place supplied. The old man won the seventh game to keep himself alive, and they traded games for bout the next twelve hours. No one wanted to leave. Sleeping out in cars in the street, under tables. Card games, fistfights breaking out. But nothing seemed to disturb the center table. Dead quiet. Just the click of the balls, ivory rolling over felt and pocket fall.

"Long about noon of the fifth day Slim commence to win. Four out of seven. Then three out of five. Two out of three. Then three or four straight. Finally the owner took his cue apart, returned it to its place under the bar, washed his hands and face. And said he quit. Tapioca. Who was next.

" 'Hold on,' says Slim. 'Don't look to me like the best shooter in all the shortgrass country ought to sell the farm till it's over.'

" 'It's over. I got no more money.'

" 'I got bout fifteen thousand here says you got one more good game in you.' And the old man plops the whole wadded bundle onto the table.

" 'And you got the deed to this here fine establishment.'

"Well, the place got mighty quiet. Slim standing at the corner pocket leaning on his cue. The balls glowing racked and ready. The owner, hands spread out on top on the bar, sleeves rolled up, vest hanging loose open. Looking at Slim. Trying to consider. A couple of minutes seems like. Like he's trying to see through the dark, but he can't.

" 'Well. What about it, Buck? You afraid of a tired old man? Your friends is waiting to hear.'

"Big old pendulum clock ticking. He reaches under the bar, pulls out his cue again. Has a little trouble getting it together. 'Let's shoot snooker.'

"So they say Sapulpa Slim's settled down now. But ever year he gets the urge, and follows the harvest hustling. Him and his two boys. That was one of them he was playing with earlier. Just a couple weeks ago they broke both a feller's arms over in Minnekahta. Tried to welsh on a bet. Yeah, they's serious pool shooters. No question about it. Is the kid still playing him out there?"

I don't answer. The toilet flushes, I lean over the sink, throw handfuls of cold water. Look in the mirror, the cowboy, short stocky. Big-headed bald, gold wire glasses askew, standing behind me devilish grinning. "Didn't know it was you, kid. Hope I didn't scare you none." Laughs, swings out the door, a quick glimpse, Sapulpa Slim standing at the table leaning on his cue.

Stench fills up. My stomach convulses. Run. But they know. Took Hank back. They know where we are. Look around the toilet. Keep calm. Exhaust fan over the stool. Go in, lock the stall door, climb up on the tank. Screwed on, fifteen coats of old paint. Try my pocketknife. No good. Sweating good now. Someone bound to come. Been in a long time. No good. Water pipes along the ceiling. Leap up, grab swing both feet crashing into the fan, push back swing again crash, metal bending crash, everybody can hear, wood splintering crash flying out fan falling to the ground outside. Me sitting in the split sill, window just big enough, I think, my hips filling it up, to squeeze out, splinters tearing at me, get the keys in my hand, shirt ripping. Caught. Legs dangling out, kicking. Damn. Foot finds something, support. Work the shoulders and head through, bleeding a little, look down.

"Howdy, Butch."

Standing on the shoulders of Sapulpa Slim's boy. The other looking on. The moon dusty yellow. Wind.

"Going somewheres?"

"Just getting a little fresh air."

Grabs for my ankles just as I leap up catching the rain gutter with one hand, feet back on the sill, I spring one leg over and onto the roof. Yelling and shouting below. I clamor to the ridge pole, look around, Slim's boys circling the parking lot. The GMC pulling out, I sprint down the shingles, leap and just clear the tailgate, up to my ass in wheat, heading north on Highway 85.

We turn east off the road and I see the '56 Ford throwing rocks and dust out of the parking lot. I vault the sideboard and double hit the ditch at twenty miles an hour, rolling forty feet into a bunch of prickly pear. Lie there hoping they didn't see. Ford drifts the corner, fishtails by almost on me in the ditch, taillights disappear in dust.

I wait. Nothing. Get up and dog out on to the dark windy prairie.

Where. They know the camp. Hank. Damn, don't get Hank.

Walk about a mile out on to the steppe. Nothing but wind. Dark. Muscles beginning to ache and stiffen. Then I hear. Carried on the wind. Dry bearing creaking metal rattle. Creak. Creak. Clang. A windmill. Pumping. Somewhere.

I walk through a long arroyo. Up an incline, table rock. Plateau. Creak. Clang. A coyote yapping. Answered. Wind moaning sighs in the draws. A tumbleweed bounces by. Prairie dog mounds. A large bird hovering before the eyes, flutters about my head. Coo-coooo. Coo-coooo.

The sky is clear now. Moon. Big Dipper. North Star. Shadows. Windmill drifting hot dry wind.

Feeling good now.

Alone.

A part of the plains.

Prologue One

Prismed morning mist rises. Commingled excited shouts. Long black-haired sweating copper women bore a litter, la Dama de Cofitachequi, Princesa de los Indios. Forest. The Spanish cavalry, snorting groaning seven hundred horses, polished armor. Silk, velvet. Lances, banners. Foot soldiers filed behind, grumbling, singing, cursing cold above iron clanging chains, collars of Tameme slaves purchased in solemn barter from chiefs for looking glasses, false pearls, glass beads, caps of yellow satin, plumes adorned with silver, velvet aprons. Knives. Carrying mattocks, spades, shoulders of bacon, quintals of cassavas, hanegas of maize. Packs of bloodhounds. Droves of swine along the ten-thousand-year-old trail.

They topped the high divide between the Savannah River and the Saluda, down into the valleys, through villages, Chalique, Gualquila, Xuala. Naked Sioux gathering along the way to gaze, offering wild hens and possum as gifts. North along the Winding Stair Trail over a craggy ridge into the foothills of the southern Alleghenies. Along the White River, skirting Glade Mountain, turning west into the highlands. Descending Cullasaja Gorge, across the Little Tennessee River on to a plain, ascending the valley of the Cartoochaye, across Black Gap, down the valleys of Shooting Creek, Hiwassee Creek to Peachtree Creek and the settlement of Guasili.

May 1540. El Conquistador, Hernando De Soto, paid visit to the Cherokee. Passing through ancestral highlands. Without trace in legend. Or myth.

But it has led to this.

Old-Timer Takes a Drink

THEM damn Indians weren't doing nothing with it. Hell." Old man unshaven, double-breasted pinstriped, crumpled. Both elbows, hands cradled round an empty shot glass. "Give me nother shot, cousin. Double or nothing."

Bartender, drying glasses, looks dubious. Considers. Looks around. Empty bar. Shrugs, takes a bottle from beneath, shielding from the old man's view. Pours. "Here you go, old-timer."

Holds the glass left-handed to the light, sniffs, eyes smiling. Takes a taste, smacking lips. "Mighty good. Let's see. Scotch. But you knew I'd get that." Another taste. "Eighty-six proof. Um. Barley." Holds to the light again. "Uh-huh. Old Smuggler."

"Hot damn." Sets him up two more.

"Thank you kindly, son. Like I was telling you. The Indians not producing a thing with all that land. Sure the Cherokees was renting grazing land to cattlemen, but when Congress outlawed that, what could they do with it? Besides, they was flat in the way of the railroads west to the coast, California and Oregon, and south to Texas. Just didn't make any kind of sense keeping settlers out of the Indian Territory. A real mess.

"Well, I was just a young whippersnapper, itchy feet you know, left the farm in Indiana and headed for the big city. Looking for work I told my ol man. In Chicago. Quite a town back in them days. Not full of gangsters like now, none of these Capones and Dillingers, Legs Diamond, like they got now. Just honest-to-God, rough-an-tumble hard-drinking swine-herding Hoosiers come to town to market the pigs and have a good time. And honest hard-working railroad men. Discovered hic, scuse me, soon discovered I much preferred drinking whiskey and playing cards to looking for work. I was tough in them days. Not enough liquor in Cook County to get me drunk." Finishes the glass off. "But there's sure enough now, friend. Try it again?" Empty afternoon bar. Bartender vacantly shrugs, wipes a glass, sets him up. "Double or nothing?"

"Sure thing."

Old man sips. "Um, lordy. Mighty smooth. You sticking to Scotch. Think maybe we didn't have no fancy stuff out in the Oklahoma District. Spensive too. Like it's too good for some ol rum-dumb, heh, Junior? That whatcha think? That this ol rum-bum Okie ain't hic ain't never had no Chevas Regal before?"

Slaps forehead. "God almighty." Pours two more.

"That's the time."

"You were saying."

"Huh? Oh yeah. Spent a lot of time in the bars and gambling houses. Seems I lost and drank gallons more than I won though. Had to find some kind of work. Well, one night I sees this drunk swineherd out in front of a saloon. Needs a drink real bad, just him and a horse. Damn fine horse too. So I sidles up nice and friendly, start a friendly conversation. Well, you know there are two things you can't talk to, and that's a preacher and a drunk, but I start admiring the horse and ask if it's his. He blinks at it couple of times, says hell yes. I tell him I'd sure like to have a horse, but all I had to my name was a fifth of real good drinking whiskey. I keep a talking, he a blathering, me bout how much I like his horse and he bout how much he needs a drink. Before you know it, I was the owner of one of the finest cow ponies ever come up the trail. And I had found my job. My career. Took that pony, and before the day was out I'd horsetraded it up to three, sold one, put the others in the livery stable and had one hell of a celebration. A horsetrader, goddamn. See this." Fumbles, pulls a gold watch from his vest pocket by the chain.

Takes it, examines impatiently. "Pretty nice watch."

Retrieves watch. Bartender still holding chain, looking at the fob. Old man opens the back, displaying engraved factory. "But look a here. Illinois Watch Company. And there's . . ."

"What's W.O.W.?"

"What?" Looks at fob. "Oh. That's Woodsmen of the World."

"Maple leaf with a crossed ax and hammer over a tree stump. And what's that?"

Taking fob. Squinting. "A bird with a twig in its beak."

"A dove and olive branch."

"Olive?"

"Yeah. For peace."

Holds at arm's length. "You don't say. All these years I wondered bout that. And the stump has a wedge in it. But I want to show you the back. See that?"

Takes watch. "A horse." Sudden smile. "Your horsetrading watch."

Impatient. "Yeah. But look at that horse."

"Yeah. He's grinning, isn't he?"

Laughs. "That's what first tracted my attention. Some feller down in Coffeyville, Kansas, was a looking for a horse. Didn't have much, wanting to get a wagon and some supplies to go down and stake him a claim. All the Boomers were gathering in Coffeyville and Independence in them days, 18—what was it—1879 must of been. Feller name of Carpenter come down from the Dakotas to organize. You see, in them days ever body was moving west. Lots of excitement. I mean to tell you the hotels and boardinghouses was full, the saloons a bustling, wagons ever where, tents and lean-tos. Campfire smoke. Steaming stews. Folks milling around, talking, singing. All looking for a homestead in the territory they all figgered was gonna be opened up soon. You see, Carpenter was encouraging ever body to come an join in an invasion. He figgered to force the opening. He'd already opened up the Black Hills few years back when they found gold, and the government really didn't do much to stop him, kind of like they really didn't care. In fact, sort of wanted the territory opened up. Needed a railroad and so on. Couldn't come right out and tell the Indians they was taking it back though. Set up another, friend."

"Okay." Goes below the bar, pours, sets glass before the old man.

"Let's see. Bourbon this time, huh?"

"Guess I can't fool you, old man."

"Ol man is right. Old Granddad."

"Right again."

"You betcha." Takes a shot, wipes mouth with back of hand. "Anyway. This young feller with the watch I was telling you about had a pretty little wife. Not many women and childrens around, but some in them days, and this feller had need of a horse, but could scarcely put food on the table, and I notice his watch. Well, I was bout half drunk at the time, and I sees this horse grinning golden and reckoned I just had to have that timepiece. Sort of tooken a liking to the feller anyway, so I give him a dandy Appaloosa for it, even trade."

Impatient. "How did you get from Chicago to Coffeyville?"

Gazing at watch. "Yeah, look at him just a grinning."

"How did you get to Coffeyville?"

"Well, I was in Chicago."

"I know."

"Like I was telling you, I was a horsetrader. Damn good one too. But had the urge to move on. The frontier opening up. Where'd be a better place for a horsetrader. And besides, I was making a few enemies. Chicago was a pretty rough town. You see, I was getting tired of paying for all my good times, and those of some of my worthless friends, with my horses. I had developed by this time quite a taste for whiskey and figgered I knew a better way of paying for it. I'd come into a place and bet the barkeep, or any other sucker. Scuse me, no offense intended. Anybody that wanted, I could identify any glass of spirits set before me. And I could, as you know."

Bartender plunks down another jigger. "Try this."

Tosses it down in one swallow. "Rémy Martin."

"Sonnuva bitch!"

"Well, one day I walks into this bar and challenges the bartender. He says okay, goes under the bar and comes up with a tumblerful. I takes a sip, notice ever body standing around kind of snickering and laughing. Like I was about to be fooled or something. Had quite a reputation you know. But they couldn't put one over on me. I sips again. Looks around says hey, this hogwash is homemade. Everbody hoots and hollers.

" 'Not too bad either. For poison. Onliest thing wrong is it tastes a little too coppery and leathery.'

" 'What!' says the barman. 'I made that personally, and happen to know it's the best goldurn sipping whiskey this side of Kentucky. The recipe my ol granddaddy give me.'

"I takes another slash. 'Did your granddaddy say to spice it with copper and leather?'

" 'Look, buster.'

"Goes to a hogshead he's got in the corner, draws off another glass of amber liquid, holds it up into a ray of afternoon sun piercing the smoky innards of the place and it shines like a torch in his hand.

" 'Mighty perty,' I says. 'And I can see the copper and leather stain from here. Whatcha do to your granddad that he'd want to kill you?'

"Ever body round laughing now. The man behind the bar getting powerful mad. I down the glass. 'But never mind the copper and leather. Where's my ten dollars?'

" 'You didn't win no bet, there ain't no copper and leather.'

"Now I'm getting mad. The man's refusing to pay up. And the people around getting mad, arguing over the side bets, jeering and a funning the bartender pushing and a shoving. Pretty rough place in the best of times and the barkeep pulls out a ax handle from under and pounds the bar. Someone crashes a glass on the floor. And I duck, not being a violent man myself, ten dollars ain't worth no cracked skull, just as someone tosses a bottle a hooch flying, and I'm wondering why such emotions is being displayed over a glass of moonshine. But don't think I'll stick around to find out. Crawling along the brass rail toward the door, raining glass, beer, wine and whiskey, I picks up a fifth of Tennessee's best rolling my way among the boots and shoes kicking and scuffling. I mean, after all I did win the bet fair and square. Meanwhile up above all hell is breaking loose. Yelling and cursing, tables and chairs crashing all over the place, a real knock-down drag-out I still can't understand, when a feller falls spitting teeth beside me, wipes the blood away with his sleeve sputtering 'goddam union fink,' jumps to his feet, two hands pound on his chest and he's back down. I looks out across the floor. Workingmen's boots, blue-and-white-striped billed caps with floppy tops. Dawns on me I'm in a doggone working man's railroad bar down by the roundhouse and they're fighting about the strike. It was, what was it, sure, bout fifty years ago, 1877. Big strike. Unionizing the railroad."

"But you were telling about the Indians and how you got to Kansas."

"Oh yeah. Sure. But let me tell you what happened. I didn't want no part in no union brawl, so I commence to scurry cross the floor on all fours again. Bout the time I reach the end of the bar some big ol feller picks up a guy standing right in front of me by the throat and crotch and heaves him crash bang against the wall behind the bar knocking the goddam shelf down with the hogshead of homemade Kentucky rolling down the plank, jumping the space between, bouncing along the bar and busting onto the floor. Man alive I'm a telling you the whiskey splashed every which a way, washing folks off their feet and slosh out into the street. And right there in the middle of the iron rings and oaken staves on the whiskey wet floor was a copper washer with a leather strap hitched to it!"

"Aw. Come on, old-timer."

Laughs till he coughs. "I wouldn't kid you."

"Get on with the Indians."

"Sure thing. But how bout another round?"

"All right." Hands up a glass of clear liquid.

Picks it up, sniffs, stumbles from the stool to get closer to the light, eyes large in terror. "What's this? Water? Gin? Vodka? Now no self-respecting drinking man's gonna touch this!"

"You said any spirits."

"I did, huh?"

"Yep."

Climbs back on the stool. "You want to double the bet?"

"You old codger. Drink up."

Tosses it down, throws head back and gargles, trickling out the sides of the mouth. "Vodka. Pushkin."

"Amazing."

Spits into the spittoon. "But you don't expect me to swallow this shit, do you?"

"Okay. Okay." Pours three fingers of bourbon. "Get on with the Indians."

"Well. I was getting restless. Tired of hanging around the big city. And besides, was finding it increasingly difficult getting any takers at the bars. The winter of '79 I believe, when I finally decides it's time to move on. Sitting in a downtown tavern one afternoon in February. Seems like it was snowing outside. In any case, cold as a well-digger's knee and wind a blowing to beat the band. Just sitting there buying my own drinks, feeling windy, cold winter. This feller sits down next to me, an Indian feller, dressed in a damn cutaway. Bowler hat. Looked mighty well-to-do. Start passing the time a day, what a cold day it is, the usual stuff. Talking bout winters we'd seen, and this Indian tells me he's a Cherokee. In fact sort of a big-deal Cherokee. A representative of his tribe to the Confederate States during the war, and so on. Course I don't believe him, but I got nothing better to do on a cold day, so I let the Indian talk. Don't hurt me none listening. I tell em I'm a horsetrader, getting the urge to move on, out west somewheres. He says maybe he could help, being a big chief or whatever. Says there's plenty of land in Indian Territory. Not even being used, Kiowa, Comanche, Apache, Cheyenne, Arapaho, Seminole, Chickasaw. Had a newspaper, the *Chicago Times*, showed me a article about it. Written by a Indian named Boudinot. Cornelius. Something like that.

" 'Who's that,' I asks.

" 'That's me,' he answers.

" 'No lie,' I says. Course I don't believe him. He hinted around he was working for the railroad and they wanted the Indian lands divided among the Indians, each one getting a few acres, and all they wasn't using homesteaded. So that the railroads could get a toehold. Land grants for building and so on. Lots of money to be made. All the adjoining states wanted it. Sending resolutions to Congress, agitating. Big business. Big money. This Cornelius Boudinot claimed he was in contact with attorneys for Missouri, Kansas and the Texas Railroad. Even showed me a map of where the land was. Said if I was really interested in moving on, there was the place to go and stake me a claim. Just a matter of time before Congress organized the Indian Territory, the Oklahoma District. It all sounded pretty good."

"Was he really a chief?"

"Naw. But I often wished I could see that Indian again, whoever he was. Think about him a lot, how he changed my life. Wouldn't think of him atall for years, but ever now and then he comes to me. Can remember as clearly as if it was him sitting in front of me now instead of you. Black sleek hair to the shoulder, down the narrow face, hard chin, firm mouth, long straight nose. High cheekbones, low brows, broad forehead and large deep dark eyes. I was drinking Jack Daniel's. Can smell the leather cushions, the cigar he was smoking. Still see the light from the gaslights, hear the wind, the stainglass windows rattle. Just like it was yesterday. Think of him when it hits me what I've done, what I was doing.

"The sky low, cold mottled blue gray cloud covering coming snow, chill wind. We're hunkered under the sandbank, in the sandhills, wind whipping the orange dormant bluestem, and sandplum, campfire smoke wispy out across the red muddy Cimarron. The red river meandering, pale yellow, white snow patches and blue. Thirty blue pony soldiers huddled below shivering, staring. Cold steel blue double barrel in my hand. . . .

"And I think of Cornelius Boudinot.

"But like I was saying, sounded pretty good. So I decides right then and there to settle my affairs and head out to the Indian Territory. Had a wagon with a few of the necessities of life, and four good Morgans pulling it, just all I needed to get started out on the frontier.

"And by God, by the time April twenty-second, 1889, rolled around I was the best damn horsetrader, hardest drinker, had the prettiest woman of any of the Sooners. You see I knew my way around by this time, and instead of lining up at the Kansas border with all the others waiting for the territory to be officially opened, me and my wife sort of sneaked in early and staked out our claim. Got there sooner you might say.

"Christ almighty, you should of seen it. Tens of thousands of homesteaders crowding into the border towns months before, rumors flying. No one knew for sure when it was gonna be opened, but knew it would be. Hotels with people hanging out the windows they's so full, tent cities building up on the outskirts. All kind of gamblers, whores and flimflam snake oil hucksters sweeping in like buzzards. And a enterprising horsetrader like myself could really make a killing. Nothing but promise of a magnificent future all round.

"When the day came, people lined up three deep on foot, in wagons, carriages, on horseback, at the border. The cavalry patrolling, burning off the prairie to keep people from entering too soon, like a damn race at the county fair, and they fire a gun and they's off in a cloud of dust and smoke you could see a hundred miles. The entire territory claimed in one day.

"But like I said, I'd been there awhile by this time. All ready to start our sod house in the bank among the chinaberry above the creek, a corral for the horses down among the three old cottonwoods in front of the red shale hills on the other side. Nothing but rolling shortgrass hills, colonies of sumac, as far as a man could see. My woman and I just standing there watching the people stream by looking for land.

"She was tall, my wife. Tall, eyes glowing black. Independent. Met her while delivering a horse, standing out among her folks by the wagon. Her ma and pa and brother Royce. The prairie behind, the sky slanted gray and white across red clouds, knew I wanted, grace of movement, should give up my wandering days, knew I wanted her. My wife. And knew I never could. Goddam woman. Should of never come—never asked her pa. Riding up on my prize palomino. Even a damn collar and tie. Damn. Woman. Be the ruin. Like an angel. An avenging angel."

"But what about the Indians, old-timer?"

"Sure. Sure there was Indians. Ride by one or two. Squaw walking alongside. Stop on the hill above. Twenty, thirty minutes looking down over the sod house at me working in the corral. Just looking, wind catch the pony tail, long black hair, blanket. Then slowly ride on.

"Yeah. I guess it was kind of nice in them days, the first few years. Working together building. A shed for the horses. Breaking ground for the crops, the truck garden along the creek to the east. The winter mighty bad that first year, '89. Damn near didn't make it. But my wife was tough, and strong-willed. Only sixteen years old. Kept us going. Sod house. Horses. Rabbits and crow. Remember snakes crawling through the walls, she a mixing up the dough for bread, reach over and whop em dead with the mixing spoon and keep on a going! Kind of nice in them days. I guess." Looks up suddenly at the bartender. "How bout anothern, son?"

"Sure. Here you go."

"Let's see. Wild Turkey."

"I'll be damned."

Old man coddles the glass awhile in silence. The bartender goes on about his business. Old man staring into his reflection behind the bar. "I guess. Guess I knew. I'd get restless one day. Think of Boudinot, Carpenter, David Payne. Instead of hoeing, just a leaning on the handle, the sun brilliant warm, grasshoppers, and I think of the Boomers again and want to go. Independence, Coffeyville. Remember Baxter Springs and my first crossing into Indian Territory, into the Quapaw reservation. It was May, a day like today. The sun warm. Grasshoppers thick flying, through the soldiers rank and file, ponies snorting and pawing the ground. Rifles reflecting sabers. Most of us honest hardworking family men. Not wanting no fight. Good churchgoing Christians. So we stake our claims while the army watches, and return back to Baxter Springs.

"But I was a young buck in them days. Looking for adventure. Wasn't real serious about the claims, the land. Even joined up with a bunch of outlaws roaming the Cherokee Outlet, running off cattle and trading whiskey to the Indians. Just generally raising hell. Not really proud of that to look back on it, but hell, I was young. And you know, it helped point out the need to organize the territory. To get some law and order down there.

"Most of the time I was a supplying horses to the Boomers, moving around from border town to border town, wherever they would gather, Arkansas City, Caldwell. Course I met up with David Payne, the Prince of the Boomers. He'd fought in the Indian Wars, a member of the 18th Kansas Volunteer Cavalry in 1867, captain in the 19th Kansas Volunteers in the wars of 1868 and '69, when they drove all the Indians out of Kansas into the territory. And Congress wouldn't even give him a pension for all he done. Made it his cause now to open up the Oklahoma Territory. I went along with him, even got arrested with him. Many times.

"Early morning. Dark. We'd slip along at dawn single file through the draws, the creek beds, along the river misty, ground fog held in the trees and underbrush. Across the border. Twelve of us, avoiding the soldiers patrolling. All the way down. East of Fort Reno, mile and a half south of the North Fork of the Canadian River.

"David Payne talking about victory, the men staking claims, me just keeping watch. And sure enough, no time till I spot a dust column on the horizon.

" 'Cavalry coming!'

" 'Be calm, men. We have a right.'

"We're all around the fire cooking up coffee, some bacon and beans. Waiting. Not much else to do. Mighty good eats too. But didn't get to finish. This young lieutenant comes prancing up, introduces himself. Payne busy with the beans.

" 'Would you care for a bite to eat, Lieutenant?'

" 'I have already breakfasted, thank you. Could I inquire what you gentlemen are about?'

" 'Certainly, sir. We are homesteaders. Preparing to work our claims.'

" 'I'm sorry to have to inform you, you must be lost. I'm sure you are aware that white men are not allowed in the Indian Territory.'

" 'No, sir. We are not lost. This is Section 14, Township 11 North, Range 3. We have claimed this land and intend to make it productive, sir.'

" 'I am afraid, sir, you are in violation of the law. I must ask you to please accompany me back to the Kansas border.'

" 'Are we under arrest, sir?'

" 'I'm afraid so, sir.' "

The old man laughs and pounds the bar, chokes and coughs. "Yeah, that was the first time, but damn sure not the last. Two months later twenty-one of us snuck back in, and were arrested again. Turned us over to the District Court at Fort Smith, Arkansas this time. Payne was fined $1,000 as leader. But the joke is he don't have no property, so they can't collect anything from him, and later that year he's advertising again that he's going into the Oklahoma District.

"The army is getting mad by this time. General Pope, I believe it was. Just trying to do his duty, carry out the laws. But it was clear the government wasn't all that interested in the laws being carried out. Pope would arrest us, carry us all to Fort Smith, and before he himself could get back to the border, we'd be there ready to go in again. Payne don't give up easy.

"About 1882 they discovered precious metals in the Wichita Mountains, and that really put the pressure on to open things up. That same year Payne sued General Pope for damages, claimed he was keeping him from what was rightfully his. Also started up Payne's Oklahoma Colony. $2.50 membership fee. We collected over $100,000. Ever body wanting to get to the Indian Territory.

"In February of '83 about 250 people, even women and children, left Ark City. Others started at the same time from Coffeyville and Caldwell. A three-pronged attack. Four hundred to five hundred of us settled on the Deep Fork. Pope knew it'd do no good to arrest us, so just took us back to Kansas and released us, and in August we went in again and was arrested at Camp Russel on the Cimarron. Went in twice more that year, and in May of the next year fifty of us were driven from the Cimarron by the army. Gunfire! Things getting tense. In June we established settlements at Rock Falls, on the Chikaskia and on the Bois d'Arc, were driven again, and Payne and me returns to Hunnewell to organize another invasion, we'd wear them down, by God.

"People getting short-tempered, tension growing. The Boomers marching in the streets agitating to get the Indian Territory organized. Singing and carrying signs. Payne, funny-looking guy, square face, short cropped hair, that crazy look in his eyes, crooked nose, droopy mustache and hairy underlip, Payne was making fiery speeches, talking of burning the country and bushwhacking the army if they didn't leave us be." Stops abruptly. Gazing at the bartender. "But poor ol Payne never lived to see the day. Died suddenly, November 1884 it must of been." Long funereal pause. "But that didn't stop the Boomers. Payne's right-hand man W. L. Couch took over right where he'd left off.

"As I recall the main invasion started in December, moving south. The army nipping at our heels, picking off the stragglers, but afraid to move against the main body, caused they knowed we meant business this time. We start making excavations in the sandhills long the north bank of the Cimarron at Stillwater Creek. Ready for a fight. And sure enough, the soldiers come. But only bout thirty, sent to arrest Couch.

"Dark cold day. Wind. Coming snow. Soldiers riding slow along the river up toward the encampment. Us a standing there waiting. I had a double-barrel shotgun, finger cold on the trigger. Shivering.

"The horses stop. Nothing but wind. Long time just us standing. Them huddled below. A few words garbled. The wind about to explode. Couch gets up on the ramparts.

" 'Come and get me if you want me! Two hundred of us say you don't want me that bad!'

"Horses breathing vapor trails, pawing nervous sand. A shouted command. The horses swirl, kicking dust blown over the Cimarron below. And move away.

"We won! We had it won. We thought.

"By middle of January there's 375 men in the encampment. Them was the days! If things could a just stayed that way. Life so simple. Ever body alive. Fighting for a cause.

"Not like later. Pretty woman make a fool of a man. Just doing the best I knowed how. I mean a man gotta make a living, don't he? I'm a horsetrader. Gotta go where the horses is and the men that want them. I mean I'd stuck around. Built a house a half-mile east of the creek where the old sod house had stood. Barns. But I wasn't meant to be a dirt farmer. And when my firstborn died . . . A man's got to take care of his family. His woman. The best way he can. I had to travel. All them years. For her. And finally a little girl as pretty as her mama, and two years later a son. Would of loved me too. But for that woman! Run me off my own land! Set my children against me! The law after me, my own land I'd fought for alongside of David Payne, W. L. Couch, the Boomers. My own woman!"

"Take it easy, old man." Bartender easing him back onto the stool. "Have another shot."

"Thank you, son." Gulps down the drink. "Hmmm. Rebel Yell."

"That's the time." Pours another. "Now get on with the story."

Pulls out the handkerchief from the breast pocket, wipes his eyes, blows his nose, empties the glass again. "Yeah. Well. It looked like we was gonna fight all right. Had to. Finally. One cold winter blowing late afternoon. Wind carrying frozen sounds of hoof fall and hoarse calling voice.

" 'Couch. W. L. Couch.'

"Him crawling out of his dugout, Winchester in one hand, brushing sand with the other, climbs up on the parapet, gazes down the river valley, crouching in his coat against the wind. A platoon of pony soldiers. One struggles up the bank in front of the others.

" 'Couch. I want to talk to W. L. Couch.'

" 'You're looking at him.'

" 'I'm Colonel Hatch of the Ninth Cavalry, garrisoned at Camp Russel. I've orders to arrest you and your men.'

" 'There's four hundred of us, sir. Figger there's only one reason we're here. And that's to fight. Figger to run your asses all the way back to Ephraim Creek, sir.'

" 'I'd hope you'd reconsider, sir. My orders are to arrest you at any cost. To shed blood if that's what it takes, sir.'

" 'You know where we . . .'

" 'Sir. Reinforcements have been dispatched, three hundred men, from Fort Leavenworth. Plus the 350 under my command already. Not really very favorable odds, sir. You can save you and your men a lot of grief if you reconsider.'

"Couch slides back down into the trench, I'm right there with him, my double-barrel cocked, other men crowded around. He looks concerned.

" 'What do you all think?'

" 'The devil take Colonel Hatch!'

"I scramble up the loose sand, swing my shotgun down the valley and squeeze off a double explosion, echo shattering in the cold. The Colonel's horse rears up, clambers down the bank, him waving an arm command, and the platoon breaking ice retreats down the Cimarron River shore. The men all shouting bring the goddam army on!"

Pause. "And we would of beat them too."

Pause. "What happened?"

Looks up slowly. "The sneaking varmint tricked us." Without interest, enthusiasm. "Too cowardly to fight us even-steven. It got colder, commence to snowing, and they couldn't get the troops down from Kansas. So the yellow bastard just moved up north of our encampment and cut off our supplies. Starved us out. Without so much as a shot being fired. Starved out like rats." Resigned. "And that was the deciding battle for the Indian Territory. We'd lost it." Looking up, bored with his own story. "But we won the war. Congress finally realized we meant business and agreed to open it up to homesteaders in 1889."

Leans back on stool. "And that's the way it happened. Sure as I'm a sitting here."

Bartender looks at him awhile. "But what about the Indians?"

Surprised. "The Indians?" Waves the bartender off. "Hell. They was just in the way. That's all." Stares a long time at his empty shot glass. "Out there on that big o prairie."

Prologue Two

THE first thing you see is the sky. Eternal changing. Vast crystalline topaz blue, fluorite green, tourmaline and spinel sunset. Particulate, water vapor, gases, heat and light. Cirrus, cirrocumulus, altostratus, cumulonimbus. Convective lifting, warm moist air from sun-heated plain, jutting thirty, forty, fifty thousand feet, cooling, tossing condensate water particles, ice, 500,000 tons about. Falling friction downdraft, violent electric discharge. Cells combine along the horizon, challenge the sun. But still there's room.

And then the grass. Rolling sea 360 degrees billow and heaves. Bluestem chased light and shadow chameleonic green springtime wind, red brown summer sun and purple copper fall. Dropseed, switch grass, Indian grass and squirreltail.

Hear it. Hissing drone. Constant. Eternal. Like a sea.

Which one time it was. One hundred million years ago. A strait, a thousand miles across. To the west the Rocky Mountain chain had begun to fold, fault, igneous intrusions, and rise, the strata to the east slowly sank, a geosyncline invaded by the Arctic Ocean and southern gulf. The mountains eroded away as they rose, more than 40 million years, rugged, washed into the sea, precipitating thick coarse detrital deposits, 850 million cubic miles, growing thinner and more fine-grained to the east. Chalky limestone, occasional loosely cemented various debris. The shore was swamp. Dinosaurs fed on abundant plants, marine life. Their fossil bones now interbedded in the coal along the western margin of the sea.

When the Rocky Mountain cordillera ceased to lift and its alluvial outwash filled the sea the water began to recede. Another 30 million years and the mountains were gone, eroded flat along the continental divide, a peneplane two to three thousand feet high. Streams, radiating away, superposed upon the buried roots of the ranges, spread a mantle of silts and muds till the sea was gone. A high plain, fluvial and lacustrine fine to coarse clastic sediments, isolated shale, sandstone and bentonitic clay remained.

Then 15 million years ago the entire region began to rise again, broad gentle arch, a thousand miles, orogeny and another cycle of erosion. The streams cutting canyons through the mountains as they lifted, the weak fill in the basins carved out and carried beyond, another broad debris apron spread upon the high plains to the east. You can see it. The remnants of the summit plain. The Bighorn River across the Owl Creek Range. The Green River cutting through the eastern end of the Uintas in Flaming Gorge. The Laramie River through the Front Range in Laramie Canyon. The South Platte through Platte Canyon, the Arkansas in the Royal Gorge. See the remnants of the basin fill in horizontal beds high up the flanks of the summit ranges. Follow the great debris apron from west to east. It slopes down from the summit of the Front Range. The fluvial deposits spread across the land, clay, silts, sands. The western and eastern margins washed away where the rivers cut across. The remaining middle, the flat, awesome prairie.

And early Miocene the grass arose. To hold the shifting loess from the wind.

Coronado's men, on their journey from Tiguex to Quivira across the Plains of the Cows, 1541, out hunting, became disoriented, lost their way and wandered days at a time, crazed by distance, space, the wind and sun. Each night roll call to see who was missing. Fired guns, blew trumpets, set signal fires. But some wandered beyond all help. One thousand horses, five hundred cows, five thousand rams and ewes and more than fifteen hundred friendly Indians and servants left no trace traveling over the prairie, passed as if nothing had been. The grass erect, fresh and straight as it was before. On an ocean there is no trail.

The first European settlers, 1820, thought they crossed a wasteland. The Great American Desert. Unfit for human habitation, sun flattened life, filled up the eyes blood-red, baked the bones, madness sometimes, suicide, you'll find me in the timbers. But a hundred years ago, the plow. Not the fragile European blade, the tough John Deere to rip the sod, the intricate root systems of each plant run a mile or more. Five oxen to pull, to lay the soil bare. Overcultivated, overgrazed. And the wind began another redistribution.

Precipitation was 500 billion tons short in 1930. The rivers that drain the area ran dry, the Mississippi was two and a half feet lower than it had ever been in four hundred years. You could wade across it. There were 362 windstorms between 1933 and 1937. The dust shut out the sun. Three hundred million tons of loess carried fifteen hundred miles in one day, 150,000 square miles blown clean of topsoil.

By 1936 the rain cycle began to creep back toward normal. A massive effort undertaken by the government to reclaim, reestablish the ecosystem. Build terraces, ponds, contour plow, but mainly plant. Bois d'arc hedgerows, cane, Sudan grass, barley cover. By 1939 the harvest was looking good. The land restored.

Finally you could look up again to see the sky.

Lyons Stops to Farm

A Swainson's *hawk riding thermals. Late afternoon. Dust rising slanted sunlight. Cowboys glint against the iridescent hanging dust, in awe. The lethal clanging bull-rope bell. The macabre spinning dance.*

She wondered if he thought of her, the baby born.

He thought the hand held tight, the turn inside. The clown thrown in the sky. The whirling vortex. Hooves. Abstract the twisted wrist, the elbow, the shoulder gone. The letting go, the ground, the ankle smashed the groin and knew. Exploded earth. Manure, dung beetle, flies oblivious inches away, the dirt catching light and shadow, gnats mites. Spittle. Blood. He knew.

He loved the bull.

Roger Lyons was a cowboy. A rodeo rider. A poet. Wrote songs, sung highways from Bogalusa, Sedro Wooley, Wahoo, Nebraska, burning oil and tires in a '31 Chevy sedan, from one rodeo to the next. The back seat gone, a mattress a bed. This is where he lived.

Blackfoot, Greybull, Wyoming. Moose Jaw, Wolf Point, Chickasha, Oklahoma.

Robert Keeper and Hank singing along. Drinking. Lived there too most times. Lyons not your ordinary cowboy. Cussed in front of women. And wasn't shy. Keeper and Hank sleeping many a night in hay barns. While he plucked his steel-bodied guitar and wooed back-seat muses. Waitresses at the diners. Bargirls small-town dreamers.

And he couldn't fight. Unfortunate for a twister claiming poetic license in bars at night. Blowing day money on bourbon if he was lucky. Borrowing if he'd drawn dead.

"Lyons, o buddy. I ain't never rode this crow-hopping son of a buck, but I do know he likes to buck with his head way between his knees. So you'd best hold her about right here." Robert Keeper measuring rein fist and extended thumb from the saddle horn. "No fancy stuff. Just good rank bucking."

Lyons weaves a horsehair in the rope to mark the spot.

"Turn her loose!"

Chute flies open, bronc flies straight up head flung back, Lyons toes out spurs the withers, rein too long, out of shape. Rolling backwards coming down lashing out twisting kick flying ass first up over the head of the horse.

Dusted. Goose egg.

Slowly picks himself up. Pounds his shoulders, arms and thighs with his hat. Limps to the fence where Keeper hangs. "I can see why you ain't never rode that outlaw. Duck his head, my ass."

"I ain't never seen him do that before. He sure did score good though."

Sitting in the bar at night, writing in his notebook with his stubby pencil. And flirting. Until some drunk cowboy starts pushing. "Writing poetry, huh, Lyons? Ain't that purty." Waitress trying to steer him back to the bar. Already interested. "Sort of taken a liking to him, huh, ma'am? Well, you should a seen him this afternoon. Rides saddle bronc bout as good as he can write."

The people at nearby tables joining in. Hank and Keeper come to the booth to help out, knowing what's coming. Lyons can't fight, but feels he has to. And besides, he knows what's going to happen. "Look, you drunken cowpoke, with that day-money horse you drew, even my ol granmother could of rode in the average."

And so on. Until a push, a shove. Hank looking at Keeper, Keeper at the ring of cowboys laughing and waiting. Had seen it all before, always good for a laugh when o Lyons is in town—pow! The drunk goes down, Lyons shaking cracked knuckles. Can never handle the drunk's buddy though and it's everybody's turn, whooping and hollering. Throwing chairs. A real you-count-them-while-I-throw-them-out.

Lyons down on the floor spitting blood, the waitress gathering up the notebook, screams, kicking shins, slapping her way to Lyons lying contented waiting, out of it, glad of it, knowing what will happen next.

She dabs blood with her apron, he smiles, weak. The sheriff coming in the front door, she looks to the rear, grabbing Lyons by the hand through the kitchen into the cool high country. Evening alley, wet brick broken bottle cowboy sleeping it off. One street over, the plains. Past the two-story buildings, high sky, intense stars and the Chevy. Along a sandy road a half-mile.

Hank and Keeper sleep in jail.

Lyons plucking singing soft. Moonlit Chevy window light across the steel-body, the knees and thighs, her breast and shadows. Singing knowing what will happen next.

No one remembers how it happened in the first place. One day they all were just tooling down the highway together. Hey, you going that a. Me too. Come along sure nough. In the '31 Chevy, pulling Hank's horse trailer behind, about half drunk on the way to some punkin roller or other. Spearfish, South Dakota, Big Timber, Montana, somewhere, nobody can remember.

Lyons with his guitar and women. Keeper disappearing every now and again. And Hank, the steady one. Quiet. Could count on him for gas money and entry fees. If he didn't win it calf roping, he always picked up a little as clown. Or hustling snooker in the evenings. Driven by dire necessity and hunger, was even known to mount a saddle bronc. Supple, sure, clingy as a cat. But it was fear of hitting the ground put him in the money most of the times he tried it. Had been one of the best. Helped organize the strike and the *Cowboys Turtle Association* at the Boston Garden in '36. Would have been World Champion at Pendleton Roundup in '37. Leading until the last go round. A hoof-shaped gash in his skull over his right eye to show for it.

"She's a high-kicking sky-jumping end-swapping bitch with a belly full of bedsprings, Hank. If you can stay on her, you got it."

Pulls a canvas bag with his *Association* saddle, pulls the saddle out, on the ground, sits on it, adjusts the stirrups, rocks back and forth for balance. Pushing back, legs snug against the swell of the cantle. Gets up, carries it to the chute. Big roan, chute fighter. Snort kicking up dirt, banging the timbers. Cinches on the saddle, takes the rein, the horsehair mark, steady big girl, wedges his legs down in the stirrups between, slamming back and forth the rails, his heels, spurs dull rowel above her shoulders. Steady now.

"Let her rip."

Big roan rears up and out, Hank heels up and spurring shoulders, front legs hit the ground lashing out behind, Hank in time, spurring half-circle flank to shoulder looking good, left hand waving. Spins two quick jarring bucks out of time spurs lifting out of the saddle over the buttocks tumbling lightning hoof cracking bone snaps the head splatters blood Hank sliding through the dirt.

Gathered up a handful of brains to carry him to the hospital.

So he hardly ever rides anymore. Retching vomit behind the pens each time. And it got around he'd got shit in his neck. So he painted his face white and blue, big red smile, cherry nose. Put on baggy pants, a floppy shirt and baseball shoes and went to face the brahma bulls.

Let me tell you about the time Hank was the barrel man. In fact the first time he ever was clown. The man saved my life sure. Lyons and Keeper out there with him, ever body worried. He'd just been out the hospital a couple a weeks. I pulled one a the rankest bulls ever to flatten a cowboy. It was ol 128. I mean even the other brahmas was scared of him. You understand what I'm saying? He wasn't satisfied with killing the twister, he wanted to get ever thing in the entire arena. When they announced he was coming out, the folks in the bleachers who knew would move back a row or two. That short-horned renegade was mean. Most bulls will try to crush your leg against the chute, know how to keep a man from getting a good grip so you're out of shape from the git-go. But ol 128 love it when you get on. Stand real still, make it easy for you. Look up over his hump at you, sort of wiggle his shoulders a little bit, you want to ride, man, I'll give you a ride, come on, motherfucker, make yourself comfortable. I got something for you. You understand what I'm saying?

Well, the gate flies open and I come flying out the chute instead of him. Like to knocked my damn glass eye out, flat on my ass. Not feeling in a big hurry to get up, when that ugly son of a bitch is snorting head down coming right for me. I don't even have time to get scared when I see Hank in his barrel throwing himself in between and, man, that bull lowered the boom. You understand what I'm saying? That barrel flew twenty foot straight up in the air, and when it come down that bull let her have it midair again and I can see Hank's feet out one end and his head out the other, ducking in as he come down twisting open end of the barrel right over that short-horned devil's head.

Well, I don't see how they's room for Hank and that bull's head in that barrel. O 128 can't see doodley squat, and he's running around in circles a shaking his head back and forth trying to throw it off. Finally bangs it loose on a fence post, and Keeper and Lyons manage to chase him back into the pens. I run over to the barrel, Hank still tucked inside. Now I'd heard the stories bout Hank losing his nerve, and was a little worried about him. I poke my head in. "How you doing, Hank?"

"I'm doing fine. But that brahma ought to do something about his breath."

Yeah. Hank, Keeper and Lyons were inseparable buddies. But one day something happened out on Highway 81. Early summer of 1939. The sun, golden fields, sunflower fence rows, bois d'arc, meadowlarks, blackbirds. Heading south. Hennessey, Dover, Kingfisher, Okarche. Keeper had disappeared a few days ago. Ornery son of a bitch. Chasing that real pretty tall drink of water, more than likely. Hank driving, pint of whiskey cradled between his legs, Lyons, boots kicked off back seat, propped up over the front.

"Can't you get them godawful feet out of my face." Plucking and singing. "An stop that doggone caterwauling." Both feeling good.

"Wonder what sort of devilment Keeper's up to now?"

"No telling."

"He'll come dragging in needing a shave and some sleep."

"You think we should of waited for him?"

"Naw."

"What if he can't find us?"

"He always does."

"Yeah. He always does."

Wind trailing dust north across a wheat field, concentric darker yellow stubble, yellow Minneapolis Moline tractor, yellow M&M combine, red wheels. A tall man and a short one standing shirtless on the platform, seat removed, tall one steering, the other backwards, wheel in hand controlling the combine header barge rolling side to side over a terrace.

Hank whooped and slapped his thigh. "Hot damn."

Lyons laughed and strummed the steel-bodied guitar.

The sun shone mellow, the wheat was yellow,

two cowboys on the road. Two happy fellow

s'and they could tell oh the farmer carried the load.

"That was awful."

"What are you? A critic?" Black '31 Chevy sedan and horse trailer behind.

"Hey, Lyons. Let's sing that one about the cowboy lover who couldn't cause a steer kicked him in the balls."

"You like that one."

"Yeah. I kind of like that one." A cloud of blue smoke acceleration to pass a tractor and combine, horse's rump swaying.

"Hank! What was that back there?"

"A combine."

"Beside the road."

"A truck."

"Standing beside."

"I don't know."

"A damsel in distress. Turn this damn thing round."

"But we don't have time to . . ."

"Of course we do."

"Well, horseshit." Sliding off onto a section line kicking red dirt, horse whinnying protest, reverse back out on the highway, accelerate back by the truck, loaded wheat. Woman standing there at the left front tire. Flat.

"Hot damn. Would you look at that. What did I tell you."

"Needs help, no doubt about it."

"I'd hope to kiss a pig. Turn this thing round. She needs me."

"Hell."

On to the next section line north. In and out, back south, and over in behind the truck. Lyons pulling his boots on, hops from the back door in the dust, bending over tugging boot top, hobbles over, stetson cocked to one side. "Howdy, ma'am. Need some help?"

"Well. Yes. I was just on my way to pick up the spare. Just isn't my day, I guess. Had a flat this morning, and now this."

"Why, hell, That's no problem atall. My ol buddy Hank here will be glad to go get the spare for you. Won't you, Hank?"

"Sure thing, ma'am."

"That's very nice. It's the first station on the west side of the highway as you come into El Reno. The name's Baldwin. This is very nice of you to . . ."

"Think nothing of it, ma'am. I'll stay here and keep you company while Hank's gone."

Pulls the guitar out of the back as Hank maneuvers back on to the highway headed south. Strums a few chords. She looks at him, at the truck, rubs her hands along the thighs of her Levi's. "Well. I'd better go ahead and get this wheel off, so I can get on to the elevator when your friend gets back. Marcus'll be waiting with a bin full by the time I . . ."

"Marcus?"

"My younger brother."

"Sure glad to hear that, ma'am."

Blushes a little. "My name's Blanchefleur."

"What?"

"Call me Blanche."

"I will not. Blanchefleur. I'm Roger Lyons. Rodeo cowboy and poet."

Smiles. Picks out a melody.

Riding along one fine day out on the o highway
saw a woman in distress, didn't even wear a dress,
stopped to help her out that day then had to go on on my way.
Now among the cow manure I think of Blanchefleur.

Picking and a grinning. She blushes again. Laughs self-conscious. Looks back and forth up and down the road, back at Lyons still smiling, turns to the truck, takes out the jack from behind the seat. Lyons strumming and a humming. She puts the jack together, slides it under the front axle, cranks it up. Wipes hands on blue jeans, gets the lug wrench, Lyons singing harvest flat tire highway breakdown. She removes the lug nuts, sweating now, wipes brow streaking grease, struggles tire off, leans it against the running board. Smiles at Lyons, still singing. Inspects the tire, finds the nail between the tread. Lyons hits a few resolving chords.

"How come you never got married, Blanchefleur?"

"Look, cowboy."

"How old are you?"

"You just keep on singing."

"You must be least 34, 35."

"I am not. I was born in 1908."

"You see. I was close."

Met a young woman who's thirty-one

looking good out in the sun.

Must admit I did admire the way she moved

when she changed a tire.

She sits leaning against the rear wheel trying not to laugh. He hunkers down beside. "Where do you live?"

"With my brother on our farm."

"How come you drive a truck?"

"We're short of help. You sure do ask a lot of questions."

Smiling at her, looking. She fidgets, tries to brush dust and grease. "I'm looking for work."

Pause. She examines him "Do you know how to drive a truck? A tractor or combine?"

"Why, Blanchefleur, they ain't nothing I can't ride." Winks. Grabs the guitar.

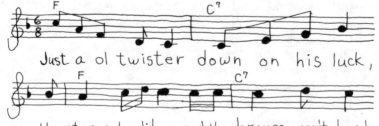

Just a ol twister down on his luck,

the steers houlihan and the broncs won't buck.

44

now I'm telling you what I want to do,
I want to cut your wheat for you.

"Are you serious? About looking for work?"
"Sure thing."
"I'll take you to meet Marcus then."
"Now you're talking."

Blanchefleur wrestled the truck across the eighty-acre field toward the domed horizon. Lyons leaned in the corner of the cab, right elbow hanging out the window, left arm along the back of the seat holding the neck of the steel-bodied guitar. Looked at her from beneath the brim of his stetson hat. Until her face intensified, not just concentration on the route from terrace to terrace, but beyond. He pushed back the hat with his thumb and squinted into the late sun to see. A man standing where contour-plowed stubbled seeder rows intersect the sky. A giant. Twice the size of the other man, there with him in the middle of the field. Waiting. Lyons blinked. The giant was still there. Lyons looked back at Blanchefleur, she smiles. "Marcus and Mackey. I bet they're wondering what went wrong this time. It's been a bad day."

"Which is Marcus?"
"The big one."
"You can say that again."

Lyons straightens up in the cab, leans forward, narrows the eyes, flexes the muscles of his back. He looks quickly back and forth, the giant against the sky and Blanchefleur banging the steering wheel play over a terrace crest. The door handle catches the cuff of his shirt and the steel-bodied guitar clangs forward against the dash. Blanchefleur laughs. "Mackey's a dwarf."

"What?"
"Only about three and a half feet tall."

Lyons peers out through the dusty windshield. Laughs. And leans back into the corner of the cab.

45

But when they get out he still has to look half a foot into the sky to see the short hard glance as Marcus walks up to Blanchefleur.

"Marcus, you're not going to believe this."

Looks again at Lyons, the steel-bodied guitar he's carrying from the truck. "I'll believe almost anything by now."

"I had another flat on the way in." Motions to Lyons. "This is Roger Lyons, helped me out on the highway with the tire." Marcus looks, the cowboy boots, guitar. "He said. He's. I told him we needed a hand to finish off the harvest." Marcus looks at the sun, the uncut grain. Back at Lyons. "He's a bull rider."

"You don't say." Back at the sun. "Can a man make a living doing that? Seems like a waste of your and the bull's time to me. You out walking down the highway?"

Studies Marcus. Big man, and lean. The right-hand thumb cut off at the top of the nail. "My buddy took my car on. Got some spare time before the next rodeo, thought I'd help you out, but if you don't need the help, I can sure catch up with him."

Looks at Blanchefleur, the guitar. "You planning on cutting wheat with that?"

"Just something to ease a troubled mind."

"When you cut wheat eighteen hours a day your mind doesn't have too much time to get troubled." The sun again. "Well, let's get going. Not getting anything in the bin standing here. Can't pay you much, dollar a day and room and board."

Looks at Blanchefleur and winks. "Sounds good to me."

"Okay, the six-speed's full. Let's hustle."

Lyons watches him stride through the stubble kicking up red dust in the wind. A big young bull. Have to work on him slow. Mackey the dwarf coughs. Lyons looks down. Reaches out his hand how you doing podner, Mackey shakes it, then heads after Marcus to the Minneapolis-Moline tractor and combine. Marcus cranks the tractor, Mackey climbs up to the header barge control wheel. Lyons looks around the field, Blanchefleur motions him toward the six-speed Ford. He stands and begins to laugh. Not really knowing what would happen next. But Lyons didn't mind. It was Blanchefleur.

Didn't mind until the first day. Seventeen hours, eating lunch standing on the tractor platform fighting the header barge with one hand, dusty chicken salad sandwich with the other. Drinking water from a gallon jug handed up by Mackey the dwarf, wrapped in a wet gunnysack stained red and dark around the bottom. Sun and wind tearing at the eyes and mouth, dry chapped hurting. Knees and thighs aching. Cowboy boots not meant for standing all day. Didn't see Blanchefleur from 4:30 breakfast, too sleepy to enjoy ham and eggs milk sliced tomatoes biscuits and ham gravy, until 10:30 dinner, too exhausted to eat fried chicken mashed potatoes and chicken gravy sliced tomatoes corn on the cob green beans with bacon hot rolls butter honey and ice tea. Too tired when he fell into the hired man's bunk on the back porch longing for the '31 Chevy and comfort of a ten-second saddle bronc ride. To think of Blanchefleur.

Lying naked a floor away, sheets thrown off perspiring in the moon through the window, in lace curtains in the wind in Chinese elms outside in mulberry trees in hedge-apple windbreaker along the hard red shale road shining blue moonlight screech owl coyote yelp, in 160 acres of uncut wheat stretching for the morning.

Too tired. To reach up to hold the sleepy vision, long blond hair in bangs and curls jarring from deep sleep four o'clock rise an shine. Marcus sat listening to the news and weather, the farm market reports through breakfast, then went out, singing the doxology, to work on the six-speed engine. Lyons too tired to talk anyway. He and Mackey pumped the five-gallon gas cans full, loaded grease guns, filled the water jugs at the well. Feeling better. Rounding the back porch he sees Blanchefleur at the kitchen sink. Stops. Looks around. Goes in just to say a proper good morning, compliment the breakfast, her embroidered shirt.

Marcus walks in on a burst of laughing cut off as he blocks the kitchen door. Stands looking at them. "Let's hustle, Lyons. We don't need you to clean pots and pans."

Mackey drove the six-speed, Lyons climbed in the truck with Marcus out to the field. Marcus didn't talk. Smoked his pipe. Pointed out a fence row that needed tightening. Lyons mumbled sure did. A big man. Mighty quick reflexes. Work on him slow.

Cool morning breeze over the field. Silent rustle of grain. Smell the gasoline, the sun in stubble red dust driving the moisture. The pop of the bearing filling with grease curling rich green from the seam. Feeling much better. Another day. Should be easier today. Mackey the dwarf drove the truck yesterday, should operate the tractor today. Lyons to drive the truck. Easy day. Sitting in the cab between rounds, driving down the back roads and highways singing to the elevator, long waits in line, just sitting loafing and lying with the other farmers. Maybe even talk to Blanchefleur.

Marcus picked up the crank, held it over his head behind his back to stretch. Cranked the tractor on the first quarter-turn, let it warm. Lyons eyed the truck, Marcus looks at him. "Lyons, you drive the truck. We're storing seed today back at the farm, and Mackey's too short to scoop it into the granary."

Scoop?

Two trucks. While Lyons scoops out one, Marcus and Mackey fill the other. All day. Sun. Heat. Wind. Back, shoulders. Hands hurt through the gloves. But at least will see, talk to, maybe. Blanchefleur.

"Speed it up a little, Lyons. The six-speed is full."

Scoop.

Small red drive-through building northwest of the house, three compartments on each side. Tongue-in-groove slats in the doors, added as the room fills up. One scoopful at a time.

"Let's hustle, Lyons. Looks like it might rain tonight."

No sign of her. All morning scooping. That man's trying to kill me.

Pulling out of the south end of the granary, he catches a glimpse. Mouth full of clothespins, stretching long, brilliant sheets billowing wind. She waves. He starts to brake, remembers, Marcus waiting.

Another jag.

Scoop.

Hunger. Heat and wheat dust condensed in the narrow stillness. Pungent. Contained. Barely enough room to squeeze between the wall and the truck bed. Sideways into the cab. Out the south end. She is waiting. "Hold it a minute. I have something for you."

Hands up a quart Mason jar condensation coruscating sun full of crushed ice lemonade pulp and seeds. Cold. Wet. Citric cringing sweet lemonade.

"Blanchefleur, you've saved my life."

"Is this a little harder than wrestling steers?"

"It takes longer."

"Here's lunch for you to take out to Marcus and Mackey."

"Chicken salad, huh."

"What did you expect, cordon bleu?"

48

"What?"

"Never mind . . . I've got to get back to cooking your dinner."

Look at each other until they smile.

"Why'd you never get married?"

"You're wasting time, Lyons."

"You reckon you could have another quart jar of lemonade handy by the time I get back with the next load?"

"Maybe. I'll see if I can fit it in."

She laughs, turns, walks a few steps, hops, runs into the back porch. Lyons heads for the field. Pulls in, tire tracks across the stubble red. Over the terraces, the other truck, the combine and tractor stopped. Damn, late again. Mackey and Marcus standing on top of the combine. Tools. Breakdown. Marcus jumps to the ground, shirt sweat mud red, face salty wet.

"Lyons, looks like we're going to need some more links of speed chain. Baling wire just doesn't seem to hold her together very long." Engine heat, straw chaff, carbon monoxide water vapor dust. Grasshoppers and horseflies. "Looks like you're going to have to go to town for the chain. Mackey and I'll cripple along as best we can."

Lyons roared back out of the field. Laughing, honking the horn, singing on into town. Loved breakdowns.

Parked in the middle of the main drag behind a '36 Chevy coupe, two pickups, a ton-and-a-half, and a Farmall tractor. Sidewalks stained red dirt, grass growing in cracks. A couple of tumbleweeds at the edge of the street. Men in overalls straw hats baseball caps. Women feedsack dresses, shawls, bonnets. Coming in to the feed store, post office. Stopping to visit or holler at each other under rusting corrugated tin awnings bent down at the ends. The Mercantile. Cream shed. Auto livery. Barbershop. Bar and Grill.

Lyons walked into the Mercantile. The clerk got the chain link, talked about the weather and the harvest awhile. Walked back out along the storefronts. Past the Bar and Grill. Laughter through the reflections, the faded lettering. Men sitting around a table. Lyons turned back and went in. Thirsty. A quick beer.

Long black-topped bar, boiled eggs, crackers, sausage jars. Round stools. Round chairs with wrought-iron legs and backs. Round tables. Cards. Dominoes. Cribbage board. Three men at one table. Older. White hair. A straw hat. One with a beard. Wrinkled. Red dust almost in the faces. Slender man in the back, stained apron and a pushbroom, sprinkling red sawdust on the floor. Leaned the broom against the wall when Lyons sat down, walked over behind the bar. "What can I do you for?"

"Gimme a bottle of Jax."

"Sure thing. You new around here, aren't you?"

"Yep. I'm helping Marcus Baldwin with the harvest."

Pause. Slow smile. Sets the bottle and glass down in front. "You don't say. You must not been with him long."

"This is the second day."

"Figgered as much. Marcus got his cutting done, you say?"

"No, not yet. Just taking a break."

"Is that right." Returns to his sweeping. "Whatcha think of this weather?"

"Mighty hot."

"I reckon it'll storm tonight. You missed the big tornado last week. Come through just west of town."

"Is that a fact."

"Sure did. Red Dog Gullet was in here the next morning. He lives out that way and so I asks him if the tornado'd did much damage to his place. Says the rain an hail knocked down a lot of his wheat, the shingles was tore off the chicken coop an the outhouse blowed over. You don't say, I says. Yep. What about your barn, I asks. Says he don't rightly know if it was hurt or not. You don't rightly know? Well. No, he says. I ain't found it yet."

"He ain't found it yet, huh."

"Nope." Laughing low-key appreciation. "Says he don't rightly know if it was damaged cause he ain't found it yet." Walks out the back door still chuckling.

Lyons turns on the stool to look at the old men at the table. The one with the white beard, large wrinkled nose, bib overalls, maroon corduroy long-sleeve shirt. An Indian, .45-calibre pistol strapped to his side, tin star on his bib. Breaks the seal on a deck of blue Bicycle cards, shuffles idly. The others looking on. Someone picks up the score pad. Examines it closely, looks back at the new deck, then at the shuffler. "Deal the cards, Sheriff." Calling to the proprietor returning with a case of beer. "Hey, Oats. Come on. Let's play some pitch."

"You know I got work to do. You're gonna have to play cutthroat till I'm through." Sets down the beer, carries out a case of empties.

Lyons picks up his glass and walks to the table. "What y'all playing?"

"Pitch. You want to sit in for Oats?"

"I guess I got time for one game."

Sits west, opposite the sheriff who deals three cards at a time around the table twice. South's bid. "I'm gonna pass on account of my hand."

Lyons taps his cards on the table. "I believe I'll leave the bidding up to my podner."

North smiles. "Give three."

The sheriff looks across at Lyons. "Well, you got to bid to win. Four."

"Attaway, podner. Lead 'em out."

"Spades is trumps." Slaps down the ace of spades.

South skims the two of spades spinning across the table lodging beneath the ace. "What you playing for low? Your character?"

Lyons pitches the little joker in. "We only bid four."

North throws the five of trump. The sheriff pushes the trick face-up over to Lyons, carefully sets down a card snapping the corner with his index finger, the king of spades. South sloughs the seven of clubs, Lyons tosses down the four of trump, North laughs well horseshit, gives up the jack of spades. Lyons, scooping in the trick, "Can't beat us today, we're sitting parallel to the grain of the table. Lead em again."

The sheriff plays the king of diamonds, South the ten, Lyons pulls a card, hesitates, looks over at North, puts it back, spins the eight of hearts across.

North slams down the ace of diamonds and rakes in the trick. "Lots of game out there." Leads the jack of diamonds. The sheriff sloughs, South plays the two of clubs, Lyons the nine of hearts. North pulls them in. "These is good as trumps." Throws the two of diamonds. Everybody sloughs. Last card. The four of clubs. "Looks like we got game."

The sheriff grumbles, plays the jack of clubs, South the nine. Lyons smiles. "I wouldn't be so sure of that, good buddy." Slips the ten of clubs under the sheriff's jack, slides the trick in. "We better count the game, just for practice. One ten, ace for fourteen, king makes seventeen, jack eighteen, plus the little joker."

"Damn, you can have shit for brains if you're lucky. You got it, eighteen a piece and you got the joker to break the tie."

"Give us high, low, two jacks and the game. Five."

"Hey. You didn't have low. I played the two of trump."

"Well, it never hurts to ask. Four of we, one for they. I do believe I need another beer after that."

Five hands and three beers later, the score ten to fourteen. Bidder goes out, North-South needs one more point to win. The sheriff over-bids North's take-out four bid, finesses South's big joker with a Bill Evans lead, Lyons runs with the little joker and they score five to win.

Lyons downs the rest of his beer. "Sure did enjoy passing the time of day with you fellers, but I got to get back to the fields."

Slowly shuffling the deck. "No need to hurry off, we got to play off the tie."

"Well. Marcus is waiting for me."

Smiles. "That's what I mean."

Lyons pulls into the field, the combine and tractor stopped. Jumps out with the chain links. "I got just what the doctor ordered."

Marcus looks up from the chain wheel. "What in Sam Patch took you so long?"

"Had a quick beer on the way. Talked to the sheriff, real nice fell—"

"What!" Standing, a quick step toward Lyons, looking hard down at him, jaw clenched, definitely serious.

"Had a beer with the sheriff, he . . ."

Calm, intense. "Get off." Mackey backing away calmly. "Off my land."

"I don't see—"

A crescent wrench in hand. "I don't want to see you around here again."

"But I . . ."

"No drop-down drunk is going to be wasting my time."

"What about my—"

Brandishing. "Off!"

Decides not to worry about his pay. "Okay. Okay. Take it easy, Marcus. I'm going."

Lyons backs a couple of steps, turns, walks off through the stubble. Then chuckles to himself.

He chased a cottontail zigzag across a terrace, turned, waving stetson across the rolling field, to the top of the knoll, yellow combine and tractor dull in the sun, the wind chasing grain all along the horizon.

Thought I'd earn me some honest meals

working all day in the wheat in the fields,

but I tell you where I'm a gonna go,

take my ass back to riding rod-e-o,

Cause I know no matter lose or win

I like brahma bulls a lot better than men.

He walked out onto the hard-baked red road. Grasshoppers, locusts drone falling off down the watershed. Piano. Orange-black butterflies buffeted, floating over red poppies and sunflowers. A horned toad, harvester ants.

Heard piano playing. The house on top of the next hill.

A buzzard, two, flapped up from the ditch, a possum carcass. A hog-nosed snake surprised, up hissing spread hood weaving back and forth.

Boogie-woogie piano from the house.

Lyons walked up the hill to the corner, along the mulberry

trees, up the steep west drive. Toward the music, Blanchefleur playing. Boogie-woogie.

Lyons walks into the back porch. Listens for a while. Through the kitchen, the living room to the alcove. Dark and wrinkled upright piano along the far wall, Blanchefleur, denim pants upon the piano bench, keeping time, the feet dancing on the pedals, hands and fingers rocking along the keys, cigarette smoke curling through her hair.

He stands there watching her. Now and then keeping the bass line going with her left hand, flipping ashes with the right. Singing outburst scat.

Her whole body rhythm suddenly stops. Snatches the cigarette from her mouth trying to hide it, turning to see. Lyons leaning against the sill, hat cocked over an eye, grinning. She fumbles the cigarette, puts it out. "You startled me."

"Keep on playing." Walking up to the piano, looking at the Methodist hymnal open to "Onward Christian Soldiers." "You're pretty good."

"I. I was just practicing. For church Sunday."

"Music like that might get me to church. What else you do that Marcus don't know about?"

"What else can you do alone on a farm?"

"There's some towns and a pretty fair-sized city not too far from here. You don't ever go there?"

"I don't know. Sometimes. To the Criterion to movies, in the afternoons, or like when I go to get my hair cut, or leave the pickup off to be worked on. I even told Marcus I was staying up with Velma Gidney once because she was sick, but we really drove to Oklahoma City to see Duke Ellington play." Look at each other a long time, till she has to look down. "You come for more lemonade?"

"No. I come for my things."

"Your things?"

"Seems like Marcus decided he can get along without me."

"What?"

"He fired me. Didn't like it that I stopped in for a beer in town."

"Oh no. I." Pause. "I guess I should have told you. Marcus doesn't put up with alcohol. Mom was a charter and founding member of the local WCTU. Used to read to us from Carrie Nation's *Hatchet Chips* before we went to bed. She even tried to organize a raid on the beer joint. Never came off though, just as well, since it's the sheriff's favorite. I don't think he would have looked too kindly on it." Stares at the piano keys for a while. "He fired you, huh?"

"Run me off is more like it. But doesn't matter."

"Yes it. I mean. I . . ."

"I wasn't much of a field hand anyway." Smiles at her. "Play some more."

"No. I don't feel like . . ."

"Come on."

"I feel terrible. About you. Being. I was . . ."

"Let's hear you play. Make us both feel better."

She glances distracted at her hands. Begins "Nearer My God to Thee." He laughs, leans against the edge of the keyboard, closes the hymnal. She looks at his hand. Up to his face. She smiles. Starts slow rolling bass. Staring back down at her hands, the melody dragging somewhere slow. He reaches down to her, slowly pulls her from the bench, she doesn't turn away, kissing, her arms dangling, fingers playing a broken measure more, then limp upon the keys.

They settle slowly. Her hands from the piano. His dusty shirt wrung perspiration red.

"I bet ol Marcus don't know you kiss like that."

Breathless. "You better get out of here."

Long pause. "Yeah, I reckon." Another kiss. "He'd shoot me like as not if he caught me still here, with his only sister."

"Where are you going?"

"I'll catch up with Hank at the Lenapah Rodeo next week."

"When will I. I mean." Long pause. "I'll fix you up some food to take along."

"Chicken salad?"

"Better than that."

Rain gusted across lightning headlight flashes. A Coffeyville schoolteacher let Lyons off downtown Lenapah. Thunderclap.

Lashing poncho around his shoulders. Lenapah Rodeo banner torn from its moorings flapping. He walked down the sidewalk laughing. See Hank again, Keeper probably there. Walked to the beer joint. The o '31 Chevy parked in front.

The door flew open wind and water flying. All turn looking. "Roger Lyons, goddamn!"

"All you bronc stompers might as well—"

"Heard you was taking up chicken farming."

"Might as well drink your entry fees tonight, cause you gonna lose them sure tomorrow now I'm—"

"What happened to the farmer's daughter?"

"Gimme a beer. I been on the road a mighty long time. Where's Hank and Keeper?"

"In the back. Come on. Let's hear about the wheat harvest."

"Hank's got a big mouth for a quiet man."

Pushes through to the back room. Hank, down on his knees, makes his point, eight the hard way, pulls the stack of bills in, Keeper yelling. "It's Lyons."

"Don't bother me, I'm hot." Throws down twenty.

A bulldogger fades him. "Come on, good shooter."

Hank wipes the sweat from the horseshoe over his eye, shakes, caresses the dice off the wall, eleven. Rakes in the money.

Lyons kneels down to the game. "Hey, Hank, lend me twenty."

"Sure, Lyons." Slides twenty to him, leaves twenty. "Let's hear it, men."

Lyons throws the twenty back down. "You're faded, Hank."

"You never were too smart, Lyons." Rolls a seven, rakes the money in.

"Hey, Hank. Loan me twenty."

"Goddamn."

Lyons throws the twenty down again. "You're faded."

"Would you let some of these other hard-luck bufords in on the action? I ain't making any headway with you around."

"Ain't you glad to see me? Come on out."

Rolls a seven. "Jesus Christ. This is like playing with myself. Would you just hold off till someone else got the fucking dice."

Lyons joins Keeper at a table. Hank leaves the forty down, he's faded, shoots a six. Makes a side bet, ten will get him fifty, six the

56

hard way, blows on the dice, tosses gentle carom, double three. "All right. Got my entry fees, now twenty more for my good buddy Lyons and I'll turn it over to y'all, cause my arm's getting tired pulling in the dough."

"You cain't quit now."

"You hide and watch, cowboy."

Rolls a seven, passes the dice, gets up and turns toward Lyons and Keeper at the table.

"Hold it, boy! Or you gonna have a heel print to match that horseshoe."

"Did I hear someone say hold it?" Turns back around to the game.

A giant 230-pounder stands. "I reckon you did."

"Hot damn. A bulldogger if ever I seen one. Turn around here in the light, so's I can get a good look at you, boy." Turns the dogger's back to Lyons and Keeper. "Now what was that you was a saying, podner?"

"I say you cain't—"

Lyons whops the duffel bag over his head, Hank knees in the balls, bulldogger doubles groaning to the floor. Grab up raincoats, ponchos, duffel bag and guitar and make for the door, Keeper staggering laughing behind, looking back. No one coming. Everyone laughing. But the dogger. "Slow down, fellers. What's the rush. Only one man interested in coming after us, and he don't feel much like it just now."

Out into the rain. "Where's Lyons?"

Back inside. Kissing the barmaid goodbye. "See you tomorrow, honey."

Turns at the door and waves his stetson. A thunderclap knocks out the lights. Shouts guffaws, breaking glass, the wind slams the bar door. Lyons on the sidewalk, can't see, blue lightning luminates, sees the Chevy, Hank and Keeper, finds his way. In behind the wheel. "How's the o rip running?"

Broken branches, garbage can, newspaper rattling water thrusting down the street. The car rocking in the wind. "She's purring like a tomcat in a meathouse."

Out of town along the blacktop, dim yellow headlit splashing frogs, white hopping barely visible through the water sheeting down the windshield. Defroster fan mounted on the steering column hums. Raindrops throw the headlights back. Drumming metal. Engine. Warm.

"Sure is good to see you all again."

Hot and humid afternoon. The rodeo grounds were crowded with trucks bringing in the stock, cowboys looking it over, trading tips, yarns. Limbering up horses, roping fence posts. Lyons weaving a new bull rope. A round manila line. Tied a honda knot, began braiding flat, nine strands, double braided over the top of the bull. Attached a cowbell. Ready.

People gathered in the stands. Sun hot. Kids running around, looking at calves, bulls, horses, cowboys. Soda pop beer. Wooden fences. Hay. Leather, sweat and manure.

The contestants meet to draw for the first go round. Keeper drew dead in saddle bronc, no chance, got a day-money horse for bareback, a gravy run. Lyons drew El Diablo.

"A real rank bull, son. But if you can stay clear of them horns you're gonna score high."

Calves bawling, horses neigh, cowboys, steers snort and bang the corral. Wives and children sit on the hoods of cars and pickups behind the chutes, on blankets on top of trailers, dogs barking, grandstands milling murmurous. The loudspeakers crackle, whistle. The grand entry. The introductions. The rodeo begins.

Bareback riding.

Keeper in chute two. Slap the ten-inch-wide leather strap around the withers, cinch down the surcingle, steady, boy, you and me going for a nice little ride. The flank strap in place. Easy, boy. Tightens on the dull roweled spurs. This is a gravy run, Keeper podner. You got the day money in the bag, and a good jump on the average. Props himself over the chute, hands and feet on opposite sides. Lyons calms the bronc, Keeper settles down, grabs the handle with his left hand, heels up over the point of the shoulders, right hand holding his hat above. "Turn her loose."

Lyons hotshots the horse's flanks, the bronc flies straight up and sideways out of the chute grunting groaning, Keeper's knees driving up and down mud flying ride him Keeper you son of a buck three seconds jarring high lashing Keeper in time rocking bouncing spurs up and snorting six seconds hat flashing sun buzzing eight seconds. Pickup men start out. Keeper vaults through the air left hand still down, knees still high spurring empty air, right hand waving free, lands on his feet trotting before the grandstands cheering standing as he bows.

"One hundred and ninety, folks! A ride you don't see every day, and the one to beat. Let's hear it for Robert Keeper!"

Calf roping.

Lap and tap because of the muddy arena. The twine around the calf's neck breaks the rope barrier for the roper soon as they leave the chute, Hank and the sorrel mare churn out. Both rating the calf. Hank twirls the lasso twice and slaps it over the calf's head. The mare slides back on her haunches, calf hits the end of the rope, jerked down, Hank leaps from the saddle piggin string in his teeth, hand along the lariat, calf struggles up bewildered, terrible scream from the horse over on her side, rope goes slack. Hank skids and falls looking back. The horse's legs flailing, froth at the mouth. Then still. Legs quiver now and then.

Keeper and Lyons jump from the fence, run out. Crowd hushed. Hank walking slowly back along the rope. Calf just standing looking on. Hank, Keeper and Lyons looking. Dead. What happened? Hank shakes his head. "Heart attack. She always was a dink. But she ain't never pulled that before."

Bull riding.

Late afternoon. Humid. Hot. And still. Lyons paces up and down the pens. El Diablo. Baleful. Ugly. Looking back.

"Let's go, Lyons, you're next."

Diablo pounding the sides of the chute. Keeper with the bull rope, flank man buckling the broad leather flank strap.

"Make her tight. Ol Diablo don't like her tight."

Lyons looking down from above. Hank outside the gate. Clown white, cherry nose, baggy pants and suspenders. Baseball shoes. Keeper looks up. "Don't be nervous, boy. He's flattened the last eight twisters to try him. So all you gotta do is stay on him and you're a winner sure. He's due to be rode. No bull ever dusted nine cowboys in a row."

"I wouldn't bet on that."

"And watch him. He's a hooker. Stay clear of them horns."

"Okay. Okay. Let's get this over with."

Keeper pulls the rope tight through the honda knot behind the shoulders, Lyons eases down on the broad gray back, wraps the flat braid over his palm twice, palm up through the fingers, clamps down the thumb across. "Let her rip."

Gate man flings open, Diablo hooking sluing straight for the fence, whiplashing hindquarters, Lyons leaning back to avoid head horns thrown back hooking plunging forward regaining balance rearing up panic blurring grandstand vision. Face. Pale. Front row. Spinning turn. Blond hair Blanchefleur. Mouth warm soft wet nicotine. Buzz. Eight seconds gone. Still here. On Diablo goddamn I did it!

Jerks the tail of the bull rope with the free hand loosening hold, Diablo another hook, Hank alongside waving the red cape in his face distracting as Lyons rolls off the back away, one last kick double gainer flop.

On all fours in the mud. Spits blood. Busted lip. The bull off after Hank digging for the fence, leaping high over as Diablo crashes in sending spectators scattering. Lyons sits there.

Blanchefleur.

Looks over at the grandstand. Tall woman at the fence looking over at Lyons getting up. Limps to his hat. Surge from the crowd, Diablo circling back, grabs his hat, dashes to the fence jumping clear. Sits on the rail, wipes the blood on his sleeve, looking down at, it is, Blanchefleur. "Howdy."

"Hi."

"What brings you to these parts?"

"I've never been to a rodeo before."

"Exciting, isn't it?"

Looking down from the fence at her. Wiping blood. Glad to see. But a little confused. Taste of nicotine, taste of blood. "Uh, how's Marcus? He come with you?"

"No. He didn't come. I. I came alone." Pause. Looking up, then down at her thumb and finger playing with the hem of her shirt. "Are you glad to see me?" Eyes frightened.

"Why, sure." Climbing down. "How about a beer after it's over?"

"A beer? Sure. I'd like that."

"Marcus won't mind, will he?"

"He. No. I won't tell."

Through the loud and boisterous smoky bar the barmaid weaved her hips to the table, slammed bottles angrily down. Lyons grinning, gave her a dollar bill. Drained his beer, grinned some more, Blanchefleur took a sip, skewing her face around the bottle mouth, withdrawing shy, began to speak, a burst of laughing spread across the room, fell silent. Lyons cleared his throat. Picked up the empty, peeled at the label with his thumbnail. Set it down, picked it up. Pointed to it and to the bar. She watched him make his way. People patting him on the back. His hands reriding Diablo, threw back his head and laughs, moves on to the bar. Piano player bangs honky-tonk, the barmaid leans over to hear. Lyons gesticulating, shrugs. She knows. About me.

What have I done. First time, frightened. Suddenly all alone. Strange noisy drunken cowboys. Smell the humid night outside so different, inside acrid sweat, beer and smoke, sweat on my forehead, armpits, the stranger at the bar trying to explain why I am here. What I have done.

When Lyons returned with two more beers, only an undrunk bottle remained, and a cigarette still burning in the ashtray. Figgered she had to go to the bathroom. Drank one beer, took out his little notebook and stubby pencil. Started to write. She didn't return.

Drank the other beer. The saloon full, jumbled light and sound of the piano joined by guitars and fiddle player. Looked around. Picked up her beer, a little warm by now. Writing in his notebook. The barmaid came by smiling. Picked up the empties, Lyons winked. She brought another, sat for a while at the table, giggled and flushed, whispered in his ear. Lyons patted her on the rump as she got up. Returned to the notebook.

Hank and Keeper came in, told him about the new horse they just bought and could he come up with forty bucks. They drank another round, Lyons peeled off two twenty-dollar bills and they left him for the back room. She must of had to catch the bus. Went on writing. Hardly see across the room. Hot. Large ceiling fan rotating overhead casting shadows. The fiddle playing and singing punctuating hoots and hollers. Long about closing time a bulldog-ger swaggers up to Lyons' table, kicks a chair around backwards and sits. "Whatcha up to, podner? Writing pohtry again?"

"Yep."

"Hey, ever body. O buddy Lyons is writing purty pohms over here." Snatches the notebook. "Mighty purty pohms. Let me read y'all a—"

Grabs the notebook back. "Well, podner, we might as well get this over with. It is getting late."

Puts the notebook in his shirt pocket. Finishes off his beer. Neatly sets the bottles with the others. Then flips the table over on the dogger, crashing stops the music shouting midmeasure bringing Hank and Keeper from the back room knowing it was closing time. Lyons throws a few punches wildly to make sure all is underway before ducking under a table and crawling along the wall to the bar where the barmaid already has removed her apron and picked up her purse. They slip out the back into the alley laughing around the building to the '31 Chevy.

Takes him awhile to realize why she swirled and slapped him as he opens the door. That it is Blanchefleur cuddled next to the steel-bodied guitar asleep in the back seat of the car.

After ten years of waiting. For Clark Gable. Spencer Tracy, Jimmy Stewart even. They never came. Just Roger Lyons. Was real enough. And Marcus ran him off.

She served the ham and candied yams, greens and creamed corn. Mackey and Marcus ate. In silence, nothing said about Lyons. She gathered the dirty clothes for tomorrow's wash. Darned socks. Marcus listened to the news and weather. They read the Bible, and he was asleep by ten o'clock.

She took the Prince Albert tobacco can from under her bed. The thunderstorms moved by south echoing over undulating landscape, flashing fitful blue green light and wind throwing the lace curtains, chastising darkness, flickering kerosene lamp. She counted the money scrimped, hidden from the grocery allowance, from her sewing held back from Marcus. Her secret guilty stash.

And decided. When harvest was over, she would leave. Three more days.

She gathers the dirty clothes, patches the knees of trousers. Marcus listens to the news and weather, reads the Bible, and is asleep by ten o'clock. She sits on her bed until his snoring fills the upstairs, takes her suitcase from beneath, packs in some clothes, the P.A. can. Looks over the things on the dressing table, hung from the walls. The books and magazines. Pictures, ribbons collected from high school, childhood, her mother. Leave it all behind. Slip out the back door down the east drive. Turn at the red shale rock garden to look back. Wind. The house hardly visible moonless night. And walk on down the road.

"You know, I've never been. Been away from home before." Trees. Night. Wind. Through the window. Inside so different. Blanchefleur cross-legged on the back-seat mattress, Lyons hands folded behind his head on a saddle, feet propped over the back of the front seat. "And I feel guilty."

"You ought to. That gal like to knocked out all my front teeth."

"I mean about leaving Marcus."

"Hell. He's your brother, not your husband."

"I know. He seems more like my father sometimes. I never knew my dad. You know all I remember about him is a gold watch with a grinning horse. He'd let me play with it sitting on his lap."

"But how come you, you never got, I mean how come you stuck around all that time?"

"I don't know. When I was young, younger, I used to day-dream a lot about the world I didn't know. I think the first time it really hit me that there was something else was when Marcus brought home our first crystal set.

"I'll never forget that, the kitchen became a magical place. A piece of mineral making voices out of air. When we got a big old Crosley battery console with short wave, I'd lean my head up against the grill cloth and listen. Strange music, static whistles and buzzes fading in and out, foreign languages. We even got ships at sea. Talking about things I'd never heard of. I'd wonder if I was there with them, or if I was in the audience. And thought sometime I'd go find out. But somehow I never made it, you know, dust bowl, depression. Just couldn't leave Marcus, but especially when Mom died. I know he seems hard, cold, but. He had to be hard to make it. He's run the farm since he was eight years old, and through hard times on nothing but will power. Still, there's more to him than that. You see he really loves the place, it's part of him and he's part of it. And his strength makes you better than you are. I guess that's it. As long as he's around I know everything is under control.

"You know, he reads everything he can get his hands on about

63

farming. Was president of the 4-H Club and a member of the Canadian County Farm Bureau in high school. He even had an article printed about terracing. I mean we built the farm together. We were the first family to have a generator-battery electrical system in the house, the first to use propane. I just wish. I don't know . . ."

She looks at him, looks around the strange interior of the car. Clutches her knees beneath her chin. "I remember the first time someone had me make them some dresses. Two of them for Marge Wiedemann for two dollars. I was so excited. Stayed up all night to finish them. And they were good. She came to pick them up, got out the money and you know Marcus took it and put it in his billfold. Didn't say a word. I mean I understood it was hard times, and we all had to do what we could. But I would've liked to be the one to hold the money and decide. Buy groceries with it, or ball bearings or whatever. Why couldn't he say I'd done good work? I mean I know it's what's expected. But that doesn't mean—I don't know. Marcus seems to think sometimes since it's expected, it's not, it doesn't deserve . . . praise."

"Why did you, I mean you must have friends, boyfriends."

"No I. Well. I was too busy. Working. I just didn't have time."

"For friends?"

"And besides, I never really felt a part of the town. Even when I was a little girl at school with the others, I knew I wasn't one of them, just couldn't let myself go, do the things the way they did. Mom made sure I didn't dress like them, talk like them. Didn't associate with them. Only at church socials, on Sundays, only at church and school. I can't remember anyone ever dropping by the farm just to visit us, to pass the time of day. So. I stayed to myself a lot I guess. Read. When I got out of high school I thought I'd go to college. My house wouldn't even have a kitchen in it. I'd be a business woman, Katharine Hepburn, and never have to cook. I was all set to go to business college in Oklahoma City. Had it all figured out. I got a room and board with a family keeping their kids. But that was just as the stock market crashed. No one had any money for anything, and I had to come back to the farm. All those years seems like the only thing you could think about was how to keep from choking to death on the dust."

Lyons rolls over, propping his head on hand and elbow, looking at her. "No boyfriends?"

She looks down at her feet. Pause. Cranes her neck, looks out the window. Smells the car. Him. Cold, black. Strange. Pulls her jacket tighter around her throat, grasps a handful of hair behind her head. Afraid. Strange. "I've never had. Had a boy. I've never been with a man."

Gets up on his knees, very near. His face to hers. The wind. Each other. Breathing. "I am with you."

Sorry Blows Off the Plains

HE woke, dream-wracked, high domed dawn rattling wind spangled slobber, deep brown-eyed cows come to watch. Galvanized water tank. Windmill turning chill morning wind. Ground hoof-beaten manure. A hundred cows around. He remembered. Stretched stiff. Looking into the eyes three feet away. Silent. Observing. He got up. The cows turned on their heels and rambled off over long shadowed shortgrass South Dakota prairie. Snooker. Hank'll get the Dodge. Sapulpa Slim. His boys. All crash back into consciousness. Air thin morning light, chilly. Looked into his face floating on moss deep water surface dissected darting water bugs, spiders and polliwogs deep. Splashed cold water. Circled the tank to the pipe from the pump, took long swallows exploding cold in his stomach going hollow from hunger. Could have won. Stripping water from the eyes to the salt lick block worn curving concave. Took a lap or two himself to cut the film from tongue and teeth. Another drink of water. Dome. Water tank. Windmill. Prairie.

Sun. Warming gradually higher above the horizon. East. Sapulpa Slim goddamn could of won what do you do now.

He stands. Muscles stiff, sore. Eyes follow grass-bare tire tracks meandering across the wide valley to the west. Highway 85 to the west. Beyond the ridge. Must be. Hungry. Sun hotter. Brown. Wind stirs up a little dust, sky grass, brown. And dark horizon.

He walked up the first bluff. Looked around. Across the plateau, another valley. Trail roaming through it. Crisscrossing cow paths dotted with cows. Walked. Road's got to be out there somewhere. Tracks lead somewhere.

He walked down across and up to the top of the next hill. There it was. Brown expanse hot sun and wind, brittle grass. The highway disappearing north, stringing off to the south. To the north on the other side of a transverse ridge. Trees. A water tower. Buffalo Gap. Will Hank still be there? Couldn't go back anyway, Sapulpa Slim's boys waiting. Hot. Highest point for miles around. Thunderhead pushing at the lower sky, dark blue beyond the brown. He strode down the path. Prickly pears. Amaranth. Ironweed. Prairie shoestring. Broom snakeweed. Silvery canescent leaves. Highway distant shimmering black asphalt ribbon cutting through the plateau ridge, gully, canyon. Arroyo. A silver speck. Blue, light blue and gray. A pickup and trailer stopped on the road.

He walked on faster, clouds building. Started to sing. Mighty hungry. Thirsty now. Gradual parallax movement of highway and hills. Land rising in front covering the pickup and trailer. Cumulus, boiling over darker blue and green clouds darkening down. Sun white anvils above. Hot, sweating walk up the trail dusty to the top, the highway again, much closer finally, can smell the rain, ice coming. The pickup and trailer on the shoulder of the high-banked road, hood up, a kid bent over under. A couple of miles now easy slope. Hank. Highway. Should have won. Storm front coming. Air thicker. The dark behind piling up over the sun, radiating fills the sky, prairie steppes, lightning interlacing. What will he, could of won all right my shot had him old man. Bad eyes. Shouldn't have run.

Run! Clouds towering churn purple green gray dust rising thousands of feet in front. Quicken the pace. The wind around gone still. Ominous. Excitement. Half a mile to the road, break into a trot. Clouds closer, higher, sun gone, prairie sudden dark movement. A lightning bolt cracks thunder explodes dry grass fire and dust. And again. Closer. Run! Fire, wall of dust, tumbleweeds, dead leaves, scraps of paper flying turmoil cold across the plains on the other side of the pickup. He sprints, head back, fingers stretch arching back thumbs perpendicular, hands chopping feet digging, kicking from the ankles dust behind laughing toward the storm gusts, a sudden wind wall, blinding dirt tossing water globules and mud. Bend into it and kick. Jump the ditch, the kid comes out from under the truck's hood, slams it shut and scrambles into the cab.

He yells to the kid, starts climbing toward the road. Lightning splits a telephone pole fifty feet away, the thunderclap knocks him paralyzed face down onto the embankment. Hands and knees, shakes his head wringing wet, blue green liquid light spirals sparks along the highwires. Panting. Blinks. Can't see. Crawls up the long embankment slipping and sliding blown to the door of the pickup, the kid inside fighting to hold it open. Up and in. Hailstones crash around the sudden interior calm. Grease and sweat. A surging din of ice on metal.

The kid pulls on a jean jacket over his wet T-shirt. "Hell of a storm." Windshield white-fogged streaking bouncing metallic rattle and roar. Shirt, jeans soaked and steaming. Shiver. "Whatever wheat there was sure nough had it now." Light lashes the windows exploding furious ice and water hurting the ears, rocking wind cold goosebump trembles. "Shit fire, I hope it don't smash in the pickup."

"Goddam big hailstones."

Wind pounding hail, the pickup rocks, jerking the trailer hitch, bounces sliding, letting go. The kid's hands tense on the steering wheel and window crank. "Fuck, we're moving!" Leg aching push on the brake pedal. Slipping. Trailer slowly slipping off the mud grade embankment, pickup turning its nose to the highway, falling. Holy shit! Stop!

A sudden thunderclap flattens the pickup. It grabs and holds. And the hail trails off.

Then the rain.

Silence.

They sit. Afraid to move, breathe. A few random drops of water. Silent. Cold. Alone. From all around last drippings. The slightest movement will send them over. Oozing down to the muddy ditch. It seems like. Shivering will send them down.

"Whaddayuh think, good buddy?"

"The situation's not only serious, but she's getting tense."

"Let's get out and take us a look."

"Our weight might be the onliest thing a holding us up."

"Naw. I don't think so."

"You don't think so?"

"Naw. I don't think so."

"Let's get out and take us a look then."

"Yeah. Take us a look."

Sit for a while longer. Vapor breath. Take hold of the door handle. Carefully. Snap open the latch. Push the door out. Ice. Three or four inches deep. Hailstones steaming, hot asphalt steaming beneath. Ease on out on the ground crunching ice. The '59 GMC pickup turned sideways in the road, the trailer hanging over the slope. Water tumbling in the ditch below. The kid comes out. The whole rig slides two inches suddenly oh goddamn both pulling, trying to hold it up.

"Don't this beat a hen a rooting."

"Ain't this a hell of a mess."

Gently turning loose. The kid pushes his St. Louis Cardinals baseball cap, bill turned up, back on his head. Paces up and down crunching hailstones blowing on his hands. Slips down along the trailer. Consults a thermometer by the door. "Hot damn. Twenty minutes ago it was a hunnert and two. Now she says fifty-two." Climbs back up to the road, offers a hand. "By the way, I'm Billy Paul."

"They call me Sorry."

"Glad to make your acquaintance." Feet fly out and falls on the bank. "Shit! Looks like we's stuck good, Sorry."

"We got one wheel on the pavement and one off. All we need to do is get some traction under this one."

"We got to get the slut to run fore traction's gonna hep us any."

"What's the problem?"

"Beats the shit out of me. She just keeps stalling out."

"Let's take a look, before some fool come barreling over that hill ninety mile an hour. We got the road pretty well blocked."

"Well, I'll give her another try."

Billy Paul eases back in, Sorry opens the hood to watch. The engine spins, takes hold, coughs and dies. Spins again. Nothing. Sorry blows on, rubs his shriveled hands together. "Looks like she's not getting any gas. Say. Before we tie into this, you don't happen to have something a feller could eat, do you?"

"You could make a dog sandwich. But the fixings is in the trailer. You reckon we could get in without pulling the whole shebang on over?"

"I'm hungry enough to give it a try."

Billy Paul gets out, walks around to the trailer door. Carefully crawls in, retrieves a loaf of bread and some bologna. They climb in the cab, Sorry shivering so much he can hardly peel the rind off the meat. Finally manages, folds a slice in half in a piece of bread. Billy Paul does the same, watches Sorry eat. "Don't you have no coat?"

"No. I left it somewheres."

"Sure could use a jacket in weather like this. You don't have any things?"

"No. Well. I . . ."

"What was you doing out in the middle of the pasture anyway?"

"Well. I ran into some bad luck. You see. I was hitching my way up north. And some fellers gave me a ride last night. I didn't know these fellers'd been drinking, or I'd have never gotten in with them. But it was getting late, and I needed a ride pretty bad, so I climb on in and they take out hell bent for leather, weaving all over the damn highway, and the next thing I know they've pulled off onto some country road and stopped. Wanting me to give them all my money, and one of them suckers has got a pistol. Well, I tell them my money is in my suitcase in the trunk, and when we get out to get it, I take off running. And that's how I ended up out on the prairie."

"Is that a fact."

"Sure is."

"Probably Injuns."

Finish eating in silence. "Well, let's see if we can get this rip started. You got some tools handy?"

"Sure."

They climb out. Sorry removes the air cleaner, looks into the carburetor. "Hit it again."

70

Doesn't start. Picks up a wrench, wrong size, another, removes the gas line. Hands shaking with the cold a little, "Try her." Gas squirts from the line. Plenty of gas getting to the carburetor. Replaces the line, removes a sparkplug wire, holds it near the engine block. "Hit it." Spark arcing to the block. Plenty of fire. Looks back into the carburetor. Takes a screwdriver. Removes the top. The needle valve must be. Let's see. Lifts out the float. Looks at it. Reservoir fills. Puts float back in, sets the top. "See what she says." Fires off, chokes and dies. Um-huh. Takes off the top, reservoir dry. Picks up the float. Let's see. She goes this a way, so that means a man would have to. So we just bend a little here, and we got it. Puts it back together. "One more time, Billy." Sputters, whines, sputters some more, dense gas vapor. "Hold it." Pulls out the float again. Eyeballs it, bends it back a little, that ought to, there we go, goddamn, it's colder than a. "That ought to do it, let her rip, Billy Paul."

She fires off, Billy Paul guns it a few times. "Goddamn if you ain't the goddamnedest mechanic, Sorry, I ever seen."

Sorry hops in, rubbing hands together. "How about another dogmeat sandwich? And let's get this baby warmed up before we try to pull the trailer up over the bank."

"They sure ain't much traffic on this road. I'd a thought somebody would been along by now to hep us."

"What about the rest of your crew? Won't they come looking for you?"

"Not before dark most likely. I was bringing up the rear."

"Well, let's see what we can do."

Cold gray blue clouds pulling low across the sky. Limp sagging highlines swaying. Brown grass melting through blue white hailstones. Rushing water, trickling, dripping. Billy Paul hunches up in his G.I. jacket, hands stuffed in pockets, inspecting the damage to the paint job, chips and dents. "Gaw odd damn. Is Marcus gonna be pissed."

Sorry rubbing hands together, blowing, his sleeveless shirt wet clinging. Looks at the back wheels again. "You lucky you were stopped. You'd been blowed clean off the road if you'd been moving."

"Damn. Didn't think of that. I wonder how the combines made out?"

"Let's worry about how we're gonna make out."

Inspects the shoulder, soft muddy. Right rear wheel sunk in a little already, left rear on the pavement. Trailer dangling over the edge. Billy Paul paces back and forth, looking at this and that, tugs at the fender, the trailer hitch, scratches beneath the baseball cap. "Whattaya think, Sorry? If we wait, someone's bound to come along."

Sorry doesn't answer. Still looking, thinking. Billy Paul inspects the hail damage some more. "Sure did peck her up."

"You got any chain?"

"Hell yes. Got some extra logging chain in the back here. You think we got enough traction to pull that fucking trailer out? Son of a bitch."

"Let's take a look at that chain."

"Sure. How bout me giving it a try? See if I can gun her out."

"You'd just bury that right wheel deeper."

"Yeah. Sure would. Right here's the chain. What we gonna do with it?"

"Need a board. One-by-six or something. Here, this two-by ought to do it."

"Yeah. What we . . ."

Sorry hooks the chain around the tongue of the trailer, looks across the highway. Strings the chain over to a no-passing sign. Pulls it tight, wraps it around the base of the signpost. Gray light level drops suddenly, heavy drops of rain. Goddamn. Places the two-by-four under the trailer hitch, cranks the tongue support wheel down on it. Unclamps the hitch from the ball, cranks it on up.

"Goddamn. I hope the fucker holds, Sorry."

"See if you can ease the pickup out now."

Spitting water. Sorry shoulders the tailgate. Billy Paul floorboards it slinging mud, digging in right rear.

"Easy, you dumb cocksucker!"

"What you say, Sorry?"

"I said take it easy, you'll bury the son of a bitch."

"Oh."

Thunderclap solarizes heavy splashing across a sudden gusting wind. Dark.

"Let me try it. You push."

Gets in, reverse, back, second forward, back, one more time forward and she walks on out.

"Attaway, Sorry! Now hook this other chain on the trailer, and pull her on out, huh?"

"We can't pull it down the road, it would just drag along the ditch, and probably tip the bastard over."

"You right about that."

"We'll have to pull it perpendicular."

"Huh?"

"Perpen. At a right angle. Ninety degrees. Straight across the fucking road."

"Oh. But they ain't much room that way."

"And this asphalt is slicker than hog guts on a doorknob."

"Yeah. Sure is. Slicker than a. Sure is. Slick."

"Well, let's see what she does."

Sorry hooks one of the chains from the trailer to the pickup. Eases out the clutch, kills it, starts, revs, clutch, left rear tire spins water steam smoke Billy Paul bouncing squeals inching forward. "Hot damn we gained about four foot on her."

Sorry backs to the trailer, almost over the hump onto the level. "Billy, pull up the slack to the pickup."

"Hit her. Hey, we got it! Let's get the fuck outta here!"

They hitch the trailer back up, toss the chain in the back, Billy Paul gets behind the wheel and they head off over the transverse ridge. Billy Paul slaps his thigh in laughing rehearsal on toward Buffalo Gap.

They pull into town from the south, rain stopped. Hardly rained at all in town. Hope Hank, the old Dodge. Hope. Passed the vacant lot. Supposed to move on north today. Some combines gone. But there's ours, and the Dodge. And. Shit! The '56 Ford, Sapulpa Slim's boys.

Sorry slid down in the seat. Billy Paul looks over. "What's the matter?"

"Oh. Just a little tired and cold. That's all."

"Where you headed anyway?"

"Headed. Headed north. I'm headed north. To see my girl. Was going to get engaged till those bastards took all my money."

"Well, I'm going as far as Bowman, North Dakota. And maybe can loan you a couple of bucks."

"That'll help a lot, thanks. Appreciate it."

They drove on through town, back out on the highway. The

cab warmed. Drone of the engine. Clothes still chilling wet. Turned on the radio, Bob Wills. Clouds moving. Ride to Bowman. Find Hank somewhere. He'll be, wait in Buffalo Gap until night, come on north, if he can find someone to. Who'd drive the truck. Maybe I could. Someone to. If. Engine road vibrations, side wind, rocking the piggyback combines pulling back south along U.S. 85, giving it up.

"Looks like we the only fools still heading north, Sorry."

Warmer now. Clothes drying, sun low through windshield hot on the face dulling thought circles Hank, snooker, restroom, pickup, Sapulpa, sleep.

"Hey, Sorry. Here we are."

"Huh?"

"This is far as I go. Wake up."

Evening. Wind blowing dust brown grassy knoll here and there trucks and combines loaded, pickups, house trailers. Lights, lanterns, voices garbled. Quarter-mile sloping down to the junction of highways 12 and 85. Weigh station. Sorry rubs his eyes, groggy, blinks. "Where?"

"Bowman. This here is Bob." Face and arm through Billy's window. "And Malachi."

Sorry's door opens, he rolls out, face to red face, long white hair white beard blowing in the wind, squinting against the falling sun. Holding out his hand. "Glad to meet you, Sorry."

Billy Paul tells how they got the rig out of the ditch, about Sorry losing his money and things. Sorry stands off by the pickup bed, tinkering with a grease gun. Everyone laughing at Billy's tale. Malachi beckons Sorry. "Youd better spend the night with us before heading on north. It's getting late. And I'll bet you haven't had much to eat today."

"Naw, that's all right. Awful nice of you but. I. I better be getting on my way. I . . ."

"Can't be going nowhere this time of night."

"I'll. I mean. Something."

"Won't hear of it. You'll eat with us and spend the night."

Malachi laughing disappeared behind the truck and combine. Sorry looked around. Other crews spotted over the hillock. No one familiar. No red Dodge. Bob slapped him on the shoulder. "Here's

74

a shirt and jacket for you. It'll be a little chilly now the sun's gone down."

Malachi returned, a woman with him. "This is my wife Viola. She'll cook up some eats that'll warm you."

Sticks out her hand. Firm shake. "Howdy, son. I'll have some food in you in no time."

They situate the trailer, level it, turn on the propane, kerosene lamps. Evening cold off the prairie, dusty stars, now and then receding diesel semis growling, air horns drifting distance from the weigh station at the intersection of the highways. Last lavender flow against the eastern sky. Malachi inspects the hail damage to the pickup, moves silently from rig to rig checking booms, braces, hitches. Red Ford, blue GMC, sideboards removed, Gleaner Baldwins chained down to the flatbeds, header barges on trailers behind. Climbs up onto the bed of the Ford, up the ladder to the combine's engine. Galvanized metal silver against the night. Malachi takes out a rag from his hip pocket and wipes the orange Wisconsin six-cylinder engine block.

Bob and Billy Paul argue good-naturedly, Bob knocks Billy Paul's cap off his head, they begin grappling, grasping shoulders turn circles laugh kicking out at ankles. Whomp. Bob goes down, Billy Paul on top, a headlock, rolling across the grass rising dust cursing laugh. Bob twists around, gets a scissor lock around the chest. Sorry stands off to the side by the trailer. Shortening sizzling smells chicken, steaming corn on the cob, lima beans, potatoes. Salivating almost double from sudden starvation. Billy Paul cries out enough, Bob laughing on his back. Billy Paul gets up dusting himself with his cap. Malachi down from the truck, Viola sticks her head out the door. "Come on y'all before I have to throw it all to the hogs."

Malachi leans back from the table, wipes his mouth and hands the dishtowel on to Billy Paul, who uses it, passes it to Bob, wipes his hands, gives it on to Sorry. Malachi gets up, kisses Viola still standing over the table, wiping her hands on her apron. "Sure you don't want no more?"

"I've had a plenty." Stands over the table looking at his crew. "Well. I called up north this afternoon. The man says the wheat isn't worth cutting, no need for us to come. I thought we could check around here tomorrow, but it's not looking good. You seen all the crews pulling back south today."

"Sure did."

"So, if it's all the same to you, I think we'll just turn on around tomorrow. Don't you think so, Viola?"

"Sure do. Wheat's only bringing $1.65 a bushel anyway."

"What do you think? Bob. You want to look around some tomorrow? I know we've made little enough money this time round."

"Naw, Malachi. We'd just be wasting our time. Don't you think so, Billy?"

"Well I. Sure, Bob, waste a time. I guess."

"I think we all been knocking our heads up agin it bout all we care to for one summer."

"That's what I figured. I already called Marcus. And he said bring them on back."

"Only one thing, Malachi."

"What's that, Bob?"

"I got a good friend I been planning on visiting up in Minot when we got up there. Now. It don't make good sense for me to be going all the way south to Oklahoma, then turning around and coming back. So."

"You want to quit here?"

"Well, yes. If it don't."

"We need someone to drive the GMC back."

Pause. Sorry looks back and forth. Find Hank but. What if, everybody heading back south. No money, clothes. Telephone. "Maybe, I mean I need a way back, food to eat. Maybe I could drive it for you."

Malachi strokes his beard, looks to Viola. "What do you think, Viola?"

"Do you have a chauffeur's license, son?"

"Sure do."

Roughs the bristle on Sorry's head. "It's settled then. Have another piece of pie."

After the dishes were done, Malachi lay down, still dressed, on the bed in the back of the trailer. Yellow green propane light. Viola, sitting patching overalls, settled up with Bob. Billy Paul, Bob and Sorry get out the cards and start playing cutthroat around the table. Billy Paul and Bob talking, swapping stories. Sorry silent, restless. "What was trumps?"

Cold wind sucking window and door screens. June bugs banging, cling. Intermittent billowing fine dust particles across the light. Hank. Home. Telephone. Bob slaps down the cards. "Hey, Malachi."

Viola biting thread in two. "He's asleep, Bob."

"It's about time I headed into town to catch the bus. You think it would be all right if Billy Paul took me in the pickup?"

"Sure."

Bob leaves the trailer to gather his things. Sorry collects the cards, shuffles, cuts, deals out a solitaire hand. Outside the slamming of truck doors, singing Hank Williams. Billy Paul watches the solitaire game, suggesting a few bad plays. Sorry preoccupied, distracted, joins in "Your Cheating Heart." Viola glances up from the sewing. Malachi snores. A diesel semi from the highway throttles through the gears over the prairie. A few flies around the light. A moth. Hank. Home. Telephone.

Bob returns. Stands at the table, hands in pockets. "Billy Paul. Let's get to going. You coming, Sorry?"

Looks up from the cards. "Sure."

Bob walks to Viola, she inclines a cheek, kisses. "See you next year."

"Let's go get us a road shortner. The bus don't come through till midnight."

They pull out of the filling station bus stop. Around the corner to the main street. Intersection town. Four buildings. One concrete block store, three wood frame houses, two bars.

"I'm not twenty-one."

"You can use my I.D., Sorry."

"But no one would believe I'm that old, Bob."

"Thanks a lot."

The place almost empty. Dark. A tall black-haired man in a white shirt with a woman. An old toothless man on a bar stool. Bob walks to the bar, Sorry turns on the light over one of the snooker tables. Billy Paul standing in the middle of the room looking both ways. Bob orders three bourbons, Sorry selects a 19-ounce cue from the rack on the wall. Motions to Billy Paul with his head to get himself a cue. Bob brings the drinks.

"Grab you a stick, Bob."

"Naw. Never took up the game."

Billy Paul breaks. Bob stands at the rail watching for a while.

Sloppy game. Loses interest, wanders back to the bar. A few others come in and out. Bob talking to the barkeep. The white shirt man comes for refills, joins in the conversation. Billy Paul scratches, "Aw shit." Sorry sips at the whiskey, wincing. Looks over at the pay phone in the corner by the bar. Nine-thirty. Woman in the booth waiting. Long muscular thighs crossed tight from under a short skirt, net stockings open-sided shoes, toe pointing, bouncing up and down. Low-cut blouse breast, corner booth maroon dark mouth dark blue green lined eyes blond, blond hair piled, shoulders long arms firm, slender wrist golden chain fingernails lacquer long cigarette between, trailing smoke. Sawdust, cue chalk, talcum, sweat. Pine-sol, whiskey through it all Sorry sensed, nostrils flaring, a woman smiled at him.

"Your shot, Sorry." Bounced the cueball off the table clattering across the floor. In a strange bar.

Billy Paul finally sank the 6 and 7, winning the game. Sorry puts up the cue. "I think I'll make a phone call."

Went to the bar for change. Barkeep looks at him dubiously. Bob and white shirt both back in the booth with the woman. The toothless old man on his stool salutes left-handed with his shot glass as Sorry moves to the phone. What to say, how. Stands at the phone, fiddles indecisive with the dime. Drops it in. Hangs up. Looks around. Billy Paul standing at the snooker table watching. Damn. Get it over. Pulls the dime from the return, puts it in, dials.

"Operator."

"I'd like to place a collect call to Alva, Oklahoma."

Distant disjointed conversations over the line, the first ring, Sorry's scalp tingling, arms weak. Come right out. Second ring. Admit. What else. Ring. Snooker Sapulpa two-fifty. Ring. Hank gone there waiting. Ring. But couldn't. Ring. "There doesn't seem to be any answer, shall I try again later?"

"What day is it?"

"Thursday, sir."

"No wonder. No. That's all right."

Thursday. Gone to the city for a couple of. Nothing to do.

"Hey, Sorry. What are you doing over there in the corner? Come on." Bob at the bar, waving a bourbon. Sorry walks over and sits on a stool between Bob and the old man. Bob slides him the shot. "What you so down in the mouth for?"

The bartender sidles up. "You sure this boy is twenty-one?"

Bob grins. Sorry rears back on his stool smiling suddenly. "How old do you think I am, sir?"

"Could I see some I.D. if you don't mind."

"Course I don't mind. I'm always flattered. You're not the first to be surprised." Pulls out the card. "There you go."

"Twenty-eight. Well, I'll be go to hell. I'd never a thought it. I sure wish I'd a looked that good when I was twenty-eight. I sure beg your pardon."

"That's all right. You ain't the first. Happens all the time."

Takes a big slug of whiskey. Fighting back tears, chases with water. Looks around to hide the shuddering grimace, woman in the booth gazing, stockinged thighs crossing still swinging her foot. Sorry hesitates, her eyes liquor fire concentric through his head, loins, he turns back around Bob laughing, the toothless old man whoopee and slams his whiskey down. Bob's hand around a glass, Sorry notices, stares for the first time. The ring and middle fingers gone gaping whiskey glass between. Bob follows Sorry's eyes. Holds up the hand. "Korean War."

"Whoopee." Bob scowls along the bar past Sorry at the toothless old man, beginning to slobber some on wrinkled pinstripe double breasted. "Ever body happy!"

Under his breath. "Fuck old people." Returning to his hand, turning palm to back. "My right lung gone too. Lucky to be alive. A MIG-17. Never saw him coming. All I remember is a dull red flash. And reaching for the ejection switch amazed at this bloody gap." Pause. Still fixed on the hand. Starts to speak. Nervous sip of bourbon instead. "Yeah. I was beautiful. A young stud in my flight suit. I was beautiful."

"Whoopee!"

"Fuck old people, Sorry."

"Jis wanna be happy."

"Man. Streaking over crumpled foothills three hundred miles an hour, wings loaded with rockets, napalm, blasting everything that moved. All the universe. Flux and motion. God. I loved it."

Silence. Sorry sips, looks around. White shirt and the woman gone from the booth. Billy Paul jangling at the pinball.

"Whoopee!"

"You're an intelligent kid, Sorry. I can tell an intelligent man when I see one. But you got too much on your mind. I been watching you."

79

"Well. I . . ."

"You know what your problem is? Huh? You know what it is?"

"No. But somehow I suspect you're going to tell me."

"You're too complicated."

"Bullshit."

"Now don't get mad."

"You've only known me a few hours."

"I've been watching. You been moping around ever since you showed up with Billy Paul, not acting like a guy on the way to meet his woman."

"I. Well. I told you what . . ."

"Too complicated. Take things simple. Like me. Life is simple. Either you're alive or you're dead. That's all there is to it, a pretty simple proposition. And a pretty thin partition between the two. I could have been a chemist, pulling down all kinds of money. Had the G.I. Bill to finish college, disability for the rest of my life. But didn't finish. College was too complicated, the professors trying to make something so simple so complex. You can prove the existence of God by the periodic tables, man. It's that simple. Yeah. I been to several colleges, couldn't finish any of them. The last one about had me arrested. Damn professor doctor trying to answer some poor dumb sucker's question, and just confusing everybody that understood it before. I just couldn't take it. Jumped up, grabbed him by the lapels shook him 'you stupid ball-less ignoramus! What the hell do you know about life and death!' and stomped out. They said if I ever come back on campus again, they'd have my ass under the jail."

"Wow."

"Make things simple. And never do anything you can't control. That's my motto." Lights a cigarette. "Have another, Sorry."

"Whoopee."

"Fuck old people, Sorry."

Silent drinking. The old man asleep, barely hanging on the edge of the bar. Sorry stares blankly ahead, Bob slumped at his glass. Billy Paul playing pinball.

Bob rears up suddenly looking at the clock. "Eleven-thirty. Time to go if I'm gonna catch that bus."

They stagger out to the pickup, Billy Paul behind the wheel, barrel down the street to the Texaco station. Circles of blue green mercury light. Empty. Weak yellow brown light rocking the corner each block up and down the street. They stop. Wait till the pickup dust whips past in silence. Bob opens the door, sits, holding it in the wind. Cold. "No need for you all to wait, you're gonna be hitting the road pretty early in the morning." Silence. Creaking. The wind. "Nice to have met you, Sorry. See you next year, Billy Paul."

"Sure."

Hops out. Grabs his G.I. duffel bag from the back, slings it over his shoulder, walks a few steps across the apron, turns, throws up a hand, first and little finger gaping silhouette. Billy spins off around the block.

Sorry wipes a hand spread fingered down across a clammy forehead nose cheek mouth chin and throat.

Strangely drunk. In a strange North Dakota town.

Marcus Has Work to Do

MOM always used to tell about the time I got struck by lightning down on the creek and she had to breathe life back in me. I was the only son, the one she counted on to build the farm, the land they claimed in '89.

We'll duck into the machine shed till this storm blows over, then get the pickup and take a ride before dark. I'll show you where it was, where the swimming hole is now.

I was six. It had been one of those days, hot and humid, when you could feel the thunderstorms, and see them coming, all afternoon long. We'd been clearing out the fence row west of the bridge, Blanche back at the house trying to get the wash done. Whenever a storm comes up to this day I think of Mom's long blue pleated dress and her bonnet.

We worked as long as we could. Till the clouds and the lightning filled the sky and the wind stopped. Then I headed off to get the cows. East to where they usually are, and it hit just as I was crossing the creek there raining to beat the band. I ran to the south-east corner and they weren't there. Over to the northeast and they weren't there. I'm ready to start crying about this time, cause I can't go back without the cows, but I realized that wouldn't do any good, and that's when I hear Mom's voice calling through the thunderclaps.

That's all I remember until I feel my nose pinched, her mouth on mine breathing in, inflating the lungs. Ringing silence, her face over me blocking the rain. And a split smoldering elm steaming on the ground. The creek was roaring thirty feet wide, Mom soaking wet, red mud smeared, had to carry me, once I was breathing, up the bank, along the ridge to the road, even the ditches hard to cross, pouring rain the half-mile to the house.

The cows were already in the barn bawling to be milked.

My dad was a drunk. It was Mom's strong will and the grace of God that kept the place together all that time. Mom always told the story how hard they worked, the two of them, the first three or four years, built the sod house on the south bank of the creek on the west place, struggled through the first summer's drought and hard winter hunger, surviving on the truck garden, what she'd canned, on corn, beets, green beans and pinto beans, the potatoes grown in creek-bottom land. See she had planned better than most of the Sooners. Because she knew the prairie is a harsh place to live. You have to make it give.

The summer of '90 they started building the house there on the hill, and my brother Cornelius was born. He died that fall of whooping cough. My dad was drinking some then, but they finished the house, and the winter of '91 Alexander was born. My dad got restless. He was a horsetrader before they claimed the land, and one day he told Mom he thought he'd take some of the best horses and head for Wichita. Do some trading, pick up some supplies to help them through the winter. Alexander died of pneumonia while he was gone. He returned two months later with nothing but a team of pissel-tail mules and a fifth of cheap whiskey. Mom said that's when she knew there was no redeeming him. He was the Devil's fodder, the foul breath of damnation threatening to destroy her life and the farm. But she knew she must endure. There had to be a son.

My dad wandered more and more. Mom suffered all those

years because he wasted everything they raised. But still she made the farm produce, grow, develop. And she waited. Then Blanche was born in 1908. And when I came in 1910, she said her prayers had been answered. She knew. Two sons dead already, that I'd live and be strong. Delivered me alone in front of the stove during a blizzard on that star-patterned quilt we still have in the upstairs chest. She said it was two days before the doctor could get there.

When I was a year old she hitched up the wagon, bundled up Blanche and me, and headed to the county courthouse in El Reno to start legal proceedings to have my dad committed as incompetent.

When he came back from one of his three-month drunks, this time on foot, and found out what was happening, he didn't even put up a fight. A pitiful man. Just changed his clothes, saddled up a horse and rode off.

We never saw nor heard of him again.

We'll drive back up the channel to the north pasture, the oldest ponds. We finished this one back in October 1918, never forget that, right before Blanche caught the flu. One of the worst times we ever had to get through. Spanish flu epidemic. Schools closed down for two weeks, everything. The governor outlawed all meetings over twelve people. More than seven thousand deaths in the state. Like I said, Blanche got it right after we finished the pond. Fever, chills, crying out in her sleep talking nonsense about our dad coming, horses, screaming out in the night. Mom stayed up with her three days straight. Moved the bed downstairs next to the stove. Wrapped her throat with a towel soaked in coal oil, rubbed skunk oil. I had to run the farm. Take care of ten horses, milk the cows, feed the chickens, gather eggs, chop wood, hitch up the team and plow.

The morning of the third day when I woke up, Mom was in the back yard throwing up. Pale. And feverish. Scared me. I was just eight years old. I helped her back inside to her rocking chair next to Blanche.

"Mom. You feeling all right?"

"I'm fine, Marcus. Just some of that cold oatmeal didn't agree with me. Maybe a touch of the flu."

"I'll saddle up Blackie and go get Doc Long."

"Doc's got better things to do, Marcus. There's folks sick around. I'll be all right. I got medicine in the blood."

"But you and Blanche."

"Don't worry, Marcus. You've got to be a man now." Her head rolls weakly, eyes straining about the room. "Get me a quilt, we'll be all right. You read to us, Marcus, get the Bible and read."

I ran upstairs for the quilt, covered her, shivering in the rocking chair.

"Have to be tough, Marcus. The plowing on the west place. Has to be done. Go on, Marcus. Get the Bible and read."

I backed away from her. The wood stove. Blanche lying in the bed staring at me. Mom staring. The room large and empty. The Bible in the alcove on the oak stand. Leather-bound. Big and heavy, I lug it across the room, Mom looking at me pull up a chair by the stove between her and Blanche. I had to. Open the Bible, the marriage date, Cornelius and Alexander, birth, sickness, and death. Me and Blanchefleur. I turn the pages, large black print, red print. Mom watching me leaf through Exodus, Ezra, Isaiah, Ezekiel, Philippians, be tough, Marcus. Don't be afraid. I just knew I had to take care of them. And the farm, medicine in the blood. And so I begin to read. Slowly. I remember pointing at every syllable.

The voice small and uncertain in the empty house.

their eyes were as a flame of fire

Distorted shadows dancing through the grate, the kerosene lamp, me reading, bent over the Bible resting on my knees.

he that hath ears, let him hear what the spirit saith

Windows rattling north wind, too scared to stop reading, to sleep.

to him that overcometh will I give to eat of the tree of life

It was me keeping them alive. If I fall asleep, I thought, they will die. Couldn't be sick.

he that overcometh shall not be hurt of a second death

I have to stay awake. The words large and black, verse after verse, column and column, stumbling, reread it till it's right, pages turning mingle hot dry dark dreaming.

and behold a white horse, and he that sat on him had a bow; and a crown was given unto him, and he went forth conquering and to conquer

Until cold settled, stillness, the wick grown dim, my head snaps up from the Bible to see her staring from the quilt. I jump up, go out back to the woodpile for more wood.

and there went out another horse that was red; and power was given to him that sat thereon to take peace from the earth, and that they should kill one another

Swing the door of the iron stove open, drop a log on the bed of coals. Blow it until it explodes on fire. Sit back in my chair, pull the blanket around, must stay awake and read. Or they will die.

lo a black horse, and he that sat

Mom talking fever babblings giant shadow across the walls and ceiling. "Your father sat. On a horse, grinning horse."

a pair of balances in his hand. A measure of wheat for a penny, and three measures of barley

"Your father. Riding up, my mother and father and brother, Royce, the wagon. Wellington, Kansas. May his soul burn."

and behold a pale horse: and his name that sat on him was Death, and Hell followed with him. And power was given

"Foul whiskey breath clammy sweating. For you, Marcus, I forced myself loathing drunken touch to."

kill with sword and with hunger, and with death

I read louder. Cannot be sick, cannot sleep. Louder than her fever. Blanche sleeping now, restless tossing, tangled in the sheet, hair pressed curls to her face, wet, red glowing. Rises up crying out for water. I lay the Bible down, take the crock out the front door to the well. The wind has stopped. The stars, the coarse rope cold, creaking pulling up echoes banging water splashes along the stone wall of the well, soft wooden, mossy bucket. Pour cold water. And back into thick dry heat smelling coal oil, skunk oil sickness. Dip the gourd and hold it to parched white flaking lips. Alone. Pick up the Bible and read.

and lo there was a great earthquake, and the sun became black as sackcloth of hair, and the moon became as blood

"Sleep, Marcus. We'll make it now. The drunkard's gone."

and the stars of heaven fell unto the earth, even as a fig tree casteth her untimely figs, when she is shaken of a mighty wind. And the heaven departed . . . and every mountain and island were moved out of their places

Sleep.

Blanche calls out in her sleep, "Daddy . . ." Soaking wet sweat. The clock strikes one.

and there followed hail and fire mingled with blood, and they

86

were cast upon the earth: and the third part of trees was burnt up, and all green grass was burnt up

Strikes two.

and the third part of the creatures which were in the sea, and had life, died

"Sweating stinking drunken moaning passion. I have borne my burden, have done my penance, I have suffered Lord God whose Son is my Saviour, Who is an angry God, why have You taken the son from my life, why have You taken him from me that I must humiliate myself the more."

"I'm here, Mom. Blanche is sleeping now."

A screech owl screams three times.

And there fell a great star from heaven, burning as it were a lamp, and it fell upon the third part of the rivers and upon the fountains of waters . . . and the third part of the waters became wormwood, and many men died of the waters, because they were made bitter

Four o'clock.

and the third part of the sun was smitten, and the third part of the moon, and the third part of the stars, so as the third part of them was darkened, and the day shone not for a third part of it, and the night likewise

I cannot sleep. Blanche is, Mom must sleep. Wipe her brow. Sweating now. Water.

"Give me some water, Marcus, for your mother."

Sweating now and sleep.

The sky going purple across the draw to the west, the mulberry trees, hedge-apple trees quiet. Violet vermillion east beyond the creek and hill.

And I went unto the angel, and said unto him, Give me the little book. And he said unto me, Take it and eat it up; and it shall make thy belly bitter, but it shall be in thy mouth sweet as honey

The shadows gone, the walls of the room return. We've made it till the sun comes up.

And she brought forth a man child, who was to rule all nations with a rod of iron: and her child was caught up unto God and to his throne

October morning.

And the woman was arrayed in purple and scarlet colour, and decked with gold and precious stones and pearls, having a golden cup in her hand full of abominations and filthiness of her fornications

The fever is broken. Yellow golden sun when the trees erupt with birds.

I had gone to bed three days ago a boy. Now I was a man.

And that was when I was eight years old.

Close the gate behind us. We'll drive south to take a look at the Smith quarter-section. We bought it when I was fifteen, put it in wheat. We were doing pretty good by then. Had thirty head of cows on the east pasture, forty horses in the barn. Mom and Blanche built chicken houses, about a hundred hens, developing quite an egg business.

I sort of had it in my head that I was going to live in the old Smith house back then. Haven't thought of that in years. Fact is, by the time I graduated from high school I thought it was time to get a wife. I'd always admired this girl Jessie Edwards, we'd had very good times together at church picnics down on Simpson's creek and the school hayrack rides. Thought we could get married, move onto the Smith place. Well, I guess I was too shy to talk much to her, didn't know what to say, but she made me feel at ease. She was tall and very smart, had had to work hard all her life because her mother had a stroke when she was young and Stephan Edwards never was a good father to her, never worth much of anything as a matter of fact. He owned the Mercantile, but was kind of a dandy, spent a lot of time in Oklahoma City. She'd been running the place for him since she was about twelve years old. Well, I was sitting in the kitchen churning butter one day when it just came over me. I'd had enough. And I got up and went out to find Mom in the truck garden.

She's over in the tomatoes. Once I get down there I don't quite know what to do. Mom pulling weeds from around the plants, looks up at me, overcast, humid day, asks if the butter's done. I don't say anything, go over to the stakes and twine lying on the ground, pick up one and start propping up the end vine. Mom, halfway down the row, looks a little longer at me, then goes back to the weeds. "With the weather we've been having, looks like all the blooms'll be setting. Should have a pretty good crop this year."

"Been pretty dry though. Winter and spring."

"Long as we get as much rain as last year."

I tie up the end plant, get another stake and move to the next, closer to her moving down the row toward me. We work on. Until we're side by side at the vines. Mom stands up, I finish driving the stake I've got, look at her, tall woman, almost eye to eye.

"What's on your mind, Marcus?"

"I been thinking." Her dark eyes glow in the humid air that never rains. Dry spring. "Instead of stakes. We ought to try putting cylinders of hog wire around each plant."

Looks up and down the row. "Not a bad idea. We got some extra hog wire around?"

"Got enough up in the machine shed to try a row or two, I think."

"Bring it down."

She passes me to the next tomato vine. "Mom."

"What?"

"I'm thinking about getting married."

She stands back up. She must be happy about it, but doesn't smile. "That's a pretty big decision. I didn't even know you had a girl. Who is it?"

"Well. She's not exactly my girl. I. She. Doesn't know anything about it yet, I thought I'd better. See what you think first."

"Who is it?"

"Well. I thought I'd talk to Jessie Edwards."

She looks hard at me, seen that anger before, her voice stays calm. "Never, Marcus. I'd never let that girl on the place."

My knees weak, chill. "But. Why not, she's . . ."

"You heard me, Marcus. We trade at the Mercantile cause it's the only place in town, but no daughter of Stephan Edwards will ever set foot in my house as long as I draw breath."

"But, Mom, what's Stephan Edwards got to do with Jessie, I don't—"

"You heard me, Marcus. Now get back to work."

She plucks a big green tomato worm from a leaf, squishes it between her fingers, turns and stoops back down to the weeding. I'm mad. Can't say anything. Just kick a stake from the ground and stomp back up the lane to the house. Sit at the butter churn, a couple of angry licks, then just stare off, across the kitchen. Trying to figure it out.

Blanche comes onto the back porch from the hen house with two buckets of eggs. Walks around the house to the well for water. She passes by me once, doesn't say anything, starts cleaning the eggs. Standing there in the kitchen door looking at me. Didn't even know she was there until she said something.

"What's the matter, Marcus?"

"Nothing."

I start on the butter again. She goes back to the porch. I stop. Walk out to her. She looks up from the porcelain bowl and waits for me to talk.

"What do you think of Jessie Edwards?"

She tries to hide a smile I think, puts down the egg she's got, picks up another one. "I think she's nice. Why do you want to know for?"

"Nothing. Just wondering."

Pause. "Just wondering, huh?"

"Never mind." Back into the kitchen.

Follows. "We were on the basketball team together when I was a senior. She was good. We didn't talk much, she was just a sophomore, but whenever I go to the Mercantile . . . Why are you so interested, Marcus?"

She's about to laugh and I'm feeling worse by the minute. "Just wondering, that's all."

I sit back at the churn, but she stays in the door looking at me while I try to get back to work.

"Marcus, you okay?"

Look at her, feeling like a bonehead fool, but have to talk to find out, to get some help to. "I. Think I want to marry her."

"What? When's all this been going on? What does she say? This is great, Marcus!"

"I haven't talked to her yet."

"Oh. . . . Don't you think it would be a good idea?"

"Yes, but."

"But what? If you want to marry her it might be a good idea to talk to her at least."

"I know, but. Mom. I talked to Mom. She. Says she'd never allow it."

Long pause. "Oh." She stands there gazing down at the linoleum.

I lean on the churn paddle. "What would you do? If you were me."

She sits down at the kitchen table. Picks up the salt shaker, turns it in her fingers. "I don't know. Mom sure hates Stephen Edwards."

"I know he's not the most admirable man around, but."

"No, it—it has to do with something he did back when Mom was alone so much. I don't know, back when we still owed a lot at the Mercantile from Dad's drinking I think. I never did find out what it was."

We sit there. A steel-blue mud dauber wanders from the back porch into the living room. Blanche looks at me. "What are we going to do?" She gets up from the table, goes out to the back porch, comes back in to the sink. Then to the cupboard to pull out a box of ginger snaps hidden in behind the flour. Sits back at the table, hands me a cookie. "You know, Marcus, I've been thinking a lot about this. What we're going to do. We're grown up now. It's time to do something. And I think. I think if you're serious, there's only one thing you can do."

Take a bite of the ginger snap. "What?"

"Leave the farm."

I didn't know what to do. I knew Blanche was right. I couldn't stay on the farm and marry Jessie Edwards. And there wasn't any other woman I wanted. I went out to the north pond to think, to try to get my courage up to face Mom. Mad at me already, and now I was going to have to tell her I was leaving.

I finally decide it has to be done. Walk back across the field, the wheat rattling ripe. One more harvest and then I leave. Montana. My Uncle Royce's place in the Gallatin Valley near Bozeman. So far away it might as well be China.

Mom is still in the truck garden weeding around the dewberry bushes. I pick up a hoe, but just stand there with it. She looks up at me. "Don't you have something more important to be doing than watching me work, Marcus?"

"I. We better talk."

Straightens up, wipes the red dirt from her hands on the apron. "Marcus. If it's about Jessie Edwards, there's nothing more to say."

"You don't even know her."

"I don't need to know her. I know her father. And we've worked too hard developing this land, already had to deal with too many depraved reprobates. Marcus, we've suffered enough hardships for two or three lifetimes wrestling this land from the wilderness and from the clutches of your father, may his soul burn in hell, and as the Lord God our Saviour is my witness, we are not going to invite another Devil incarnate on the place."

"But Jessie's not—"

"Marcus, I know you're a young strong and healthy man, but you're going to have to use your head. Bad blood is bad blood. For generations. Your father and Stephan Edwards. We didn't sacrifice and toil to give the land over to the combined issue of such as they. Jessie Edwards is not the woman for mothering grandchildren of mine."

She goes back to pulling weeds. Want to turn and run. But I can't. Blanche is right. I have to leave. "Mom."

Not looking up from the dewberry roots. "What."

"I think. I'm going to leave the farm."

Stands back up, removes the bonnet and wipes the sweat from her forehead. "Marcus. I thought you were going to bring the hog wire down from the machine shed for the tomato plants."

"I mean it, Mom."

Stand facing each other almost eye to eye. "I see you do. Where are you planning on going to, Marcus?"

Can't back down now. "I was thinking I would go out to Uncle Royce in Montana."

She walks over to the water jug leaning against a peach tree. Puts down the adz. Takes a drink. Hands over the jug, a stern smile plays across the dark eyes. "When you planning on leaving?"

I take a drink. "I'd wait till harvest was in."

"We'd be a little shorthanded for plowing and getting the seed in."

Take another drink, put the jug back down under the tree. "I know. But you could get help from some of the boys around, a hired hand somewhere."

She looks at me. "I guess I could manage awhile." Picks up the adz. "Young man has to stretch his legs a little. Think things over. Royce always says he wants us to come out. Probably do you a lot of good to see the country." She smiles. "We'll talk about it at supper." Leans down to the dewberries. "Now get back to work."

Well, I was surprised. Mom thought leaving was a good idea. So after harvest, I went to tell Jessie Edwards I was going. Couldn't tell if she was sorry to see me go or not. But when I finally got up enough courage, standing there in the Mercantile by the baling wire waiting for the place to empty out, to ask if she would write me while I'm gone, she said she would. And with that to lift my sinking spirits, I headed west.

I'll tell you, it was an amazing place, between the Madison and the Gallatin ranges. The river tumbling through the winding narrow canyon coming in, over stones and boulders, so cold and clean you drink right out of it, like nothing I'd ever seen before. Hilly green meadows and pure clear air the sun would turn to gold, make the sheep and Charolais cattle glisten. There was a trout stream ran right through the barnyard, go out and catch a few for breakfast when you're hungry. Uncle Royce was glad to have me. Taught me a whole new way of doing things, ranching instead of farming. They'd been irrigating in the valley since 1902, he said. The government provided money to develop the system. All the ranchers in the valley cooperated. A network of ditches running swift cold water from the mountains, see the bottom ten feet deep. Everybody shared it. Made my work back home look like beginner's stuff. Really made me step back and take notice. Thought I'd found paradise for sure, all I had to do was get settled, then write Jessie Edwards and ask her to come out and marry me.

But you see a strange thing happened. After I'd been there awhile, I started feeling uneasy. Just thought I was lonely, a little homesick for Mom and Blanche. Jessie Edwards' cards not coming so often anymore. But it was more than that. The mountains were always there when you looked up, very beautiful, but blocking the view, the morning sun, cut off the light much sooner in the day. I began to feel hemmed in. The nights began to get cold long before they should and the air so still. I missed the wind. Hearing it, feeling it, seeing it surge through the grass. I even missed, maybe most of all, the shale red dirt of the farm. The smell of it in the sun just turned with the plow.

So when I heard Blanche was leaving the farm to go to business school in the city, and Mom's letters began to tell of the drought back home, and the market fell, and it was the middle of a winter like I'd never seen and I don't know, all the cowboys sitting around the stove spitting tobacco juice telling me what a mild one it was, holed up in the bunkhouse days at a stretch with nothing to do but waste time playing cribbage and dominoes, I knew Montana wasn't for me. Mom needed me back on the farm. I'd have to have it out with her. I dreaded it like the dickens, but I couldn't see any other way.

I was nineteen. Haven't thought of that in years. It was a sad countryside I came back to. The stock market crash didn't really bother us much. Hurt the bank some, and the businesses in town. Wheat got mighty cheap. What really hurt was the crop failures brought on by the drought. I'd been preaching since I was in the eighth grade to anybody who'd listen. If your land is going to take care of you, you'd doggone better take care of it. The farmers in the state, in the entire southern Great Plains, were taking, but not giving back. Living on borrowed ground and time.

Anybody with any sense living on the prairie ought to know it's dry, uncertain rainfall. And windy. The soil type is loess. Fine-grained, dropped here by the wind in the first place. And the Lord isn't the only one that can giveth and taketh away. Anybody who thought about it would know that the native grasses, waist-deep rolling in the wind, hissing green blue springtime grass is what holds the world in place. Roots go down fifteen feet. And it ought to be obvious when you plow the grass under, millions of cows chew and trample it to the ground, and the wind keeps right on blowing forty miles an hour night and day, you're going to have problems holding onto your farm. You're going to blow away.

But there didn't seem to be anybody with any sense, anybody who thought about it in the entire one hundred million acres filling the skies in the thirties. You see, almost all the homesteaders planted row crops, wheat, oats and rye. They say the wheat acreage tripled from 1914 to 1919 because of the high war prices, and increased another fifty percent in the next ten years. Well, high prices, and the development of tractors and harvester-threshers, farmers doing good. Taking while the taking was good. Like I always said, I'm out trying to make a living, and everybody else is out making a killing. By 1935 half the land was cultivated and the other half overgrazed. It was clear what was being killed.

And along about 1930 the rains stopped coming. I remember it was one of those things, like growing old, happens so slowly you don't realize it until one day it's there, and you know it's been there a long time. But I saw it coming for years, could tell, feel it, uncanny sixty-degree winter days, spring wind, a little dryer, a little hotter, moaning telephone wires and barbed wire, splashing trees, the leaves more brittle, the cows crowding, perforating muddy banks of shrinking summer ponds, turning their backs and bawling with the wind. Walk out mornings through dusty grass instead of dew. Could feel the sky tighten. Grow dense. Thick. And dusty. See the sky on fire burning evening sun. The little rain turned muddy globules bursting blood-red, scattered over the six-speed windshield, then gone, residue turned to dust. The roads were red powder, hot. Ditches, pond bottoms cracking, the creeks a trickle, and then gone. The daylight dimmer, dust showing paths of wind, ridges and ripples at first, behind the granary, the hen house, the hedgerows. Flowing through the tractor and plows sitting idle in the barren field. The low spots and hollows filling up. Drifting. Fence rows buried to the bottom wire, the middle. Then the top. Fine as sifted flour. Piling up fine around the cracks of doors and windows. Billows and swirls around your shoe, covering it on the floor where you step. You could taste it, feel it grit your teeth, in your mouth, in your throat, your lungs, mud lining lips and nostrils, caking in the corner of your eyes.

In the first black blizzard, in the Dakotas, blotted out the sun, the wind howling unhindered across the high plains. The sky dark the next day over Chicago, and the next day after in Atlantic City, New Jersey. And the dust settling on the decks of ships at sea.

The dust bowl had begun.

"What profit hath he that hath laboured for the wind."

"In the sweat of thy face shalt thou eat bread, till thou return unto the ground, for out of it wast thou taken. For dust thou art, and unto dust thou return."

And believe me, there was plenty of dust. You could see some storms coming hours before they hit. First you'd see just a dark line on the horizon, black, slowly building, until the bottom half of the sky was covered, grown heavy churning swirl boiling over the land. Towering seventy-five thousand feet, three hundred sixty million tons of earth. Until it all collapsed unspinning, black out the sun, choking abrasive dark. Some storms you feel it. Sifting in, a dense fog along the ground. Slow, calm, filling up the world. Drive with your headlights on, and you still couldn't see. It rolled over the windshield thick as water. The bandana around your face turned your breath to mud. You could not breathe. And the sky never cleared.

If any crops sprouted, they'd be burned off at the root. Static electricity generated in the hot dry wind, horn tips of cattle glowed blue at night. I did a lot of traveling around the state for the Farm Bureau after I got back, trying to help farmers keep hold of their land. But too late to do any good. We saw lots of rundown, abandoned farms out west, in the panhandle. Fallen-down outbuildings, paint-scoured houses buried in desert drifting dust to the second-story windows. The machinery polished dull gleaming from the wind abandoned in the field in dusty sun. Dust-blinded cows, run bawling circles until they drop, suffocated, nostrils clogged mucus mud. Jackrabbits huddled close to the ground, face away from the storm, downwind wake settled dust. You'd find them next morning, buried hillocks, just the caked noses twiching out. And ever now and then an old farmer who didn't make it. Even too hot and dry for the flies.

There'd be harsh changes in the weather. I remember one February it was sixty degrees at four o'clock in the afternoon and a front blew through, temperature dropped to sixteen below by six. But never any snow or rain. Six months at a time. Then you got the whole year's supply in one night, flash floods washed away the bare ground the wind hadn't taken.

One afternoon back in '33 I was trying to get home before a storm hit. Started hailing just as I topped the hill by the Stout place. Henry Stout had died the year before, and Willa Stout was trying to hold onto the farm all by herself. I pull in to find her, and maybe take cover myself, and she's standing out on the back porch watching. Raining and hailing to beat the band. All of a sudden it stops. Still as death sky icy green purple, and we see the tornado funnel drop out of the boiling sky and touch down not a hundred yards out in the wheat field heading right for us. We just stand there watching. Henry had bought a Gleaner combine right before he died, hoping there'd be some wheat to cut one of these times, Willa trying to keep up the payments although there hadn't been a crop in two or three years. We could see it sitting out by the barn starting to shake and dance around like St. Vitus. Then hover and slowly whirl and float right over our heads into the clouds and dust and debris. Willa, who was a faithful churchgoer and one of the finest women in the town, stood staring at the sky where it'd disappeared. "Well, goddamn. There goes my combine."

We jumped into the pickup and headed after it. Followed for about a mile and a half until we came upon it, sitting in the middle of the road right in front of Ed Treach's old Model-A skidded off into the ditch. Ed standing there in the mud, hands stuck in his overall pockets, looking puzzled up to the sky.

The only thing wrong with the combine was the axle sprung a little.

Because of the rain the storm had brought there was a cover of green that spring. But it was devoured by a ravenous plague of hungry rabbits and grasshoppers.

It was like a funeral. And the earth herself was the corpse.

But we kept on. Blanche had to come back from the city, the family she worked for couldn't afford her anymore, she couldn't find anything else. Anyway Mom needed us on the farm. It was a struggle to keep ourselves alive, the constant wind and dust. Seemed like there'd never been anything else. I kept thinking I'd know the time to go to Jessie and ask; when to challenge Mom. But. There was always something. I kept thinking there must be better times than these. Blanche kept telling me, you've got to do it, Marcus, now.

Blanche and I trying to set out the tomato plants, early spring, 1931. The wind out of the southwest, hot and dry over New Mexico and the Texas panhandle, desert wind stinging dust and sand. The plants we'd started from seed on the back porch. We set them in the hole, water, see each one dry up before our eyes, the leaves wither and wilt, stem cut off and tumble across the patch and catch in the chicken wire fence before we get the next hole dug. Blanche looks up at me, watery eyes turned to mud, chapped cracked lips, looks up at the sun clogged dust in the sky. "Marcus. Let's go into town to the Mercantile, see if we can get some gallon buckets to put around the plants. We're wasting our time fighting this wind." Wipes the mud from the corners of the eyes. "And you can talk to Jessie Edwards."

We drive the six-speed in. Blanche goes around back to look

for empty gallon cans and I go inside to find Jessie. She's talking to Blackjack Hennessey and a man I don't know, sort of huddled near the counter, drinking grape pop, hiding from the howling in the ceiling vents and gusting down the street. She sees me come in and smiles. What can I say to her? The wind blowing us all away. Mom. Blanche and me. It all seems so senseless. I look at her. Then tell her I'm looking for gallon cans to put around the tomato plants. She says sure. Might be a few out back in the shed. Take whatever's there. The man says he thought he'd found a dime out on the sidewalk turned out to be a gallon bucket lid. We all chuckle. Yep. Sure is hard times.

And I go back out to help Blanche load them up.

About six months later Blanche tells me Jessie Edwards has married a fellow from Edmond she'd met when he delivered feed to the Mercantile. They're living with his folks, expecting a baby.

I walk out onto the pasture, grass turning to dust where I step, billowing eddies dancing off across the rise before me. What could I do? I had work to do.

I tell you, it doesn't matter, good times, bad times. You have to work just as hard. I am my mother's son. Farming is what I'm meant to do, a steward of God's soil, and it's a tough way to serve the Lord. But everyone has a calling, and all are equal in His eyes. He doesn't care what you do, but how you do it. So you go about your business with the same resolve, doesn't matter, trying to sow seed in parched powder whipped a hundred and ten degrees scathing wind so hot the meadowlarks hunker down in the shade of fence posts, or getting up to thrash dew fresh sunrise, pure air churning ripened wheat as far as you can see. You do what has to be done. And it would be of little meaning, of no consequence to do it gladly only when all was ease and bountiful harvest. It's hard times that test the will and spirit, when a man really needs to be glad.

Well, because of the work we did on the watershed the creek usually had a little water. Not all the ponds dry. The windrows we'd planted, the terraces. It all helped. We had the truck garden. The chickens, eggs and some milk left over to trade. Could hunt and trap for food, and sell the skunk and possum pelts. Blanche and I would go along the creek at night with gunnysacks catching frogs to sell in the city to the hotels. Two dollars a dozen. Some years even some money from the wheat, but you considered yourself lucky to get back your seed. Usually didn't even pay to cut it. In 1934 only three percent of the crop harvested in the state. Only brought twenty-five cents a bushel. Just plow it under and hope for something better next year.

Lots of people lost their land. Went into debt at the Mercantile, Stephan Edwards suddenly back in town taking an interest in running the place. They couldn't make their payments to the bank. And they foreclosed. Stephan Edwards and the banker got lots of cheap land. But Mom, Blanche and me stuck it out. And just as it looked like we had it made, a rainy spring, the ponds filling up again, just as it seemed like we'd be able to reap a little of what we'd sown, that the drought was over, an economy put back together, Mom took sick and died.

Early on Sunday morning. Blanche had been up with her in the night. An early morning thunderstorm throwing trees outside along the walls and ceiling, rumbling booming blue gray moisture thick air, water splattering against the windows low against the floor, running down in streams changing quick trails gather in the corners, trickle off dissolving in the rain again. Mom breathing easy, pale, her eyes closed. Blanche feeling her forehead. "She's still burning up, but sleeping for the first time. Was awake most of the night talking out of her head again. About you and Dad. I think we should get Doc Long."

"She doesn't want a doctor. She's got medicine in the blood."

Blanche looks at me for a while. Gray striped wallpaper, white enameled closet doors. Mom's face gray between the window on the west at the head of the bed, the north window, spotted drops running water gray. White blue gray patterned quilt. Smelling coal oil and lard. Urine standing in a crockery bowl on the floor. Slow thunder trembles across the room. Blanche looks down at her. And leaves. Flash cracking thunder shakes the house rattles the windowpanes. Her eyes open. Shining dark. "Marcus."

"How you feeling, Mom?"

"Open the north window. Smell the wet trees."

Thrust of colder air. Wet. I sit on the edge of the bed. She closes her eyes, seems to sleep again. Peaceful thunder rolling down through the elm trees in the north yard. Clumps of mistletoe in the

99

branches glistening new leaves gentle green and water. Honeysuckle on the hog-wire fence. The six-speed. Two shovels, a pry bar in the back. A coiled rope. A pile of chicken manure near the tailgate. The tires. Stained, all stained, wet, red mud. The dog curled beneath.

A fit of coughing shakes her awake. Breathing hard. Rattling in her chest. Looking up into the room. "Seems like all my life. I've been waiting for it to rain. The soil light. Moist. And easy to spade."

"It's going to be a fine wet spring."

"I did it for you, Marcus. The farm. For generations."

Coughing, tears. Not sadness, straining. Breathing hard, sweat beading, curls of hair matted to her forehead. Deep dark water eyes looking. Wanting to say. But can't. Just coughing, foam at the corners of her mouth. I dab with the edge of the sheet. Wants to say. Rattling phlegm gurgling in her lungs. Can't. Raises her shaky shrunken hand in the empty air, the smell of new leaves, tracing letters. An *L*. Tracing, I think an *A*. Trembling, coughing drops her arm struggling to breathe, eyes open burning wide, at me, coughs, chokes rasping breath, moans softly, face settling within itself. Closes the eyes. And doesn't breathe again.

The wheat on the west place made twenty bushels to the acre that year.

Shall we receive good at the hand of God, and shall we not receive evil? Like Job. That's what life is. Deceptively beautiful sometimes. A windless long slow soaking rain. Sunrise slanting light on sloping green pasture grass along a watershed marked by sandplum, sumac, chinaberry, persimmon trees and the song of birds. A full moon diffuse through altocumulus motionless, a lower lamina gray and blue veil, altostratus moves silent, indifferent across. The wind. Silent. A cow calling out from the east pasture.

Stand in wonder.

And go on.

A year after we buried Mom, Blanche left home. Without a word. I woke one morning, right after harvest, the house cold, no aroma of eggs and bacon, no biscuits baking. No sound of her singing filling up the stairwell of the house. Cold empty. Her room. Suitcase gone. I ran around the place like a crazy man, calling, looking in closets, like we were playing hide and seek, outside yelling my head off, cursing, the machine shed, chicken houses and barn. Along the creek. But she was gone. You know, I've never told anyone this. I sat in the rocker in the front room and didn't move the whole morning. Mackey finally made me breakfast. I couldn't eat. Just sat there wondering. She'd be back. I thought. Write. If that's what she wanted, but. How could she? Where would she go to find a life? I thought she understood. Working together all these years, milking cows, quiet dark dawn, just me and her in the barn, the cows.

Lean our faces against the warm flanks and milk. Together. Steam rising from the hay damp manure. Kerosene light. The cats rubbing up against your leg, flies scattering from the slapping tails. Empty the pails into the milk can. Pitchfork in the hay, cajole old Betsie and Roan and Ring-eye into the stall, their heads in between the upright two-by-fours to lock them in. Smear Raleigh's Brown Salve on chafed teats. And milk. All those years. No time to talk, it seemed like. I didn't think we had to, thought she understood. Bundled in a blanket in the wagon on the way to school, snow flurries swirling down the red packed road. It wasn't all so hard. Before the drought. She was my big sister, I counted on her, she should have, I was proud of her at school. Why didn't she say something to me?

I couldn't waste time looking. She would come back. I thought.

But I've never seen her since, nor heard a word.

And that's been twenty years.

It hardly seems possible. All that time. You stand in the east yard at night and see the lights of Oklahoma City. Growing. We'll drive over to the west place, I'll show you the airstrip I've got over there. Right above the bank where the sod house was. Well, a smooth place where Raymond Herold can land his Piper Cub, or any of the flying farmers when they come to visit. Always meant to learn to fly, but haven't gotten around to it yet. But it's a real thrill for me to be up there. Raymond at the controls, hopping the high-wires and terraces, the wing tip knocking off the heads of the wheat sometimes on a turn, and me there with my 12-gauge hunting coyotes. Or soaring up with the hawks over the land, to see it all at once, the relationships of hills and gullies, watersheds, creeks and dams. Trees, grass, the gridded fence rows, plowed ground and terraces. To see how it all makes sense, it's all a pattern. To see El Reno, Okarche, Yukon and Oklahoma City, and the network of railroads, section lines and highways. Can almost feel what the Good Lord must have felt resting on the seventh day. That it was good.

"Every man to whom God hath given riches and wealth and hath given his power to eat thereof, and to take his portion, and to rejoice in his labour, this is the gift of God."

A lot has happened in those twenty years. Hardly had time to stop and think about it. Where she is. What she's doing. Why. Hardly had time to wonder.

Until the harvest crew came back from North Dakota. With a young man who called himself Sorry.

Keeper Takes a Woman

Whᴇɴ Robert Keeper answered the phone he hadn't thought of Saskatoon.

A long time since he'd looked at the '31 Chevy, Lyons fidgeting his hat, pawing dirt with the toe of his boot. Fast rewind jibberish through his mind. Gazing out through the window by the phone, the barn and field behind. Blowing away 1940. Chute number two coming out. The highway. The backroom dark. Smell of blood. The doctor quiet.

Had always meant to tell.

But time.

And hadn't thought of Saskatoon. Thought of rodeo in years.

Hank and Roger Lyons were hard-luck cowboys, figgered he was hard-luck too. Never stopped to wonder where the money came from when they borrowed entry fees, whiskey money or Keeper paid the barbecue ribs and gas. Always figgered it was winnings. Never stopped to add it up. He never won that much. Always figgered him for a ordinary drifting bronc stomper like themselves.

He wasn't. Had a share of a big wheat farm in Oklahoma. His dad's. Given to him as he grew.

But he *was* hard-luck. Played baseball, semipro. Traveling around the state, second base, not too bad. Maybe a shot at big league ball. Hot field, cow turds, clumps of clover, dandelions, goatheads, buffalo grass, spots of blue red shale where not much of anything could grow, sometimes surrounded by a board fence, barbed wire sometimes no fence at all. Taken out over second, first half of a double play, by a big o fast boy, broke his elbow, right arm. Healed all right, a little stiff, and couldn't make that good off-balance throw from way behind the bag on the third base side any more. Gets all its snap and power from the wrist and elbow. He favored the elbow, put all the strain on the shoulder, and it started to bother him at the plate. Couldn't fight off that tight inside fast ball like he used to could.

Each year his share of the farm was getting bigger. But he was restless. Sat around a lot at the elevator or Mercantile telling baseball stories.

He'd always wanted to ride rodeo as a kid. Lassoing calves bringing in the cows for milking. Trying to ride the bull. Bulldog. His dad wanted him to go to college, *dreaming hot night manure light bright rodeo,* learn to be a scientific farmer, take over the place when he was gone, *sweat creaking leather snort ripping air,* gave him cows and pigs to raise, horses, knew he wanted to ride. His dad signed over the south forty when he graduated from the eighth grade. First calf sold at the county fair 4-H winner, he took the money and run off. Hitched his way, 13 years old, to Liberty, Texas, and laid it on the line, entry fee for bareback bronco riding.

Found him two days later, still knocked out in the hospital. Run off to Waycross, Georgia, when he was 14, Dothan, Alabama, at 15. Next to baseball had always wanted to ride. So instead of loafing and a lying at the Downtown Recreation, since a stiff elbow doesn't keep a man from waving his right arm in the air for eight seconds or so, he went to his dad to tell him he'd decided to give rodeo a try. Bareback and saddle bronc. His dad just looked at him in that silent way he had, for what seemed like five minutes. Sitting, both of them, across from each other at that old round oak table they used to have, kerosene lamp on the lace doily. Drank cup after cup of coffee. Had a long talk that night. Made a deal. The harvest done, plowing through in the fall, go ahead. Until his dad couldn't work the farm alone. Sure would rather he'd go to college. But as long as he was home to help, he'd get his share of harvest.

And that's how they came to ride the circuit together all those years. And when he'd disappear every spring, Hank and Lyons figgered it was on a drunk, or with some waitress, although neither of them ever saw him do either, and never questioned.

Like Keeper and Hank never questioned the morning in Lenapah when Lyons, downright embarrassed, and neither of them had ever seen it before, confused, uncertain. Fidgeting his hat, pawing dirt. Trapped. Told them Blanchefleur was gonna travel with them for a spell.

Uneasy at first, down the road. Lyons not singing. Hank silent from the back seat with Keeper. It's all right with me, goddamn, can do what he wants. Goddamn. And besides, she won't last too long anyhow.

Blanchefleur riding amazed, remembering distant, near, from over a hood, a bus, a '31 Chevrolet, ribbon road, slowly faster flashing blurred. Her hands folded, his hands on the wheel, on her, her cheek, her lips, neck, breath, moon, breath breast, blouse gone breathing, bra gone touching, touch pants underpants sweating belly, moon, thighs, what's happening what am I, are you, touch touching touch me, trembling hand never touched before, am with you round languid liquid sweating hot hair heavy bobbing thighs quiver weak, finger soft rippling warm oh, oh are you are you. Time. We got time, Blanchefleur. It, feels so. Time, there's time, first time. To feel so good. Don't stop.

Anticipation along the highway. In a car hinting body smells. Leather saddles, gunnysacks and rope. Of three strange men.

What am I doing. Here.

What is she doing here. Must be plumb loco. Not like me at all. Blond. Long legs. But. A. Never before. First time at thirty-one with me, come after me, chose me. And couldn't tell her no. Didn't want to tell her last night goddamn long tall drink of water goddamn goddamn Marcus you lost. Goddamn. What have I gained.

Sudden laughing along the highway.

What is that boy laughing at. Plumb loco, I should of knowed three weeks ago on Highway 81 never to stop when we seen her with her flat. Mighty pretty gal though.

Strumming along the highway. In a car glinting morning sun southeastern flint hills grass, on steel-bodied guitar through the back seat window. Play it, Hank. Play it blue and low down. Cause Lyons o buddy has met his match.

And Robert Keeper leans back laughing too.

From rodeo to rodeo. Blanchefleur was one of them it looked like. Lyons happy. It looked like. But Keeper watching, from the back seat, from the bar stool. The barmaids sullen huffy cool, distant. Hank and Blanchefleur joking talk drinking beer. Lyons motionless now, except the thumb peeling the label of the bottle squeezed in hand. Eyes blank. Silent. Didn't write anymore, no more brawls to end the evening. No more songs. Just old ones over again. Blanchefleur joining in not knowing when why to who. Knowing just the peripheral waitresses, rodeo followers in all the little towns and stops, diners along the way. Each one farther, each one longer away and gone.

And Keeper watching.

One day sudden, one week maybe, she didn't laugh so much, or sing. Nervous. Red worn watery morning eyes one day, one week. High-cheeked wrought, sun brown, but tired. Maybe only Keeper saw. Watching riding, silent, cuddled sleeping as Lyons drove.

An overcast day, humid. Cool. U.S. 59 north of Ottawa, Kansas. A native stone filling station and garage. Outside hydraulic lift, red chipped and scratched, white coarse gravel splattered oil, slick water puddles. Short sunflowers in the wind in front of the outhouse buzzing flies. The horse trailer sitting to the side beneath a native elm, tail and rump in the shadows, shaking clomps now and then and whickering inside. The Chevy at the pumps, Keeper pumping the glass globe full, filling the tank. Hank and Lyons talking to the mechanic shaking hands and laughing. Blanchefleur walking slowly along the highway, out onto the prairie, looking at wild flowers, anthills, just walking, hands in the pockets of her jean jacket, tossing her hair, swaying her upper body as she goes. Keeper watches her, puts the gas cap on, Lyons starts the Chevy up, backs around, pulls up, guided by Hank, onto the lift, raise her up. Drain the oil, lubricate. Start working on the brakes. Blanchefleur returns, watches awhile, goes inside. Sits gazing out the window eating potato chips and a Snickers bar. Keeper walks around, wiping his hands on a Kex rag, enters, leans one foot up on a chair, stares out the window too, still wiping his hands. For a minute or two.

"Must be the weather."

"What?"

"Must be the weather makes a man feel so lowdown."

"Yes. Must be. Cool and muggy at the same time. Thick wind." Continues eating. Examining the Snickers closely before each bite.

Looks at her for a while. "What do you? I mean." Trailing off silent.

"What?"

"Nothing. I mean, I was just thinking."

"About what?"

"It's none of my business."

"But?" A friendly smile.

Laughs, relieved too. "No, I was just wondering about, about your family, you look a little homesick."

Eyes moisten, go blank, down, turn away. Back up. Look him in the eye. If she could trust the stranger riding quietly in the back seat looking at her a lot. Looking now. "Hasn't Lyons told you about my. About Marcus?"

"Nope. Well, I did hear him sing the 'Cutting Wheatfield Blues' a time or two. But that didn't tell me much."

"My brother is the only family I have. Had left."

Pause. Anxious. He seems to decide. "How come you left, I mean. I don't know. You just don't seem to be the type to follow after the rodeo. After a guy like Lyons."

Eyes empty again. Runs her lower lip under the front teeth, looking away. "Does it seem so unusual I should, I mean can't I. Love him?"

"I guess he is a lovable cuss. But still. You'll have to admit it doesn't seem like the most obvious matchup in the world. It's not just busting out all over with future. I mean how long do you figger on trailing along from one pumpkin roller to the next, what kind of life is that for a girl—"

"Goddammit! I'm almost thirty-two. I'm a woman." Throws down potato chips and candy, leaving Keeper standing. Walks quickly down the road. Then stops.

Looks confused at the grease rag, wipes his ring and little finger one more time, pitches the rag into the barrel in the corner, goes out after. Approaches cautiously. "I'm sorry, Blanchefleur. I was just."

Without turning. "That's all right. It must be the weather." Starts walking across the pasture. He follows, walks alongside for a while, down by a little pond, some willow trees. She doesn't look. "I can't just go back and face Marcus. Not right now anyway. Not now." Wipes the inside corners of her eyes with thumb and first finger.

"I guess I shouldn't say anything. I hardly know you at all. But. I'm probably all wrong, but it seems to me. You're making a mistake. Fighting against the, the way your people, your brother, the way you lived. You know what I mean." Doesn't respond. Keeps on walking. "I mean you must have been unhappy with that way, but you must have liked it too, or thought you should like it, cause you're going about it in a way that'll make you more unhappy. You see what I mean?"

She stops. Looks quietly at him. Tears welling. He wants to touch, to cup her face in his hands. To. "Shut up, Keeper."

They pulled into Strong City, registered, paid entry fees for the rodeo. Found a cabin with kitchenette outside Cottonwood Falls. Blanchefleur and Keeper silent all the way. Cool evening. Frying chicken in the cabin, Blanchefleur starts to sing Methodist hymns. Hank out exercising the horse. Lyons and Keeper sitting on the front fenders of the Chevy, Lyons abstractedly chording the guitar, Keeper whittling. Blanchefleur comes out awhile. Leans against the car with her belly holding Lyons' leg as he plays. Keeper doesn't look. She reaches up and kisses Lyons before going to turn the chicken, never looks at Keeper. Lyons sings a few bars of one of his old songs, then hums and mumbles along. Grows silent. Keeper looks over at him sitting still fretting staring over into the trees. Takes a few licks more with his knife. "What's going to happen with Blanchefleur?"

Long pause. "What you mean, good buddy?"

"I reckon it's none of my business. But. She just can't keep on following us around like this, you can't. I mean, she's not like all the other waitresses and barmaids."

Strikes a sharp metallic chord. Then picks out a gentle melody. "The hell she isn't. More to the point, the hell they aren't like her. They're all women, Keeper, human beings lonely looking. Trying to find a home on these hot and dusty, windy plains. Just like you and me. And just cause her brother owns a farm doesn't make her any different, any more complicated, any more sensitive, her need, her desire, one bit greater than any woman slinging hash or serving suds in some two-bit dive in some ramshackle roadhouse out on the highway."

Pause. "I. You know what I mean."

"No, I don't, good buddy." Keeper resumes angry whittling. Lyons keeps on strumming. "I didn't ask her to come along. That's her business. I couldn't stop her."

"She says she loves you."

"I guess I am a lovable cuss." Changes keys. Keeper hacking away at the stick. "She just told me her friend's three weeks late."

"What friend?"

"Period's three weeks overdue."

"What!"

"Yep. Looks like I'm gonna be a daddy."

Throws down the knife and stick jumping coming around the radiator face to face. "You sonuvabitch!" Pulls Lyons from the fender. "What ya gonna do now!"

Holding guitar by the neck grabbing Keeper at the throat with the free hand spinning around slamming him against the car door. "Take it easy, good buddy. There's not much I can do now."

Gone limp. "But what about the baby?"

"He'll make it just like me."

"What if it's a girl?"

"Then she'll make it too."

"But the kid'll need a dad who can. A father."

"Hell." Letting loose of his shirt. Keeper slides down to the running board. Props his face in his hands. Lyons steps back, gets up on the fender again. Another peaceful melody tossed about by the poplar trees. "Who needs parents."

They rode from one town to the next, one pumpkin roller, longer and longer, bigger. Belly swelling. Tension sometimes. Keeper irritated, Hank keeps the peace. Blanchefleur sensing, some mornings, see it in her eyes, could be if, could vomit if she thought. But didn't. Couldn't. Not with Lyons, not with Keeper. Couldn't be sick. Couldn't be afraid.

Snuggled winter nights in roadside cabins, magnolia and pine moonlit on the windowsill. He would talk about his boy, hand on her belly laughing when the rascal kicked. Feel good then, the warm hand, the laugh, but always contained, knowing not to ask, not to mention the things he wouldn't hear, or never think about. And panic when he sleeps, leaves her aching bloated alone in a strange dark cold southern cabin, something frightening alive kicking at her heart.

Too proud to talk to Keeper. Or what. Couldn't go to him to admit. See him looking when she sat alone at the table in the tavern. Could tell he knew. She didn't want to be here, but afraid not to come. The barmaids slim and mobile. But Lyons always bragging and showing her belly off, had people feel the little cowpoke crow-hopping rank bucking outlaw, and laugh. Proud. He was proud.

So what's the matter, woman?

What makes the time so slow?

Keeper just waited for the time. Had it planned. He'd have to tell, admit to them he wasn't one of them. Had a farm, and didn't know why he thought it would make them mad. But someone had to plan. She couldn't have it in the back seat of the '31 Chevy.

So he waited. Six months, seven months, eight. Her belly large breasts and proud now. The anxiety of the early months seemed gone. Changed from jeans unbuttoned shirttails hanging, to long dresses sensuous curving contour rounding cloth. Walking regal grace and balance moving. Anxiety gone. It seemed. But must be worried, be concerned. I can't be the only one to think.

The time has come.

They were heading north for Saskatoon. Farther from Oklahoma every day. The ride back too long, can't wait too long. Keeper got up from the cafe booth, Cut Bank, Montana, "Got some business to take care of." Walked down the street to the general store where the bus would stop. This is it. The end of it no more rodeo, what will Dad say now, too long. Waited too long. Messed up again baseball rodeo, Dad will say. And Mom. The bus. Too long. Will be through about six in the evening heading south. Get two tickets. Walk on back to the cafe. What am I gonna say. To Dad. To Lyons and Blanchefleur laughing as he approached the table. Sat down. And waited.

"Well, Keeper o buddy, you bout ready to hit the road?"

"I got two tickets on the bus."

All look at him. "What for?"

"Blanchefleur can't be bouncing around in that damn ol Chevy anymore. She's due."

She looks quickly apprehensive. At Lyons, at Keeper. "Where are the tickets to?"

"Well. I. You see, I got a farm, that is my dad and I, and my mom, we have a farm in Oklahoma."

"What?"

"A farm."

Lyons breaks out laughing. Leans over the table grabbing Keeper's shoulder. "You full of surprises, ain't you, Keeper?"

"Well, I think it's time she had a place to rest up and someone to look after her, and the baby when it comes. So I got the tickets."

"Why the hell didn't you say something earlier, you tight-mouthed sonuvabitch. We could a made some plans, stead of waiting till we was plumb to Canada."

"I . . ."

"I can't take off and leave now. I got to win some money. Got to have a stake for my future son." Putting hand on her belly. She looks from one to the other. "And besides, how would I know where your place is? Your dad would probably shoot me on sight. Naw, I got to go on to Saskatoon. You'll have to take her on back for me, Keeper, o buddy."

"I didn't." Looks at Blanchefleur.

"Hank and I'll be down soon as the rodeo's over. Sure wished to hell you'd spoken up sooner. You better take her."

"Well I." Looks at Lyons. "Sure. Someone has to go with her."

The first contraction was on the bus to Enid. Had been a week, from town to town day and night jumbled lights and dust. Wind flashing lightning rain. Layovers filling stations general stores isolate, dark, missed connections, taverns, drugstores, diners, heavy hot colorless sun. Transfer, ride, wait. Breakdown Deadwood hot sweating silent ride. They didn't talk. Blanchefleur determined, holding belly blankly staring glowing saline red.

"How you riding?"

"I'll make it."

Lyons attached the bell to the woven riding rope. Had drawn

Duke Morgan. Rankest bucking brahma in seven states and two provinces of Canada.

Keeper and Blanchefleur got off the bus at Young's Garage in Alva, sat on an overturned 55-gallon drum among rusty red dirt brakeshoes, wheel rims, cauter pins springs sickle guards nuts and bolts and grimy grass in the shade of a mimosa tree. Sun hot grease and oil, gasoline.

"I'm going to find my uncle. He'll take us on to the farm. Make sure Doc isn't too drunk. Be right back. How we doing?"

"Every twenty minutes or so. I'm fine."

Squeezes his hand. He smiles. The first time in a week, walks off down the street. Leaving her sitting on the drum.

Where her water broke. Sitting alone and hot.

Hank paints his cheeks and forehead white, a crimson grin, adds a cherry nose. Puts on a striped referee shirt and steps into baggy red suspendered trousers. Laces on baseball shoes.

The old pickup rumbled off the blacktop onto the sandy section line, swerving a controlled fishtail accelerating dusty wake. The doctor's car from the opposite direction close behind, slowing to let the dust blow clear, follows. Hot morning, getting hotter, pickup cab windshield filtering sunheat powdery surges wind whipped at the open windows. Cottonwoods glittering yellow green along creek beds. Cows huddled in the shade turning to watch. Blanchefleur turning to watch, hair twisting flies dancing around red sweating face, impassive. Exhausted. Alone. Eyes widen, bites her lower lip. Every ten minutes. Fence posts clattering by. Crest a hill, Keeper points. "There it is."

Foreground windmill churning, pumping, long rusty pipe to galvanized tank. Moss circling the edge hanging, brim dipping trickle, meandering path through bare trodden ground, past the concave salt lick into buffalo grass falling away rippling heat quivering to the far section line corner. Hedgerow. Trees. A red barn. A silo. Modular structures outbuildings. The house. The farm.

Lyons stares through the planks at Duke Morgan, baleful big brown eyes. Snorts stringing saliva in the air. A cowboy, short, stocky. Big-headed bald, gold rim glasses askew devilish grinning rolling a cigarette on the top rail looks down at Lyons, back at the bull. "You know, I tried to ride that outlaw just last week. Blame near killed me." Lights up. Offers a drag.

Savors the smoke, exhales. "Is that right?"

"Yup." Takes cigarette back. "Flattened me in zero point zero."
*Inhales. Blows smoke through nose and mouth. "You see, he's a
spinner. Tight to the right. And he ain't satisfied with just dusting
you. He's out to kill you sure." Looking up at a hawk soaring. "Sin
Miller tied into him last month in Missoula. Bucked him forward
spinning, caught the horn tip in his mouth, o Duke shook his head
like a hound dog holt of a bullsnake. Sin was lucky though. Just
knocked out all his teeth like laths in a picket fence and broke his
jaw. Wired her up and he was back at it next week's rodeo. Junior
Sidle ain't tooken a step since he drawed the Duke last year down in
Swift Current."*

"You don't say."

"Yup. He'll kill you if he can."

Keeper's dad and mother come out to the pickup pulling into
the drive. Blanchefleur watches from the front seat, the hug, the
handshake, words, gestures toward her through the windshield.
Another contraction cramping around down her abdomen. Exhausted. Been on the road, fitful dreaming connecting Cut Bank,
Lyons and all *this*. Burning sun through glass on her belly, the
smiling kind woman at the door, pickup door open breeze evaporation perspiration cold cloth against skin. Her hand upon her
forehead reassuring gentle cool. Dust drifting by, the engine cut,
the doctor walking up from behind. Looking in over the woman's
shoulder, smiling. "I see we made it. How often are the contractions?"

"They hurt, Doctor. More and more. Longer."

"How often?"

"Ten, five minutes."

"Well, let's get into the house."

Mother helping her out. "You must be worn out. I've got the
washtub out in the cream shed full of hot water. Just what Doc
ordered. Right, Doc?"

"It wouldn't hurt. You been seeing a doctor?"

"I don't. I've never been to a doctor. In my life."

"Oh. Well. You just relax in the tub for a few minutes, and
then we'll have a quick prenatal exam. If it's not too late." Laughs
quietly. "And maybe get a little sleep."

She goes with Mother Keeper to the cream shed. Removes her

shoes. Cool smooth concrete. Smell the butterfat, the cows drifting in the windows. Alfalfa. Contented clucking of chickens. A mud dauber in the rafters. Removes her dress, wet sticky, pants and bra, releasing swollen breasts rung red wrinkled imprints around, shoulders, back. First time naked in a week, first time standing stretching, looking down, caress abundant body full, first time in a week feeling healthy tall strong pregnant good. Standing eyes closed, flowing air across her body, alive moving inside concentrating focus out. Impending birth. Steps into the oval metal tub. Hot. Stands motionless scalding feet. Adjusting. Chills running along her back. Then slowly doubles down, wringing clenching ache through the womb. Shaking chills and hot water mix steaming humid rush filling face and nostrils. Inaudible moan. A long-hair yellow cat sitting in the door watching, detached curiosity. Warm gentle hands on her shoulders, neck, massaging.

Breathe deep and slow now. Don't fight it, breathe along with it. Relaxed and deep.

She breathes, that's the time. Slow and deep, hands laving body water steaming vapor from breasts and knees, trickling down her back and arms hot soothing breathing warm moist thick air slow rhythm sloshing water soap and hands over arms and back and armpits and breast. Coming to life again. The milk, the chickens, cows, cat and wasps, a woman's hands and water interweaving aching grip breathing in and out. In. And out. Letting go. Hands submerged unclenching. Flowing out, away. Dissolving heated water, creamshed air.

Lyons puts on spurs. Testing locked rowel partial spin with a fingertip. Shaft slanted up to grip broadside burly bull. Firmly strapped. Touch the toes, a few deep knee bends, vomits behind hay bales, spit, walked to the chute, Duke Morgan chute fighting, banging boards from side to side snorting angry head. Hank looking in from the arena painted grin a fraud, absently fingering the hoofprint above his eye, looks at Lyons, giving thumbs up. Lyons climbs the fence, hovers over, flank man throwing broad leather flank strap round the loins. "Easy, you goddam sonuvabitch. Gonna cinch this down good and tight. Don't like that so much, do you, Duke."

Man with the manila bull rope trying to stay clear of the horns, bell banging, throws it around the shoulders, mashed against the rail, shit, pulls it through the honda knot, Lyons lowers down. The fatty gray brown hump bristling snaking mad. Easy you devil easy. You might as well settle down. Goddamn. Man pulls the rope tighter. Shore is an onry varmit. Lyons wraps the flat braid across his palm twice, clamps his fingers down, thumb across, pulling tight, Duke Morgan banging the gate, he's ready. Lyons takes a slow deep breath, looking out, Hank moving back, a red cape, tractor inner-tube, the gateman looking, waiting for the sign.

The doctor pulled down the shades. Blanchefleur lying on the bed on her side. He washed his hands. "Bout three, three and a half fingers of dilation. Everything is looking good." Wipes rimless glasses clean, the sweat from his face. Talking quiet, calm. "You're doing very well. Don't fight it, don't be in a hurry. Breathe deep. Let it out slow. That's the way."

Keeper's mother by the bed, talking softly. The room dark, hot. Blanchefleur not noticing. Thirsty. Not so much afraid. No need to be so hard. Alone. Mother gives a chip of ice. Rubs her back. Smell the clean sheets. The house. Tired. Sleep.

Until the next contraction racked her wake.

"Stay with it, Blanchefleur, breathe it out slow."

Mother's hands. Doctor gray hair gartered shirt sleeves standing near dusky heat. More ice. A piece of horehound candy. Breathe. And sleep. Lyons' mother near, her hands. Keeper.

"Relax. I'm going to see how we're doing now."

"Okay."

"Four fingers. Thin as a kid's circus balloon. You're coming right along, right along."

"I want to push."

"Not now."

"Who's having this baby!"

"You are. And doing real well. But don't push now. Breathe fast and shallow. That's it."

"I. Want. To."

The gate open dust and Duke Morgan spinning inside once twice Lyons out of shape. Tries to bail out three four five feet and legs flying jerked back tethered hand and arm to the bull rope bell clanging six seven flopping hangs on the side of the brahma hooking spins eight nine shouting Hank desperate lunge for the tangled rope end horn snags the groin slinging him up and out of the mortal dance sucking Lyons limp whirling under. The rope slips loose. Eyes. Final.

Indifferent. Hank lies cramped and bleeding. To watch a Swainson's hawk watch Lyons down.

"Push. You can push now, Blanchefleur. One more."

"I feel it, I."

"One more time. It's crowning."

Dark hot. Blanchefleur squatted at the head of the bed, mother holding massaging. Doc's shirt clinging sweat, smell mucus amniotic fluid, blood. There it is! The head squalling anger. Doc suctions out the nose and mouth. Keeper comes in from the other room to see. Doc bending over. Low soft voice. "Easy. That's the time, one shoulder at a time. An easy birth. There we are, a boy." Lays him on her belly till the cord stops to pulse. Takes two pieces of white string, Blanchefleur's eyes wide amazement, awe, ties one close to the belly around the umbilical, the other a thumb's breadth from the first. The crying stopped. Takes a pair of blunt-nosed scissors and cuts the cord. "There you are. You're on your own, little man." A few gasping quiet sobs. Doc lifts him up, misshapen bloody vernix smear, eyes wide bewildered staring here and there tentatively moving arms and legs unhindered space. Places him in a tub of warm water speaking soothing. Drawing out the words. "Look at me. What is happening to me." Smiling, almost laughing, Blanchefleur laughing too, the doctor raises him from the water, places him at her breast, she cradles him closer, Mother Keeper shows her how to guide the nipple between her fingers to his mouth. His eyes looking in her eyes from wrinkled forehead, matted hair, begins to suckle. Doc leans back. "Little man."

"We have a baby."

The telephone rings.

"It's him!"

Keeper goes to the phone. She watches through the door. The wooden box, two bell eyes and drooping mouthpiece nose, crank and receiver.

"Hello. Yes, Mabel! Hank!" Raising voice. "Louder, Hank." Startled, the baby cries. "You'll have to talk louder." Looks to Blanchefleur, quickly back. "What?" Hand cupped over the vacant ear. "He." Swallows sudden. "No. It." Long silence. "No." Keeper slowly, blankly nodding. "Okay. I understand." Louder. "I understand." Everyone looking at him through the door. Trying to control. Blanchefleur growing pale. "Sure, Hank. We'll be here. Ask anyone for the Keeper place. What? Oh. Fine. She's fine. Delivered just"—sob interrupting—"a few, few minutes. Ago. A boy."

Hangs up the receiver. Pauses. Turns, sees her looking through the door, chalk-white, baby at her breast. Hesitates. Swallows. Looks out through the window by the phone, the barn and field behind, back to the bedroom. Dark. Smell of blood.

Blanchefleur stares. Slowly whispers. "He's dead."

Silence. Suckling child. Slowly lifts the baby from her breast, he complains, looks at him, tears welling, trembling bloodless lips. The doctor whispers. "Come on, Blanchefleur. We're not finished yet."

"I'm cold."

"Get back up on your pillows. This shouldn't take us long."

"I'm cold."

Places a pan beneath her, two contractions more, to deliver the afterbirth. She sinks back down, staring intently at the baby. The doctor pieces the placenta together on a blood-stained towel, bit by bit, looks up anxious, back down, around. Not all there. Looks at Blanchefleur as a crimson scarlet burst of blood fills the eyes, nostrils, fills the room flowing out.

"I'm dying, Doctor."

"I'll do what I can."

She looks at the baby. "Waited a long time to see you. Now this. Have to call you. Sorry."

Keeper sitting by the phone at the kitchen table, staring, vision blurring tears through the door.

And hadn't thought of all of that in years.

Until he asked his son whose rig it was he drove from North Dakota. And Sorry said a man by the name of Marcus Baldwin.

Prologue Three

THEY settled the prairie. Anglo-Saxons, Scandinavians, Germans, Slavs. With stops in Massachusetts, Pennsylvania, Indiana, Kentucky, Missouri, Mississippi and Arkansas, where the humidity is high and the rainfall dependable and a man can make a living on 80 to 160 acres. They came onto the semiarid plains, disregarding the people already there and what they could learn from them.

The Comanche, Kiowa, Apache, Blackfoot, Arapaho, Cheyenne, Teton-Dakota, Gros Ventre, Sarcee, Assiniboin, Crow. Accommodate themselves to the cycles of the prairie. Nomadic, they do not till the soil. They use dogs, until horses appear to help them follow the harvest and the herd.

The Texans, most of them from Spain, already knew something about dry conditions. Developed wandering armies of horsemen, the Texas Rangers. Gave up the long rifle, requires both feet planted, braced in the crook of a tree. They used the Colt .45.

And the cattlemen. An entire European culture adapted to the prairie, an institution without counterpart in the humid East. Cities did not arise. No formal government. Constant movement of stock from one range to another, to the railheads and the markets. The range was open and free. No one owned the land. The ranch house was built on a river or a creek, near water, and the customary range could be anywhere. Appropriated by personal decree through notices in the closest weekly newspaper, listing the brand, the boundaries, usually the divides of watersheds, and the landmarks of the range. It was all on file in the brand book of the territory. The local Cattlemen's Association controlled use of the public domain, settled disputes over boundaries, winter and summer grazing lands, waterholes, creeks and reserve feed. The State Cattlemen's Association regulated the cattle drives. Bedding, watering, feeding and traffic on the trails.

But the industrial revolution ignored all this. They had their old institutions from the East, all they needed was land. And they used it like humid timberlands. Railroads were built, someone in Illinois invented barbed wire, they made the windmill better. You could breed blooded stock. The whole economy of the prairie started to change rapidly. And finally the small farmers, grangers, the nesters moved in and drove everybody else on out.

Seventy-five delegates attend Montana constitutional convention. Nine born in Europe, two in eastern Canada, thirty-two in New England, twenty-one in the Midwest, east of the Mississippi. Only eleven come from the plains. Only half had lived here for ten years or more, fifteen less than five. The constitution for North Dakota was written by a professor at the Harvard Law School who'd never seen a prairie. No one interested in new institutional devices suited to sparse populations spread over wide unpredictable costly space. Cycles of drought. Floods. Insect infestations. They section the states into many small counties, townships and school districts with overlapping jurisdictions. They are committed to private ownership. A good-sized farm is 80 to 160 acres where they come from. And that's the size plots the homesteaders get on the plains. In Europe and New England credit and foreclosure are used to protect against bad character. But on the prairie it's more often than not the lack of rain, or a horde of grasshoppers, green bugs or black stem rust that leads to default. In God we trusted. In Kansas we busted.

The plains become a colony. The food and fiber are shipped out to the rest of the country for processing and distribution. The farmer gets the Minneapolis price for wheat minus freight, pays the Minneapolis price plus freight for bread, oil, natural gas and coal. Tractors, plows, drills, combines, trucks, hand tools, all come from the outside. The Farm Bureau and national farm policy are dominated by states east of the Mississippi. More and more farmers are forced to give it up and the land falling into the hands of absentee owners. At the same time the unrelenting reality of the place is reforming the people who stick it out. They are becoming people of the plains.

The two world wars draw them from parochial to regional, regional to national, slowly, finally from national to international involvement. The boom of the first war. The dust bowl. Then the boom of the second. The total income of Oklahoma grew 132 percent during World War II. Kansas made B-17's and half of all the B-29's. The world needs the wheat, corn and cotton grown on the modern frontier.

Politicians can't be like they used to be. Not like Oklahoma Governor "Our Jack" Walton back in 1923 throw a barbecue for the inauguration. A mile of hickory and blackjack pits broiling beef, buffalo, reindeer, antelope, chicken, turkey, possum, rabbit, pheasant, quail, prairie chicken and crow all round the capitol and two day knock-down-drag-out inside fiddle contests. Hoedown, cakewalk clog dance square dance spreading through the four stories. Smoking jackets and evening dress strung pearls jostled among the cowboys, Indians, dry-land farmers in overalls and cow manure, spill whiskey on the carpets, put out cigars and track red mud. Can't be like Alfalfa Bill Murray, chain the chairs in the governor's office to the wall so sinister lobbyists can't edge too near. Call the graduates of the University of Oklahoma high-toned bums and send the National Guard to collect tickets at the games when the NCAA investigates the football team. Or seize the oil fields when the price is too low. Can't be eccentric rustics, rough-and-tumble outlaws or champions of a single cause any longer. The modern frontier is based on industry and connection to the international interests.

Inspired by the prosperity of World War II, the politicians and business leaders of the plains states decided to do something about this colonial relationship. Vote in tax incentives to attract eastern investment, establish processing plants for the agricultural products within the area. Industry and business based on humid-area ideas: Man can conquer nature; natural resources are inexhaustible; habitual practices are best; the owner can do what he likes with his property; has to make his own decisions; the factory farm is the most productive; free competition makes an effective balance between agriculture and industry; land values will rise indefinitely and the economy expand forever.

There is extensive technological change, the development of fertilizers, herbicides, insecticides, fungicides, sophisticated machinery. But it is not enough to overcome the problems of institutions tied to a high-technology industrial state. The cozy triangle of government, land-grant colleges and agribusiness requires long-term planning and control. Predictable conditions. Conditions which, despite high-pressure deep-well irrigation and petrochemical intervention, and maybe even because of it, remain capricious.

And the people living in a system designed for certainty, for stability of income, for contract performance, for predictability of the future, living on the prairie where conditions are uncertain and harsh, where you have to have mobility, flexibility and reserves, where you have to live at the level of greatest stringency at all times, bust or boom, the people living on the prairie must adapt. Or get out.

Isadora Faire Quits Her Job

B EEN watching too many soap operas. Read Rex Morgan, M.D. too long. Young Dr. Kildare, I guess. Florence Nightingale of the plains, or something. My mother's a nurse as well.

Besides, what else is a young girl to do. Marry Erwin Hebb, stay pregnant most of my years, boiling hot dogs, frying eggs and washing greasy mechanic shirts with his name embroidered over the pocket. Sit alone at night in the mobile home reading *True Confessions* while he's out drinking beer and playing cards or doing God knows what with his ignorant friends. Laughing loud vulgar jokes. Banging me from my sleep pressing hair curlers in my skull, painful slobbering kisses, calloused stubby hands groping all around. No. I've talked too much with other women to know that wasn't for me. Not for a sensitive, intelligent, idealistic lovely girl like me. I'd be a nurse. Romantic helper of suffering humanity. And marry me a doctor. Have cultured children, dance for the daughter, piano for the son, be chair of the Heart Fund drive. Have United Way ladies over for tea.

Bull.

Empty bedpans, sponge-bathe wrinkled moribund flesh, audit halitose lonely nightmares in dark rooms orange-lit nocturnal nurse's call. Inquire how a carcinomic corroded world is doing today. Pass out pills. Pass out pills. Laughing at sexual innuendo repeated, stranded, from a hundred beds. So many goddam beds.

I should have known better. Mother didn't marry a doctor. Worked graveyard shift for twenty years, still working it today, to put me through high school, nurse's training. So I could amount to something. And it never occurred to either of us, instead of marrying one, I could have been a doctor too.

There have been moments, I'll have to admit. Intense. Rewarding even. When it seems I've truly helped someone, some human being, not just a diet card or list of medications, milliliters, grains, minims, drams, temperatures and pressure. Another human being. Out of all the people, sickness, heartache, death, that passes before your eyes, there are those that catch and hold, who knows why. Haunting combinations, sounds and smells, medicinal, muffled conversations, flowers wilting, rented televisions of a desolate Sunday morning, stirring indistinct abstract sadness and sympathy for humankind. A woman wheeled down the hall from recovery, pale, shivering, cracked lips white dried spittle. Intravenous bottles vibrating stainless steel. And all the ward, miseries forgotten, problems and capricious concerns drop away and watch her pass. Abruptio. Emergency C-section. Baby gone. Empty aching thirst. Loss. Impersonal kindred understanding, common suffering. The wrought gaunt face of a man bending over to hear.

"Did you see her?"

But it's sort of rare. Mostly mind-numbing routine. One day, one night flowing into the next. Amazing how trite the human body is. How unimaginative it is in choosing ways to fall apart. You'd think something so damned complicated would offer up a little more variety.

And the people you work with. No imagination, no awe at what they do, not even pride. Everybody's got to do something, and this beats waiting tables. You might as well be sitting in your mobile home watching game shows, I swear, as to be talking to some of these folks.

Of course the hospital structure, the administration, certainly don't encourage initiative, self-reliance or original thought. Let you know in more ways than one, they've got their rules, their procedures, and by God you'd best not deviate from them.

The hospital's a bureaucracy these days, run by business administrators. Medicine's no longer the art of healing. It's an industry. Puts out a product and expects to make a profit. Our product is promoted by massive public relations and advertising campaigns. The image of the hospital is what is important, not what actually goes on in the wards and labs and surgical theaters, the daily struggle with life, death, pain and loss.

Naturally people expect a product to have a guarantee. And when it fails—but I don't even want to go into that. I just wonder if it was all that naïve of me to think that nursing, or doctoring for that matter, was something you went into because you wanted to help people. Someone other than yourself. I'm just tired I guess. Working too hard. It's not all that bad all the time. It does seem though like I'm tired more and more lately.

Friday night. Emergency. A bad night in Emergency. About to go off duty. Midnight, and damn glad of it, when this drunk comes in. The last thing in the world you want to see at quitting time on Friday night in Emergency is a drunk. You get to where you hate them as a matter of fact. Staggering up to me at the desk. "I been. Run over. By a Volks. Wagen."

Sure enough. Could see the tire track across his T-shirt. But he doesn't seem to be hurting too bad. As I'm filling out the forms, he's trying to talk some line to me, the same stuff you hear from a million drunks a million weekend nights in Emergency, getting real fresh, stinking brewery slobbery unshaven goddam drunk, and he's wasting my time my.

Well, anyway. I took him into the examination room, and there he was, a new intern, marry me a doctor, my oh my, tall muscular black curly hair glistening in the examination light, packing away his gear, getting ready to call it a day. I hesitate, don't hesitate, don't let him know I'm looking to see if he's hesitating not hesitating not letting me know he's looking to see the best-looking nurse in Rapid City Regional looking to see the best-looking intern in all of South Dakota looking. My attitude toward the drunk becomes suddenly solicitous, concern for the well-being, strictly professional you understand, stethoscope, eye ear nose and throat light, all business, wipe your brow Doctor, no, I fantasize, not in such a hurry to go any longer. Don't let him see looking to see to see looking to see.

Damn.

Didn't know I was so horny. Smell his perspiration through medicinal sterile, mixing booze and burnt rubber of our buddy. Rippling forearm veins hair, long fingers, delicate brain surgeon's hands. Strong. Soothing lilting voice. Smooth. To see looking. Impatient. Self-conscious. Deliberate. Definitely looking to see me looking. Hurry up to get this bum out of here so.

"Looks like you're all right, sir, but I'd stay out of joints like that if I were you." Drunk jabbering nonsense down the hall and out. "Thank you, Nurse. I believe we can get out of here now. I'm exhausted. See you tomorrow."

Picks up his bag and leaves.

What. That arrogant bastard. Knew I was, was himself, and then all he says is see you tomorrow. Not if I see you first, buddy. Not until.

Until two days later. Emergency surgery. See them wheeling the man past to the theater. Looks familiar. Of course. The drunk with the VW track across his belly.

"Dr. Concord report to surgery. Dr. Concord."

Dr. Concord. Yeah, the intern, the arrogant s.o.b.

Five minutes later the head surgeon walking slowly down the hall with his arm around Concord's shoulder talking fatherly. I can't help but overhear. Ruptures, internal bleeding, peritonitis. "We'll have to take out a yard and a half of gut. Now I know you're good, conscientious. Big-time medical school in the East and all. But the next time a man tells you he's been run over by a Volkswagen, why not take a few X-rays? Just in case he's telling the truth. Okay?"

Concord nods weakly. The head surgeon slaps him on the back and walks on down the hall, pinching a nurse leaning over a linen drawer on the butt as he passes.

I watch smugly, but a little sympathetic too. He sits down in a wheelchair cupping face in hands. Slowly remembering where he is, that someone is watching, that I am watching, looks at me embarrassed.

"I guess I fucked up."

"Don't take it too hard."

"I should have . . ."

Walking off down the hall, giving the ass a little extra, white stockinged legs, styling, timing, stop and turn. "You were just distracted, that's all."

He is distracted. I'm smiling big, getting out of control, feel my face flushing, but keep looking him straight in the eye, struggling wanting to look away, to giggle, he's looking to, starting to laugh loudly as I laugh. And turn the corner.

Laughing a lot the rest of the night. When I remember. Sensuously self-conscious of my ass.

That night he was waiting at my car in the lot.

"Dr. Concord. What a surprise."

"Now don't get the wrong idea."

"What idea's that?"

"That I'm going to suggest we go somewhere for a drink."

"The bars are closed."

"Right."

"So? Who had such an idea. See you tomorrow."

"Wait. Don't you want to know what I'm doing here?"

"It's a public parking lot."

"Seriously. I was going to suggest. That you take me home. I don't have a car."

"Sure. Get in." Starts the engine. Pulls out of the lot in silence. "How did you know where my car was?"

"You'd be surprised the records a hospital keeps. I just happened to be looking at the parking permits and the roster at the same time."

"Sure. Where do you live?"

"That's not the home I had in mind."

"Oh? What ho. Um. Oh. You arrogant bastard."

Looking at each other, green dashboard light, bursting out laughing. "Besides. The bars are closed."

He was an arrogant bastard. But he seemed sincere. Or at least I was taken in. It sure looked like I'd found my man anyway. That first night I thought sure he would make a pass, thought sure it would be the same bullshit over again that I'd put up with before. Even as we were pulling into my drive I was wishing I hadn't said okay. In fact was getting mad at him for what I expected him to do.

But he didn't.

We drank Hearty Burgundy and talked the rest of the night, amazed to see the light sky creeping around the shade, and he apologized for keeping me up so long and left. I couldn't believe it, no pass. Not the slightest hint. Talked about his plans, desire to be a physician, to help people. He wanted to be a country doctor. Live in some small community where he was needed. With no bureaucratic tangle like at the hospital. I started fantasizing again. The husband-wife, doctor-nurse team. A unit. A community. And I was halfway mad at him when he said see you tomorrow, and left. Without even making a pass.

The arrogant bastard.

It looked like, after about our third or fourth time together, talking at my place, going to a movie, my uncle's tavern, eating out, that if any passing was going to be done, I'd have to be the one to do it. I was beginning to wonder. That I was all wrong about his arrogance, that he wasn't even aware of the sexual implications of what we did, that such a handsome hunk of man was a faggot or something. I didn't know what to think. Until bang.

And that was it. So to speak. I had a roommate.

We never did talk about the future. Who needed to at first. There was so much else to think about. And do. Always on the go. I don't remember when it started bothering me, when it happened. I suppose it was the invitation to play golf with the head surgeon, although I didn't think much other than that's nice at the time. We usually did something together, a ride in the country, picnic, on Sunday. But what did a golf game matter.

Until it started happening every week and he decided he ought to buy some clubs. And shoes. And all the rigmarole that goes with it.

"I think I should join the Country Club."

"Why?"

"I've got the clubs, might as well use them. I need the practice."

"You're going to play more golf?"

"I need the practice. And besides they have squash courts. We're going to start playing squash Wednesday mornings."

"We?"

"Me and some of the other doctors."

"Oh."

But I guess when I really sat down and started to think, really noticed that something was going on here I didn't like was, it wasn't even when he started sleeping over in his room on Tuesday night because it was closer to the Country Club, it was when he came back one Sunday from golf.

"I think I need a car. I'm going to buy a car."

"Oh really. That's good. What kind?"

"I've never owned a car in my life. You know that? Not even a hotrod dragster when I was in high school or college."

"What kind you thinking about?"

"I'd like a Cadillac, or a Mercedes. But that's a little out of my reach right now. Something like the new '63 Chrysler, or Buick maybe. Lots of the young docs drive Chryslers."

Now everybody needs a car. But something in the way he said it made me sick. Mad. And very unhappy. And started me thinking. His internship would be over in six months. What would happen then? What did I want to happen then?

Didn't have long to wait to find out.

"You know, baby. What I'm going to do when my internship is over?"

"What?"

"Become an anesthesiologist."

"A what?"

"Yeah. I've decided."

"What about the practice in a small community?"

"Oh. Well. Anesthesiology is where the money is. I've got these damn debts to pay. And the hours are much more reasonable."

"I see."

I saw. The writing on the wall. And we didn't need to talk too much about anything anymore. Wasn't even upset when he started staying in his room Saturday night too. The Sunday golf. Closer and all that.

And when his time was up. He was gone, it's been fun. Next time you're in Chicago look me up. Dr. Concord, in the phone book, bye.

And you know. I'm sure I could have married him if I would have wanted to. If I would have asked him. Would have looked good lounging around the pool suntanned string bikini at some

Chicago Country Club or other. All the young docs in their Chryslers would have clicked their tongues some woman you got there Concord. Squash on Wednesday. Tea with the muscular dystrophy matrons.

I didn't want to.

So here I am, 31-year-old nurse. And we all know how them nurses are. Going nowhere. Crabby childless old maid tyrant. Nurse. Whispering behind, giggling. Easy lay, no strings attached. There must be a better way. Gotta get out of here. Somewhere. Out in the country. Never see another person, another form. Just me and the chickens, cows. Enough of this human husbandry. There must be a way.

Like the advertisement for the Datamate Computer Dating System Nurse Little keeps after me to try. Sounds like a joke. Or something.

Almost asleep at my station. Nodding over the magazine Nurse Little gave me. Bored. The double doors swing open at the end of the corridor. Several orderlies shove a stretcher through. From Emergency. Stop to give me papers. A young guy. Not unusual. Good-looking, well-built sun-brown body, I look again. Roll him on.

Nurse Little following behind with a paper sack. Hands it to me. "He sure is pretty."

"What's this?"

"His hair."

"What?"

"Shaved it off. Long blond beautiful. I just couldn't throw it away."

I look in the sack. Sure enough, hair, the same color as mine. Nurse Little watches them turn him into Clarence Krupp's room. I look at the papers. Possible skull fracture, concussion, lacerations. "What happened?"

"Some rancher found him out west. Had gone out early in the morning, before daylight to tend his cows, saw a cloud of dust spiraling up on the horizon. Thought he better check it out since it looked to be coming from his pasture. Got closer he could hear an engine. And something else. Strange, music he said, drifting over the ridge and an engine pulling uneven, low gear growling. The man didn't know what to think. Got out his twenty-two and crept up over the rise. White pale morning sky, and this old Chevrolet driving around in circles. Wearing a path in the grass, round and round. Empty. Except for the music. Said it was unearthly. A harp. A guitar. The rancher just stood and listened, almost afraid. There's been some strange goings-on out in the pastures lately, sexual mutilation of the livestock and so on, so he watches until the engine sputtered and died. Out of gas. And the car and the music rolled to a stop. He eases up, twenty-two cocked and ready, looks nervous into the front. Nothing. The hand throttle pulled, steering wheel held fast with baling wire. Carefully opens the back door, jumps back, rifle level. And there he was. Lying on a mattress, dried blood black from one nostril, left ear. Lifeless. Barely breathing. Hands folded over the strings of a steel-bodied guitar."

"Is that right." She's still standing looking at the door to his room. "You'd better get back to your station, Nurse."

"Yes, ma'am."

An orderly brings his clothes and the guitar. I take them to the room. Enter quietly. Krupp asleep, snoring lightly. Room dark, mournful. I stare at him lying on the bed. A tube running down his nose. Dark blue circles under his eyes. Didn't matter. He was pretty. Just one of those. Out of the several. I like. I stare at him unconscious on the bed a minute or two longer. Put his clothes and the stainless steel guitar in the corner, and leave.

He was different. Unusual. Not like the normal hernia of Farmer Brown, or Ma Frickert's gallstones. A mysterious and, I don't know, romantic aura about him. You get the idea only uninteresting people get sick sometimes, although that's unfair I know. Nobody's at their best holed up in a hospital. But I always looked forward to his bed, I mean room, when I made the rounds, and ended up spending all my free time, just like any soap opera episode you'd see, talking to him. I had to work a double shift that day. Get off at four and back at midnight, and all of a sudden I didn't mind anymore.

Silent twilight halls, I find myself thinking about him, when Clarence Krupp's call light blinks on. One of the county commissioners in for malignant prostate surgery. Not in the best of moods when he thinks he's healthy, which is rarely, being somewhat of a hypochondriac. My heart thumps like any country girl's. Not for Clarence.

Walk in on all hell.

"It's bad enough the butchers here cut me up, but now I'll probably contact some social disease just from being in the same room with this godless beatnik. What is this goddam bag of vermin-infested hair?"

"What do you mean godless! I am a Christian missionary out to save the heathen from internal damnation. I am a martyr set upon by a band of devil-worshiping heretics, who, save for the miraculous intervention of our Lord Son of God and Divine Saviour, would have thrashed me to death!"

"What's going on here?"

"Nurse. This, this beatnik was playing his guitar and singing. In the middle of the goddam night."

"What? The man is dreaming, what sort of drugs you been giving him?"

"Now both of you calm down."

I look around. The guitar in the chair in the corner. Hadn't heard any guitar. I calm Krupp down, bring him a sedative.

Back out in the hall. The night passing slowly. Thinking of the stranger with the guitar. Clarence Krupp's light again. I laugh to myself, on the way to the room. Nurse Little already there, trying to restrain Krupp climbing out of his bed. "That beatnik is playing and singing again. I swear, Nurse, if you don't put a stop to this I personally will see to it that all county funds to this hospital are withdrawn. Put him in another room!"

I look. The guitar in the corner. He's lying fetal position, eyes closed, groans now, rubbing eyes, rolls over. "There is no other room available, Mr. Krupp."

"Stop the guitar playing!"

Sleepily. "What? Nurse, you've got to stop him from waking me up."

"Get him or that guitar out of here!"

I shrug, pick up the guitar, no resistance, take it out to the nurses' station, take another sedative to Krupp. Wait in the room till things are quiet.

"Were you really playing your guitar?"

"Yes."

"What for?"

"To ease my headache."

Put my hand on his forehead. "I'll go get you something."

"Naw. Don't need it. Got medicine in my blood. But now that you're here, we could talk a little."

A couple of hours later, that dead stretch of night, I'm back at my station reading this magazine and Krupp's light is on again. Nurse Little goes to the room, muffled, then not so muffled voices along the dim orange-lit corridor. "Mr. Krupp, he doesn't even have the guitar now!"

"That doesn't keep him from singing."

"What's that old man dreaming this time?"

Nurse Little comes out to the station pantomiming strangulation. I chuckle, get a sedative and we go back to the room and calm the situation. Krupp dozes off again.

"Your head still aching?"

"Not so bad. I was lonely."

"And since I'm here anyway . . ."

"We might as well talk."

"What happened to your head?"

"Well. I was on my way north to see the old maid aunt who raised me. I'm an orphan. She's dying of old age and heartbreak. I stopped to pick up this hitchhiker. And the sonuvabitch pulls a knife on me and tries to steal my money and my car. Well, I managed to disarm him, and we commence fighting. He gets hold of the jack handle and hits me over the head. But somehow I get away, I don't remember how. And the next thing I know I'm waking up with a strange fair maiden staring down at me."

Nurse Little sits on one side of the bed. "What do you do when you're not fighting off bandits?"

"Oh, that's all I do. Roam the country looking for injustice. And for love."

I'm blushing, what is this. Sit down on the other side. "Having any luck? Finding love, I mean, I'm sure there's plenty of injustice."

"I'm looking for a new way of living, a place to settle and found a shining city."

"Sounds like that jack handle did more damage than we thought."

"Does that sound crazy? What are you looking for?"

"What makes you think I'm looking?"

"Everybody is."

Nurse Little laughs. Who is this guy. "Well. I guess what I want doesn't have to be a shining city. Just somewhere I can work, help. Like family, I guess."

He looks at me from the bed like he's just thought of something. A long time. "Like family, huh?"

"Yeah."

"That does make sense. Everyone needs a family. Me, as an orphan, should know that. So simple."

Silent middle of the night hospital. Electric hum and troubled breathing, night sighs. Illness. Then I laugh. "Well, it's not so simple when you get right down to it. You're an orphan and I'm an old maid nurse. Just like your aunt."

"Aw, come on. There must be dozens of rich handsome doctors around here. You must have lots of boyfriends."

Staring down at the magazine I've still got rolled in my hand. "Don't let the soap operas fool you."

Nurse Little takes the magazine from me. "As a matter of fact, I've been trying to get her to use the Datamate Computer Dating System."

"What's that?"

"A computer service that matches people up."

"Oh yeah? . . . So you mean people looking for family can find it in a computer?"

"That's what they say."

"Let me see that." Takes the magazine. Reads. "Sure. Nothing to it." Looks up at me, big smile. "Are you going to try this?"

Blushing again. "You never know."

A sudden moan, then wailing echos through the wing. Trouble in 503. Nurse Little and I jump up, say goodnight. He smiles, closes his eyes, the magazine open, face down on his chest. I watch him awhile, then follow Nurse Little down the hallway.

Next morning I told him the sheriff was coming to talk to him. I don't know what about. He shot out of bed, standing bouncing on the mattress for a second, head bandaged, hospital gown, looking from side to side, bounces toward Clarence looking on in terror, God bless and goodbye, over the bed again, slides around me heading for the door, slipping and flopping back to the bedstand to grab the magazine folded open and out the door flying down the corridor bare-ass open gown flapping past the nurses' station grabbing his guitar, me giving chase by this time, yelling, nurse at the station yelling you can't leave without signing out, you can't, hurdled a stretcher coming from surgery, ducking into the express elevator between the closing doors, and that's the last me, Clarence Krupp, the hospital business office, or the sheriff ever saw of him. I looked out the window, the sheriff's car pulling up south, an old Chevy heading off north. Laughed. Turned and took an empty catheter bottle and a sedative to Mr. Krupp.

Back to the old grind.

Sure did like that guy for some reason. Really did. Just goes to show.

Found out later he was probably the one who almost beat my uncle McMorold to death over in Mud Butte.

I'm standing behind the desk. Sunday morning. Empty time, melancholy. That's what it is. Hollow. A taxi driver comes up to pick up woman checking out. Recto-vag-fistula. I get the forms. Hand one to the cabby waiting for her to pack her overnight. "Sign here."

"What?"

"You have to sign here."

"I'm just a hack driver, ma'am."

"You still have to sign."

"I don't even know the lady."

"You have to sign before she can leave."

"What?"

"You have to sign before people are released."

"A cabdriver?"

"Yes."

"Me?"

"Yes."

"I'm new in town. I didn't know."

"Sign here."

"How did people get out before I came to town?"

"Would you just sign here."

"Or is this the first person ever to get out of this place. Cause I finally showed up?"

"Sign."

"No."

"What?"

"I don't know this lady."

"It's hospital policy."

"That I know her?"

"That you sign."

"I've never signed before."

"You were never here before."

"Then how did they get out? If I didn't sign and—"

"*You* don't have to sign!"

"You just said it was hospital policy that I had to."

"Not you!"

"Then why are you bugging me with this piece of paper?"

"Because you've got to sign."

"Make up your mind. You said I don't now you say I do."

"Not you. Somebody. Goddammit! Sign the damn form!"

"Easy, Nurse. I'm just trying to get this straight."

"Somebody has got to sign before this woman can get out of this hospital."

"Oh. I see."

"So sign."

"No."

"Somebody has to si—"

"So you sign it."

"I can't."

"Why not?"

"I work for the hospital."

"I work for the cab company."

"You sonuvabitch! Are you going to sign this goddam form or not!"

"I'm getting out of here. This is too fucking crazy for me. Tell the lady I'll be waiting for her down at the curb."

He's right. Too fucking crazy. The woman comes from the room.

"I'm ready. Is my cab here?"

"It's down at the curb. But I'm afraid you can't leave yet."

"What?"

"He didn't sign."

"Who didn't sign what?"

"The cabby. You can't leave until the cabby signs this form."

135

"The cabby?"

"Yes."

"Sign this form?"

"Yes."

"What for?"

"So you can leave."

"What if I didn't call a cab?"

"He wouldn't have to sign."

"Okay. I didn't call him."

"Yes, you did."

"No, I didn't."

"I heard you. You. Hold it. Hold on a goddam second. Too fucking crazy. Sam."

An orderly comes over. "Yessum."

"Sign here."

"Is he a cabby?"

"No. He's not a cabby. Sign."

"Yessum."

"And bring her a wheelchair."

"Yessum."

"A wheelchair?"

"Sam'll wheel you out."

"I don't need a wheelchair."

"It's no big deal, it's—"

"I don't need a wheelchair."

"It's hospital policy."

"That I need a wheelchair?"

"Enough! Enough of this bullshit!"

What would I have to lose. Fifteen dollars to the Datamate Computer. And wait and see what happens.

Sorry Learns Who He Isn't

SORRY didn't know what to think. Tired of thinking, just wanted to sleep. It had been a long three-day drive south from North Dakota, bucking headwind all the way in Marcus Baldwin's GMC, the Gleaner combine chained down on the bed behind and pulling the header barge trailer. Plenty of time to run it over and over again. The snooker game, Buffalo Gap, Sapulpa Slim. Wonder, worry about Hank, and mumble imagined phone calls with his dad into hot dry turbulence through the cab. Billy Paul's idle talk St. Louis Cardinals cap, bill folded up, pushed back on his head, crouching beside the highway out of the swirling dust and sun eating noontime bologna sandwiches, mayonnaise, raw onion, tomato and dill pickles. Malachi dozes against the dual wheels of the Ford and Viola looks at Sorry, smiles and seems to shake her head in a private disbelief. The miles longer, thoughts jumbled dull sweating reverie, the farther south they came, Nebraska, Kansas, Sapulpa Slim. Finally the soil turned red. The mileage chopped chunks of hours, still towns to go, the Northwest Highway, Sorry singing himself hoarse to keep the mind awake. Shouting invectives to Sapulpa Slim's boys and pounding the side of the door when the signals on the Ford in front finally begin to flash a left turn off the concrete three lane into the trees. Sorry snaps the axle down, shifts into second, steers north from the highway down the red shale hill into the dense shade and sudden cool of a creek channel rumbles across the wooden bridge into the dusty wake. A gradual rise for three-quarters of a mile. Sees the trees, the house and barn on the next hill, drops down through the dry creek bed, climbs the long grade to the corner. Straight ahead west of the house, turns east up the steep drive and sees him standing in the granary door watching his crew return. Marcus Baldwin.

Didn't know what to think. Watched him through the window, his head almost touching the top of the door frame, sleeves rolled up, arms hanging loose, hands and fingers evening light, calm, the wind dying down with the sun. A pipe slipping smoke from the corner of the mouth. The eyes meet, the GMC rolling easy low gear between the granary and chicken houses.

Marcus' gaze goes distant, the truck cab passing by.

Sorry pulls up behind the Ford. Malachi climbs out, stretches, comes back to the GMC, tells Sorry to leave her there, we'll unload the Ford first. And goes on to meet Marcus walking up behind. Sorry takes a long drink from the water jug and jumps to the ground. Feels good to stand still while Malachi and Marcus talk at the header trailer. Chickens beginning to roost. Marcus looking over at him, Sorry, listening to Malachi explain. They walk toward him, Marcus still looking, extends his hand, thumb cut off at the top of the nail. They shake, Marcus holds a little longer. Sorry looks to the ground, back up at him. A big man. Billy Paul comes up from parking the pickup and house trailer down by the barn. They unhitch the header trailers, pull them into the machine shed. Malachi backs the Ford up to the loading dock, they unchain the combine, Billy Paul backs it off. Sorry maneuvers the GMC to the dock. The sun's gone behind the hedge row. Billy Paul backs the Gleaner off, puts it in the machine shed. Viola calls from the house that supper's almost ready.

Sorry didn't know what to think. Just wanted to sleep. Sitting on the couch in the living room opposite the buffet. A dwarf came in the kitchen from the back porch. Talked quietly with Viola, looking through the door at Sorry, came in, the picture on the buffet, looked at Sorry, said his name was Mackey, shook his hand. Strange house, picture. Sepia tone and old. Brown. Young, long blond hair. A girl. Young woman. Marcus came in. Sorry. The picture. On a doily, between ceramic men bowing to women in long petticoated dresses. Other pictures, Marcus, obviously, young gaunt serious high school senior. A man and woman with a baby in front of a wooden frame house, treeless expanses of grass. Tall dark-eyed woman, same one, holding. Must be the arm of a man cut out by the picture frame. But Marcus looking at the picture on the doily. "That's my sister Blanchefleur. She. She's gone, doesn't live here anymore."

"She . . ."

"Left home twenty years ago." Marcus looks at the picture. Sorry standing by him in front of the buffet. Young woman. Marcus' sister. Familiar. Like all high school senior pictures. Marcus heads for the kitchen. "You can wash up in through the bedroom there. We'll be eating in a jiffy. Viola, how's it coming?"

Sorry stood at the portrait. Then went to the bathroom, washed his hands with 20-Muleteam Boraxo. Threw water on the face. Went back through the bedroom past the door to the stairway, stopped in the south door to the kitchen from the living room. Sees Mackey first, looks to Marcus, quickly back to Viola, Billy Paul and Malachi turn in their chairs to see. Air saturated off-white kitchen harsh-lit overhead bulbs. Viola is at the stove, a steaming pot, talking across the white wooden table to Marcus. Sitting at the head, by the east door to the back porch. The empty chair by him on the northeast corner. Mackey the dwarf northwest, Viola behind her chair on the west end. Malachi and Billy Paul on the south side. They all go silent when he enters. Two moths flutter sudden shadows, Viola points with a wooden serving spoonful of mashed potatoes. "Sit right in behind here." Sorry moves behind Billy Paul by the sink, Viola at the stove, scoots along the north wall around Mackey. Sits. Looks at his hands on his thighs.

Started to eat. They'd catch each other's eye and look away. Marcus talking to Malachi about the bad harvest. Sorry pushed chicken and homemade noodles around his bowl with the spoon. Sitting next to the dwarf who made the soup. Have to call. Home tonight after supper. Snooker game. Buffalo Gap. Sapulpa Slim.

After they had eaten they took the jumper cables to the barn to start Billy Paul's '48 Mercury. Then Malachi and Viola left. Sorry returned with Marcus and Mackey alone to the house. Empty and dark. Mackey went up to bed. The radio on the back porch, news and weather. Marcus lights his pipe. Would have to phone.

"Marcus, could I use the telephone? Need to call home, I've been sort of out of touch the last few days."

Marcus strikes another kitchen match, watches Sorry across the bowl of the pipe, puffs of smoke. The way he moves. Points the mouthpiece toward the living room. "Sure. Help yourself."

Sorry dialed the operator. Marcus turns off the radio, sits on the back porch in the dark. Pipe smoke through the kitchen. Living room. Buffet.

Keeper laughed when he answered. "Sorry. Sure is good to hear from you."

"Hope you weren't too worried, Dad."

"Naw, I'm used to it. Where are you now?"

"It's a long story."

"I talked to Hank this morning. I've heard part of it. Says it's just like the old days. Sure glad to hear you, knew you'd be all right, but if I didn't hear by tonight I might have begun to get a little nervous."

"How's Hank?"

"He'll be in tomorrow sometime. Picked up some fellow in Buffalo Gap to help drive the rig home. Said there were some pretty tough hombres hanging around in a '56 Ford looking for you though. Got to know more than where to spot the 5-ball when you shoot serious pool, son."

"Yeah. I found that out all right."

"Hank says he's got to take part of the blame, seeing as how he's your teacher and all."

"Well, I'm sure going to watch who I hustle next time."

Laughs again. "Where are you now, Sorry?"

Sorry chuckles. "I spent the night out on the prairie, just me and the cows, then I found my way back to the highway and got on with a crew coming back south. Just happened they needed someone. Been on the road three days. Just got in tonight."

"Glad you called. I just got back from the city myself. When Hank called. Whose harvest crew you say it was?"

"A man by the name of Marcus Baldwin."

Long pause. Moon on the white wooden table in the kitchen. Pipe smoke hangs in the light in front of the east door to the back porch. A spiral eddies through. Marcus. Keeper's voice almost inaudible static on the line. "Well, I'll be damned."

Blanchefleur, why did you die. Keeper pulled up in front of the two-story house. Evening. He cut the engine and waited in the car beneath the native elm trees bending north over the drive. Marcus Baldwin and Sorry sitting on the front porch in aluminum chairs. Brick pedestals, elongated wooden trapezoidal posts. The well at the east end, dark green ivy climbing up around the shalestone. Hog-wire fence, honeysuckle.

Keeper sat in the car. *Why did you die.* Looked at the house. Where she, Blanchefleur grew. Marcus stands. Keeper looks at him a head taller than Sorry. They come down the walk to the gate. He has to. Keeper has to get out and speak, not laughing, grinning, glad to see. Has to hold out his hand to Blanchefleur's brother, can't look him in the eye, Sorry holding strangely back behind. They know, all of them, this place knows. Keeper the intruder now has to say. What? Blanchefleur. Here. Brother and son.

They walk to the porch. Beautiful day for a drive. Not a car on the road. Could use some rain though, always use some rain. Marcus pulls a chair across the concrete, Keeper remains standing at the top of the steps by the well. Some rain before we plow. The harvest bad. Sorry hasn't looked, sits. Looks now at Marcus, Keeper standing, looking east toward the horizon, southeast where the hill slopes off toward the city, the first tall buildings shimmer there.

"Nice place here. Nice place you've got." Marcus sits and waits. Silence. Sorry sits. Keeper starts to slowly pace.

"I guess I always knew I'd run across you someday. And have to tell you, Marcus." Sorry leaning forward in the chair, elbows on the armrests, hands clasped in front, looks down at a spider dangling above the floor. "Sorry . . ." Keeper stands in front of the well. Dark circles under the eyes, hesitation. Head down, voice thick and sad. "You'd think I would of had it all thought out by now." Marcus sits. Placid. Arms folded. Looking right at Keeper.

Sorry looks up at each. Somehow all this has to do with. The house. The picture on the doily on the living room buffet. And Keeper so miserable afraid.

"I know what you have to say." Keeper looks up. They study each other. "Blanchefleur is Sorry's mother."

They wait. Sorry can't connect. Looking each to each. Mother. Sister. Uncle. Father. But they don't know. Each other. Never met before. What. Just another South Dakota highway. Never heard. Why, fighting back the tears. Marcus keeps looking to Keeper, waiting.

Keeper drops his eyes to the tips of his boots. "Was. His mother. She's dead." Marcus shuts his eyes. Then opens them again. "She died when Sorry was born."

Cold galvanic sweat across the back. Marcus' eyes, fixed on the porch chair, then at me, Marcus looking. My hands on my thighs. See only fingers, knuckles, dim evening. My other.

"And you're her husband."

Keeper tries to look at Marcus. At Sorry. "No, I'm not." It doesn't connect. "He's dead too." Keeper finally looks at Sorry. He hasn't realized yet.

Her husband dead. My. The. Night crashes down. "What?" Glance back and forth. Keeper looks back down. Start to speak. Stop. Turn away. Her husband my father. "Dead? You're not my."

Keeper stands, head bowed. Marcus, right ankle propped on left knee, arms folded across his chest, stares at his high-topped shoe, dried red mud in the seams, in the crux of the heel, brass grommets and clasps, worn knotted shoe strings. Colorless night light. A sharp metallic concrete clattering when Sorry flies from the porch chair, through the front gate out on the drive. A swatch of moon. Stops. Stands. Then starts out around the drive toward the barnyard.

Keeper yells "Sorry!" watches him stalk around the trees behind the cellar mound. Turns to Marcus still contemplating the shoe. "Marcus. I know I owe you an explanation. But I owe it to my. To Sorry more." And follows Sorry down the lane east into the pasture.

Sorry stands on the swimming hole grass. Fists clenched on the thighs. Stares at the steep far bank hillside, red mud margin, a large green yellow bullfrog peers over dark lambent green. Sorry kicks a cowchip in the water spreading concentric ripples, the bullfrog slips baffled into the silent waves. Sorry spins, starts up the slope, sees Keeper's silhouette, stops, turns toward the road.

"Sorry!"

"Leave me alone!"

"Wait! We got to talk."

"What's there to talk about?"

"About—"

"You lie! It's not true what you told me, not true."

"But I—"

"Why should I believe you? Huh? Goddammit. Tell me why, what else isn't true, is that what you want to talk about? Well, I don't want to hear any more of it, okay? Leave me alone." Up on the dam now, paces back and forth. "None of what you told me is true. About you. About my mother."

"It is, Sorry. True. About Blanchefleur."

"What's true? That she's dead, married a man Marcus didn't even know and died and Marcus didn't even know, you knew and didn't even tell. What the fuck is this all about? I'm run out of a pool hall, meet a total goddam stranger broken down in a goddam cob floater and hailstorm, drive all the way from North Dakota, I've got to drive a strange truck all the way to Oklahoma to find out it belongs to the brother of my mother! Who I've never even heard of! And now you want me to listen to you talk. Bull. Shit!"

Keeper hunkers. Looks around. Pulls a halm of grass, sets it in his teeth. Wipes his eyes. "It's true." Voice weak, cracking. "What I told you about Blanchefleur."

"That she was your wife?"

"I never told you that."

"You never said she wasn't!"

"No. But."

"But what? You said she didn't have a family."

"But."

"She was buried in California."

"But."

"Other than that it was all true, huh? Well, that's all you ever goddamn told me! Except that she was beautiful and young and smart."

"And it's true. She was. Beautiful and smart."

"Great. How old was she?"

"About 31."

"About! You don't even know?" Pause. Looks for the first time at Keeper, down from the dam at him, small, darker, squatted, forearms on the knees, hands hanging limp, chin almost resting on the pectoral arch. Sorry takes a few soft slow tentative steps down the dam toward him, father stranger. "How come you never showed me any pictures of her?"

Looks up at him. "I only have one, and she's with Lyons, with your dad."

"Only one?"

"We didn't know her very long."

"With my dad? Lyons. My father is . . ."

"Roger Lyons."

"Who rode rodeo with you and Hank, wrote those songs?"

"He met her fixing a flat tire, came to cut wheat, got run off by Marcus, she came after him to Lenapah and—"

"Hold on. Not so fast. My. I'm a little. Not so fast, I got to think this over." Sits down beside Keeper. Deepening night silence. "Sorry I yelled at you."

Left hand on forehead, turned away, waves off with the right. "That's all right. Don't blame you none."

Last light. Dark. Frogs and cicadas call and answer. Tremble, the water grass, the leaves of trees, breathe and think. Listen. Keeper removes the shoot, an aspirate pop of the tip of tongue on the upper lip. He sets the stem between the teeth again. And starts to tell the tale. Soft. Slow. Chuckling soon, remembrance, pain. Sorry on his haunches beside him. Intent listening. Then smile. Quiet laugh. Keeper, Hank, Lyons. A father, two fathers, a friend he never knew. All old, all new. Strange. A mother. Stood here, grew up here, chased cows, waded the creek, caught frogs and red horse minnows. Little girl to woman here, till Lyons. The '31 Chevy. The old Chevy out in the shed, Lyons'. Sorry used to climb through the window to play, sensing somehow the ominous forbidden adventuring. Conceived in the back seat bed. Growing in Blanchefleur's womb, warm unknown mother's womb kicking bouncing over narrow rhythmic thumping concrete highways. Where strangers, mother father strangers lay. Stories. Touch these things and shatter, shaken they fall suddenly in place.

Loud laughing.

No, it's not in place, still laughing incredulous. A story not in place or time. Simple, unfolding flow.

"Why didn't you tell me before?"

Keeper stopped silent. Laughing tears turn into tears. Pinches the bridge of nose, looks away a moment. Then back, cannot speak. Starts, hesitates. They sit and look, darkness glistens about the eyes. Keeper stands, walks to water's edge. "It was too sad to tell." Hot summer, windy day. Blanchefleur's casket in the house. Gentle dust settling, wipe the dark wood and brass, billowing motes, a blue, uncertain fly caught the stifling room. The windows failed. And look at her. The face. Like the inside of an apple spoiling in the air. Then sit on the porch. "Hear you bawling in the bedroom. See the dust cloud moving down the section line, the '31 Chevy's wake, a dirge. Watch it getting closer. Wait for Hank to pull into the drive. Pale, unshaved, blood soaked through the bandages, the trousers. Sweat and grime. He had to sell the horse to pay the undertaker, not even enough left over for the doctor who'd patched him up. Sold the saddles for gas. A week's funeral drive, Lyons bouncing along in the horse trailer behind. All the way from Saskatoon." Pause. "It was just too damn sad, Sorry. To tell."

Nighthawks dart and dive cawing over the pasture grass. "Dad?"

"What?"

"I think. You'll always. Be my father."

But I knew it wasn't true. Somehow. I couldn't trust anything again. I felt, I don't know, contaminated somehow.

We sat there for a long time on the bank of the swimming hole not saying anything. Anger, the resentment was gone. A vacuum. Dad and me. Partly not wanting to move, to break the last tenuous bond. And not wanting to go back and face Marcus. Not wanting to explain again. Could see it in his eyes. Sudden welling in my sinuses, catch it in the throat. Too much to think about now to push for meaning in the tears. I know it was on his mind, he'd have to tell him. I wanted to know it too. "Why didn't you ever try to find Marcus? After Blanchefleur died?"

Picks up a piece of shale, examines it. Plunks it in the water. "I don't know." Weakly. Almost a question. "I didn't know where she was from."

"You knew his name."

Another piece of shale. "It wasn't that simple. I. She didn't tell much about her family, we never even talked much before she died. She was with Lyons. With your dad."

"But you could have done something. The state police would have, it seems like, I mean." Keeper staring at the opposite growth of trees. "You could have."

Silence. "Yeah. I reckon I could have found him. If I'd wanted to." Slowly two more strata of shale. "I guess I really didn't want to."

It was an August night. Hot, dry wind. But it was suddenly all different to me. New. Uncertain. And alive. Nothing necessarily connected to any other thing. The billions of stars. A meteor shower and restless bats among agitated trees. Marcus still sitting on the front porch when we got back to the house. I left them there to talk. Walked down the hill to the west, over the next, to a bridge. Climbed through the barbed wire fence and down to the creek. Took off my shirt and boots and waded through tepid water running over moss slick slabs of rock, deep shale gravel bars. Two raccoons reared up to peer at me, then scrambled up the south bank into a dugout foundation. Cottonwoods opposite, leaves clattering in the stars and wind, an old broken-down corral among the shadow flow. I stood there. Water gurgling about the feet. The stars that fell. I was alone. My life about to change.

When Sorry got back they were just sitting down to supper. They ate in silence. Then Keeper left to go outside. Marcus and Sorry alone at the table. It was getting late. Marcus poured another cup of coffee. Sat holding it in both hands in front of him. After a while he looked over. "You know. You look just like Blanchefleur."

Try to smile. "It's very strange. Looking at her picture."

"Blanche and I built this farm together. With Mom. Your grandmother."

Looking around the kitchen. "It's a great place."

He pours more coffee. Stirs in sugar. Not knowing what he

wanted. Say something. Go to bed. All these years, some part of Blanchefleur. The kitchen table, hum and creaking of the house, all these years. "How'd you like to come. Visit. Stay awhile?" Sorry doesn't look up from the pattern of tablecloth around the plate in front of him. "See where your mother lived."

Looks over at Marcus, looking back at him, bright kitchen light. "I was planning to go to college this fall. I don't know. I've got lots to think about I'd never heard of yesterday. I don't know."

Leans back in the chair, yawns and stretches the left arm straight up toward the ceiling, right parallel toward the back porch door. "I think we all do. Well. You're welcome here anytime. This was Blanche's home." Rocked the chair back to the floor, stood up. "It's getting late. Time to hit the sack."

A big strong man. "Thanks, Marcus. I'll think it over."

It was a long, hot, quiet ride back home. After all the amazement wore off, I wasn't very happy all of a sudden. Distant from Keeper, Dad. I mean not really, but not the same anymore. I wasn't mad at him. Anymore. But it wasn't the same. I didn't trust things, that's all. Even the countryside, used to seem solid, the given texture of the world, now it looked ominous, cold. Indifferent. My buddies and my old girlfriend. The town, the farm, it was all strange. We'd hang out at the Downtown Recreation, they seem young and silly. How we used to carry on in high school. Just a few months ago. But seems like years. Like it never happened, a dream redreamed, transposed, shattered, cut off. From who I was. Who I am to be.

I didn't really want to do anything. But work on the '31 Chevy. The old padlock on the shed was so rusty we had to saw it off. Hank and me. Creaked the door open and there she was. Dust, chickenshit, bird droppings, mud daubers, nests, feathers and straw. Mice musty, eggs, grease. 1940 plates, 1931 Chevrolet, my dad's, my car, where I was conceived, up on blocks, opened the door, chewed gnawed moldy. Stained. Driver's seat. With. Blood. Mattress stained. It must be. Pretty strange to see.

We look it over. Key still in the ignition. I knew. Still see my childhood handprints and smears. Mysterious, remember now. The glove compartment. I open it and it's there. A map of Saskatchewan. The receipt. From a Canadian mortuary. Hank looking through the window, slowly shakes his head. "Well, let's get to work. She was running mighty good when we put her in here."

Changed the oil. Greased her. Oiled the throttle cable. Poured in gas. Pumped up the tires, by God they're still holding air, checked the wiring, a little chewed in the insulation here and there. Cleaned the spark plugs, distributor cap and points. Put in a battery. Hank steps back admiring, rubbing hands together. "Fire her off."

"You think she's ready?"

"Sure thing."

"Then let's get her off these blocks first." Jacked up the front, removed the blocks, then the back.

"Okay. Hit her, Sorry."

"Maybe you better do it. You know more bout this baby than I do."

"Nothing to it. Pump her five or six times, hold the footfeed halfway down, set the choke about right here. And let her rip."

I pump, hold the footfeed halfway, set the choke, turn the ignition, hit the starter with my foot and she's purring like a tomcat in a— Hank looks at her dour. "She never would hardly start."

We started on the inside. A new mattress in the back, new lining, replaced the wiring. Sanded it down, filled in, worked out, the little dents, a few rusty spots, and laid down seven coats of black lacquer, hand rubbed, like you wouldn't believe. That sucker looks like she must have in 1931.

And as we worked Hank and Dad started to talk. Stories about the car at first, that dent there, the race with the Oldsmobile down K-15 that time, and the stories grew, expanding from the center, from the car, self-conscious at first, uneasy, after all these years not talking, busting forth all of a sudden. Laughing. Remember.

And I'd withdraw, polishing chrome or into the corner of the kitchen, or a back bale in the barn, and just listen. Invisible for them, let them forget. Wrapped in aromatic hay loft cow manure. Ride the rodeo again.

"Remember the time, Hank, down in Texas when Lyons stole the Greyhound bus?"

"Yeah, said he'd always wanted to drive one."

"We were walking down the street, damn quarter to seventeen in the morning, two-thirds drunk, down in Laredo. He'd just won the bull riding the day before, so feeling pretty good when we come by this bus sitting by the curb in front of a all-night diner. Idling. With the door open. And no one in it!"

"We admire it a spell. And I tell him now's your chance, Lyons. I'll tell the driver you'll be right back."

"So Lyons and I get in, leaving Hank on the curb. Just wanted to go for a little spin around the block you understand, but we got off on the back roads, just a little bit turned around, off on the damn highway, little loop through old Mexico I think, lots of folks running around hollering a foreign tongue, didn't even know where it was we were trying to get back to."

"And meantime I'm standing at the diner, trying to explain to the driver where his bus is, and to the sheriff who was attracted to the scene by the enthusiasm of our discussion."

"And by the time we get back, they're just a standing there like old friends."

"Cause I've convinced the driver that the last thing he wants to do is press charges and explain to his boss what it was that the bus was doing at the curb empty with the motor running and the door open in the first place."

"And how about the time in Nebraska he jumped from the second story of the hotel into the water tank out back."

"Yeah. Claimed just for the fun of it, but I'm not so sure."

"Seem like I do remember a little gal down at the tavern there with a awful big corn-fed husker of a boyfriend and—"

"When the night clerk came to complain about the noise—"

"Lyons jumped again."

"Yeah, Sorry. Your ol man was quite a guy. Quite a guy."

Sitting listening. Driving the Chevy over the plains. Yellow brittle newspaper stories and pictures. The old photograph. Took from the chest of drawers, from the wrinkled envelope. Put it in a frame on the bedstand. Examine it before I sleep, drawn in, subtle grays blacks whites and silver world, two dimensional taking on depth. Explored it with a magnifying glass. A car. A Chevy. The Chevy, '31 out in the shed, 1940 license plate, the same as now. Objects unreal black and white, real in the mind, in the shed, two people standing. Look at the faces. Smiling. Young happy cowboy hat tipped back, blond curling hair, not really blond, off-white and grays, silk bandana blowing wind petrified in time. Background trees frozen unfocused motion. Chemical patterns burned on paper. Me. See me in the faces. A cut on his forehead. Real flesh once, blood. Touching the old Chevy where I can touch. Long dress caught on the bumper. Mud on the shoes and boots, mud under the

fender, mud there now. And belly. Belly bulging. Me. That's me.
My mom and dad.

Started playing the steel-bodied guitar serious now. Dad's
guitar. Old. His fingers wore the frets, the neck, brass sounding
board. And whose before.

And the notebooks Hank had saved of the songs and poems.
Smudged number two pencil. Misspelled words. Songs, poems. All
dated. Columns of figures added, pitch scores, gas mileage, phone
numbers, names. Rough, bold, large printed writing.

Afraid to read them at first. Funny, raucous. Rodeo cowboy
songs, women and horses, fighting and on the road songs, hello and
goodbye songs, sure am feeling blue songs. But some different. The
last one was written the day I was born. The day.

> What drives there are to put on spurs
> And spend a man his life.
> The livestock didn't choose.
> Never think there is a wife,
> Don't think of danger, what of hers?
> Just you and the brahma. Pull
> Tight the honda knot. The grandstands disappear.
> Just breath and heartbeat. And the only fear
> That's real, not theirs, not hers, not his, refuse
> To see but yours as you mount the bull.
> And the ceremony reoccurs.

Drive the Chevy across the plains. The earth domed, to the
sandy cemetery, the highest spot in the entire county. A bald swelling bluestem mound, a foot higher than the surrounding wind-
blown field, jutting rotting tombstones, wrought-iron fences, a
clump of old cedar trees bending north in the corner. Withered
wind-eaten wreaths. The wind. And stand in front of the two marble markers. Land fallen away contoured amber orange grassland,
furrowed plowed ground dusty uncertain light low on the horizon.
The sky. The cedars crying. The marble slabs. To get some feeling,
some meaning. Fingers along the cold chiseled script.

Roger Lyons	Blanchefleur Baldwin
?–1940	?–1940
He Could Trace His Family	She Knew But Didn't
Seven Years	Have The Time To Say
Duke Morgan Did Him In	She Bore Their Son

Stay there all day sometimes. It did not become less. Irresolute each time the first anticipation beneath the trees, dark damp desolate. To seek some contradiction, to stand so often long, to hear crepe tumble snag the iron gate. Why see, finally, lost, and the flag faded frayed popping early autumn shifting winds. White glimpses sudden magpie wings, phlox. Dried petals rattle. Cold red sundown cloudy tentacles surrounding before I leave.

Big Liz Gets Drunk

SORRY walked alone. Cold mist, dark wet red brick up 14th Street to Ohio. Into the Jayhawk Cafe. Warm. Mumbling jumbled voices. Stood at the door looking up and down the long narrow building. The glass counter to the left, cash register, Mississippi Crooks, Dutch Masters, Muriels, White Owl, Redman Chewing Tobacco, Camels, Lucky Strikes, Chesterfields, Winstons, Baby Ruth, Oh Henry, Snickers, Heath bar, Butterfinger, Lifesavers, notepads, typewriter ribbons, ink, ballpoint pens and pencils. Then the bar, round revolving stools. The serious drinkers, down to the window to the kitchen clipped green orders dangle over humid platters banged out kitchen light. The center row is headed by the jukebox, double booths opening left and right, high Naugahyde partitions. Booths along the right-hand wall to the pinball machine and toilets.

No one he knew. He sat down in an empty booth on the left side of the center row. Opened the calculus book. Exam tomorrow.

Skinny kid in an inside-out sweatshirt and apron takes the order. Chicken-fried steak and a beer. Sorry puts out a pencil and yellow note pad. Began working: $y = f(x)$, $x = g(t)$, $y = h(t) = f[g(t)]$. Simple. Bob. Windy brown North Dakota. Periodic tables. Simple. $dy = f'(x)dx$. $dy/dt = (dy/dx)(dx/dt) = f'(x)g'(t)$. $dy = [f'(x)g'(t)]dt = f'(x)[g'(t)dt]$. $g'(t)dt = dx$. So $dh = dy$ and $dy = f'(x)dx$. Simple.

The waiter set the plate down and brought the glass of beer. The place is getting full, noisy. Festive. Alexandra laughing, a group of regulars around the cash register. The jukebox Isley Brothers, "Twist and Shout."

Sorry ate two or three times a week at the Jayhawk Cafe. Where the unaffiliated, the estranged, off-limits for sorority girls and even the women's dorms, too strange a place, too many beatniks came to eat and drink and talk unheard things at Bufie's table.

"Riffle a Bud."

"Groundround a pair."

"Eighty-six!"

Bufie, short, toadface, horn-rim glasses and apron, and Alexandra, his sensual wife, usually presiding. Bufie gone to Kansas City, just Alexandra tonight.

Sorry came across the Jayhawk Cafe right after freshman registration. Walking the streets of Lawrence when the third floor room drove him out restless. His life up till then didn't make too much sense anymore.

When the work on the '31 Chevy was done he paced about the house, Keeper's farm, his farm, where he grew. It was time to pack for college, the semester began in a week, the football scholarship, like he'd always planned. But it didn't make sense. He walked out to the Quonset barn where Hank was changing the oil in the Dodge pickup. Sat on a old tractor tire and watched. Hank drains the last can of Quaker State, pulls out the oil spout, wraps it in a Kex rag, tosses the empty into a 55-gallon drum, wipes his hands on the old piece of workshirt tucked in his belt. "What's on your mind, Sorry?"

Gets up from the tires, dusts off the seat of his britches. "Let's go get a beer."

"Sure. See how this old Dodge is running."

They drive into town to the Downtown Recreation, not the same, inside and sit at the bar. Old Dodson brings two draughts. "Hey, Sorry, how's the KU football team going to be this year?" Dead cigar butt in his mouth. "But you won't be playing varsity, will you?" Sorry looks into his beer. "Naw, I won't be playing." Dodson goes back to brushing down the snooker tables. "We'll all be waiting for next year." Hank gets a bag of pistachio nuts and they crack shells and drink for a while.

"When you planning on leaving for college, Sorry?"

Sips the beer. "I don't know."

"School starts pretty soon, don't it?"

"Yep." Few more pulls on their beer. "I don't think I'm going to go."

Old Dodson stops whistling "I Walk in the Garden Alone." Hank looks over at Sorry, rubs the horseshoe scar above the eye. "Why's that?"

"Oh, I don't know." Cracks a nut. "What would you do? If you were me."

Leans back on the stool. "Well. It's not ever day a man gets the chance to go to school."

"I know. But what I'm going to learn there isn't what I need to know right now. Things just don't seem right anymore."

They sit for a long time. Finish off their beer. Hank signals Dodson for another round. "You think you'll be staying around the farm?"

Folding and unfolding the beernut cellophane bag. "I'm thinking some about going to stay with Marcus awhile."

Long silence. "Have you told Keeper yet?"

"Not yet."

"He's feeling pretty low lately."

Pause. "He's not the only one."

It didn't make sense, but he had to. He knew it. Keeper knew it. Sitting in the kitchen at the round oak table, a pot of coffee rat trap cheese and saltine crackers. Sat there over an hour, not really saying much, not too much to say really. Words condense, precipitate tears.

"Sure would like to see you go on to college, Sorry. My daddy always wanted me to go. And since I never made it I was hoping you'd."

Cuts another slice of cheese, puts it on a cracker. Takes a bite, picks up the dill pickle. "Dad. It's just not the same."

Pause. "Well. Maybe it would be a good idea to stay here. Until things. I don't know. Sort of settle down."

A bite of pickle. "I can't stay here. I've got to. I mean. I can't be satisfied with the way things were now. I've got to try to put them together again. And Marcus seems as good a place as any to start."

Pours another cup of coffee. Sips at it awhile. "You know. It's kind of funny. Dad and I sat at this very table over twenty years ago. I wanted to leave home to go ride the rodeo. No good reason. Just felt I had to do it. I guess I've got to admit now you've got plenty of good reasons. And I guess Marcus Baldwin's farm isn't so far away that we'd never see you again."

Long pause. Keeper staring into his coffee cup. Eyes and mouth working around the tears. Sorry finishes the cracker, stirs sugar and cream. "Sure. Things will work out."

"And you can always go to college later."

Sorry packed, walked around the house, would be good to take the time to think about it. Explain what is lost. Long childhood afternoons. And why. Walk around, hints of it, the buildings, dry-land farm, intermittent showers, but didn't know exactly what it was anymore. Alone out on the prairie with the cows, overfull, vast and distant. Touched and interwoven, a long new thread in a sequence of images now confusing to endure. Finally say goodbye. Constricted, numb. Keeper Hank chickens dog and cats, had to say goodbye and finally leave. Expecting. Something. Anything. Nothing.

He didn't call to say he was coming. Pulled away from Keeper's farm, first cool fall morning break in the dog days of September, pushed tears from the eyes and drove to Marcus Baldwin's farm. Parked by the propane tank behind the house in the north drive. No one home it looked like. Through the back gate to the back porch. Hollered. Went in. The living room buffet. Picked up the picture of Blanchefleur. Wiped the fine particles of dust from the glass, the picture of his grandmother and grandfather, the house and the baby. Must be her. He walked up the stairs, stood above the landing outside the southwest bedroom must have been hers, the door closed. Looked around the hall, old chest, uneven board floors painted thick chocolate brown, slowly opened the door. Stepped into the room. Where Blanchefleur grew up. Blue and white. Magazines, books, ceramic zebras, medallions, a program picture of Duke Ellington. Clark Gable. Newspaper clippings brittle yellow. School plays. Yearbooks. Blue and gold ribbons, Canadian County Track Meet, Girls' Basketball. Clothes hanging in the closet. A picture of three women in flapper dress crouched in Charleston pose tacked to the back of the door. Blanchefleur the middle one. Looked. Touched. Giggly accounts of school trips she wrote in the town paper. Can't be so hard. To find a mother.

He started suddenly. Lace curtains billow Prince Albert tobacco traces, the air, tingled perspiration along the spine. Caught. Turned quickly to the door, listened for the stairs. Silence. Heartbeat. Glanced around the room, an ashtray on the bedstand, two spent kitchen matches ashen residue. Sorry held his breath until the silence was sure, then stepped quickly into the hall, back down the stairs and out into the yard.

He heard a tractor, dust from the east field at the top of the hill. Got in the '31 Chevy and drove up to look for Marcus. He waited at the edge of the unplowed ground for the Minneapolis-Moline to make another round. The right front wheel bouncing along the furrow, Marcus leaning against the yellow rear fender watching the moldboard plow behind. He passed, saw Sorry, slight toss back of the head, arched eyebrows, and turned to cut the throttle and disengaged the hand clutch. Vaulted to the ground. His face red dust except the eyes and teeth and upper forehead when he took off the cap and smiled. Held out his hand. "How you doing, Sorry?"

"Not too bad." Shakes the hand. "Mighty good-looking field you're plowing here."

"Try to keep it that way." Looks back at the tractor, pulls a rag from his pocket and wipes dust from the engine. "What brings you to these parts?"

Walks around the radiator of the M&M to the plowed ground. "Looks like you've had pretty good rain. Ground nice and moist."

"Forty-five hundredths last week." Begins checking the radiator hose. "How's Keeper?"

"He's doing good."

Goes back to wiping dust. Then looks up. "What you have on your mind?"

Pause. "Last time I was here you. I've been thinking it over. Was wondering if you could use an extra hand."

Marcus looks up at the sun, back at Sorry. "How do you mean?"

"Well." Pushes a lump of plowshare polished earth with the side of his boot, breaks it up with the toe and heel. "Just thinking." Looks back at Marcus a red mask of dust over the yellow engine cowling. "You said, if I wanted to, to think it over. I believe I'd like to stay, work for you awhile."

Marcus stands there at the tractor, like he's mulling something over. Puts the rag back in his hip pocket. "What about going to college?"

"I decided not to go. Not this fall anyway." They stand there. "I mean, I just thought. It would be good to think things over." Pause. "But if you don't need, I mean . . ."

Tractor loping idle. Marcus something distant caught in his mind, looks back at the sun. "Well. We're not getting much done just standing here." Smiles. "Mackey and I are a little short right now." Smiles again. "Sure could use a good worker. Hop on, let me finish up here and we'll go find a place to put your things."

They climb back up on the platform. Sorry watches him set the throttle lever, engage the clutch, stubby thumb, veins along the muscles of the forearms, legs spread apart standing at the steering wheel, eyes set shining concentrated mask of dust. The contour of the field ahead, the plow rolling soil smooth red, falling off behind. Early September afternoon sun congeals the face, fresh-turned sod, gasoline and grease, sunflower jointgrass bindweed wheat stubble sweat and dust. A deep breath and long exhalation. Relax. Engine steady rhythmic pulsing. The furrow track. Marcus. Now and then a shouted comment above the drone and Sorry nods. Can't be so hard.

They finished up the field and returned to the machine shed north of the house, unhooked the plow and put the tractor in by the combine. Walked between the granary and chicken houses to the back porch. Got the enamel bowl and washed up in the east yard.

Not much conversation at the supper table. Uneasy. Mackey ate, left the kitchen before Marcus and Sorry were done, went into the front room and sat rocking in the rocking chair.

Sorry brought the duffel bag and steel-bodied guitar into the living room. Marcus took the guitar. Held it awhile, glanced from it to the buffet and back to Sorry. "You play the guitar, huh."

"I pick and strum around a little."

"This is an out-of-the-ordinary instrument you've got here."

"Yes. It is."

Silence. Then Marcus leads the way upstairs. Sorry stops in front of the southwest bedroom door.

"Not in there. That's Blanche's room. You'll be staying in the junk room."

Leads on through the northeast door. Two chests of drawers, an old buffet, stacked dishes, cups, candlesticks and kerosene lamps. A tin-topped kitchen table and three chairs. A sofa. Marcus puts the steel-bodied guitar on the brass bed in the northeast corner. "The closet is full of sheets and blankets, some of Mom's old clothes. We'll have to make room for you tomorrow."

"No problem."

They stand awhile, both looking around the room. "Well. Let's go get in the pickup and take a tour of the place before the sun goes down."

Sorry climbed into the cab and waited for Marcus to unload the two five-gallon gas cans in the back. The chicken coops, the house and the barn. All strange, alone. Watched Marcus in the rearview mirror. *What's he thinking. Why did I come.*

Marcus got in behind the wheel, took the pipe from his shirt pocket, the can of Prince Albert from the glove compartment. Stuffed the bowl. Struck a kitchen match on the steering column, two billows of smoke. Started the engine, a few more puffs, put it in gear, clunk of the driveshaft taking up the differential slack. And they moved around the drive and west to the site of the first sod house, the old corral.

They came back to the north pasture, the network of ponds along the watershed down to the swimming hole. Talked about technique, machinery, drought and thirteen-inch thunderstorms. Sorry stood a little longer after Marcus went back to the pickup. The dugout foundation, the dam of the oldest pond. Where Blanchefleur operated the drag bucket, escaped the prairie fire. Almost see her on the land, and wondered why. A cool evening, standing beside Marcus on the east hill, new moon, a billion stars. He was content to wait to hear.

Marcus listened to the news and weather, read the Bible, then went to bed. Mackey already asleep in the rocking chair. Sorry stood in the yard, unknown mother's yard. Then walked up the stairs, past her bedroom, to the northeast room that was now supposed to be his. Lay on the bed and wondered. Began to drift.

A board creaking jars him awake. A door bolt falls into the latch. Blanchefleur's room. Footsteps along the hall, hesitate before the junk room door. Listen. The southeast door. The downstairs clock strikes midnight.

Marcus finally began to snore sound asleep in the southeast room. The wind rises along the windows. Warm. Safe. Marcus Baldwin's house. And hers.

The next morning the homecoming was over. Four-thirty A.M.

"Hustle, Sorry. Mackey, cook this man some eggs and bacon. Here's oatmeal and sorghum. It's a beautiful morning. Mackey, you finish up your work on the truck garden fence. Sorry, how'd you like to do the plowing on the west place while I go into Yukon for fence posts and wire? I'll be back in time to feed and water the chickens and gather the eggs." Marcus steps to the back porch carrying his shoes and socks, stretches assessing the weather through the back door window. "Up and at em. I perceive that there is nothing better, than that a man should rejoice in his own works. For that is his portion. For who shall bring him to see what shall be after him."

And walks barefoot on out into the yard.

Sorry sat there. There must be more to it. He picked up the calculus book and opened it, put it down beside his chicken-fried steak platter. Lyons on the farm. Why Blanchefleur left. Sorry tried to eat and read at the same time. The Jayhawk Cafe filling up, loud and raucous students. The pages of the textbook fluttering closed. Two years. Sorry shut the calculus book, no use. Slowly chewed a mouthful staring out over the Naugahyde, neon saturated smoky nebulae. Two years. We worked. As if nothing had happened, there must be more.

Marcus and me out in the machine shed, mounting the right rear tire on the tractor. It's coming on evening and we've about got it done. The M&M is jacked up, the tire is on the rim and we've just finished getting the rim on the axle. Marcus has got the water poured in for weight and I've taken out a sparkplug and I'm screwing on the hose to use the cylinder compression to pump her up. We've been working on it quite awhile. Quietly. We're a pretty good team by now, used to each other's moves. But.

Just as Marcus is about to crank her up, Simpson, the neighbor to the west, bounces over the crest of the west drive in his pickup, a cloud of dust around the granary and slides to a halt in front of the machine shed, yelling out the window.

"The bastard's broken down the fence again! Gooder's Hereford bull, got into my pasture and he and my black Angus are going to kill one another! That son of a bitch got into Dickerson's pasture last year just as his bull was mounting a cow, butted him sideways and broke the bull's dick clean off. Had to make hamburger out of him. Come on!"

Simpson spins around kicking up a cloud of dust and heads back to the road. We grab rope from the wall, call Peewee the runt German shepherd, she jumps into the pickup and we tear off after him west a mile then north sudden drop down over the creek to the gate. Gooder is there, dogs barking bull roaring from the trees in the southwest corner, Peewee leaps from the back before we come to a stop, sprints off south through the broomweed toward the commotion. We set out trotting, Gooder leading the way.

The Kiley twins are already there, we make our way down the embankment, chinaberry and wild grapevine, out into a clearing at a bend in the creek. The two bulls face each other on a long wide shalebar on the south side. Snorting saliva slobber stringing the air, pawing gravel dust distracted by a bluetick hound, a mongrel dalmation-looking feller and Peewee circling around the bulls barking, darting at their heels. The Hereford spins around, head lowered horns butting, Peewee leaping splashes across the water out of range while the other dogs are nipping in behind. The Angus attempts two jabbing feints at the Hereford's exposed flank, pelted by shouts and stones, the Kiley boys whipping at the Angus with their ropes, and the Hereford swirls back from the dogs to face him. We ease around them both, whistling, shouts, dogs scattering then regrouping around the Angus who lets out a loud bellow and the Hereford answers. Red dust hangs in the trees, excited panting of bulls and men and dogs. Dusk. Peewee slips in closer to the side of the two bulls. They both stare. Blood on the Angus's neck. Gooder wades the creek and slaps at the Angus with his lariat. The bluetick attacks the Hereford from the rear, Hereford turns and charges, bluetick retreats, the other dogs follow them across the creek and up the bank north crash into the undergrowth and disappear. Simpson drives the Angus the other way, him and Gooder got things pretty much under control. Marcus and me and the Kiley twins take off after the dogs and the Hereford bull.

It's mighty dark by now. Overcast. Pretty much just follow the yelping of the dogs. Sounds like the bastard's headed for the open pasture across the creek again. We spread out, the Kiley boys one way, Marcus and me the other. But the barking's confused now. Damn blue must be sidetracked after a coon or something more fun than herding an angry bull back to the barn, not sure which way to go. Marcus and I walk along the high ground north of the creek looking for a good place to cross. The dogs gone silent for some reason. Approach the dark line of trees along a cow path. Not even frogs or crickets. Blotchy patterns moving among the shadows. Marcus to my left. We drop down a steep slope. A branch snaps. Look out!

The bull charges right for me, whiteface and horns flash in the dark. I watch him come. Until the impact, burst of air from the lungs, and it's Marcus has me around the chest flying to the ground as the Hereford bull thuds sudden exploding hooves and barking dogs past us on up the hill. Marcus back on his feet above me. Reaches down to pull me up. I slowly take his hand, get on my feet. Dust myself off. Marcus on the cowpath watching me.

"Thanks."

Looks a little longer. "Keep your head cut in."

The bull and the dogs are at the top of the rise. Standing around breathing hard. They've had enough. Marcus and I climb silent back up the worn rut. Call in the Kiley twins and we all amble back to the pickup. Gooder chases the Hereford on across the road. We reinforce the broken-down gate.

"Why don't you all come on over to my place? I got a whole case of Falstaff in the pumphouse."

Sounds good to me, I'm mighty hot and thirsty. But Marcus is already in the pickup. Gooder looks at me, the Kiley boys laughing, horse around with the mongrel dalmatian, I look at Marcus. He starts the engine. "Well, Gooder, we got to finish up the work on the tractor. Come on, Sorry."

Gooder smiles at me. "I know how it is, Marcus." I climb in the cab. And they're already telling each other about how they broke up the bullfight as we pull out the gate and are gone.

Marcus. When are we going to take a break and talk. This isn't a contest, is it? We're all over at Meivas' place gelding hogs. The whole damn town there almost, we had to castrate about thirty young boar, five or six men got them rounded up into the corner lot of the pigpen. Kids running all over screaming and giggling, then dead silent watching. Elva, Joy and Irene had a couple of bonfires going, big iron skillets and a pot of coffee. Table piled with potato salad, cole slaw, Jell-O salad, lemonade, ice tea, a couple of pies and an angelfood cake.

We'd three or four of us wrestle a pig to the ground on his back, squealing and a kicking, everybody not blaming him one bit, kind of a sympathetic whine ourselves. One man with the knife, another the smear, everyone of us hurting, tightening jerk through the loins, the scrotal sack, spurts of blood and a handful of smear. The raw gonads thrown into the gory pail, two teams of us, on to the next struggling hog. Sweat pig piss and shit, blood and smear. Evening campfire smoke, pain, clamor and we work our buckets full. One of the kids hauls buckets over to the fire and Elva and Irene cleaned and dressed, began to fry the mountain oysters up.

After we're through we all walk down to the creek. Strip and wade splashing and talking out into the foot-and-a-half deep pool under the cutbank down by the bridge. Throw water over chest, along the arms, thighs and genitals, relieved and hungry. Even Marcus. Two-toned cream and brown bodies. The sun almost gone. Late summer festive mood, jovial, sort of ceremony. The strong aroma of meat when we get back to the fires and Marcus says we ought to be on our way.

"What?"

"Better get on back home."

Look at all the folk around the board set across two sawhorses, bowls and pans spread out. "Don't you want to eat something first?"

"Got to check on Mackey shingling the east chicken-house

roof. Don't forget we're going to be widening the spillway on the lower pond and planting grass tomorrow and the day after."

Starting to get angry. "Well. I think I'll get a little something to eat before."

"Sure."

And he walks to the pickup and leaves. I join in the feed. All of us standing around the yard by the pigpens. Billy Paul, Gooder and Irene starting to sing barbershop. I get out the steel-bodied guitar, first time in a long time I realize. Whenever I got it out, seemed like Marcus would just stare at me. Think of something else needed to be done. Hardly played at all since I came. I get it out, Marcus not here anyway, and start to play and sing along with them. People my mother grew up with, Sunday school, Algebra I, mixed glee club together, here maybe, this same wicker chair beneath the catalpa tree. Talk and slap me on the back, Elva touches my hair.

"Sorry, I swear you look just like her. Blanche and I were best friends in school, you know. Always a lot of fun, but never talked as much as we used to, after I got married and had the kids. She had such plans and I'd always sort of imagined she'd make it big. Come back to town someday riding in a Cadillac and wearing expensive clothes!"

"You know, Sorry. I was a little sweet on your mother myself back in high school. Didn't have too much luck though. I remember the time Chester Yowell and me went out to the Baldwin place, we must have been sophomores or juniors, went out to do some sparking one night. We parked Chester's dad's Model-T on the east side of the hill and walked to the drive south of the house and started hollering her name. Sighing, moaning, wanted her to come out to the road, nonsense like that. Carrying on. It was dark and cloudy, and Marcus. Your Uncle Marcus is a hardworking man, and we all respect him for the way he took care of the farm with his mother, could tell even then he was going to be a pillar of the community. But I'm afraid your Uncle Marcus can't take a joke, if you know what I mean. Like I was saying, he must of only been about fourteen, already a big man, it was a dark and cloudy night, and we're standing on the shale rock garden where the mailbox is, and Marcus circles out around by the west road and slips up behind us.

"Now Marcus had a mighty good baritone voice even then. He

163

may keep to himself the rest of the week, but you can count on him booming out 'Holy Holy Holy' or 'Old Rugged Cross' of a Sunday morning at the Methodist Church, overpowering even Hod Spivey's bass, slightly off key it has to be said, floating over from the Southern Baptists. Like I say, a mighty voice, especially on a late dark road unexpectedly right behind you when you thought you were alone.

" 'I'm gonna start swinging and when I get done, there won't be nobody left standing but me!'

"Well, we jump up about three feet, Chester just hanging there in the air a minute or two seems like, then slipping and sliding on the rocks trying to control his voice, falling down busting his backside on the red shale wall, jumping to his feet trying to see through the darkness. I don't know about mine, but Chester's face is pale. Trying to get tough. 'Wha. Who. Marcus? Marcus, that you? Just you. What you going to do? Two against one!'

"Marcus is already six foot two and a hundred and eighty-five pounds. He stepped forward, we step back. 'We don't want to, to hurt you, Marcus. Just funning your sister. That's . . .' Another step, we step back two. 'Marcus, we're warning you.'

"He starts walking toward us, we start backing up, faster, stumbling turn, running down the hill. Chester faster than his legs. Chester always did have a little trouble negotiating this world. You met Chester? Just last year he got the toes of his left foot cut off by a train ran into him down at the county road crossing coming into Yukon. Lost the right leg to diabetes, left hand when the tractor flipped over on him ten years back plowing the Reddog forty and I don't remember how come he's got the glass eye. Velma says by the time he's ready to turn in at night, she doesn't know which pile to get in bed with. Anyway. We're running down the hill toward the creek and Chester belly-flops right before we get to the bridge. Limps up the hill, cursing, to the Model-T. Well, neither of us ever bothered Blanche much after that!"

"With you and Chester carrying on like that, and living with Marcus so hard, I declare it's really no wonder she left. I'd known Blanche ever since she was born, used to teach her in Sunday School and keep her and Marcus both sometimes when they were little and Mrs. Baldwin took the eggs into the city to sell. We sort of helped each other out, both being women alone. Blanche was sharp as a tack. She could talk like a grown-up by the time she was two and a half and knew what she was talking about too. I remember one time one of Smith's calves had been breaking into Mrs. Baldwin's lot, and she had an old heifer that never was too smart, and that yellow calf of Smith's would get in and suck her dry, and her own calf was about to starve. Smith would show up a few hours later chewing on a straw and spitting, ask if anyone'd seen that yellow calf. Finally Mrs. Baldwin told him if he didn't keep the calf out of her lot she was going to shoot it. Next day here come the yellow calf. Mrs. Baldwin grabbed the old Colt .45 revolver used to belong to her husband, just wanting to scare the calf off, she was standing clear up in the yard on the cellar mound, and good lawsy if she didn't hit the critter right between the eyes. She felt awful bad about that. Loaded the carcass up and took it down to the Smith place, and since there was nobody home, left it on the front porch. Smith didn't show up at the Baldwin farm for about a week, and when he did he didn't say a word about what had happened. I was over there with my eggs when he came up the drive to see if he could borrow some wire to mend his fence. Now Blanche was only three years old at the time, Smith and Mrs. Baldwin talking out on the front porch, and she walks up, a grass shoot in her mouth, thumbs hitched in the suspenders of her overalls, takes the straw out the mouth and spits. 'Anybody seen that yellow calf?' Yes, Lord. That child was something to behold.

"It always made me sad to think about her staying around here never getting married. She used to stay up till late at night, when everyone else was asleep. I'd see the light on way off and wonder. I think it was the only time she had to herself. It's really no wonder she left. And a shame we had to go as long as we did before we found out she died. But still. You've got to feel a little sad for Marcus too. All those years alone. You know, Sorry, you're his only living relative."

I sit there, the steel-bodied guitar on my knee. Only one left alive. Hadn't thought of that. All those years alone. But damn. Why wouldn't Marcus stay here tonight? Trying to prove he can work harder? This is as much a part of the job, more than just duty. Why not?

"Who did you say your daddy was?"

I look around. The yard. The pigpens. Rooting hogs among squat huts and pigweed, banging buckets, scratching against the fence posts, ripples, campfire, frying pans, blankets and quilts spread on the grass. Men women children of the town. Neighbors. If you look back hard and far enough, probably kinfolk after the chores. Celebrating. And I begin to spin together stories, threaded through, here and later, patchwork what we know into a fit of who I am. And we eat and talk and sing until we can hardly stand.

But it all came unraveled. Planting grass with Marcus on the west place down by the creek where the old sod house foundation's dug into the bank. Before it all was found and formed.

"Better hustle."

Marcus and Sorry together to pick up rocks below the spillway of the lower pond. Sweating. Hot day already. Just the morning project, finishing up from the day before. Planting grass in the afternoon. Blanchefleur's brother and son. *My mother can't be so hard.*

Marcus wrestles a hundred-pound chunk of shale, it explodes hissing evil vibrating tangled rattlesnakes underneath. Sorry jumps back heebee jeebee and they slither various directions into the grass and rocks. Marcus doesn't even flinch. "Let's go, Sorry." And heaves the shale crashing onto the pickup bed. Sorry stands amazed. Laughs. Then carefully lifts a slab by the corner away from him peeking over. Marcus carrying on like there's not five or six rattlers wriggling about. "Let's go, Sorry. Let's get this rock over in the draw and see if Mackey has the sod turned yet."

Sorry lugs the last mass of shale into the pickup. He knows it's time. Circles around the truck, throws a shoulder up to wipe perspiration, red dirt from the forehead, gets in beside Marcus. Smell the sweat, distinctive, topsoil, grease, gasoline, Prince Albert tobacco smoke from Marcus' pipe. Pitch and yaw slowly over the pasture, Marcus pointing out the last dam project, completed the year before the shelterbelt planted early spring three years it's been. Talking about the grasses, things he wants to do next. Sleepy heat. Sunrays through the windshield. Body glowing. Sound of the six-cylinder, the transmission, the springs, in low, crawling among the cows over uneven hillside. Calm deep voice. The sun. Prince Albert. Sweat. He knows. And still.

He loved his uncle.

Two years of this. We work. No more talking. Always something needs to be done. Make the place look like someone lives here and you got to do it right cause you don't want everybody who drives by to see every bonehead mistake you make. And what Marcus means is you don't want the prairie to see, he doesn't want to see it. The first winter, spring, the harvest. Maybe the second autumn, now the third coming on, the routine established. You'd think there'd be some time. Only living relative. Why are you so hard. And me getting so mad.

If any talking is going to get done, I guess I'm the one who's going to have to do it. Now. At the dinner table. Mackey sullen. Malachi. Quick silence when I come in from the back porch. No more easy laughter. Not like home. Keeper, Hank. Viola moving pots and pans from the stove to the table, roughs my hair and smiles when I move by her at the stove. But Malachi doesn't look. Marcus comes in and we begin to eat. Hot. A fly buzzing about the tabletop. Marcus grabs it out of the air. "Sorry and I finished up the spillway this morning. Mackey's got all the sod turned in the east pasture. We'll load it up and plant after we eat. Get it out of the way and we can start on the plowing tomorrow."

Mackey scratches his nose. "Shall I do the plowing?"

Marcus looks from Mackey to Sorry. "Let Sorry do it. You need to wash and candle the eggs. Clean the chicken houses. Sorry's getting to know the contours of the fields pretty well." Mackey looks back at his spoon. "Then we can get the north pond siphoned out and get in there with the drag-bucket, we'll have plenty of good fill and double the reservoir capacity for the rains next spring." Everyone silent. Mackey slight rocking stares through the light, Malachi studies the linoleum between his shoes. "Trade in the old pump we got, and we'll have the water and the equipment to deliver it to the yard, the truck garden and orchard. Sorry, I'll put you in charge of that, should have it done before next year's harvest run."

Malachi looks up. "I was thinking I was going to do that."

"Let Sorry do it, get used to the pond system."

"But . . ."

"You and I'll be overhauling the combines."

Viola gets up and goes to the back porch. I look around the table. Like one of his own. Another worker on the place. Like I'd been here all my life. Am I the only one wondering? Viola brings a cherry pie. Looks like it'll have to be now. Shit. "Marcus. I been wondering. What happened when Roger Lyons was here?"

Pauses with the pie wedge in the air. "Who?"

"My dad."

Everybody gets real still. Marcus scoops out a piece of pie, hands the wedge to Malachi. Reaches to the middle of the table for the cream pitcher, pours cream over his pie plate. "You know. Ever since Keeper told me about that, I've been trying to remember him. And for the life of me. I can't."

Look at him awhile. How could he not. He's looking at me, holding a forkful of cherry pie, really trying to remember. An insignificant two days of his life, breakdowns, flat tires trying to get the harvest in before the storm, which storm was it, the year Blanchefleur. Stir things up goddammit. "Why, do you think, did Blanchefleur leave?"

Very long pause. Marcus sets the fork down beside the plate. Elbows on the table, folds the hands in front of his face. Then reaches for the toothpick he wears over the right ear. Works on the top incisors between the canines. I wait, breathing hard. I got him. He leans back in the chair, still looking, cleaning his teeth, every now and then forcing air in then out with the tip of the tongue through the space between his incisors. Wipes the toothpick dry. Replaces it above the ear. "I don't know." Picks up the dishtowel. "And never had much time to think about it."

Malachi, Viola, Mackey all staring at plates and spoons and hands around the white wooden table. I've gone too far. I'm the one out of place. What difference does it make, why do I ask why. Marcus sure doesn't. Talk about what, where, when and how. Never why. Twenty years ago. When you get right down to it there really isn't much time to think about it. He's right. Why come searching for a lost mother? What can she teach you, why get mad about what you can't change? Why stay here with Marcus anyway.

He's sitting there at the table. Six feet four, two hundred fifty pounds, not an ounce of fat on him. A tough man. Only one thing certain. We're gonna plant grass all afternoon.

We pick up the sod from the pasture and bring it to the yard east of the house and start hoeing holes and putting chunks of buffalo grass in, every two or three feet. And it's hot. Bending over to tamp it in, carrying the water bucket over to water, carrying it back and forth to the hose for more. And Marcus won't stop, won't take a break.

Well, I figger I'm as tough as the next man, and I'm younger, I can outlast him. If that's the way he wants it. I mean all of a sudden it seems like I've been waiting two years just for this. You sit down, Marcus, I'll finish this row. A hundred and twelve degrees. In the shade. We're out in the sun.

Well, I guess I'm gonna have to wait some more, cause he doesn't slow down. And I'm pooping and a falling.

Naw. That's not really it. I'm not tired. Tough as he is. What I really want is to stop and talk. He's got to remember, to wonder about it. Why couldn't we talk it over, it should be clear to him I'm thinking about it, and he must be too. I mean he's kept her damn room clean for twenty years. If we spend so much goddam time making the place look like somebody lives here, wouldn't it be nice if, instead of just work here, we take some time off and did live here ever now and again. Marcus. What are you trying to prove?

Anyway. We finally get the patch east of the house done, and I'm looking forward to a glass of ice cold lemonade, he hustles us all into the pickup over west to the bridge where the county'd done some roadwork. Tore all the grass out and we're going to sod the ditch.

I bear down. But getting mad. And that's what's wearing me down. I'm psyched, having trouble keeping up with him. You got to stay calm when it's 112°. But I'm getting mad. He's got the hoe in one hand, armful of sod, gray Sears pants and shirt, large wet discolorations down the armpits and back. Pipe in his mouth, gray billed cap. Impassive. Only stopping now and then to wipe the sweat from his eyes, remove the hat by the bill running the forearm across his two-toned face forehead and cheeks to the shoulder, replace the hat in one motion. The whole bowl of earth throbbing. Floating in heat. Silent. Sun.

It's a contest between him and me. Something inside, and I've taken sides, Marcus. And he is tough.

Simpson tells about the time Marcus was helping him thrash wheat, back before they had combines, had to cut and bind the wheat into shocks, then bring in the steam-driven thrasher. Marcus caught his gloved right thumb in a chainwheel, spun his hand around. Went ahead and made the adjustment he was trying, thrashed wheat another eight hours, about 110 like today, didn't take the glove off until ten o'clock that night. Threw the tip of his thumb to the hogs before sitting down to supper. And for some crazy reason I'm standing here on a sloping red dirt hillside wanting to take him on. It doesn't make any kind of sense. It's definitely time. I've got to get away. From Marcus. I slung the armful of grass down to the ground. "Marcus! Let's take a break." Trying to control the voice. "It doesn't make sense working nonstop in this sun."

Turning to look. Expressionless. Passive. Fixing with his eyes. "The water bucket is almost empty. Better go down to the creek and draw some more."

Mackey picks up the sod I threw, looking from Marcus to me, walks over beside Marcus and continues planting. I stand my ground. My face congested heat. "Let's take a break, Marcus."

"Man goeth forth into his work and to his labour until the evening." I want to charge headlong, bury the head in his gut. He's standing there like he knows. Towering in the sun, him and his shadow. Head in the gut.

Stand tense. Sweating like a stuck pig, back aching hands raw, fingernails bleeding. Sun. Oppressive. I can't do it. What good would it do. He's too damn big.

I pick up the bucket and go down the long embankment to the creek. Drop it in the thick warm water. Look at the shalebar across, the remains of the old corral. The old well cover, the hollow place against the hill. A house of dirt and grass once, turned from the rolling prairie above it. Same grass I'm planting now. Been growing here ten thousand years. A drunken father, hard-willed mother. Marcus. Every day. Wind. Cold. Heat. Rain. Hail. Sleet. Ice. Drought. Disease. And death. He's right. You had to be hard. Back then. And now.

I stand in the shade of old cottonwoods, water moving over moss-strung strata. A dragonfly quivers incandescent blue black dappled water grass and dart. Cottonwood leaves shudder glittering movement of sun and air. It is me out of place. I have to leave the farm.

Sorry let the calculus book drop by the empty chicken-fried platter. Looks over the partition toward the front of the Jayhawk Cafe. "The Duke of Earl" from the box. A milling group around Alexandra at the cash register, music laughter voices wineglass and smoke. Finished off his beer.

So he came to college. As if nothing had happened. Like he was planning to do before the harvest, before Sapulpa Slim, like his dad, like Keeper had always wanted him to do. In the '31 Chevy.

Packed in the duffelbag, the notebooks and Lyons' old steel-bodied guitar. Drove into town. Slept down by the city park, back seat mattress. A week. Found a room. Went to orientation. Talked to advisors. Enrolled. Walked. Rounds of rush week parties. But not really. Standing off in a corner watching the piano man play, hands dancing on the keys while young kids tried to be cool and drink too much beer. He knew more than them. He knew he didn't know.

Just like they'd planned. But it didn't make any sense. Nothing settled with Marcus. He didn't really leave. The only living relative, mother's brother. Uncle. Go back summers for the harvest. Help put in the truck garden over spring break. Out of kilter, oscillating around a disturbed equilibrium. Walked a lot. Hung out at the Jayhawk Cafe. Sometimes played pocket billiards with basketball players in the student union basement. Silent tolerance at first of the silent stranger, then thinking they had a mark, Easy Money man, accepting him into the towering circle to shoot some serious pool. Got excited about what he was doing in class sometimes. But without system, direction. Not studying to be a farmer. Just taking what came. Math. Philosophy. Literature. Geology. History. And late at night, fall evenings, sit trying to read under the sultry bare bulb fixture, exotic singing from the Pakistanis across the low dark hall. He'd drop the book. Pick up a hand mirror and look. And think. Of a hard luck rodeo cowboy.

> *You can't trust a steer.*
> *He don't know what you're about.*
> *Much better sitting here,*
> *Wink at the waitress, drink your beer.*
> *Tell dogging stories, laugh and shout.*

Toss the mirror aside and go walking. Where students wouldn't go. Dark lit streets, cars rusting, faded paint brown gray bondo poxed, bashed ragged fender. Garbage cans newspaper old tomatoes grapefruit rinds and flies. Buckled sidewalks growing grass in cracks, broken wine bottles in paper bags. Urine. Boarded windows, doorways lurking. Mexican cantinas, downtown snooker bars. Bring Lyons' notebooks to read, the steel-bodied guitar and sing for pocket money.

Return through empty early morning to Tennessee Street and the ominous dark house, climb the back stairs to the narrow rafter room. Where Marcus waited silent. Blanchefleur's son. Not working.

Sorry gathers up the calculus, yellow pad and pencil. Sits awhile. Exam tomorrow. Better get on to the library.

"Heh, Sorry, man, what's going on?" Honest John from English 221. Sits down. "What you up to?"

"Test tomorrow. About to head for the library. What you doing?"

"Thought I'd better have a beer to celebrate. You'd better have another one too."

Looks down at the calculus script across the yellow pad. What the hell. "What we celebrating?"

"My brother in the army. Special deal, training in the jungle." Signals the waiter. "Riffle a Bud!"

"The jungle? The Russkies don't have any jungle."

"Who knows what they're up to."

The waiter brings two more beers. They drink, watching the cafe around them, the jukebox turned up a notch, the voices from all the booths keep pace. Honest John picks up the calculus book. "Pretty heavy stuff, man."

"Not so bad once you get into it."

"What are you majoring in?"

"Who knows."

"You mean you don't have your curriculum and life all planned out?"

"Not yet. How bout you?"

"I stopped going to class a month ago. Except for English, I go but don't do any of the work. I've made straight A's ever since I've been here. Now I'm going to show everybody I can make F's too."

Sorry looks at him over the rim of the beer glass. Laughs. "Well, everybody's got to do something. Riffle a Bud!"

Honest John empties his glass and hands it to the waiter. Gets up and goes to the toilet. Sorry takes the yellow pad and stares at the formulae. Then chuckles to himself. Loud laughter from the front. A chess game in the next booth. Honest John comes back carrying the two beers. "You know, man, there sure are some good-looking chicks in here tonight. What's going on anyway. It's almost closing time and the place is jumping."

"We're celebrating." Raises his glass. "To an unburdened future."

Honest John clanks his up. "And the jungle. Wherever it may be."

Bang!

A gentle arc parabola over the tall partition between the booths. A half-pint bottle spins slowly, stops. Neck pointing toward Sorry. They look startled at each other and laugh. "It's getting wild in here tonight." Sorry picks up the bottle. Southern Comfort. Empty. Grabs a napkin, a pencil, points with the eyes to the other side, writes.

> *There was a young man in a booth*
> *Who wondered what it meant in truth:*
> *When a bottle comes flying*
> *Is there sense in denying*
> *That someone is being uncouth?*

Stuck it in the bottle neck and pitched it back over the partition. The jukebox turned up louder. Eleven-thirty already, almost closing time. Forget about studying.

Bang.

The bottle again. A napkin stuffed in. Sorry unfolds it.

> *Uncouth? What mean you brothern?*
> *You notice the Comfort is Southern,*
> *and believe me mister*
> *This here sister*
> *Is pouring herself anothern.*

Sorry gets another napkin, scratches his head, laughs. Honest John orders two more draughts.

> *We don't want to seem impolite,*
> *But it hardly seems to us right*
> *That we're drinking beer*
> *While someone so near*
> *Is consuming such southern delight.*

173

Sits back with a big grin waiting reply. Shouts, handclapping from the front, big crowd around the jukebox. Bufie's wife Alexandra doing the Twist with one of the regulars. Midnight, closing time. But beer still flowing, the blinds drawn. Begins to wonder about the bottle just as it rises at the top of the divider, faint glimpse fingers distort refraction through reflections, teeters, falls down the Naugahyde, bounces off the napkin holder, shoots across the Formica top, Sorry lunging to catch it one-handed grab a foot from smashing the floor. Pulls out the napkin.

> *Someone in my condition*
> *Should not make a proposition.*
> *But I've got at my font*
> *Everything that you want*
> *If you'll just come around the partition.*

Sorry hands it to Honest John. They look at each other, at the throng up front, shrug why not.

The booth on the other side is filled with women. Two on one side, and Big Liz on the other. "My name's Liz." With another half-pint half full of Southern Comfort and a Coke. Three hundred pounds at least. "Which of you est le poète?" Shoves forward the napkins with the limericks. "Qui est-il?"

Sorry nods. "I am."

"Sit down, mon ami."

Honest John already slipping in the other side. "Thanks. My name's Sorry."

"Ah, Tristesse. Quel nom unique. Mon cher. Have a drink." Drinks down half the Coke, pours in the entire contents of the half-pint flask, gulps down half the glass again, reaches in her purse, pulls out another half-pint, shoves it dizzily toward him. "I am getting drunk, Tristesse."

"Is that right."

"It is." Downs several large swallows of Comfort and Coke. "Open this, mon cher."

Opening the bottle. "Are you French?"

"That's why I'm getting drunk." Picks up the Southern Comfort, assiduously pours into her Coke glass, Sorry glancing to the others for explanation. Nothing. All three sitting motionless large grins watching. She then takes Sorry's not-quite-empty beer glass, pours, offers what little remains to the other side.

"Why are you getting drunk?"

"My boyfriend left me."

"What's that got to do with French?"

"He's a Frog."

Silence for a while. She drinks, Sorry sips. Honest John makes talk with the redhead next to him. Laughter and louder music. Bunch of people have joined Alexandra twisting the night away. Honest John takes redhead by the hand and weaves up the aisle. Sorry glances at Liz, across the table at the dark woman still there. Leather headband, narrow face, long black hair to the shoulder. Gaze at one another. Slowly smiles. Light rhythm space jumble up, Sorry sniffs the Southern Comfort and beer, swallows, powerful stuff, perfume, dark woman's body wafting. Liz bangs her glass down empty. "I'm getting drunk cause he's a sombitch. Why are you here? Let's philios-ophize bout the meaning of life. Why are you here?"

To the dark woman. "How much has she had?"

"Trishtesse, you're ignoring me. I've had all. Cept for a few sips to my friends." Sorry looks to the dark woman. She confirms. "I love it."

"That's quite a bit, isn't it?"

"I'm quite a bit. Takes a lot to get the job done, mon ami."

"You do this often?"

"Never has liquor touched my bought red mouth. I am a serious student of premedicine. He, le Frog. Le Frog. Has driven me to this. Answer my question."

Looks over at the dark woman receding in the corner deep red as if to listen. "Well. As a matter of fact I was thinking of that very thing just before this Southern Comfort bottle fell into my lap. It was my uncle drove me to it. Planting grass in a hundred and twelve degrees of sun."

"Ah. You're making that up, Trishtess."

"Seems that way, doesn't it."

Liz not listening all of a sudden. Passed out on the tabletop. Sorry looks at the dark woman. Still sitting in the booth. Large eyes, high cheekbones. Laughter and music. She leans forward from the darkness. "Let's go dance."

The Jayhawk Cafe very hot. Pounding jukebox bass rhythm, sweat beading, trickling down faces, the space at the head of the center row of booths jumbled mechanic rocking back and forth seesaw up and down, knees, elbows, hands, asses flowing over into the aisle on either side. Booths full of people playing cards, amorous entanglements, hearty discussions. Alexandra back behind the bar surveying it all.

Sorry and the dark woman push into the Peppermint Twist. Bumping hips and butts tangling legs and feet in the crowd, pushed closer together, hot, laughing, tighter, sweating, dark eyes body moving. Close. Warm saline acidic body, touch the hand, touch and hold. Sway arrhythmic aromic, arms hands shoulders. Half-time press closer, thigh and thigh and belly, Joey Dee and the Starlighters Chubby Checker touching mouth to hair neck, the ear. When Alexandra pushes through to shut the jukebox down, two-thirty, time to quit. Loud complaining, "Come on come on, if the police would happen by they'd close us down for good. The place is supposed to be empty by half-past twelve. Let's go."

Sorry and the dark woman standing face to face.

"Let's go."

"Where to?"

"I live just around the . . ."

"What about Liz?"

"Liz."

Make their way back to the booth, darker than before, large heft inert in the corner, head down tangled blond, turned toward mouth open eyes rolled back. Right hand limp on viscous tabletop. Open tube of lipstick on its side pointing to soggy napkin lipstick lettering.

HELP!

They look at one another.

"What to do?"

"Don't know. Don't really know her. She came with Carol."

Look around in the dark cafe, lights being turned off, Honest John, Carol nowhere to be seen. Sorry tentatively taps Liz's shoulder. Nothing. A little firmer. "Liz." Harder. Louder. "Liz! Hey Liz!" Nothing. Punches, shouts, "Hey, Liz, up and at em, time to hit it."

Arm flails violently, Sorry jumping back, she bursts up from the depths shaking the floor toppling glasses and bottles, spewing wild-eyed pupils swirling gossamer saliva from her wet chin red creased cheek. Pirouettes, stumbles, wobbles, ricochet rumbles down the aisle to the front, folks scattering from her way. Stops. Turns bewildered among a group of laughing strangers, wipes both hands confused down the clammy dress. And topples backward into the right-hand booth, enormous gams blubbering forth from flowered panties. Very loud laughing, shouts. Except from Alexandra. "What are we going to do with her? She can't, I mean this will cost us our license for sure. Even if she makes it home, her dorm mother finds out where she's been."

The regulars gather round to confer. Boisterous merriment.

"She can spend the night at your place."

"My place! No man, I've got a weak floor."

"Call her a cab."

"She's a cab, definitely that big."

"Just send her off into the night."

"Come on, we've got to do something with her."

"Who the hell is she anyway? Where does she live?"

"Some dorm I guess."

"Somebody do something!"

"What? She's out like a cold jack mackerel. That's too much dead weight."

Sorry and the dark woman watch from down the aisle. No one to help. Sorry takes a step forward, looks back at the woman, walks the row of booths looking at the crowd lining the bar, peering over booth partitions taking it all in, what the hell, no one knows me, gigantic legs teetering out blocking passage, he bends over, supporting on the back of the booth, leaning way over, the belly, breasts, straining for the cheek and ear. "Liz."

"Hey, Sorry, hooray," Anonymous voice from cafe innards. He turns and waves to the crowd bursting out cheers, turns back to the task.

"Liz, baby. Time to get going, rise and shine, up and at em."

"Ooh. Urum."

She stirs, Sorry grabs a chubby hand, strains, pulls, "Come on, Liz, you can do it," pulling harder, the feet on the floor. There you go, she blinks against the remaining light, mouth slack slobber, a close circle around of regulars, Alexandra's concern turns to hope. Liz wavers, loses balance, regains, Sorry supports she blinks some more, recognition trickling in. "Ooh. Trishtesse, c'est mal. Très mal."

"It'll be all right. Going home now. Take a couple of aspirins before going to bed and you won't feel a thing in the morning."

"I've never done this before. I'll take four aspirins. I'm pretty big."

"Right. Four aspirins."

"I'm dying, help me."

"You're all right, just keep those eyes open. We'll get back to the dorm, you'll—"

"Dorm! The dorm mother will kill me. What weell I do, mon Dieu."

"You'll walk straight, not say a word, walk straight to the elevator and—"

"Take six aspirins. But sign in, I gotta sign."

A cab honks outside the Jayhawk. A corridor opens Sorry and Liz to the door, Alexandra presses a ten dollar bill in his hand, he looks back in. The dark woman. She comes and takes Liz by the other arm, and they swarm out into the street, suddenly joined by three or four others crowding into the cab, scrambling for room, coats books umbrellas. Somehow Sorry ends up on the floor of the back seat at Liz's feet. Can't let her pass out again, it could be terminal. Reaches up over her bulk to pat her cheek. "How you doing, Liz, wide awake?"

"Em shleepy."

"Not yet, Liz, hang in there."

"Get your hand off my boobies."

"Excuse me, just trying to keep you up."

"I'm gonna be sick again!"

"Hold on, Liz, goddammit I'm down here!"

The cab rolls over the hilly campus, slowly emptying bodies at each stop, down fraternity row, the sororities. Sorry lying on his back now, hands folded over his chest, head resting on the driveshaft hump legs tucked up, somebody's feet stretched out resting on his knees. Stockinged calves, thighs, light patterns playing slowly over the roof of the cab, smiling to himself calmly blathering to Liz, making sure she's still awake.

Last stop, the women's dorm. They struggle Liz out, down the walk, now stand up straight, no staggering, the dorm mother must suspect nothing, no loud singing now, that's the way. Stop at the door, ring the night bell, wait. It opens, the house mother glaring out. Evening. A little car trouble, had to take a cab, sorry we're late, church meeting out late, dark woman goes to sign her in.

"All right Liz head for the elevator, that's the time." She doesn't go. Stands outside the door. As in a trance looking at Sorry, go on girl, mouth falls open, Sorry smiles at the house mother, punches Liz secretively. Liz starts, turns to the door, turns back to Sorry. "Keess me, Trushtesse, mon cher ami."

Puckers her lips, closes her eyes. Tilts her head back throwing her off balance. Sorry catches her, looks around perplexed.

"Kees me, mon très cher."

House mother's arms folded hostilely over the bosom. Sorry gathers courage, an inward shrug, kisses the sour mouth. "Reservoir, baby."

The door rumbles closed. Sorry starts to turn. Wait a minute. The dark woman, who is she? Where? Looks through the glass door as the elevator glides shut.

Oh well. Heads back to the cab but it's gone. Didn't even pay. Looks at the ten dollar bill in his hand. Up and down the street. Precipitation falling now. Mixed sleet and freezing rain. The only sound. Starts walking back toward Tennessee Street. Singing to himself. And some unknown cowboy.

A chill. A presence down the spine. Walking silently over asphalt, concrete, wet brick sidewalks. Streetlights, parked cars beading water ice spectrum puddles.

Marcus. What future is there, do you work for? All alone.

The street growling louder filling headlights, a street cleaner swishing brushes past, throwing haze leaves and twigs, scraps of paper. Strange. It had to be. I wouldn't be. If you Marcus hadn't. Here. Be me. Through freezing mist, hilly town, Colorado sandstone buildings bottomlit confusing saturated night. Wouldn't be me.

On the way back to the little room.

Sorry Figgers It Out

THE wind rippled hot bearded wheatheads across terrace ridges over an expansive sink sloping away flattened then rising toward the higher mounded horizon. A gully washed soft contours along the foot of the dome, becoming less distinct, vanishing in wheat on the basin floor. Clear sky. Wind. Hissing rattling grain. Bob snaps a head from its shaft, thrashes it with his fingertips in the palm gaping middle and ring fingers. Sifts from one hand to another, chaff and beard bits drifting in the wind. Tosses the handful of plump moist berries in his mouth. Chews. Squinting into the sun, watches Malachi, Sorry and the manager nearly waist-deep ten yards out in the field. With this hot wind, be ready to cut day after tomorrow. Thirty-five bushels to the acre.

Malachi turns first, irritated, starts for the fence. Sorry and the manager still talking, finally follow. Malachi grumbles past Bob. "Day after tomorrow. Thirty-five bushel."

Sorry and the manager laughing, Sorry gesticulating broad sweeping gestures. "Day after tomorrow."

Manager nods. "About thirty-five, thirty-six bushel to the acre. That's the kind of production the board predicts. Let's hope no anomalous contingencies occur. The prognosis was this good or better two years ago, and the night before the harvesting phase was to begin it came a three-inch rain. The kind they calculate for April, but is counterproductive during the harvest cycle. Rained four days straight. Then turned so hot the product that hadn't been knocked down was burned up in the field before the machinery could be brought on line without bogging down to the goddam axles in mud. This sure is good next-year country. Let's hope she goes a little better this time."

Bob steps on the middle strand of the barbed wire fence, pulls the top with his hand. The manager, then Sorry, duck through, Sorry takes the wire for Bob. Sorry in the ditch, Malachi standing in the road, long white beard in the wind. Sorry takes the manager's hand to shake. "We'll sure get it done for. Who did you say you represent?"

"Holding company in Minneapolis."

"Well, you tell them we'll get her done for them. Ten percent of the crop and a nickel a bushel to haul." *What's eating him?* "Won't we, Malachi?"

"We always have, Sorry. Always have."

Bob watches the manager, Malachi and Sorry climb in the cab of the pickup. Definitely trouble. Ever since Sorry joined the crew in Bowman, North Dakota, been three or four summers ago. Very interesting. Cutting wheat like a crazy man, eighteen, nineteen, twenty hours a day when it was dry. Malachi sitting nights silent in the trailer table booth, Viola at the stove. The crew, shirtless, slurping and smacking. "Sure damn good chicken." "Mighty fine." "Viola, you done it again." "Makes it worth coming on this godforsaken harvest." "Pass the ice tea." "Dee licious." "Gimme some more of them sliced tomaters." Sorry glances to Malachi, looks away. Viola carrying the bowl of mashed potatoes from the stove for refills. Billy Paul tilts his plate toward her, here you go, Viola. Flips a dollop with the serving spoon ten feet across the table plop on his plate. They all laugh. Eat. Viola reviews news of the harvest picked up at the grocery store. "Some more beans, they's plenty where." "Heard a thunderstorm knocked all the wheat down north of town." "Hot damn, who got the gizzard?" Only Malachi sitting silent carefully eating at the head. "That's the best gravy I believe I ever tasted, Viola." Plop of potatoes across to Bob. "Have another roll." "First good crop in three years flatter than a pancake." "Pass the butter." "Man, I wonder what the poor folks is doing." "Herumph." "Damn if it don't look like a coyote didn't kill a chicken on Sorry's plate." "Save some room now, I got a cherry pie coming out of the oven in just a minute." "Don't worry none about that, Viola." "Wheat's up to a dollar-eighty a bushel, that little sprinkle we got is going to slow us down some." "Just one more little piece ought to do me." Clanking silverware, dishes and glasses, slowing. Moans of pleasure. Sighs.

"Mighty good."

"What do you think, Sorry?"

Wipes his mouth on the dishtowel, glances at Malachi staring into his coffee mug. Back to Billy Paul. "Looks like a good night for a beer and a game of snooker to me."

Billy Paul takes the towel. "All right. Let's hit it."

Viola at the stove, looks apprehensive.

Bob sitting back watching it all. Good year, bad year, crazy carousing across the gridwork harvest, dusty plains when it's too wet to combine. Sometimes hitching rides or walking back to camp to explain to Malachi where Sorry was. Somewhere. Back seat '31 Chevy, moonlight and the steel-bodied guitar.

Or stumbling out the snooker bar, Billy Paul, baseball cap pushed back on his head, counting wads of fives, tens and twenties. Climb into the car, "Hot damn, Sorry, that was some shooting." To drag Main Streets of wheat-field towns from Oklahoma to North Dakota, from one end, red brick laid tree-lined, Apco station to the A&W root-beer stand on the other.

"Man, there's three good-lookers in that '54 Hudson. Get on their tail."

"What do you think I've been doing the last five passes, checking the price of gasoline?"

"They know we're after them. Pretty fancy maneuvering."

"And they drive good too. Look out!"

"Goddamn. Did you see that left turn from the right-hand lane between the Ford pickup and that Plymouth!"

"Well, Sorry, your U-turn and ninety degrees after them wasn't too bad either. Where the hell they going anyway!"

"I don't know, but we're going to find out, hang on!"

"Hot damn, an S-curve at fifty in a residential. That broad can drive. Shit, she's rounding the block to try it again at sixty. Can this old Chevy handle it?"

"You hide and watch."

"We've lost them. No, wait a minute, they're waiting for us up there. Hot damn."

"Ah, Sorry."

"Now where they going?"

"Sorry, old buddy."

"What you want, Bob?"

"As good as you and that woman are doing, there are some other things worth our attention."

"What's that, Bob? I thought I was the one made things too complicated."

"Well, this isn't all that damn complicated. Have you checked the rearview mirror lately?"

"Um. I see what you mean. How long they been back there?"

"I first noticed them the first time through the S-curve."

"The bull?"

"Not unless they drive pickups around these parts."

"Pickups?"

"At least two."

"Well, hell. Let's see what they do with a quick one-eighty and a run back through the S-curve. This old Chevy can outdo any number of pickups any day of the week."

"Holy shit!"

"Now hang a quick left. How we doing?"

"Sorry, old buddy, that was some good driving but this is Saturday, technically not a weekend day."

"What's that got to do with it?"

"I realize you were busy double clutching and didn't have the extra time to be reading, but if you would have I'm sure you'd have noticed the bridge-out sign on that last left you negotiated so skillfully. By the way, the pickups are still behind us."

Very interesting.

Bob closes the pickup door behind the manager for the Minneapolis holding company. Sorry behind the wheel, Malachi in the middle. And definitely trouble. Bob looks back out across the wheatfield, thirty-five bushel, day after tomorrow, then climbs up into the truck bed and sits down on a five-gallon grease can covered with a gunnysack. They start toward town. Dust flying wake curling inward, expanding out across the fence rows, drifting off north behind. Bob watches. Fence posts blurring, ditch, sunflowers, joint grass, thistles, volunteer oats and corn. Wheat. Roaring, up over the edge of the basin, down along the river bottom, trees. Shadows sunblobs pounding the eyes, hair face, tears streaming from the corners of his eyes along the temples pound roaring Sabre jet engine strafing skims Korean rice river paddies dikes roads and bridges. Bob stares down at the oxidized red gasoline tank between the gap, missing ring and middle fingers.

"Not much to do till day after tomorrow. Let's go into Mud Butte for a beer."

"Might as well. Can't dance. And too green to combine."

"I'll go find Billy Paul."

Bob left Sorry strumming the steel-bodied guitar lying on his back in the '31 Chevy. Parked along the railroad tracks, out behind a cluster of Butler corrugated bins. Walked over to the trailer. Nobody there. Viola gone to town for groceries. Malachi over working on the Ford. Found Billy Paul asleep in the shade of the GMC bed, St. Louis Cardinals cap covering his face, head propped almost under the rear tires. "Billy. You ignorant sap." Billy starts awake. "What the hell you think would happen if someone decided to move this rig?"

"Huh? Wha?" Wiping sweat from his eyesockets, trying to tell what his mouth tastes like. "Whatcha say, Bob?"

"What would happen if someone moved the truck?"

Looks around blinking the eyes, sucking on the upper front teeth. "Are we pulling out?"

"No."

Looking around under the truck. "Moved the truck, huh? Guess that would depend on which way they moved it."

"You ever seen a watermelon fell off a truck and been run over by a car?"

"Yep."

"Well, that's what your head would look like. And I do believe that's as bout as smart as you are. A watermelon."

"That smart, huh."

"Let's go to town."

Sorry walked laughing over to the Ford. "Malachi, you need anything from town? I think Bob, Billy Paul and I are going in for a spell."

Looks from under the hood. "No, I guess not." Pause. "You got everything in shape here?"

Looks around at the rigs parked beneath the trees along the railroad tracks. "Well, I think so, Malachi. We're not going to be doing anything till day after tomorrow. You don't need any help on the Ford, do you?"

"No. No, I can handle it myself."

Malachi goes back under the hood. Bob and Billy Paul standing back by the GMC. Sorry leans on the fender of the Ford watching Malachi work for a while. "I don't think there's anything needs done around here then."

Malachi looks back up at him. "You go on. Do what ever you think is right."

Looks at him. Starts to say something. Doesn't. Turns away. "See you later, Malachi."

"Sorry."

Turns back. "Yeah?"

"I know Marcus put you in charge of this harvest crew. But I'm keeping my eye on you."

Long pause. "Sure, Malachi. And I appreciate it too."

The bar was crowded with harvest hands. Oklahoma, Texas. Very quiet. Good South Dakota harvest, lots of money. Sunburnt skin sweat brown khaki denim lining the bar. Gathered around the snooker table. Can't dance, too wet to plow.

They found an empty table, ordered beer. Drank the first round in silence. Billy Paul got up to watch the snooker game. Had learned a thing or two about it since knowing Sorry.

Bob watches Sorry closely. Sitting silent looking at the bubbles rising in the beer glass. Bob lights a cigarette. "What's on your mind, Sorry?"

"Huh? Oh. Nothing."

"You and Malachi not hitting it off too good seems like."

"Naw. That's not it. That's just part of it. I don't know."

Long silence. "How's things at college?"

"They're all right."

"What's your status?"

"Status?"

"With the draft board. Any danger of you getting drafted?"

"Drafted. Don't suppose so. Not while I'm in school. I don't even have a draft card."

"Never registered?"

"Yeah. I registered. In Rushville, Nebraska. Right before I met up with you, with Marcus. Forgot all about it. They were supposed to send the registration on to my local board. I haven't heard from them since. Damn. Isn't that something."

"That's not your problem anyway."

"No. That's not it. Nope." Long swallow of beer.

Billy Paul comes back to the table. "Hey. Who can loan me bout fifty dollars for a second?"

Bob looks back over his shoulder at the snooker table. "For a second? What you need fifty dollars for, for a second?"

"Been having a little bad luck at the snooker table, but I'm getting hot now. Have my money all won back in a jiffy."

"Sorry, why you ever taught this boy to shoot pool I'll never know. He can hardly keep track of his money when it's in his pocket."

"Come on, Bob. I'm gonna teach that slick dude a lesson."

"Who you playing anyway?"

"He's the owner of this place. Been taking all the harvesters' money all day. Cleans them out every year. Hardly a snooker-shooting harvest hand ever leave this town any way but broke."

Laughs. "You getting hot, huh?"

"Sure am."

"You better be, boy, cause I'm taking this out of your hide if you lose it."

Bob watches Billy Paul swagger back to the table, a few comments from the harvesters and some of the local haunts. Bob shakes his head chuckling. Turns back. Sorry hunched over his beer. Bob orders another round. Drink in silence. Orders another. Sorry looking blankly at his hands cuddled around the beer glass. Bob drums his two fingers. "Sorry. If you weren't so busy sinking into yourself, trying to separate the flyshit from the pepper, maybe you'd see some things clearer."

"What things?"

"Malachi, you and Marcus. You got to simplify the way you look at it, if you don't mind my saying so."

"What?"

"That's right. You think it's two things conflicting. But what the periodic tables teaches us, or any serious study of the world, is the unity of the universe. You should know this by now, doing all that math. Just because it looks so various, you think it is."

"Shit, Bob. Here I am, the man's only living relative, which gives me some responsibility for him and to him, but God knows what that is cause all he wants to do is work, and you're coming at me with some bullshit about the periodic tables."

"Now don't get impatient, Sorry. Goddamn. Give a man a chance to develop his idea. Let's get another beer. I can see you're gonna be hard to convince."

Bob turns looking for the waitress just as a burst of clapping, laughing swells from the snooker table. Billy Paul hurries through the bystanders up to Bob and Sorry, brandishing his cue. "Quick, Bob. Loan me another fifty. I got the sucker right where I want him."

"Right where you want him? What happened to the other fifty?"

"He made a couple a lucky shots."

"A couple, huh."

"Yeah."

"Well, Billy o buddy. You and he cleaned me out. You heard of the good-money-after-bad theory of betting, haven't you?"

"How bout you, Sorry? I know I got him."

Sorry looks over at the snooker table. The owner leaning on his cue right hand over left, looking back at Sorry, through drifting eddies of cigarette, cigar smoke. "I don't know, Billy Paul. The man's looking pretty mean to me."

"Come on. Ain't you got confidence in your student? You know what I can do."

"That's what I'm afraid of."

"Come on."

"Tell you what I'll do. I'll advance you fifty against your pay."

"You won't regret it, Sorry."

"I know I won't. I'm not so sure about you though." Billy Paul goes back to the snooker game, enveloped in the crowd around. Silence. The click of balls, gasps, curses, applause. Sorry looks at Bob. And laughs. "Now what was it you were saying?"

"Well. I see it this way. Work and play are really the same thing when you get right down to it."

"Now that don't make no sense."

"Sure. Take your daddy Lyons. You tell me he rode bulls, drank beer, sang songs. Why do you think he did all that?"

"Cause he was crazy."

"Besides that."

"Dunno. He did what he pleased. I guess you'd have to say."

"He was what you call your hedonist when you get right down to it, right? He enjoyed it. From what you've told me. Now take Marcus. You'll have to admit, won't you, he's your ascetic. Doesn't give the flesh no slack."

"No doubt about that."

"But why does he act the way he does? Work all the time. Does he seem dissatisfied? Unhappy?"

"No. He's the most self-satisfied man I've ever come across. But . . ."

"Exactly. He's that way because he enjoys it."

"Aw, come on. You don't know what you're talking about, Bob. It's more complicated than that."

"There you go again. I tell you they're both the same. Let's have another beer."

"Why not."

"You see, that's the way it's got to be. Look. In order to survive in all sorts of conditions, a man's got to have a well-developed sense of enjoyment. Take war. Me flying sorties over Korea. MIG-17 could jump me anytime, did many times, and you never know when it's the end. But damn if it wasn't the ones like me, who enjoyed ever second of it, that survived. Take the dust bowl and the depression. Could be blown out anytime. Starve. And damn if it wasn't the ones like Marcus, who enjoyed ever second of it, that survived and prospered. When the shitstorm comes, you've got to be prepared for anything. For survival, it's your duty. To enjoy it. Why do you think I go on this godforsaken harvest every year? I don't need the goddam money, I get disability, man, Uncle

Sam. I enjoy it, that's why. The harder things are, the more pleasure there is. It takes much less to be a feast. When it's twenty below outside, zero seems warm. Hundred and ten degrees, tepid water and some shade is paradise, taste better than champagne wine."

"Horseshit."

"Now listen, Sorry. What you think is a conflict is really an illusion. You make it up. Your enjoyment of drinking, fucking, playing the guitar and shooting snooker is the same enjoyment as cutting wheat seventeen hours a day, repairing a bent sickle bar with nothing but a pair of pliers and a big rock, reshingling a barn, bucking bales or planting grass. And the only reason you think they conflict is you confuse the external circumstances. You can't let other people's shortcomings slow you down."

Sorry looks incredulous at Bob. Smiles. Shakes his head. "You know, Bob. Somehow I think there's more to it than that."

Sudden uproar around the snooker table, crashing cueball on the tile floor, rolling up to Sorry's feet, Billy Paul slams down the cue stick, "Goddam sonuvabitch," runs, pouncing on the ball. Crouched for a second. Sorry looking down at his back, back up at the owner flanked by several regulars. Menacing, still holding his cue, legs widespread. Billy Paul looks up slowly at Sorry. "I miscued."

Owner holding out his hand. "My shot, friend."

"I had him, Sorry. Just needed lots of reverse english, and I had him."

"Scratch seven, friend. And hand over the cueball."

"I was thirteen ahead, Sorry."

"The cueball."

Billy Paul limply hands it over his head, still looking at Sorry. The owner takes it. Smiles at Sorry. "You next, farmer? Your boy's down quite a bit now. Course I can understand you not wanting to put up any more cash."

Winks. Returns to the table, sinks the 7-ball. Pockets the wad of bills, leans on his cue looking over. Billy Paul looking up from the floor. Sorry looks at Bob. Bob smiles, empties his beer. "Seems simple to me, Sorry."

Sorry looks down at Billy Paul. "Some pool shooter you turned out to be."

Empties his beer. Walks up to the rack, selects a cue. Rubs in talc, chalks the tip, approaches the table, propels the cueball right-handed around, banking each rail twice and dropping in the corner pocket. "Tell me something, good shooter. How much you won off these wheat cutters today?"

"Hard to tell, farmer. I'm not finished yet."

"No. But you'd best get the bartender to start counting it out. Cause I'm winning it all back. And if you need to piss, you'd best do it now, cause we ain't slowing down till this here party is over. And since I realize this is a small-town establishment, I'm gonna be shooting left-handed."

Pulls out the cueball, caroms it around the table twice, falling into the corner pocket in front of the owner. "Lag for break, good shooter."

Bob moves up with Billy Paul where he can see. The owner fishes out the cueball, tossing it up and down sizing Sorry up. Places it down on the table, chalks the tip of the cue, leans over the rail and eases the ball up and back, almost freezing it against the head rail. "How much you want to shoot for, farmer?"

Glances at Bob. "I only got bout forty dollars change, guess that'll have to do for the first game."

"You gonna lag?"

"Your break, good shooter."

The owner circles the table once studying the rack, places the cueball and breaks, sinking a red ball. Then the 6. Sinks six more red balls, alternating the 6 and 7-ball, finally missing a thin cut on a red ball in the side pocket. Sorry takes over, finishes off the red balls, scoring 5's, 6's and 7's. A five-point lead, but is lucky to even get a piece of the 2-ball, leaving the owner an easy run of four balls, but he can't get the 6 to drop dying right on the lip of the corner pocket. Sorry finishes them off, winning 64 to 60. Bob collects the money, starts to rack the balls, but the bartender won't let him. Does it himself.

Sorry loses the next, wins two in a row, $80 up. "How much you down to this feller, Billy Paul?"

"Well. Let's see. Fifty I borrowed from Bob, and a hundred and ten of my own. That'd be, ah . . ."

"Hundred and sixty. Eighty dollars on the next game, good shooter?"

"Your break, farmer."

Bob surveys the crowd. Getting drunker and noisier. Some mighty tough characters around, not all friendly. Bartender racking the balls, at least six-three, two-fifty. Hasn't smiled the whole time. Returns to his position behind. Hand-carved sign hanging on a golden chain. *McMorold's Tavern.* Sorry looks back at McMorold, smiling, leaning on his cue. Better make this the last beer. McMorold's a sore loser.

Sorry breaks, doesn't sink anything. McMorold runs eighteen balls before he scratches. The pressure's on Sorry. Has to run the table to win. Goes to the wall, rubs on talc. Bob studies closely. Seems calm. Chalking the tip, pacing up and down the side rail. Looks at the light, rubs his eyes, smiles over at McMorold. "An old eye disease. Bright lights, you know."

"Shoot, farmer."

He runs the table. The harvest hands the only ones laughing and talking. Local clientele sitting around ominous. Bob collects the money, turns to Sorry. "We better be heading back, o buddy."

Sorry waves him off, circles the table with hands raised quieting the hubbub. "How many Okies we got here?" Loud chorus hoots and yells, stomping feet, glasses pounding on the bar. "How much you hard-luck Okies lost to this man?" Cacophonous splattering of figures, Sorry raises his hands for quiet. "One at a time."

"Twenty bucks." "Thirty!" "Fifteen!" "Sixty dollars, man!" "Bout thirty-five." "Down ten." "A hundred."

"Ya'll sure ya'll Okies now?" Even louder ovation. "Okay, good shooter. The bet's three hundred."

Bob takes Sorry aside. "Think we'd best be going, man."

"What do you mean? I'm making things simple. It's my duty to enjoy this, isn't it?"

"But I'm afraid this hedonism is gonna turn ascetic real quick if you keep on winning."

"You suggesting I lose?"

"No. I'm suggesting we get our asses out of here while we still got just one asshole apiece. Have you taken a close look at the bartender and some of his buddies lately? They're not enjoying this show atall. And they are all big, and McMorold ain't no punk himself."

"Three hundred it is, farmer."

Sorry looks at McMorold, back at Bob. "No turning back now, Bob. Can't let the Okies down either."

"Let's hope the Okies remember that when the shit hits the fan."

Glancing at the men's room. "Important thing, I remember."

Walks slowly to the head of the table, takes the cueball from McMorold's hand. "My break, I believe." Sets it down between the 3 and 4. Returns to get his beer, gulps down a swallow, throat cracking, nerves, looks at Bob. Billy Paul, the Okies. The bartender. Eyes. Sapulpa Slim Hank Buffalo Gap prairie grass, three hundred. Marcus. Back at Bob.

"Let's go, farmer."

All the same. Shoot. Yeah. A little talc on the stick, grease on the main cylinder, chalk the tip, fluid, Okies gathering round, "Counting on yuh, Oke, counting on yuh." Move the cueball an eighth to the right, check the rack again, circle the table, lean over the red balls, move the cueball back a sixteenth. Smile at the bartender, McMorold, wave to the Okies shuffling feet, brandishing beer bottles. Tavern full, filling, light and smoke shouts, yellow green, swirling brown gray and blue, chalk at the tip and break.

Red ball drops.

Quickly now, it all seems clear, patterned, simple, the body reacts. Sink the 7-ball, respot at the foot spot, sink a red ball, the 7 again, stride around the table smiling at McMorold, body before the mind, simple, shoot, red ball, 6-ball, respot, red ball, 7. Respot. Fast around the table, leaning over, bridge flat and steady on the felt top ready before the cueball even stops rolling, shoot before it hardly stops, red ball 5-ball, around the table, still smiling at no one, all blurring round green yellow red blue brown gray, light and smoke, jumbling sound table patterned balls and pockets. Clicking balls, clicking body mind, red ball black 7, respot, white cue rolling flux and changing relations ball to ball clicking body movement, round the table, over the rail, pressure swing cut english, red ball 6-ball roaring hum click flowing respot red ball 7 red 7 red 7. Balls rolling stopping at my will, back off watching body eye arm and hand separate, Sorry shooting snooker. Bob and Billy Paul. Me. And the bartender, McMorold grimly looking on.

Stops. For breath. A swig of beer. Next shot suddenly a little tough. But loose. Warm sweat down the armpits, back. Hair lightly lying on the neck. There's McMorold. The Okies going wild, bursting yells and curses.

I've won.

The red balls gone. A hundred and five points already. Only twenty-seven left on the table and McMorold hasn't even shot.

"Goddammit, Oke, if that ain't the damnedest snooker shooting I ever seen."

Sorry smiles at McMorold. McMorold pounds the butt of his cue onto the floor, walks past the table toward the bar, turns to Sorry. "You're cheating, farmer."

Sudden silence in the tavern. Bob looks widened told you eyes to Sorry, his gaze to the bartender, three or four other burly regulars at the bar. Sorry calm, quiet. "What you mean, good shooter?"

"You're cheating."

Even the smoke in the air is still. "Could you please explain to me and my Oklahoma friends just how that is."

"You're cheating." A few more steps to the bar. "You're getting no money from me."

Not quite so calm and quiet. "Look, man. The balls went in the pockets, your balls, your cue, your table, now get back and—"

"No way, Okie. I didn't hear you call those shots."

"Well, I'll be go to hell." Turning full circle on the spot appealing outspread arms to a surly silent crowd. Leans back over the snooker table, one hand flat, the other cuddling the 7-ball. "Look, you goddam sonuva—"

"Out of here, Okie!"

"Not without the money."

"All of you out! Before I call the sheriff." The bartender moves from around the bar, the burly regulars start forward.

Bob looks for the door, looks for Sorry. Goddamn, the goddam southpaw rearing back, hurky jerky high lead leg kick, and fires a fast 7-ball across the tavern deep into McMorold's belly. Loud gasp scattering Okies several directions, Sorry explodes across the snooker table, lays the doubled McMorold out against the bar with a forearm shiver. Bob takes on the closest man to him and Billy Paul joins those making for the door. Peripheral skirmishes settled quickly. McMorold recovers enough to break his cue over Sorry's head. Sorry crumbles momentarily, rises up, turning black-eyed yelling "Goddam bastard," leaps at McMorold, down to the floor, on top, hands around the throat, bangs McMorold's head against the brass rail. The bartender clears a path through the remaining harvest hands to the snooker table, apparently spent, amazed, disbelieving, watches Sorry pull his money from the cash register and drop to his knees by McMorold. Sorry sets the cueball on McMorold's chin. Stands, walks slowly, wobbly, out the door.

Bob is dropped by his man going to the aid of the fallen McMorold, and eases his way through the door in time to see the '31 Chevy roaring out of town.

And to miss the sheriff running in.

Bob sat at the table in the trailer. Viola at the stove cradling a cup of coffee. White yellow propane light. Malachi stroked his beard and snorted through his nose. "When did Sorry say he'd be back?"

"He. Well, plenty of time before the wheat's ready. He just wanted to visit this college friend. Some little town nearby."

Malachi got up, went to the door and looked out. "Wheat'll be ready day after tomorrow. He can do what he wants till then." And walked on out to the Ford. Viola looked at Bob. He shrugged I-don't-know-what-the-hell-happened-to-him. And went out to try and get some sleep.

Bob and Billy Paul snuck back into town the next day, looking for the Chevy, for any sign, listening for rumors of the fight, the whereabouts. Nothing.

Billy Paul spent the rest of the day in sunglasses hunched down in the cab of the GMC reading comic books with the doors locked.

Ate a silent lunch. No one said a word but Viola trying to pierce the tension. Flies buzzing at the trailer screen door. Sun reflecting off the Butler buildings, hot dry day. Bob and Billy Paul shirtless, sweating at the table, Malachi, bib overalls and long sleeves, lights up his pipe after the peach pie, looks glumly at Bob. "Wheat'll be ready early in the morning with this low humidity. When Sorry say he'd be back?"

Billy Paul excuses himself, lopes back to the GMC. Bob wipes sweat from his forehead. "He'll be back in time."

Four-thirty A.M. Bob starts up in the cot beside the Ford. Looks around quickly. No '31 Chevy. Rubs the corners of his eyes with thumb and little finger, clears his throat and spits. Swings feet into the dry grass. Be cutting by six. Pulls on jeans, walks around the header trailer to piss. First sunrays catching face and beard of Malachi coming up behind. "Not here yet, huh."

"Don't look like it, Malachi."

"We'll do it without him. Like we always done before. Wake up Billy Paul."

Aroma of coffee. Bacon and bread. Another hot hard day to come.

They left the pickup and header trailers in the yard of an abandoned farmhouse, drove down the road a piece to the high banked ditch to unload. Malachi backed the Ford around perpendicular, back wheels easing into the ditch, running the truck bed into the bank right at the top. Bob and Billy Paul jump on the back, remove the chains holding the combine down, Billy Paul climbs up into the seat and starts the engine. The truck bed just wide enough. The outside edges of the combine's large front tires hang over the sides. "Back her off easy now, a little to the east, come on back, thataway. Take her west not too much, you got it straight on back."

Billy drives along the crest of the ditch to where it's shallower, cuts across onto the road and guns her bouncing back wheels off to where the headers are. Bob and Malachi unchain the sideboards from the middle of the truck bed, begin putting them up. Sun already hot. Malachi pulls the Ford out, spinning wheels kicking dirt a little, and then goes over to help Billy put on the header barge. Bob backs the GMC up to the bank, removes the booms and chains, backs the combine off. Pulls the truck out of the ditch, parks it along side the gate to the field. Grabs a head of wheat, checks it for moisture, ready to cut in an hour.

By the time he gets to the abandoned house the first Baldwin is ready to go. Malachi tightening the last bolt on the unloading auger, Billy Paul greasing the main bearing. Bob pulls around to his header trailer, eases the snout up, backs off, corrects a half-inch to the north, gently guides the cylinder housing into the slot of the header barge, cuts the engine, jumps off and begins bolting it on. Billy Paul pumps his combine full of gas from the tank on the back of the pickup and is ready to hit it. Sun higher hotter in the sky.

"Okay, Billy. Cut out about a forty-acre patch, and I'll be there with the truck time you finish the first round."

Throttle out, deep-throated drone, Billy Paul shifts to high, wheels out onto the road, rear wheels bounding out of control, downshifts to second and heads for the field.

Good cutting. Heavy yield high protein. Hot sun no wind. Engines droning, throbbing synchronized closing, separating. Pattern swath dust and light playing over heat trembling expanse of yellow white grain. Modulating. Amber waves of grain, amber waves of. Smell hot dry stalks, chopped sunflower, joint grass, bindweed, dust grease gasoline, vinyl sweat. Waves of grain. Hawks circling, soaring, rabbits, field mice, bullsnakes pheasants sparrows grasshoppers potato bugs ladybugs horseflies. Sicklebar cylinder bulk flow speed chain augers bearings belts moan banging hiss, cycling amber waves of grain.

Malachi takes her a round or two. Bob climbs down, gets in the cab of the Ford, pushes it into low, lets out the clutch, shudders, moves slowly surging over to the uncut wheat. Billy Paul rounds the corner, pulls alongside the truck. Grins down at the cab. Removes sunglasses to wipe them clean, St. Louis Cardinals cap, dust-covered face ringed eyes dull perspiration sheen, rivulets cutting down along the cheeks, old flowered Hawaiian shirt sleeveless burnt umber dusted muscles sunlit bleached down hair, Billy Paul reaches for the water jug Bob is handing up.

Bob vaults over the sideboard into the wheat knee-deep, grabs the scoop shovel to level the load. Billy Paul singing barely discernible human syllables, cuts a quick step on the combine platform, slaps the steering wheel a few licks with the free hand, lifts the water jug to his mouth overflowing down the chin and chest watering Hawaiian flowers and mud.

Grinding unloading auger clamors louder and the grain stream stops. Dust and chaff. Bob wades over to the cab, jumps to the ground. Billy Paul hands down the jug, singing and a grinning, tap dances to the gear shift, clutches into second, one thumb up in the air, jerks on forward garbling Wisconsin six.

Bob pulled out of the field and headed for town in the truck.

Harvest!

Semitrailer hoppers, air-conditioned combines, FM radio headsets on blank-eyed drivers. Sure not like the old days. He honks and waves, no one hears, double clutches clicking the two-speed rear axle down, and groans on over the hill.

Wonder where the hell Sorry is.

The day wears on hot and still. Dry. Evaporating sweat to cool. No sign of Sorry, no word at the elevator, no mention more of the snooker game, the fight. No Chevy to be seen.

Viola brings fried chicken, potato salad green beans and ice tea with Malachi returning from town. Take turns eating in the shade of the Ford. Viola talking about the price of wheat, the yield, to Billy Paul, then Bob.

"The food sure is good."

"Mighty hot day."

"But the humidity's low."

"Wheat sure looks good."

"Yeah, thirty-five bushel to the acre."

Viola, her knees gathered in her arms sitting on a towel gazing out across multitextured movement. The field, the road slight wriggling, ditch, grass, telephone poles lined perspective diminishing wires sagging.

Bob pitches chicken bones away. Looks at Viola sitting pensive. She smiles, gets up, replaces the Tupperware lid on the potato salad, covers remaining chicken neck and wing, shoos the flies from atop the cherry pie, digs out a piece for Bob to gobble down. Malachi rounding the corner. She recovers the pie, stands, hands on hips squinting into the sun. "Wonder where the dickens Sorry is."

Heat. Long trance afternoon. Numb. Torpor. Mirage shimmering silver blue. Circling closer to the center of the field, farther from the fence, the road, isolated, dumb, slow dumb beast consuming swaths of ripened brittle dusty heat. Turning thrashing, spreading dusty straw, dusty stream of wheat.

And then a change of light, a slant, spectrum shifting. The temperature eases. Finally Viola again. Ham sandwiches, tea and apple pie. Shadows lengthen, sun dropping down large red sudden resurgence, energy. The air glows, western stratocumulus a golden saffron red. Stubble straw and wheat, deepening seeding row shadows. Cool. Birds gather, grasshoppers calm mandibulation on the steering wheel golden green brown yellow glistening evening light.

Billy Paul gives out a high long happy yawp and giggle. "You can't cut wheat like me!" Reaches back into the bin and tosses a handful of wheat berries into his mouth, chews them into gum.

Sun gone beyond the rise. Red darkening maroon, violet distant eastern fields still light, blue to purple reflection in the eastern sky. The field matting gray blue and black. The combine running good. Easy, muted, flowing night. Venus, the moon. Bob turns on the combine headlights pulling alongside the Ford to unload. Malachi climbs up to the platform. "I'll take her a round or two."

"She's running good."

Bob drops to the ground, walks out into the stubble away from the truck. Pisses. Looking at the moon. Stars large across the heavens. Hears the Gleaner shift into second, the clutch released, engine bog, governor brings the rpm's back up, and the combine recedes into the dark field, final swishing straw-spreader lingering behind.

Bob stands there. Then ambles back to the truck. Takes a long drink of water. Climbs up into the cab. Both doors hanging open, gentle breeze drifting through. Dark. Cool. Alone. Silence. Reaches to the radio, turns it on. Blue light flowing on the fingertips, dials through the spectrum slowly auditing buzzes warps, whistles, KOMA, modulations fractured voices, codes, beeping, hums panting, tones. Piano. Distant. Ease the knob closer, swelling louder, clearer, fading. Flowing broad clear distant tones filling the cab, drifting wind into the field. Slow. Headlights on the distant hillside flickering reelslats turn, an orange ball moving light across the night. Undertone engine throb. Pulsing music disintegrating electronic distortion, reforming louder clear soft gentle phrase. Dark. Arpeggio. Concerto largo. The moon. Float blue across the empty field.

A sweep of light on the horizon. Piano. Light moving along the road. Orange ball trembling across the hillside. Combine engine. Engine. Piano. Along the road. Light beams sweeping the sky. Turning into the field. An engine. Car engine. Chevy engine.

Bob slowly steps from the cab looking toward the light. Definitely turned into the field. Bouncing along over terraces toward the opposite combine light. He reaches back in, turns on the Ford's parking lights. The car turns that direction. Definitely a '31 Chevy, definitely Sorry is back.

Bob walks toward the car shielding his eyes as it stops in front of the truck, cuts the headlights. Sorry swings out of the door. Amber parking light, pale, dark ringed eyes. Flash reflection yellow green. Bandage around his head. Bob stops in front. "Well, I'll be damned. Where the hell you been?"

"Had a little bump on my head, that's all."

"But what . . ."

Brandishing a rolled magazine. "And I've figgered it out, Bob. It's simple."

"Hold on now. That looks like more than a little bump."

"Medicine in the blood, just a night in the hospital and I've figgered it—"

"Hospital? Wait a minute . . ."

"Had a long talk, fantastic woman, tall strong thighs, simple."

"You ain't making any sense, boy. You sure you're all right? And what's that you got on?"

"Hospital gown. Left in a kind of hurry, but it's simple, Bob, just like you always said it was."

"What's simple?"

"Resting my head, talking to the nurse I figgered it out. You're absolutely right, it's obvious." Unrolling the magazine, leafing through the pages. "Marcus needs to have a child."

Selected Letters

Dear Mr. Baldwin,

I guess I should call you Marcus, but I feel a little strange about it in this first letter. Somehow, when I got my addresses, I didn't expect the computer to include someone like you. I almost want to say a "real person." I really didn't expect anything I guess. In fact I was saving writing to you, I suppose, postponing what I thought surely must be a disappointment. So you can imagine how happy I was when you wrote first. Frankly, I'm not sure I would have had the nerve to write at all.

Excuse me for going on about something of little interest to you. I know from your letter that you are a busy man. Your description of the farm sounds marvelous. I hope it's not too forward of me at this point to tell you how much I'd like to see it. You see, I feel sort of lost when I think about where I come from, city or country. My mother and father lived on a farm in the southwestern part of South Dakota, but my father died when I was very young and my mother and I moved to Rapid City. Too large to be rural and too small really to be urban. So I don't know much about farm life, nor much about the big city. What I'm getting at is that I really think I'd like to live in one or the other. And lately I'm feeling I'd enjoy tending animals much better than people.

You see, I am a nurse at Rapid City Regional, just like my mother, but I'm getting fed up with the place I'm afraid. It's becoming bureaucratic, run by business administrators, losing sight of what the hospital should be in the first place. And I guess I am getting a little lonely. I hate to even mention this, but you must understand, otherwise you wouldn't have turned to the computer yourself. I don't know why I'm so nervous about this, I should be telling you all about myself and my life, but can't really get into that, since actually I can't imagine talking, that is writing, to a real person just now. You seem more like a fantasy. I find it hard to believe I really filled out an application for a computer dating system. It's not really like me, and you must wonder what kind of person would do such a thing. (There I go again apologizing, when you yourself did the same thing. In this modern world, there's nothing wrong with availing ourselves of modern technology to solve the age-old problem of human relationships. Why should science only be used to keep people apart and unhappy?)

But I ramble on. I wanted this to be a cool friendly letter. I'll probably tear it up and throw it away when I reread it. What I'm saying is that I think we should meet each other face to face, soon. I've got lots of vacation time saved up, and I could come down and visit you on the farm sometime.

I hope you don't think me a flighty person. I'm not. I'm just excited thinking of the computer paying off in some way. I sent in my application on a lark, not expecting much to come of it. Not that I really expect that much now, you understand. But from your letter it sounds to me like we might become good friends. I am a hardworking individual, you have to be to be a nurse nowadays, and you will see this when we meet.

> Hoping to see you soon.
> Sincerely,
> Isadora Faire

P.S. I'm enclosing a photograph of me. Please send one of you in your next letter, if you have one handy. I hope you can write soon.

Dear Isadora,

I was very happy to find another letter in the mailbox this morning. I hope too we can really become close friends. And who knows what that might lead to. I'm glad to hear you are interested in farm life, because the farm, which was settled almost single-handed by my mother, is very important to me, and I could never leave it. That is the main reason I haven't married yet. It must be someone who would want to share the hardships of rural life. And there doesn't seem to be many women locally who have been both willing to do that and available at the same time. I am very active in the Methodist Church, I attend all the ice cream socials, bake sales and the like, and believe me, I've looked around for eligible women, and in a small town like this one they are not plentiful.

It is good that you are a hardworking person, because we do work hard on the farm. Some would even say too hard maybe, but I hope you won't feel that way. If you are to make the land produce, especially the shortgrass prairie, you must be willing to put in long hours. The reward for this labor is considerable. There's no administration telling you what to do or when, your work develops from your own notions of what is necessary and desirable. And what could be better than moving around outdoors all day long every day of the year. The sunshine and fresh air. My only fear is that the many years of hard toil, ever since I was eight years old, has affected my social skills. I hope I will know how to act when I meet someone like you. Because the only thing missing to make the farm really seem like someone lives here is a woman, a wife and children maybe even, to give me something to work for besides work itself, so that all the effort up until now will not have been wasted.

I certainly do look forward to getting to know you, especially after seeing your picture. I didn't expect to get in touch with someone who was interested in farm living and so attractive. However, I don't think it would be wise to meet each other so soon. Our expectations might be too high and we would be disappointed. Besides, this time of year is particularly busy on a farm, and I wouldn't have time to devote all my attention to your visit. So I think we should continue writing, getting to know each other that way before coming face to face.

Well, I've got to go gather the eggs now. Write soon. Oh yes, about the picture of me. I don't have one right now, I'll send one as soon as I get one.

Yours truly,
Marcus

P.S. Call me Marcus.

Dear Marcus,

Just a quick note between classes. College is going well this semester. I am enrolled in some very interesting courses. I think I've about decided to major in mathematics.

The weather has also been excellent. A good rain last weekend, but since then nothing but fantastic Indian Summer. Highs in the 70's, lows around 50. The maize harvest should be great in this area. Have you got all the wheat seeded by now?

I don't know why this occurs to me now, but I've always been curious to know. Have you ever thought about getting married? I've just been wondering what you thought about it.

I'd better get this on to the post office if I don't want to be late for class. I'll be having Thanksgiving with Keeper and Hank, see you Christmas.

S.

P.S. I don't even have a picture of you. Could you send one in your next letter?

DEAR SORRY,

WE HAD AN EXCELLENT WEEK WITH THE EGG BUSINESS. A HUNDRED DOZEN. SO AFTER MACKEY AND I DELIVERED THE

REGULAR ROUTE, WE STILL HAD ENOUGH LEFT OVER TO MAKE IT WORTH OUR TIME TO GO TO THE FARMER'S MARKET TO SELL THEM.

THIS AFTERNOON WE ARE GOING TO CLEAN THE CHICKEN HOUSES AND SPREAD THE MANURE ON THE WEST PLACE. THEN WE WILL CULL THE HENS. WE HAD A SIZABLE NUMBER OF PULLETS THIS YEAR.

THE PRICE OF FEED HAS GONE UP AGAIN. LOOKS LIKE WE MAY HAVE TO RAISE THE PRICE OF OUR EGGS. I HOPE NOT, WE'RE ALREADY GETTING HARD COMPETITION FROM THE BIG PRODUCERS. THEY'VE GOT THE EDGE SINCE THE MOTHER COMPANY ALSO OWNS THE FEED MANUFACTURING BUSINESS.

DEVELOPERS HAVE BOUGHT THE SECTION EAST OF THE SMITH PLACE FROM BILL WILSON'S KIDS. CAN'T REMEMBER IF YOU KNEW BILL. HE WAS KILLED COMING HOME FROM HIS CITY JOB ON THE NORTHWEST HIGHWAY ABOUT A YEAR AGO. HIS KIDS LIVE IN THE CITY NOW, AND ONE GIRL WENT TO DENVER. THEY SAY THEY'RE GOING TO BUILD A LAKE AND SOME HOUSES. I HEARD DOWN AT THE MERCANTILE THE OTHER DAY THAT THEY MIGHT BE PUTTING IN AN OILWELL ON SPRINGTOOTH JACOBSEN'S PLACE. IT'S REALLY AMAZING WHEN YOU THINK OF THE PROGRESS THIS COUNTRY HAS MADE JUST IN MY LIFETIME.

THE SUNRISE WAS MAGNIFICENT THIS MORNING. FIRST TOUCH OF AUTUMN IN THE AIR. THE FIRST FROST COULD COME ANY DAY NOW. THE *FARMER'S ALMANAC* SAYS IT'S GOING TO BE A BAD WINTER. I'VE NOTICED THE WOOLLY CATERPILLARS HAVE THICKER COATS THAN NORMAL, AND THE SQUIRRELS HAVEN'T BEEN LEAVING MANY BLACK WALNUTS LYING AROUND EITHER. IF WE DO GET LOTS OF SNOW AND A RAINY SPRING THE WHEAT HARVEST AROUND HERE COULD MAKE AS HIGH AS FORTY BUSHEL. I REMEMBER WHEN YOU WERE LUCKY TO GET OVER EIGHTEEN. ALL THE SPRAYING OF HERBICIDES, PESTICIDES AND FERTILIZERS NOWADAYS HAS REALLY MADE A DIFFERENCE. I READ IN THE *OKLAHOMA FARMER* THAT THEY'RE ALREADY EXPECTING A RECORD HARVEST ALL THE WAY TO THE DAKOTAS.

WE'LL BE LOOKING TO SEE YOU CHRISTMAS, WE'VE GOT TO REBUILD THE PUMP ENGINE AND CLEAR OUT SOME BRUSH FROM AROUND THE SWIMMING HOLE.

MARCUS

Dear Isadora,

Another letter from you today! They are becoming more important to me every one I get. As winter approaches, a severe one by all indications—the thick-coated caterpillars, the squirrels flitting about the black walnut trees—even the *Farmer's Almanac* agrees, it will be a test. But I see even more dangerous signs, a bigger threat than icy roads and bitter wind-chill factors. A developer has bought land nearby and plans houses and roads. An oilwell is being drilled. All this growth! And I feel even more alone, realize how important it is to me not to be. I look at your picture and can't help but think you are the one. Together we could hold on to all I've worked for, it would make sense, there would be a reason and a future, not just developers and salesmen and oil company lawyers circling around waiting for me to sell out or die so they could move in and divvy up what is left behind.

You would love it here this time of year. The air is clean and crisp, fluffy fair-weather clouds white against the blue sky, the cottonwoods showing traces of yellow among the green, the rusty yellow stubble and red plowed soil of the fields in autumn afternoons you'd think would last forever.

This is the place for someone seeking a life within the scope of their own imagination, unbounded by the vastness of the sky. You should be here when the milking's done.

Love,
Marcus

Dear Marcus,

I've been thinking about you a lot, especially now that winter seems to be here, and earlier than usual. Cold weather is not my favorite. And things are getting more hectic by the day at the hospital. I reread your letters. I'm surprised to see how many already. I try not to, but I can't help fantasizing about your farm, what it looks like, what you look like. I wish you would make a special effort to get a picture, any old snapshot, just go to some Fotomat. It wouldn't take too much time.

I suppose you're right about getting to know each other by mail before visiting, but I wonder if leaving it up to our imagi-

nations for so long is good. Reality might be hard put to rival what we've cooked up in our heads. It is very tempting to take a few days off and come and surprise you sometime. Maybe you should send your telephone number, so at least I could hear your voice.

I've been given a promotion (given—ha! I earned it). Anyway, I'm now a clinical leader. It's nice for the money and recognition, but it's just one more step away from the patient. I will probably forget all I ever knew about nursing and medicine. I have to start learning how to push paper, read computer printouts, even go to school to learn to program the damn things (pardon my language) and learn statistics. I'll have to talk about the "product capacity," and that's in terms of "beds," not people, "curable units" as opposed to "terminal units" and "transient units," "time modules," "customer modules." I'll have to admit, Marcus, I'm really looking forward to the day when I can tell them to—that is, tell them I quit.

Keep your letters coming. I look forward to them, and am disappointed on days when the mailbox is empty.

> *Love,*
> *Isadora*

Dear Isadora,

I too look forward to your letters, and know the emptiness of mailboxes. But work must go on.

I am tempted to use the phone, but must resist. I just know it would be bad. Standing there with this cold piece of plastic in our hands, some electric tickling in our ears that's supposed to be a voice of someone we know, or are getting to know, humming and buzzing. I'm just uncomfortable on the phone, always have been. I wouldn't be myself. We'll know when the time is right. And whatever you do, don't surprise me with a visit! You see, I might not be there. I travel around the county and state a lot. It's best we have no extra surprises. Let's save the best surprise for when we actually meet.

I can sympathize with your feelings about the hospital. I see the same thing happening in farming. Agribusiness. Someone dies and his land is sold to pay the inheritance tax, and the only people who can afford to buy it are either large corporate farms or land developers. The tax law is supposed to eliminate inherited wealth and power, but actually insures it.

The work on the section southeast of the farm will be beginning this spring. Subdivided, houses crowded in, stylish apartment blocks for Now-generation singles and suburban families. The skyline of the city is pushing over the horizon, the dawn and evening sky, even the afternoon sky dulled by yellow brown haze.

I look at your picture often. I will make a special effort to get you one of me.

Love,
Marcus

Dear Marcus,

I would really like to have a photo of you. Anything. Sometime when you're in the city on egg day stop by the bus station or a K-Mart and take a picture in a machine. I'd like to have one.

It snowed about six inches last night. Real heavy wet flakes. It should do the wheat a lot of good. This morning was only five degrees above zero.

I won't be coming directly to the farm for Christmas vacation. I'm going to visit Dad first. I've always wished he'd get married. It's so lonely for him living alone all this time.

I'll see you about December 28 or so. Will we still have time to get the pump fixed?

Work at school is going well.

S.

DEAR SORRY,

THE RECENT SNOWS HAVE DONE THE WHEAT A WORLD OF GOOD, BUT HAVE DELAYED OUR WORK ON THE NEW TERRACE SYSTEM IN THE NORTHEAST CORNER OF THE EAST EIGHTY. I WAS

HOPING TO HAVE IT DONE BY CHRISTMAS, BUT IT LOOKS LIKE
WE WON'T MAKE IT. ALSO MACKEY HAS HAD THE FLU.

I'M THINKING OF SELLING OFF SOME OF THE CATTLE THIS
WINTER AND EXPANDING THE SHELTERBELT ALONG THE EAST
FENCE ROW INTO A GAME PRESERVE. THE COWS ARE BECOMING
MORE TROUBLE THAN THEY'RE WORTH. I WILL JUST KEEP
ENOUGH TO LOOK RESPECTABLE AND KEEP THE LOCKER IN
YUKON FULL.

GIVE MY BEST TO KEEPER. AND TRY TO GET HERE AS SOON
AS YOU CAN. WE FOUND OUT LAST WEEK THAT THE WEST
CHICKEN HOUSE HAS A LEAK IN THE ROOF WHICH NEEDS TO BE
RESHINGLED.

MARCUS

Dear Marcus,

Thank you so much for the gloves. They are beautiful.

*This is just a quick note between hassles at the hospital.
I've got a meeting coming up with the board to discuss the cost
analyses of my department. But I wanted to thank you for the
present, but also express a nagging concern. I'm almost ashamed
to mention it. I tried to call you when I got your gift, I couldn't
help myself, but Information said there was no such listing. I
didn't think much of it, thought maybe the phone was still in
your mother's name, you've lived there so long. So I tried all the
Baldwins listed, and they said they'd never heard of a Marcus.
I'll admit that upset me a little. I think you can understand
why. I'll admit I started this whole thing on a lark, but it's gone
quite a bit beyond that. And even on a lark I don't like being
made a fool of. I'm sure there is an explanation, and I'd like to
hear it. And soon! Before this whole project gets out of hand.*

Love,
Isadora

Sorry sat on the narrow mattress on the floor of the Tennessee
Street attic room. Thick aroma of curry down the hall. A fitful,

fine, early morning sleet rattled the roof shingles, brittle brown maple leaves in the rain gutter and dirty windowpanes. Isadora Faire's letters scattered over the G.I. blanket. Her picture thumbtacked to the wall. A real fine mess you've gotten yourself into this time. He got up and went to the typewriter, put in a piece of paper and typed.

Dear Marcus,

About marriage. Why don't you say something, goddammit!

Pulled the sheet out of the carriage, wadded it into a ball and threw it across the room. Whatever made me think this would work. I should have known I was in for trouble filling out a questionnaire. Which qualities do you value most in a date? What would your ideal future dating relationship be?

He went back to the bed and reread a few letters. I'll marry you, Isadora, let Marcus work himself to death. Hell. Looked at the calendar, one more week before Christmas break. Come this far, got to ride the son of a bitch out. Face to face with Marcus. This time for sure. Hell. Why wait a week, get it over with.

He got his duffelbag out of the closet, stuffed it with a couple of pairs of underwear, socks, a shirt or two and sweater, put on his mackintosh, grabbed the steel-bodied guitar, said goodbye to the Pakistanis down the hall, and headed for Oklahoma.

It took him twice as long to get there. Icy roads. Windshield coated frozen rain. The sleet finally gave out outside Okarche. The sky low and dark, blustery cold northwest wind. Patches of powdery snow clung downwind clumps of dormant buffalo grass, forbs and low places of the fields. Marcus and Mackey were mending fence in the northeast corner of the east pasture when he pulled in. Sorry watched them through binoculars from the cellar mound. Then walked around the house, out to the barn. Waiting. Thinking. How to say it. Up to his room, Blanchefleur. Isadora Faire. And Marcus. Until they returned.

Marcus was surprised to see him. They unloaded the pickup, put up the fence posts, wire stretchers, hammers, dikes, barbed wire and staples. Mackey went to gather the eggs. Marcus and Sorry took the pickup to the barn and loaded it with hay and a new block of salt and carried it to the cows in the north pasture. Drove back south past the house. "We'll take a ride over to the Smith place before it gets dark to see where they're planning to put in the lake." Rode silently. How, when to say it, what to say.

They pulled into the field at the top of the hill. Got out into the wind, cold overlook. The skyline. The channel of the creek.

"They're going to build the dam west of that stand of trees, you see, about two miles to the southeast there, and put in a marina on the north shore and houses along both sides clear up to the section line."

Face to face, as good a time as any. "Don't you think it's a shame to flood out all that good farm land?"

"It's progress. Do the community a lot of good."

Pause. "What kind of progress is that? Kill all the trees, destroy the creek, cover forty acres with water. Bring in commuters from the city. Is that why we kill ourselves planting grass and building terraces, what you're working for? So some city slicker can pave it all over for a shopping center, Marcus. What kind of a future is that?"

Looks over, kind of astonished. "This country was an arid wilderness before Mom came here. And now there will be boating, fishing and houses. That's what Mom was working for. To develop the land, make it produce, a place to live and . . . "

"And what?" Marcus looks over the land, hunched in his jacket, last curving weak winter sun seeping through low cold purple blue horizon behind. Hesitate, not what you came to talk about, come on. Get it out. "Marcus. Didn't your mother want. Don't you think you need a family. A wife. Someone to work the farm when . . . "

Marcus standing beside the pickup. Slowly looks to the ground, searches the grass with the toe of his shoe. A long silence, cold wind crystals of ice. "Sometimes the Good Lord doesn't want things the way we would like. You're the only family I've got. Since Blanchefleur."

Long pause, heart pounding, short breath whipped vapor eddy and gone from the lips. *He's talking.* Force out the words low excited trembling cold. "Marcus. I don't. I can't find my mother here. I've got to face it, she's gone. Lost. We've both got to."

Marcus looked at him. Then looked away. They stood on the

windy hill. The watershed recedes, cold gray. Dark dendritic where the lake will be. Dust and powdery snow. Until all light is gone but the cold loom of the city on the eastern sky. They got back in the pickup and returned to the house.

After dinner Marcus watched the news and weather, read the Bible and went to bed. Sorry sat up in his room. Didn't exactly say what he wanted, Marcus didn't exactly respond. Hadn't exactly known what to expect. What to do next. Tomorrow another day, chicken roof and pump engine to break down. But Marcus had started to talk. Hell. Ride the son of a bitch out. Get a piece of paper. A woman, watermark, shades of ink, stamps and envelopes upon her tongue. Somewhere tonight, some touch of flesh, created, caught up in all of this. And begin to think of what to say, to write another letter to Isadora Faire.

Dear Isadora,

You'll have to excuse the long delay in answering your letter, especially since it was something that required a prompt reply. But unexpected problems came up on the farm. The chicken-house roof needed fixing, the pump engine had to be rebuilt, the normal holiday rush of church functions, visitations and so on. Anyway, Happy New Year!

I must apologize for being so thoughtless. It's just one of those things that you take for granted, and don't even think about until it's too late. You see, the farm is in Oklahoma, not Kansas. It never occurred to me that you didn't know that, I've been using that Lawrence address for so long. It's too complicated to explain in detail, but I've mentioned how bureaucratic and involved farming, agribusiness, has become. My lawyer advised many years ago that I could get a break on state taxes if I was some sort of interstate commerce. My lawyer will have to explain how it works. Don't think me a crook, but the address is my nephew's, who forwards all my mail. Please forgive me for making you wonder and worry.

I think of you often, imagine you with me in the pasture, the winter wind ruffling your hair and the world about us pale white frost and snow. Isadora, Isadora, we will have much to say when we meet.

                    Think of me and do not doubt my love.
                    Marcus

Dear Marcus,

Perhaps you're wondering why I too have taken so long to answer. Marcus, the fact is I've taken about as much of this as I can. First you never sent me a picture, then you don't have a phone number, you wait a month to explain why (very strange explanation, but at least an explanation). You can imagine, can't you? what I was thinking all that month. Well, your idea of getting to know each other through letters has outlived its usefulness. It's time to see each other, I don't think I can stand the suspense much longer. I know it's ridiculous to speak of love, but something has been developing in these letters, some emotion, desire, desperation, whatever, that's too weird attached to someone you haven't even seen, who you doubt even exists sometimes, or who you think is playing a cruel joke on you. The unreality of this whole thing is too much to bear. I must see you, hear your voice. Or I'm telling the computer to cancel, delete, clear screen, null and void.

Marcus, I know I rant and rave, but you've got to understand. It's not good for, nor conducive to, stable moods or meaningful planning of one's career to be missing, longing for, sad and happy about someone who is just a figment of your imagination, words written on a piece of paper.

I've got some time off coming up in April, and I'm coming to see you. And if you say no, you might as well not say anything. We can just consider this experiment with modern technology, as usually seems to be the case, a failure.

Please. I know this sounds like an ultimatum, a threat, but you must understand, I can't go on without meeting you. My imagination has done all it is capable of doing. We must move on to the next step, the sooner the better.

                    Isadora

Sorry Fesses Up

Mackey leaned on the posthole digger, drew out a red bandana to wipe sweat from his brow. Watched the pickup joggle up the hill. Loaded with Chinese elm saplings and young cedar trees. Marcus climbed from the cab with the water jug, handed it over, took the posthole digger, kicked the balled moist soil from the blades, continued chopping along the row. Mackey returned the jug to the cab, circled around and gathered an armload of Chinese elms, carried them to the holes and began tamping them in. Marcus stops, looks at the sky. "A man couldn't ask for a better March day than this."

"Sure couldn't, Marcus."

Back at chopping holes, Mackey still looking, staring at a long vapor trail moving slowly across. Silver speck. Barely perceptible movement. Almost audible jet engine among the movement of pasture grass and trees in the established shelterbelt, among the sounds of the brain, shovel thrusts and breathing. Mackey shielded the eyes and watched. Listening, garbled up in the trail, far behind the silver shining pin point of light. Goes back to setting trees.

Returned to the pickup for a cedar, noticed the faint red dust haze, dust trail rising between the hills west of the house, become thicker as a car topped the hill, turned into the drive, circled the house, dust slowly drifting over the tops, reappearing in the pasture over the dam. Sorry.

Mackey drags the cedar off the tailgate and lugs it around. Plops it in the hole, starts pushing dirt in packing it tight upon the root ball, pounding with clenched fists. The '31 Chevy pulls behind the pickup and stops.

Marcus turns from his digging to look after the engine has stopped, the door opened and closed. Hardly changes expression. "Sorry. Good to see you. You having a vacation?"

"Just a weekend trip. Have something to talk to you about."

"Well, good to see you. You take the postholer and I'll help Mackey with the planting."

Mackey handed the creamed peas over to Sorry, studying him closely. What this time. Looked over to Marcus. Eating contentedly. Swiss steak, watched the overhead light glitter in Marcus' eyes telling tomorrow's chores. Hot new-baked bread, tomato sauce and pepper. Commingling. Mackey savored, leaning back now and then, seated on a pillow and chair, stretching free-dangling legs and back, a little sore from carrying, balled roots cedar, elm saplings. Knees raw from crawling, hands from tamping, scraping dirt with fingernails. Looked at Sorry towering above the board, spooning out mashed potatoes. Long blond hair paler through rising steam. Gleaming eyes. Waiting for what?

Mackey clutched a gigantic spoon in his fist, pushing on the pile of potatoes in front, eye level, on his plate, forcing a crater. Absentminded. Observing. Listening. Waiting. Leaned forward reaching for the gravy. Marcus pushes it closer. Mackey ladles brown sauce into the center. A moth circling the light, fluttering flapping against ceiling and bulb. Mackey picks up the fork, pushes dikes up higher around the gravy reservoir trying to surround it, cutting too thin, trickling, finally pushing in the dam erupting gravy running down the slope onto the plate into tomato sauce.

Mackey picked among the fried onions and peas watching the

blade of Sorry's knife back and forth through meat, the fork tines from plate to mouth, jaw muscles contracting relaxing. Watches Sorry push a strand of hair from the perspiring forehead with the fork hand back. Sorry smiling intermittently at what Marcus says.

Marcus, Sorry, Malachi in front of the stove. Viola in from the back porch. She ruffles Sorry's head, high above, fingers wedding glow golden band on the free hand interweaving. Looking down. At Mackey. His plate. "You've hardly touched your food. No dessert for you."

"Not too hungry tonight, Viola. Not feeling too well. Probably got a little overhet planting trees."

"You better eat something more. Get some rest."

"Yeah, I think I'll hit the sack early tonight."

Got off the chair, made his way behind Malachi between the chair and stove. Ambled into the living room, climbed up into the large stuffed rocker, legs stretched in front, picked up the *Daily Oklahoman*, looked blankly at the front page. B-52's refueling in the air. Heard the clatter of saucers, the knife cutting pie. Rattle of ice in the tea glasses. Forks on plates. Chairs dragging on linoleum. Began rocking back and forth.

Malachi helped Viola with the dishes. Marcus and Sorry came in the living room, turned on the TV to wait for the weather. Mackey pretended sleep in the chair.

"Well, Marcus. I've got someone I want you to meet. A woman."

"A woman? Well. Who is she?"

"I think she'd be a good wife."

Looks at him closely. "Sounds serious."

"I mean for you."

Long pause. "A wife? For me?"

"Yes. I think it's time you have a family." Marcus says nothing. "I mean, it doesn't make sense being here alone." Nothing. "I'm not going to be around, more than likely. I've got a life to lead." Still nothing. "I think your mother would want you to get married." Silence, Marcus looking at Sorry as if the words had no meaning. "Say something, Marcus. What do you think?"

Looks quickly around the room, to the kitchen, at Sorry and away. "I don't. Don't need any help from. Who is this woman anyway?"

"She knows all about you. I've told her, and she's really, she wants to met you. Her name's Isadora Faire. She's a nurse."

"And how do you know her?"

"Well I. Well actually. Uh. You see, I figured you should have a family. And being so busy like you are with the farm, the egg business and all, I thought. Well, there just aren't many eligible women around a little town. And so. Now, Marcus, this isn't so weird as it may sound."

"I don't follow you yet."

"Here. Here's a picture of her."

Looking at the picture. Snorts, rubs the pointer finger along the side of his nose. Lays the picture on the coffee table, takes the pipe from the shirt pocket. Walks out of the room through the kitchen to the back porch. Sorry clasping hands, elbows on knees, staring at the floor. Sighs. Marcus returns with the can of Prince Albert, a couple of kitchen matches, sits back down. Begins stuffing the pipe examining the photo lying on the table. Mackey eases open one eye. Malachi and Viola quickly say goodnight, leave through the back porch. Marcus strikes a match on the sole of the shoe, puffs billowing blue gray smoke into the room. "Mighty handsome woman. A nurse, you say."

Perking up. "Yes. Very interested in farming. Animals."

Another match to the pipe bowl. Flames suctioned in, flaring out with the cloud of smoke. "Where you say you met her?"

"Met her. Well. You see, since I figured the chances of meeting someone around here weren't very good, well, I sent your name into a computer service."

Mackey starts. No one notices the rocking. Marcus looking severely at Sorry. "A what? You did what?"

"A. You see. A computer. Service. For getting people with common interests and . . ."

"A computer."

"Yes. People send in their interests to . . ."

"The computer matches them up."

"Yes."

"Well, I'll be. Don't that beat all." Laughs loudly. "A computer."

Sorry tries to laugh. Uncertain. "That's progress."

"Sure is." Looks at the picture on the table again.

"I've been writing letters to her. For—"

"Sorry. That is the beyond a doubt the dumbest thing I believe I've ever in all my born days heard tell of. A lonely hearts' club, huh?"

"No. It."

"And you've been writing letters to her, signing my name? Sorry, whatever got into you?"

Looks back at the picture. Relights the pipe. Picks the photo up. A few minutes. Sorry slowly coming out of shock. "What would it hurt? I mean. To meet her."

"Absolutely not. A mail order bride? Come on, Sorry. I don't have time for such foolishness."

Jumping from his chair. "Why not? Come on, Marcus. Just because you met her through a computer, she's still a human being. What could it hurt to meet her? There's more to life than work and this farm." Pacing up and down angry now. "What are you gonna do when you're old and alone? Sitting here with the place surrounded by high-rise apartment buildings, McDonald hamburger stands and filling stations. Think about the future! At least give her a chance. She's a human being and she wants to meet you."

Sorry stops, arms raised to shoulder level, looks at Marcus still seated chewing on the mouthpiece of the pipe, slowly releasing flowing smoke. Slaps his arms to his sides and stalks out of the room, up the stairs to his room.

Marcus pounds the bowl in the palm of his hand, drops the ashes in the tray. Picks up a pipe cleaner, screws the stem off, runs the cleaner through a few times. Blows through it and the bowl. Puts the pipe back together, back into the shirt pocket.

Watches the weather.

Gets up, turns off the TV, the lights, covers Mackey with a blanket. Walks back to the coffee table, looks down. Picks up the picture, goes outside, looks at the sky, the thermometer, pisses. Comes back in and climbs up to his room.

Mackey slowly opens first one eye, then the other. Stares into the darkness. Watches the moon on the elm branches tossing in the wind outside the window. Begins rocking his head. Forward and back. The chair slowly picking up the cadence.

Mackey stood on the chair at the stove, frying eggs and bacon. Five A.M. Marcus lumbered down the stairs, turned on the radio for the farm report, the news and weather. Walked out barefoot into the yard, dew wet. Over to the cellar mound to look. City lights, coming sun. Broke loose the opening verse of "Little Brown Church in the Wildwood." Checked the thermometer, came back inside. "Forty-three degrees, Mackey, it's going to be another fine day."

Picked up the plate of eggs and bacon, poured a glass of milk, dished up a bowl of oatmeal, began eating, listening to the market report.

Sorry drags in rubbing his eyes, yawning. Mackey cracks a couple more eggs into the skillet, looking from one to the other. Sorry sits, fills a bowl with oatmeal, not looking at Marcus, pours on sugar and cream. Eats silently. Light rising outside the window. The clock in the living room strikes the half-hour. Mackey sets the plate in front of Sorry, climbs back up on the chair and puts on two more eggs, butters the toast, carries it to the table, leans over to the bottom cabinet behind Marcus and pulls out the gallon can of molasses.

Marcus turns off the radio after the weather, knifes off a six-teenth pound of butter onto a saucer, pours molasses from the can onto it, mixes it with the blade, applies it to toast one bite at a time.

Sorry finishes, pushes his plate forward. Sits silently. Mackey watches first sunrays move down the wall.

Sorry clears his throat. "I'm sorry about last night, Marcus." Marcus continuing to eat. "It was a stupid idea. And I had no business interfering with your life. I don't know what got into me. I just thought. Well." Picks up a piece of toast, tears off a bite. Another. "I'll have to write her and tell her the whole thing was a mistake. That I. I'll think of something to tell her. I guess."

Mackey's eyes shift to Marcus finishing up the molasses. Wiping his hands on the dishtowel, placing it by Sorry's plate. Marcus takes the toothpick from over his ear.

"Well, Sorry. I'm glad you realize it was a bonehead thing to do." Smiles. Sorry looks over for the first time. Smiles miserable self-conscious. "But since you've gone to all this trouble. And the woman does want to visit the farm, I guess it couldn't hurt to meet her. Could it."

Marcus stands up, congratulates Mackey on the fine breakfast, goes back upstairs. Sorry left with his mouth open. Mackey slowly turning his spoon in the light across his plate. Marcus returns with his shoes and socks, looks at both of them, clicks his tongue come-on-let's-hustle. "Neither did we eat any man's bread for nought, but wrought with labour and travail night and day."

And Mackey watches Sorry amazed watching Marcus walking down the red dirt-stained walk to the gate, singing loudly.

"Onward Christian Soldiers, Marching On."

Five, afternoon should be warmer than it is. Streets crowded around the hospital. A damn traffic jam here. Isadora Faire, tired, irritated, alone, depressed. Sitting in the car moving slowly toward the parking lot exit. Radio playing loud screaming, pushes the button for another channel, loud DJ talking groovy, another button mechanical teeny beat, selling jeans, cosmetics, Coca-Cola, strident jangling nerves snap the radio off. Listen to the car exhausts, horns honking. A siren. Screeching tires. Damn. Damn.

Looks down at the pile of computer readouts on the front seat damn the goddam computer, goddamn, slams on the brakes bucking to a stop a half-inch from the bumper in front, throwing readouts onto the floorboard. Ga odd damn! Goddam computer. Goddam Marcus Baldwin! Pulling such a trick, a game. No answer, has to be a game. Should have known better with that bullshit about the Kansas address, the telephone. Should have known. Why doesn't he answer? How could he write such letters and not answer? Probably got wife and kids, gets his kicks seducing computer maidens, an electronic freak. Damn his eyes.

Finally pulled out into the street, made her way past the rush to leave the hospital and the rush to visit. On the verge of tears. Marcus, the hospital. A cold drizzle falling by the time she got home.

Got out of the car, went around to the other door, reached in for the readouts, leaning in out of balance, knee presses painfully on the doorjamb, gathered up the paper, lifting, middle slithering out flop on the floor again goddamn goddamn, raining harder, pushing the sheets sloppily together, pulled it up rising bang! her head on the edge of the roof bursting out shit crying flinging the readouts onto the drive splattering raindrops, sees the paper welting up water, cries louder fuckfuckfuck scooping them up in a wad and running weeping into the hallway.

Dark. Warm. Leaned against the wall, eyes closed clutching the mass of paper, tears streaming down the cheeks.

Finally opens the eyes, sniffs a few times, looks down at the kid gloves holding the readouts. Tears welling up again. Stood until they passed. Opens the eyes, sees the letter in the box.

Put the readouts on the floor trying not to look again. Get the key. Open the box, it was. A letter from Marcus Baldwin.

Isadora Whitehands
Casts a Spell

ISADORA Whitehands opened her eyes. Lay in bed. Night sky turning red in the east. She walked to the window, stood naked looking across brown earth toward the summer kitchen. Cool white south wind. She blew four times on her hands, upon her breast, turned to the closet, took out a cotton shift, lifted and let it settle over her arms and torso. Thinking of the blond-haired stranger. Was this what she wanted. Great-great-grandfather Kilakeena, the Buck, sent off from Georgia to the Foreign Mission School in Cornwall, Connecticut, changed his name to Elias Boudinot. And almost lynched, presuming to love the daughter of Headmaster Gold. Before the trail of tears. Before the tomahawk seven-cleft his skull. Seven. For treachery. Aunt Ruth, full blood in the kitchen of her parents' giant house, cooked their meals, washed their clothes, raised them, Isadora Whitehands, her brother Gordon and Richard Chewey standing in the enormous kitchen to hear her, hair pulled back and tied behind the head, laugh and talk and sing the Cherokee songs and spells. The way it was. The way it is. To heal the sick. To make men lonely. Rebeautify, discomfit. And to kill.

Isadora Whitehands had learned them all.

She returned to the window. Must decide. The sun almost up. What good is remade tobacco now? Is there treachery in the blood?

The earth brown, purple cloud covering, white south wind blowing clear. The east turning red. Cardinal and Whippoorwill. The old Chevrolet sedan black in the drive. But east turning red.

She stepped to the night table, almost ashamed, embarrassed. Opened the drawer. The silver pipe George Washington gave to some ancient chief. Found it with Uncle Stand Watie's things in the attic before the lawyers came after her parents died. Held it in her hand, imagined hands, is there magic in the touch, the tobacco, wizards and the songs? It has led to this. The Mason jar of *Nicotiana rustica*. She removed the zinc lid, took out a pinch of tobacco in the left hand, replaced the lid, put the jar back in the drawer. Slipped quietly through the house and out into the white south wind.

Self-conscious soul a tobacco moth.

Treachery in the blood.

She walked across the pasture, wind pressing the white shift against her body, kneading the tobacco in the left hand, thumb and four fingers. Across the swell of broomweed and grass. The black western horizon receding, purple clouds turning blue. Toward the trees blue and black against the red clear eastern sky. She began to sing softly in the dawn. Three times singing to the creek.

> *Anagali:sgi gigagé:i iyú:sdi*
> *U:ghvhada iyú:sdi*
> *Dhlv:datsi iyú:sdi*
> *Wahhya gigagé:i iyú:sdi*
> *Hida:we:h(i) iyú:sdi tsinanugó:tsi:gá*
> *Tsada:n(v)dho:gi ayv aye:hliyu gai:se:sdi*
> *Gha?! hna:gwo tso:la uné:gv tsugh(a)sv́:sdi tsa:yalv́:tsi:gá*
> *   tsugh(a)sv́:sdi.*

She made her way down the dark familiar path through the trees to the clearing below the limestone bank. Water trickling over moss rotting stone. The cottonwood trees. Rising light of morning.

She faced where the sun would appear. And sang the fourth time.

Like the red lightning
Like the fog
Like the panther
Like the red wolf
Like you, you wizard, I have come to make my appearance.
I will be walking in the very middle of your soul.
Now! now the smoke of the white tobacco has come to wing
*   down upon you.*

She stuffed the pipe, laid it on the rock ledge, knelt down to the water, scooped handfuls cold onto her face, laughing now, stripped water from the eyes, shook it from the hands, dried with the hem of the shift. Began to gather drift debris from the edges of the stream, leaves and twigs, piled them below the bank from the wind. The sky gone red. Took out a wooden match from the shift pocket, carefully set the driftwood tinder ablaze. Let it burn down. Daubed a pinch of ashes on her forehead, rubbed it. Another on each breast. Picked up the silver pipe, blew on the embers of the fire, the first shaft of sunlight through the branches of the trees! Picked up a coal in the bowl of the pipe. Inhaled two or three quick times, white smoke. *Nicotiana rustica* burning in the sunlit silver bowl of the pipe.

She climbs back up the path to the pasture. Walks back toward the house. The blond-haired stranger waits. His sad-eyed smile. A shiver through her body.

Treachery in the blood.

Walks back along the cow path to the house.

She stops beneath the canopy of the yard. Four puffs of smoke from the silver pipe. White smoke blown and drifting toward the summer kitchen where he stands looking out from behind the old distorted windowpane. The white eyes meet. Cannot turn back.

Isadora Whitehands slips into the front door to the middle of the house. The very middle of the room. And knocks the ashes from the pipe.

Sorry. I will be walking in the very middle of your soul.

Hank and Keeper
Remember How It Was

LYING back with feet propped up on the front seat, strumming and a singing. Sorry had a college degree. At least that much was certain. Hank and Keeper the only ones to make it to graduation. Came up the day before. They all piled into the '31 Chevy, bottle of whiskey, steel-bodied guitar, and headed out across the Flint Hills. Hank driving. Keeper in the front seat with him. Sorry singing in the back. Wind popping hot in the windows. Wide high blue light, white dissipating contrails, bluestem just hinting yellow-brown drought and summer. Black Angus. Whiteface Hereford spread across the wandering watersheds and limestone draws. Distant tree alone against the folds and swatches, leaves and branches slow movement with the air. Smell the grass and sun. The distant tree. And cows. Hank slapped the steering wheel and honked the horn with the beat.

"Goddamn if I didn't know no better I'd think I'd just woke

from a long fitful sleep and it was still 1938. If you stay to the back roads and the small towns, this country looks just like it did. The same goddam filling stations, the same goddam bars, the same goddam Chevrolet, running just as goddam smooth as she ever did. And if I didn't look in the rearview mirror, I'd swear that was Lyons back there singing up a storm."

"You're mighty right about that." Keeper looking back, looking away. "Goddamn, Hank. Where's the nearest rodeo? There must be a rodeo somewheres around here. Some punkin roller. I just got the urge to see you rope a calf."

"And I'll bet you can still ride saddle bronc in the average."

"Why the hell not."

Sorry stops playing. Looks at his hands, the reflecting sunlight on stainless steel, suddenly overwhelmed by it all as Hank wheels into a filling station to ask where a feller might take in a weekend rodeo.

Pulled into Cottonwood Falls curving over the bridge by the dam still flowing heavy over cottonwood elm tree trunks and branches, brown thick water from recent lines of thunderstorms. Along the wide red brown brick Main Street. Rodeo banners stretched across billowing wind swaying polar gridded wires. Rolled past one- and two-story buildings, brown brick, native stone off-white, cornice, corbel, brickwork friezes, white, green copper flashing, past pickups and cars. Kansas Pioneer Light, VFW, TG&Y, I.O.O.F., Oklahoma Tire and Supply. IGA. Apco. Wide sidewalks, benches here and there old men sitting. Tin awnings. The post office. Focusing up the domed street to the square and the county courthouse. Red tile roof, cupola clock topped in wrought iron, romanesque arch over the central three windows flanked by circular glass above the steps and portico. Converging walks. A statue of a World War I soldier, a World War II cannon set among native elm.

They idle around the square and back down Main. Stopped in front of the large red Coors sign, *bar and grill.* Sat watching heat ripple brick and stone, street and walls and walks. Hank finishes off the whiskey bottle. "The goddam place hasn't changed in twenty-six years. We sat in the same car in front of the same bar, and I killed the same cheap whiskey back in 1938."

Keeper grins squinting against the sun. "It's not gonna surprise me none when we go in and see the same hard-luck cowboys belly-ing the bar."

"Let's go then."

They get out. Sorry following cautious into the dark interior. Stand until sight returns. A CB radio monitoring traffic. Cowboys lining the bar. Young. Fancy boots, flared jeans, expensive sheen cowboy shirts, long hair and shades. Mustaches, a beard or two.

"Not the same, Hank."

"Sure ain't."

They sit at a table. No one says anything. Listening. Draws, stock, houlihans, pigging strings, hooey, flanking, added money, day money.

"Sounds bout the same, Hank."

"Sure does."

Sponsors, endorsements, stocks and bonds, brokers, invest-ment.

"Or maybe not."

"Yeah. Maybe."

A plump woman at the bar, gray hair, tired face, chatters idly, automatically with whoever. Picks up a cloth and walks to the table, wipes it bruskly, looks at Hank. "What'll it. Be."

"Three beers."

Continues looking. "Three beers coming up." Pause. "You know. You sure look familiar."

"Well. I been here before."

"It's the hoofprint above your eye. If you don't mind my saying so. You used to know a man, a rodeo cowboy, bull rider played a metal guitar and wrote poetry?"

"Sure did."

"You knew Roger Lyons?" Eyes intensifying. "Well, I'll be." Looks at Sorry a moment, back at Hank. "I heard about what happened up to Saskatoon."

Hank and Keeper, Sorry shift uneasily. Uncomfortable pause. The woman staring, in thought. Hank looks to Sorry self-consciously examining fingernails, coughs nervously. "Well. Yeah." Pause. "You know, this here is Lyons' boy. Sorry."

"Oh." Almost a surprised whisper. Reddens. "I didn't know he. I. I'm."

Starts to extend her hand, then suddenly she turns from the

table, goes off into the back room. Nobody looks at anybody. The linoleum floor patterns, the ceiling fan slow turning. A few flies. The jukebox comes on Chet Atkins, the cowboys talk, hound dog asleep at the end of the bar blusters and paws. Sun glaring on the brick Main Street outside the door.

A hobbled old man brings the beers, mumbling to himself across the floor grinning a toothless white-whiskered grin. Hank and Keeper look very tired all of a sudden. Drinking beer in silence. Sorry looks around. Rapid gulps of beer.

A burst of heavy motorcycle engine outside. Silence. A cowboy in silk shirt, embroidered jeans and denim jacket, silver-studded boots swaggers in, the place explodes—welcome, back slapping. A young woman who replaced the plump one behind the bar joins him at a table. Hank and Keeper drink up sullen. Withdrawn. Get up and leave. Sorry watches the man and the girl exchange soft greetings, then follows.

A crowd of kids around the Harley chopper. Chrome extension tubes, teardrop tank flowered swirls and a *Rodeo Cowboy Association* emblem. Hank standing with the kids looking. Not at the cycle. The emblem. Not looking, standing there in the heat with the kids in front of the bar, the domed brick street rising to the courthouse, standing there lost in thought in years standing lost.

Sorry climbs in the back seat of the Chevy. Hank finally slides in beneath the wheel, sits. Then starts the engine. "Well, we better be heading on back. Sorry's got a big day tomorrow."

The Chevy was packed with what he had. Two pair of Levi's, one wool slacks, one white shirt, two cowboy shirts, two cotton knit sailing shirts, striped, one corduroy blazer, three pair of Munsingwear horizontal fly, five pairs of socks, one black stretch, two wool, two white cotton, one green Hudson's Bay Company wool sweater, his G.I. feel good jacket, a WWII great coat, one bandana, faded red, pair of worn sneakers, one pair of Florsheim wing tips, black, and swimming trunks. Wearing the oldest cord pants, Sears workshirt, broad leather belt with saddle bronc champion buckle, the Calgary Stampede 1937, boots. One G.I. blanket. Dop kit, Palmolive soap, toothbrush, Dr. Lyons tooth powder, Old Spice, mug and brush, Williams shaving soap, Gillette adjustable, Wilkerson sword blades, tube of Prell shampoo. Calculus books, matrix theory. Set theory. Probability and statistics. *Catch-22, Sometimes a Great Notion, V, Life Against Death. Main Currents in Modern Thought,* notebooks from class, Lyons' songs and poems. Silvertone stereo. Chuck Berry and Bob Dylan records. Steel-bodied guitar. And a college degree.

Said goodbye to the Pakistanis across the hall and climbed up 13th Street. Deserted. Turned at Chi Omega house past the student union, Greene Hall, Frazier Hall, the library, the School of Journalism, Strong Hall. Now and then still a grandmother and grandfather taking a picture of the grad. Some foreign students. Squirrels. Buildings and Grounds crews. But mostly empty and vast. To the Campanile, and down along the lake, through the student union silent out the front and down 13th again to Ohio Street and the Jayhawk Cafe. The old Dodge pickup out front. To meet Hank and Keeper.

The place empty except for voices in the dark glow red Naugahyde from the booths along the bar on the left. Laughter. The smell of a season's groundround, chicken-fired steaks, hamburgers, cigarette smoke and beer clinging to the surfaces. A patina, dark and rich. Transition. The laughter, the voices. Hank and Keeper, Bufie and Alexandra in the booth finishes the story as Sorry comes up along the bar.

"Well. Speak of the devil."

"Who was?"

"How's it feel, grad?"

"Bout the same."

"You really have some son here, Mr. Keeper. What are you going to do now you're finished?"

Sits on a stool opposite the booth, picks up a salt shaker, turns it in his fingers. "Rest. Think it over. Cut wheat."

Bufie cleans his horn-rims with a napkin. "That's the right idea. No need to run into anything hastily. You never know what's in store. I was going to be a Latin scholar and look at me." Circling gesture holding glasses by the right eye with the thumb and forefinger over his head. "You know, I looked at this place as something temporary until I could get a position teaching. And the irony of it is that I've done more to promote scholarship serving up

BL&T's than I ever could have hopping around behind a podium in the dusty attic of some remote building on some little schoolyard or other. I've had poets, writers, Russian historians, comp. lit. Joyceans, medical illustrators come to maturity right here in these booths eating chicken-fried steaks, drinking Pepsi-Cola and beer. That ought to be my motto, engraved in Gulden mustard over the portal. *Servit Et Qui Moretur.* 'He Also Serves Who Waits.'"

"And look at the bright side. If you'd have been a teacher, you'd have never met me."

"I often think of that, Alexandra, my dear."

"I was his first bookkeeper, and soon keeping more than the books."

"Always did suspect that imbalance that had us poring over the midnight accounts that time was intentional." She pokes him in the ribs, he hops rolling his bulging eyes. Replaces the horn-rims. "No, my dear, you would have found me, even if it required matriculation in Virgil one and two. A match like ours is made in heaven. Like thunder and lightning."

"With that it's time to clean the kitchen, Bufie. Give these people a pitcher of beer as a graduation present and let's get on with it."

"As you say my dear, riffle a Bud."

He slides out from the booth and circles the counter to the tap, pulls a pitcher from beside the stainless steel sink and draws it full, hands it to Sorry across the bar. Alexandra gets up, takes Sorry by the free hand, "Take it easy now," and goes off after Bufie into the kitchen delivering orders as to what should and shouldn't be done first. Sorry carries the beer over to the booth and sits. Pours the glasses full. Watches the bubbles rise, the head foam, dome, drip around the rim rill upon the tabletop. Keeper lifts a glass yellow light dull from the partition edge, the front window matt afternoon and humid warmth, oak and maple fronting, roots buckling brick walk and curb of Ohio Street. Sorry looks from the window, the glass. Silhouette shadow red across the arm, the faces. Hank and Keeper sit. Hank pulls a glass toward him, Keeper holds, eyes shining in the little light. "Well, goddammit. We finally made it. Too bad Mom and the old man couldn't be here to see it. Sure did want me to go to college. But now you've done it. Good work. I'm mighty proud of you."

He drinks. They drink. Sit quietly. Keeper wipes the back of his hand across his nose. "Too bad Blanchefleur isn't here to see."

Sorry looks up. Looks closely at the man across, sips his beer still looking. "What was she like? You never told me."

"You never asked."

Pause. "I guess not." Falls silent. But Keeper still looking. *Never asked. Keeper and Blanchefleur. Of course.* "You know. It's funny I was always thinking about Marcus. The man takes up a lot of space and time. When I thought of Blanchefleur I always thought of Marcus. Sure." Looks at Keeper, Hank. Nothing. Keeps going, after something. "There's more to it . . ."

The rattle of the front door causes him to trail off. Two students, one tall skinny black plastic rim glasses, the other shorter, dark black curly hair, wearing blue blazers, identical crests on the breast pocket, a gold and blue *P* encircling a globe. Carrying yellow notepads, German-English dictionary, a thin volume. Pass Sorry and Hank and Keeper watching them. Sit in a booth toward the kitchen. Bufie comes out. "Kitchen's closed. Just selling off excess beer."

"No peach pie?"

"Eighty-six."

"A beer."

"Pepsi."

Bufie moves glassware, taps beer, the heavy snap of the cooler door open and shut beneath the bar. Returns to the kitchen. Sorry looks back to Keeper. Lighter now, more blue in the red booth, almost noon. Have to leave soon, have to. Keeper tops off the glasses from the pitcher. "She was quite a woman."

"But. You and her."

"No, Sorry, I . . ."

"You didn't find Marcus. Brought her home from Montana, took her away, you. Were taking her away from Lyons?"

"No!" Swallows beer slowly. Puts the glass down. Sits. Starts to grin. Breaks out laughing. "Hell yes. I was taking her away. Lyons, goddamn you, I was trying to take her away! I wasn't going to be a rodeo rider all my life, time to start thinking, about Dad and Mom, about the farm. Too bad you weren't old enough to know Dad. Quiet. Never said much. Almost enough to make you afraid of him if you didn't know better, and I was always letting him down. Trying to show him I could do it on my own, what I wanted. I never did somehow. Didn't make the big leagues. Only thing I even got close to doing right was bronc busting. And now that was messing up, cause I was going to take her away, and that sure as hell was gonna mess things up with me and Lyons and rodeo. He loved her, don't get me wrong, loved her like hell, in his way, would have loved you too, but he couldn't change, couldn't be what he never was and never wanted, never even thought of being." Stops. Pinches the eyes with thumb and fingers. "But just couldn't do, didn't make it. Too late. I waited too long. And lost her before I even got her home a day." Drained his glass. Poured more beer. Sips for a while. Muffled discussion from the other booth. Sorry waits. Keeper finally looks back up. "I worked for her and you all these years. I'm proud. I still had some of her, wouldn't give that up. You didn't go so much for baseball, but then. Well, football is all right. Not the game baseball is, but. And you off to college, like Mom and Dad wanted for me, but I don't know. Marcus. After all the years. Hank and I running the place, keeping it going, the old International Harvester so old hardly worth the trouble anymore. Specially with you off with Marcus. Hardly makes sense." Looking at Sorry. "What are you planning on doing, Sorry? I know I'm in a funny position now, deserve anything you think. But still. We can't just ignore all the years, act like they never happened. I'm your. Did a damn good job of it. The only father you'll have."

"I." Shrugs.

"It's time to start thinking about it. Comes a time when. Well hell, I guess I'm not your pa, but. Seeing you coming down that hill in those black robes, put a lump in your old dad's throat, just like I really was your old dad. I mean since you left it's been pretty. I mean Hank and I, we sure miss you back home. Sure would." Sniffs. "Would be nice if, you ought to give it some thought, to coming on back home. I mean."

Looks away to Hank, sitting calm and silent. Sorry looks down. Clears his throat, hoarse. "Sure." Reach out, embrace, but can't. "Give it some thought. I've already. I." Falls silent. "Got to go piss."

Turns out of the booth before they see the tears, moves unsteady past the two leaning over the scribbled yellow page, sweeping a hand in shadowy air, and banged into the toilet.

Nowhere to go.

How can it be, the years, days, gone. How to think about it now. Complain. Glides and flows, unhindered, sifted from silent, like a strange mongrel dog. A hundred years from the daguerreotype sod house, sepia gray silver white stories, notebooks and coffins gather dust.

And one with me.

As if my very hair.

Nothing to do.

But wash the face with cold water and finish off the beer, the unsaid silence. But walk into the brilliant warmth. Trees and tall houses, steep ragged grass and grown-over fallen-down brick retaining walls, winged maple seeds twirling through. Nothing to do but climb in the cab of the old red Dodge, into the back with the cans of grease, gunnysacks grease gun pry bar chain splintered two-by-four and grain of all those harvests. Drive around the block to Tennessee Street to the Chevy. Nothing but start her up and drive out across the Wakarusa Valley. To Emporia. The turnpike entrance. Shake hands. Stand. Paw gravel with the toes of rough worn boots. Shake hands again and cannot look. Nothing to do but wave as Hank and Keeper pick up a ticket at the booth and drive on down the Kansas Turnpike. Nothing to do but climb in the Chevy and head west on U.S. 50 alongside the long freight train a quarter of a mile to the south. To Strong City, south on 177 out across the Flint Hills. Through Matfield Green, Cassoday, prairie chicken capital of the world, through El Dorado to U.S. 77, Douglass and Winfield, Arkansas City into Oklahoma.

Nothing to do but head on back. Unsettled. To Marcus. The farm. Another harvest. Dust. Wind. Flowers. Sun. Shadows of earth. And think. Of what to do when winter comes.

And Marcus has a wife.

Marcus Takes a Woman

THERE'S no getting around it. Look in the mirror, and think about it awhile and you have to admit it's not a 20-year-old man you see. Look away and I sure feel the same. Same Marcus, strong as ever. But it's been over twenty years since Mom died. All the life, glided unhindered over from little boy, silent, mum, a stranger to me now. Fragmented. Standing frightened in pee-soaked red-dirt-stained nightshirt, looking up at a monstrous horse snorting and steaming cold autumn air. A whiskered man with a gold watch swinging up, towering out of vision, whirling and gone. And the next thing I know I'm a man. Wondering in front of the mirror.

Only the land, the willow trees on the oldest ponds, the pasture hills, and grass are the same. Surrounded by independent development. The house expands in the mind, takes on a bathroom and porches, trees grow up around the yard, a fence, the potbelly stove disappears and the stairs suddenly curve at the bottom. The skyline of the city looms. The developers come. Progress. And it all means time. Measured by Mom's hand tracing the moist air of death.

And I think I know what she meant now, what she was trying to say. A family. Even Sorry understood that. He wasn't enough.

The eligible women at the church socials sure didn't offer much. In fact, about the only one unmarried is Mabel Preaby. And she's just not the type of woman I could see as my life's partner. I know you should see to the beam in your own eye, but it's generally agreed in the whole town that she's crazy as a loon. Suppose she takes it after her mother Maude. The sheriff alway likes to tell about the time Maude and Clyde Turner got married. Both in their eighties, and Maude figured there were too many people in this world for her to ever live alone, so she and Clyde decide to pool their Social Security checks. And about two, three times a week the sheriff would get a call from her saying there was a strange man in the kitchen drinking her coffee and eating her Lazy Dazy cake. Well, the sheriff would have to go over every time and explain to her that that was Clyde Turner her husband.

Now Mabel, after Maude and Clyde passed on, sort of went off the deep end. Let's face it, anyone who, after seeing a program on "You Asked for It" about running the rapids on the Colorado River, puts all her savings, mostly crumpled one dollar bills, in the trunk of her '52 Hudson with all the chicken feathers she keeps there for a feather bed she plans on making one day, and pulls out for the Grand Canyon, knowing only that it's west of town somewheres, sticking to the back roads because she's afraid of gravel trucks, and actually makes it, and has an interview with the governor of the state to explain all she knows that her daddy Cecil Preaby had taught her about the prevention and care of soil erosion, anyone who does that, even though she does sing a mighty fine soprano in the church choir, and can be counted on for cow tongue salad at any picnic, cannot be considered seriously as a candidate for mother of your children.

So after Blanche left and all those years alone, it seems to me Sorry was the only family I could expect.

Anyway, when he came up with that harebrained scheme for me to meet Isadora Faire, how could he know. That I was lonesome. I don't know why folks think I don't have feelings like them. By the time she came to visit I was nervous as a schoolboy giving a recitation. Never felt so ridiculous in all my life. Almost turned back on my way to the bus station in the city. Morning rush hour traffic so thick I could hardly breathe, cars cutting in front, crowding the road, and impossible to find a parking place anywhere near, almost kept on going, "Well, I tried, but no place to park, too bad, maybe next time, some other time," ridiculous notion of Sorry's anyhow. Besides I wouldn't even know her if I was to see her, all I have is a picture, circling the block cussing and fussing, and there she is. Standing at the curb with a small suitcase. No question about it. I'd know her anywhere. I think. Almost run right over the fellow in front of me. She looked so, so handsome. She is coming to see me. I'm sitting there, put on the brakes so hard I'd killed the pickup engine. In a dern pickup! Smell the grease and sweat, muddy coil of rope in the floor, chain, crowbar and Stillson wrench. Red dust on the dash, old rags and P.A. can. Whatever came over me, to pick up a woman in a. And by this time she's looking in at me through the side window, unsure but pretty sure, eye to eye it's too late to do anything else.

"Isadora? I . . . "

"You must be, I thought I recognized you from your . . . "

"Picture, yes, me too, I was looking for a place to park and. Well." Honking from behind. "Get in."

Marcus jumps out of the cab, the car behind squeals around shouting. Another honking in its place. Picks up Isadora's suitcase and places it in the back of the pickup on top of the fence posts and barbed wire, turns back face to face, they stand there. Finally she offers her hand, Marcus reflex jerks his hand up, then back to wipe on his trouser leg. They shake hands, words of welcome drowned in cement diesel cursing around the pickup. He opens the door, removes the gunnysack from the front seat, dusts a little with it and she climbs in. Marcus checks the suitcase again, knew he shouldn't have, up against the fence posts, black creosote smear on the canvas plaid side, a little gasoline ought to, tried to find another place, but watch the barbed wire, another bonehead move. Returns to the window, asks Isadora for the gunnysack, more honking and shouts behind, well-coiffed three-piece business suit in a Volks getting irate. Marcus walks slowly back to the car, leans down over, elbow resting on the roof. "What's got you in such a hurry this morning? Afraid you'll be twenty seconds late when you hit the hay tonight?"

The Volks gulps back, darts out in front of a bus and around, mouthing his reply from the corner stoplight where he barely avoided rear-ending a young dude's souped-up Pontiac. Marcus wraps the suitcase in the gunnysack and they start back for the farm.

Rode silent for a block or two. Isadora looking over the interior of the pickup, the buildings going by. "Looks like it's going to be a nice day."

"Mild cold front moved through last night, high pressure behind, should keep the temperature down in the mid-eighties." Voices echo metallic pickup cab. "Only about a ten percent chance of rain tonight. Sure could use a good rain."

"It's been a dry summer." Marcus keeps his eyes on the road. "I didn't realize Oklahoma City was so large."

"It's really growing. When we get out on the Northwest Highway, you'll see nothing but new houses and apartments, all put up in the last four or five years."

Silence again. The city gives way to residential, the new developments, the topology abstract rooftop cedar shingles gabled flowing contours below the highway gradual slope vertical sectioned red brick chimneys light poles and gridwork antennas. Falling away into hazy white gray oily indigo, insolation scattered through.

"How was the trip down?"

"Not too bad. One night on a bus isn't a total disaster. I had a seat all to myself, could curl up and sleep some."

"That's good."

More silence. Off the highway to the farm. Around the back gate, pulls the pickup in by the propane tank at the northeast corner of the yard. Marcus gets the suitcase from the gunnysack. "I'm afraid I messed up a little, some creosote on your bag, but a little gasoline ought to take it right off."

Looks at it. "Oh, that's. Sure, a little gasoline."

"I'll get it right now. Why don't." A broad gesture around the farm.

"I better unpack it first, I . . . "

"Okay. You, I thought it would be. You'll be staying with Viola and Malachi down the road, but right in through here." Heading for the back porch. "There's the downstairs bedroom, unpack there, and change, the bathroom here."

Takes the bag from him, puts it on the floor by the bed. "Don't want to get creosote on the bedspread."

Marcus takes the empty suitcase out to the garage, gets a can of gasoline and a rag, puts the rag over the spout, turns the can up and back, dabs at the creosote. Isadora Faire comes out, changed into jeans short-sleeve blouse and sandals, watches Marcus, then walks around the yard, around the house looking, the trees and vines, the well, meets Marcus on the east side carrying the suitcase. "Good as new."

"Very nice, thanks."

"Well."

"Well. Good to see you."

"Yes. You too."

"This is a little strange, isn't it?"

"You can say that again."

"Your farm is beautiful."

"Well. I try to keep it looking like somebody lives here. Would you like to take a ride over the place? Before we." Darn Sorry's eyes, how did I ever let him talk? "Well, Malachi and Viola'll be coming by directly to help with cleaning out the chicken houses, I hope you don't, I mean." Handsome woman. "I'm afraid it can't be put off." Clean out the chicken house, but what else. "And we better find Mackey, he's out in the north pasture gathering dead branches and trees with the tractor. I don't suppose this is what you expected but . . . "

"Sounds great. I want to see how the farm runs, I can't think of a better way."

They climb in the pickup. Damn his eyes, get me into this, drove out the west drive north a couple of hundred yards up the gradual rise and down to a gate, three-strand barbed wire. Normal day, clean the chicken houses, a woman all night on the bus to see, and all because of Sorry, and clean chicken houses. Got to. Slowly over the pasture.

"Those ponds we passed there north of the house are the oldest on the place, put in by Mom. These old willows been there a long time. That's fore Dad left. This one here's a different branch of the watershed. The first pond I ever dug, drug out with a drag-bucket and a team of mules, me and Blanche. Must of been ten I guess, Blanche was twelve. The Bermuda grass you see all along the spill-way, well, that was nothing but shale. The channel'd made a cut through a shale bluff here where we dug the thing, so nothing would grow very well, and come a big rain, four to six inches in an hour, the kind you can expect every twenty years or so, and more than likely you're going to lose your dam. So we loaded some dirt off the top of the hill there northwest and sodded the whole area. And sure enough, it wasn't two years later came a rain like a cow pissing on a flat rock one Wednesday night. I know it was Wednesday, because Mom and Blanche had been to choir practice, and the storm blew up before they were home. The lightning spooked old Portia and she run the last mile, Blanche hanging right in with her about bouncing them both out of the wagon. The old road over east where the swimming hole is now didn't go straight across the creek then. We'll see that after we find Mackey. It took a dogleg through the coffeebean over a rickety old flat-bottom bridge, and Blanche took that wagon full tilt right through the curve, best horse handling I've ever seen. Anyway, it was coming a real toad-strangler, thundering and lightning to beat the band, and Mom and Blanche headed for the cellar. But I just had to see how my sodding job was going to hold up on the spillway, so I take out barefoot, Mom calling out what a fool I was, she'd already had to breathe life back into me once when I was struck by lightning, didn't I know someone tall as me bound to attract the stuff. I could hardly breathe the water was so thick in the air, the drops so big I thought it was hailing there for a while. You see that old bois d'arc over there? Well, the water got up past it, almost to run over the top of the dam. That would mean it was about four foot deep running over the spillway. I just stood there watching in the flashes, wind just a roaring, rain, water over the spillway and down the channel. Very impressive. Thought I was going to lose my dam for sure. Next morning when I came back out, the runoff was down to about six inches deep, and I could see she was good as new, the Bermuda laying pretty flat to the ground, but not a cubic foot of dirt missing. That Bermuda is some grass."

"That's really something. Wow. And it's so beautiful."

"How did I ever get into, let myself get into this. "I hear the tractor up behind the trees above the pond, we'll go check on Mackey."

Pickup lumbers up on the dam and across. Stops in the middle, Marcus gets out, Isadora quickly follows.

"From here, you can get a good look at most of the draining basin feeding this dam." Pointing over the trees in the channel. "You see that horizon to the northwest there. About three or four hundred yards into the next section. That's the highest point of these four sections, so we're very near the head of the watershed. That feeds into the North Canadian River. Over the rise north feeds the Cimarron. The grassy channel you see above the dam is an ephemeral stream we call it. It's above the groundwater table most of the time, like right now, and there's no water running in it. The channel only carries surface runoff, except in real big rains, like the one I was telling you about, when the groundwater table will rise temporarily, because the basin has a high infiltration rate. It's covered with grass and trees. But you see the plowed ground over in the next section? Well, there's a lot more runoff a lot faster when the ground's bare, but you notice the terraces"—she squints to follow his pointing finger—"the pattern of them, how they channel the water back and forth across the face of the gradient, that slows the water, it's not going down so fast, and it has farther to go, so more of it will soak in. It took some doing for me to talk old man Moffet into putting in those terraces. He was losing his field and the silt was filling up my pond. But he finally was convinced when I got him over here and showed him all the fine topsoil in the bottom where there used to be shale. Now remember I said when I came out the next morning after that big rain, the water was still running six inches deep over the spillway, even though the rain had stopped over eight hours earlier. Well, that's because the groundwater table had risen above the channel due to the high infiltration rate. It was an effluent stream for about the next day and a half. But like I said, we only have rains that big once every ten, twenty years, or if we have an unusually wet spring and the ground stays saturated all the time. When we follow this channel on down to the big pond above the swimming hole to the southeast, you'll see it becomes effluent below the dam all the time. Now that wasn't the case before we put all these ponds in here. That's one reason we survived the dust bowl on this watershed when some of the neighbors didn't do so well."

"That's amazing. Fascinating. I."

I think she means it, haven't been talking her ear off. "Well, it is pretty interesting when you get to doing it. I've been working for ten years to get an upstream flood prevention project on the next watershed over. Finally overcame the opposition and got through all the red tape and got approval for three retardation dams. Huge structures, perfectly engineered and constructed, and we're very proud of them." Stops. Talk too much. "We better find Mackey."

They get back into the pickup and continue across, around the pond to the northwest. Mackey bounces on the yellow M&M, red wheels, dragging a large dead trunk toward a pile of brush. Feet dangling from the seat springing with the land lay on its iron tongue. He sees the pickup, strains forward to disengage the hand clutch, cut the hand throttle, slip her into neutral. Throws his right leg over, hanging from the seat, down to the platform, down over the hitch to the ground. Walks to greet Marcus and Isadora Faire. "Howdy, ma'am. Sure nice to meet you."

Can't suppress a glance from Mackey to Marcus and back. "It's great to be here."

"Well, I better get back to work."

"How much more you got, Mackey? Malachi and Viola'll be here in about half an hour."

"I should be finished up by then."

"Okay."

"See you later, Mackey."

"Sure thing, Miss Faire."

They pull across the pasture along the slope, over a divide and down into a draw, another branch of the watershed, another pond. Drive up on the dam, covered with whiteface cows.

"This is the second pond we put in. See where this channel, so flat above the dam you could hardly call it a channel, where it meets up with the one from the drainage basin we just left? It does some serious work. You can see, this side of the heavy trees, how deep it's cut through. Well, I used that gorge for the big pond. Don't ever wade out in it when the water's low, she'll go from four feet to thirty-four in one step. We'll drive over to it."

They wait for the cattle to lope on off, cross on over the dam.

"Up in the northeast corner is the shelterbelt Mackey and I put in a few years ago, doing real good. Those elms and cedars were just six inches high when we set them in there. Already attracting pheasant, rabbits. Hawks and coyotes."

"Isn't that bad, hawks and coyotes, aren't they predators?"

"Lot of people think so, but lot of people are ignorant too."

"Don't they kill chickens, calves and lambs?"

"You even hear stories of them carrying off human babies. But hawks kill a hundred times more rats and mice than they do chickens. The same is true of coyotes. They help control the squirrels, rabbits, woodchucks and raccoons too. I guess out west in sheep country they probably do kill a few lambs every year, but that's part of the price you've got to pay. I don't know where people get the notion that they can reap the benefits of the land for free. That it all belongs to them. Humans sure as shooting don't work for free. You get someone to rid your house of rats and termites or cockroaches, he doesn't do it for nothing, so why do folks think the hawks, eagles and coyotes will. The few chickens or an occasional lamb they take is their share. And they earn it more honestly than a lot of the humans do. Every year the birds and worms take their share of the apples, peaches and dewberries. You plant corn in the garden and the crows and the coons are going to get their part of the harvest, in fact raccoons know better than you when it's ready. There's no getting around it. You've got to pay, and when you think you can get away with not, you're in trouble."

"Makes sense."

"Here's the big pond."

"It is big."

"About ten thousand cubic yards of dirt."

"Covered with Bermuda grass to keep it from washing away."

"And you see that nice clear water in the creek below? Stays that way year-round, except in times of extreme drought."

"It's so beautiful here. Your farm is." Trails off, looks at him, then around over the trees.

Looks away from her. "We better be getting back to the house. We got to unload these fence posts and the wire before we start on the chicken houses." Chicken houses, what is she going to. "I hope. I guess you and Viola can visit some while . . ."

"Uh-uh. I came to visit you. And if cleaning the chicken houses is what you're doing, then that's what I'm going to do."

Looks at her again. "Well. We can always use another hand."

Isadora Faire rolled her sleeves, her pants legs, took off the sandals, picked up a scoop shovel and started moving manure and straw. The pickup backed up against the side of the west chicken-house window, screen removed. Mackey with a pitchfork, Malachi a scoop. Viola drove off to town for groceries.

We carried out the water cans, feed troughs, chickens scattering over the drive to scavenge. Then load the pickup, turning saturated straw heavy vapor moist thick, tossing it through the window into the bed. Isadora streaming sweat. I've got to hand it to her, she went after it like she meant it. When the pickup was full we drove over to the rye patch southeast of the house to spread. I drove while she stood in the back and shoved it out over the terraces. A strong woman. And I was still cussing Sorry for getting me into this. But she would smile, soaked to the skin, joke. She'd look at me sometimes and I wouldn't know what to think.

When we got back Viola was there with a gallon crock of lemonade. I thought Isadora would go help her in the kitchen, but she drank down the lemonade, picked up her scoop and went to loading manure again. Filled up Malachi's pickup, spread it, and Viola brought out a bunch of chocolate chip cookies fresh out of the oven, and we kept on shoveling, each load followed by more lemonade, more cookies, chicken salad sandwiches at noontime, and Isadora kept out there with us all the time.

Afternoon came on hot and still. The air and everything in it seems to vibrate, we're all sopping wet, shirts, trousers, hair. The heat in the coops when you walk in from the outside where now and then a breeze would cool you, would almost buckle your knees with the weight. No one smiling so much anymore, but she doesn't quit. And Viola keeps bringing the lemonade and the cookies.

We got the west house and half the middle one cleaned right before supper time. The sun easing up a little. That time of day when all of a sudden you know you've beaten it. The drop of one degree is all it takes. When it's been ninety-eight it's amazing how cool ninety-five can be. We go down to the barn to get some fresh straw to cover the floors, and she comes along and bucks bales with us.

After we spread the straw over the floor, change the laying cubicles, we all pile into the pickup to head down to the swimming hole to cool off before supper, and it didn't even occur to any of us until we pull up on the rise above and get out and start to strip down. Isadora! We were all halfway embarrassed, Malachi started laughing and she did too. So we have to designate the swimming hole as hers and the big pond as ours, leave her off, and watch in the sideview mirror driving toward the dam, see her walking down the slope unbuttoning the soppy shirt. Come to see me. What has Sorry done.

Viola outdid herself for dinner. Roast pork from the hog they'd butchered, squash, green beans and corn from her garden, tomatoes and potatoes, all from the garden, and home-baked bread, with peach pie from the peaches she'd canned from the truck garden, with homemade tutti frutti ice cream. Only thing storebought was the butter we put on the bread and the n   and sugar in the ice cream. Mighty good.

Isadora had put on a dress after we came back from the swimming hole, her face and arms glowing red from the sun. Tall, strong like Mom, a handsome woman. Wondering I'll bet what sort of yokel, I mean coming all this way to clean chicken houses. We're all sitting in the living room, no one hardly even moving we'd eaten so much, worked so hard. I'm trying to think of something to say, she had hardly said a word at the table, Malachi and I talking about wheat futures and sow bellies. I can't think of anything. Time for the news and weather anyway, so I turn on the TV. Viola and Isadora start talking in the kitchen, come out with coffee, go out on the front porch. Mackey dozed off on the couch, Viola and Isadora sitting, voices drift through the screen, the june bugs trying for the light.

"Have you and Malachi lived here all your life too?"

"Goodness no. We done some serious traveling before we settled here. I was born down in the southeast corner of the state, near Broken Bow. Down where ol King Cotton reigned, used to anyway. My daddy was a tenant farmer, getting by pretty good, never too well off of course, but still. What with the war, World War I, I mean, demand for cotton was high, production went way up, we made a decent living. But after the war things got pretty bad. Not only did demand drop way off, the prices collapsed cause of everybody growing so much, the freight rates were high and set in favor of the eastern processors anyway. Not only all that, but the o boll weevil come to get him some too. Everybody going into debt, and you know the first to hurt is the tenant farmer. Folks started packing up and leaving, looking for greener pastures. People always say the depression started with the great crash of '29, but believe me, Isadora, we saw it practicing long before that."

"What did you do?"

"Well, we moved west. Up near the panhandle. Mom and Dad ended up working a farm between Waynoka and Fort Supply for the owner, one of those still-faced boys, a banker, lived in town. Didn't know too much about growing wheat, but figured we would learn. And did real soon.

"Along about 1927 we was able to buy the place. Seemed like heaven. The prices up, lots of rain, good crops, enough money for the payments and for food and clothes. Dad was proud finally taking care of the family. Well, long about 1935 the dust storms got so bad finally we just couldn't grow anything. And the bank foreclosed on the mortgage. Everybody was talking about California, the promised land, could live out in tents all year-round, plenty of jobs, and the main thing, no dust. So we managed to scrape together enough for an old Ford truck, poured it full of gasoline and loaded on everything we had left, which wasn't much, mostly the furniture the bank didn't think was worth taking and our musical instruments. We used to sing and play a lot back in those days, bout the only thing to do. Sure weren't no crops to be tended on the farm. We'd huddle around the living room, so dark most days we couldn't even see with the lamps burning. Stuffing rags in the cracks around the doors and windows, but that didn't do no good either. Tell stories, talk politics and sing. Mostly to try to drown out the lonesome howling of the wind. We got by on sugar syrup and cornbread. And for variety, we'd roast the cornmeal in the oven to make imitation coffee out of. I remember my uncle, G. O. Palmer, died of the dust pneumonia. He'd gone blind a few years before. We took turns sitting up with him, cover his mouth and nose with a wet cloth to try to protect him from the dust. Good ol G. O. High spirits to the end. Used to play a pretty mean banjo, him and his brothers and cousins played at the inauguration of Governor Our Jack. Anyway, I came in the night he died, could tell it wouldn't be long, saw his banjo hanging on the wall. 'Hey, G. O. You still play the banjo?'

" 'Hell yes. I'd play it for you now if I thought it would do you any good.'

"Last words he ever spoke.

"But like I was saying, when the bank foreclosed in '35 we had no choice, we were dust bowl refugees. So we piled into the Ford, rocking forward and back, rolling from side to side, and headed out for the ol peach bowl. Good lawsy, what a trip. Most things that happened I can remember what, why, when, where. But not who. Me, Mom, my sisters. It's all one big wad of home-churned butter. But I don't think I'll ever forget that trip to California as long as I live on this earth. Headed through the panhandle of Texas, McLean and Amarilla, into New Mexico. We was doing all right until we came to the first mountain pass. Way up yonder on a mountain road, like a bunch of flatlanders never seen, had a breakdown. My dad about to have a nervous bustdown right there on the spot, some feller in a little filling station trading post, said he was a mechanic, said it was engine trouble. Which helped us a whole lot, said he couldn't fix it, didn't have the part. But did allow as how we might be able to find it if we could make it on in to the next town. Course even if we found it we probably couldn't of paid for it, but we didn't have any choice, and the feller said it was downhill all the way in, so Dad decided to coast as far as we could. We all hop out and start pushing, get the Ford rolling, jump in and commence coasting. Picking up speed. Pine trees going by a little faster, starting to blur, hurt my eyes to look at them, Dad a pumping on the brake pedal don't seem to be doing any good, and a hairpin curve. We didn't make it. Man alive, flying over the ditch through the trees, pots pans fiddles and the guitars, little sisters, Mom and me flying, scattered all over the side of that old mountain. I don't know to this day how we kept from all being killed.

"Well, we were about the same as dead. The old Ford sure was. We gathered up whatever we could carry on our backs and started walking, trying to hitch rides. Finally made it into town about half starved and completely wore to a frazzle. It was coming on dark and we had no food nor place to stay. I don't remember how we was paying for gas, cause we sure didn't have cash money. But we did have our instruments, so my sisters and I got out on a street corner, looking real pitiful, and believe me we didn't have to playact very much, wearing the only feedsack dresses we had left. To sing for our supper. Mom and Dad passed the hat, telling our tale of woe, kind of a talking blues, and darn if we didn't get enough for some food out of the performance and a haybarn to sleep in. So that's how we made it on out to California, walking, hitching, and believe me we walked a lot farther than we hitched. And singing.

"But it wasn't no paradise when we got there either. We even had to sneak in. Wouldn't let us cross the border, had to wait till night and crawl through a field like we weren't even Americans. I remember the first night in the state, thinking we'd reached the promised land. Dad snooped around until he found a spud or two and Mom made some slumgullion. Mighty thin stew. Could read a magazine right through it.

"It also turned out all the jobs that were supposed to be out there weren't. The growers had been handing out handbills back home just to get as many people as they could to come out so labor would be cheap. We ended up living in an old shack, lucky to find it at that, made out of orange crates, old car fenders, flattened gallon buckets, pasteboard and a wagon sheet spread over for the roof, out in the middle of a migrant camp on the Sacramento River. What made it so bad, was that we were camped right across the river from a big old peach orchard loaded with peaches that the growers were just letting rot on the trees. You see, the C.I.O. had broke away from the American Federation of Labor and was trying to organize the Okies and Arkies to try to get decent jobs of work and living conditions. And the growers were refusing to hire anybody, thugs were coming around to break up meetings, terrorize the camps. I'm telling you it was hard times for sure. My sisters and I kept singing, but not for our supper anymore, cause everybody in the camp was hard up as we were. But to keep up everybody's spirits, and courage to fight for what was ours. And that's how I met Malachi."

Gets up walks to the door. "Malachi! You and Marcus turn off that durn TV and come on out here on the porch and be sociable." Back to Isadora Faire. "Can I get you some more coffee?"

"Oh no, thank you, Viola. I don't think anything could keep me from sleeping tonight, but I'd better not take any chances."

Malachi and Marcus come out on the porch, dark hot evening. Isadora looks at Marcus, smiles, he turns to the well. "Anyone like some water?" Drops the bucket down. Malachi sits by Viola. Marcus draws the water, offers the dipper dripping to Isadora, she reaches, squirming her knees to avoid water drops, touches his wrist hand, reaching for the handle, and the dipper clatters to the floor. Dark water spreads across the concrete. Marcus retrieves it, Isadora scoots the chair away from the water, nearer the empty chair, he brings more water. She drinks. He sits. Long silence. Crickets and tree frogs.

Bonehead move. Can't even hold on to a water dipper. Some day. Darn Sorry's eyes.

Viola breaks the silence. "I was telling Isadora about the old days, how we met, Malachi."

"I hope you didn't believe everything she said about me."

"Well, she didn't really get to that part. What shouldn't I believe?"

"I wasn't as wild as she tells it."

"Oh. You were wild?"

"I suppose I was wild enough."

"Just how wild were you, Malachi?"

"Those were wild times. You had to be a little wild to keep up. Now my daddy was wild. No doubt about that."

"You grew up in California?"

"Nope. Cromwell, Oklahoma."

"Oh." Pause. "Viola said you met in California."

"Yep. That's right. We did."

Pause. "How did you get to California?"

"Well. That's a long story."

Pause. "I'm listening to stories tonight."

"Well. My daddy was in the land business back in Cromwell, buying and selling, and could whup anybody he couldn't outtrade. So we were doing all right until one day somebody come roaring into town all covered black, yelling they'd hit it, a gusher, struck oil, we're rich, the whole town is gonna be rich! And Cromwell, and me, my daddy were never the same again."

"Why's that?"

"It became a boom town. Over night the streets seemed to jam full of mule teams and wagons carrying boilers, drilling rigs, lumber, iron and steel and pipes. The streets and saloons filled up with mule skinners, roughnecks, roustabouts, tong buckers, block-and-tackle men. And more saloons, and bars and gambling houses to take up the money being made in the oil fields as fast as it was brought into town. Whores, dope pushers, bootleggers, gamblers, speculators. Nothing but noise and fistfights. And bankers. Real estate men. The real sharks. And my daddy had met his match. He couldn't outtrade them. And couldn't get close enough to fight.

"But it sure seemed great at first, especially to a young kid like me. Could think of nothing better than rolling up my sleeves with the tough men I saw streaming into town and making my fortune. I mean, these were men right off the farm, tougher than an old boot, born working gonna die working, and if there's work to do, we'll get it done, work until we drop, put up a forest of derricks, drill down into the ground until you hit oil, tap it off, and set to pumping, keep those cars and buses, factories and big eastern cities running, then move on to the next town broke as when you come, to Smackover, Arkansas, Bristow, Oklahoma, Drumright, Sand Springs, Bow Legs, Kilgore, Texas, Longview, Burke-Burnett, Electra. Wherever. And after they leave, there's sure not much left.

"You'd see the rivers and creeks suddenly start flowing black, swirling in the current, sun reflected golden rainbows churning with the turmoil of the dying fish. The grass dying, the grapevine, then the trees along the shore. The fishermen sitting helpless along the gray dead bank, among empty whiskey bottles and a broken-down hay rake, to see the belly-up fish and oil-soaked boards drift slow in dog-day heat and stench that filled up the countryside. The smell of oil, the smell of money, smell of death.

"One day a well blew right on the outskirts of town, boiling oil and fire a hundred feet into the air, catching the next and the next, sludge ponds, seemed like the earth itself aflame, till it reached the shotgun boardinghouses. Firetraps if there ever were ones. Mazes of cardboard, tarpaper and cheap dry lumber, whipping up a convection wind roaring through those shacks like they was made of kindling. I don't know how it kept from killing every man woman and child living in them. Mostly young girls come to town, boom-chasers, looking for work or adventure, some kind of job, taken advantage of, turn on to alcohol and dope and turned out on the streets by the vermin that swarm wherever money's fast and easy. But most people made it out of town all right. A few old folks and drunks lost, but most of us made it to the hill outside of town to watch the fire spread, cracking popping from one building, one street to the next. Watched the trees wither and explode. The night red golden roily domed blue black flowing embers drift and eddy like miracle stars and comet tails. A fine dank ashy mist falling down wind. And pale smoky dawn. The town was gone.

"Daddy drifted off to Texas, had relatives there. I followed the boom awhile, but like I said, there's not much left for a working-man to do after the oil field is in. And the early thirties filling the skies with dust. Depression. I did what I could, which sometimes wasn't much. Even acted for a while. Well, one time. For an auctioneer who went around the countryside selling repossessed farms. He had such a hard time attracting buyers. Can you imagine that. You had trouble attracting interest in farmland. So what he did was put on a little tent show to gather a crowd. A string band, and a few playactors to do a skit, and then he'd try to auction off the land. Well, this one time I thought I'd give it a try, promised us meals and a dollar, something like that, and we all piled into the back of his truck and headed out for some godforsaken panhandle town, Hardesty I think it was. I played the banker. That was before I had my beard. Didn't grow that till I was riding the rails out to California. That was 1935.

"My daddy had ended up in Pampa, Texas. He ran a boardinghouse. So I went down there and worked for a while as maintenance man for him, mostly sweeping up dust. That old building could hardly be called a building, the dust choking everybody out, town dead, old folks dead and babies dying, people leaving out for California. And I remember back in 1935 a big old dust storm filled the sky. April fourteenth it was. Daddy hadn't been able to pay me in over a month, and I looked up and saw that old black dirt, the entire western half of Kansas and most of eastern Colorado rolling in, look back down at the fine sifting dust in front of my broom, spit a mudball poof into it, tossed the broom aside, went and found my daddy and told him I'd had it, heading to California on the next thing smoking, so long, it's been good to know yuh. And walked out to the highway and stuck my thumb up into the heart of that old black blizzard.

"The last time I saw my daddy alive.

"I jumped a freight, along with about eighty other men, in New Mexico. Bout killed myself hanging on the iron ladder between the cars to keep out of the wind, till my hands almost froze, fingers lose their grip and slip and fall, and those old iron wheels rolling over you and the iron wouldn't even make a funny noise. Got beat up by railroad dicks in Albuquerque, had to bum frijoles and rice to get me on to the jungle camps of California. And things out west almost made the dust storms look good.

"But that's where I met Viola. Coming into camp one night raising Cain, a bunch of us coming in from an organizing meeting, and we saw her and her sisters singing out in the middle of camp, down by the one water spigot for the whole several thousand of us there. And everybody calmed right on down. And I knew right then and there I'd found my bride."

"Aw, Malachi, you sure can tell some tales. Once you get started. It was some mighty stormy courting, Isadora, before." Looks closely. "Well, I'll be. The poor woman is sound asleep in her chair. Dead to the world. That's the usual effect of your stories, Malachi."

Marcus stands, yawns. "I doubt she was expecting to work all day scooping out chicken houses."

"She sure did a whale of a job."

Looking at her asleep in the chair. "Sure did that."

Viola stands. "Well, Malachi, I hate to wake her up, but we better be going. She's got to catch a bus tomorrow early, and we got another coop to do."

"She sure did a whale of a job. And a handsome woman too." Standing above on the dark porch. Looking. Handsome woman. Come to see me.

The next morning I dragged out of bed, hardly slept at all, got to go pick her up at Malachi and Viola's and take her into the city to get her bus back home. I dreaded seeing her. Almost decided to call Malachi and ask him to take her for me, make some excuse about work to do. But I went to face her feeling like a fool.

As I stepped out the door I saw her walking down the road toward the house, shoes in her hands. Could hear her singing, puffs of red dust drifting across the fence row each step she took. She saw me and started running along the mulberry, right up to me.

"Marcus. I've never slept better in my life. Sorry I fell asleep last night on the porch, the stories were so interesting. But I was dead tired, and it was so peaceful out there. It was a tremendous day. Your farm is beautiful. I had a great time. I'm coming back as soon as I can."

And she kissed me on the cheek.

I just stood there like a bonehead fool. Realizing all I've ever done all my life is work.

Sorry Picks Up
Where He Left

THEY work all day. Each time Isadora Faire came to visit, the same thing. Marcus would curse the bonehead foolishness of it all on the way to the bus station, but Isadora Faire came to join right in, sleeves rolled up and bandana tied around her head. She gathered eggs, cleaned and candled them, loaded hay, gathered brush. Even road construction, she learned to handle the tractor and drag-bucket, cutting off the crown of the hill east of the house. Better visibility for cars meeting at the top. Marcus stern, excited, giving instructions leaning over her, feel the breathing, the pounding of the heart, his hand on hers to shift to a lower gear. Short weekend stays, always sleeping at Viola and Malachi's place. Always rushed to make the bus, dread another two weeks, another month at the hospital, settling down in a window seat for the dark empty bus ride north. Isadora Faire would try to think about it, Marcus and the awkward goodbye kiss at the boarding gate, about what she wanted. But the diesel engine rumble, moon flat prairie gliding through green blue glass bus windows, thought dissolved restless, exhausted into sleep.

When her two-week vacation came in the spring, she spent the whole time on the farm. They put in the truck garden, she planted petunias, morning glories, iris around the house. Made the place look like someone lived here. Laughed and sweated. She bought Marcus trunks, the first of his life, and they swam in the swimming hole. Attended an ice cream social and bake sale at the Methodist Church. But did not talk about what each was wondering, trying to decide.

On the last night before she was to leave, both of them agitated all day long. Wild spring night, violent thunderstorms, tornadoes moving through, filling up the house, electricity gone, intense and concentrated fitful discharges throw borders of trees around the rooms and leach the yellow orange kerosene lamplight, thunder rattles the dishes in the living room buffet, crashing hail, branches stripped leaves scream slashing across the yard booming over the watershed. The telephone lines are out. And finally they go down into the cellar.

Soaked to the skin. Marcus fidgets in the night dark damp dirt, last summer's remnant potatoes onions turnips apples dusty Mason jars, egg crates, cob web, candle flame. They sit. Hailstones pounding on the tin cellar door. Marcus up to check the storm again, wind, water and ice bouncing down the passageway when he raises up the door bucking in the turbulence to look. Isadora Faire watches him in the lightning flashes, shirt and trousers adhere, back and buttocks. Down the stairs. Excited. Frightened. But not of the storm.

Sudden thunderclap, reflex Isadora Faire grabs his arm. He looks at her. "Isadora?"

"What?"

Almost yelling against the crashing hailstones and wind. "Will you marry me?"

She sits there shivering. They sit there. The hailstorm swells and ebbs, then dissipates. Rain, distant thunder and silence. They sit. Water dripping around the hinges of the cellar door.

"Mom had a vision of what the land could be. And I've worked hard to fulfill it for her. But no matter how hard I've worked, there's always been something wrong. I hardly had time to think about it. Ever since Blanchefleur. Until you came along. I haven't been alone. With. Someone like you, with a woman since. Since I was in high school. Like I told you, me and Jessie Edwards. I know all my work will go for nought if. But I think she would approve of you. If you would . . ."

They sit. Isadora Faire trying to decide. What did she want, why did she keep coming down here, if not for this. Marcus, looking straight across the candlelit cellar to the eggs she had packed the week before. Water trickling from the edges of the arc above the passageway, collect and rivulet along the red-dirt-stained stone sides of the steps. Water soaking down the earthen walls. Cold heavy humid air. She turns. Reaches a hand to his face, must decide, the bus ride back, the hospital, 31 years old, a farm, flowers pounded into mud outside, the land. Marcus. A big strong man. Turns his face, her arms around his shoulders, his arms, hands and stubby thumb.

"Marcus. I think. Yes. I would marry you."

Sorry, Billy Paul and Bob removed the headers from the combines, cleaned, loaded, chained them down to the truck beds, another harvest done. Pulled into the parking lot of Bill's Tavern north of Grassy Butte, North Dakota, where they'd camped the last ten days cutting. Eighteen, nineteen hours a day. Last night. Shoot a little friendly snooker, drink a few beers, laugh and talk a lot. And touch football with a roll of toilet paper in the pasture behind against the bartender, his two cousins, and his brother-in-law on Sorry's team. And thrashing sleep on iron cots beneath a wagon sheet slung between the Ford and GMC. Folding northern lights flow across the sky.

Sunrise still crisp cold. Breakfast in the trailer. And Sorry watches them pull out south and gone. He climbs in the '31 Chevy, heads out west, steady rise with the light, ten miles, high plains shortgrass pasture. Turns through an iron pipe cattle guard and half a mile to the cow hoof cobbled ground around a windmill, water-tank and salt licks. Prickly pears and cow chips. Stripped off his dusty jeans underwear and sleeveless shirt and washed the car. Singing. Already hot thin air. Then plunged into the tank.

Feeling real good about it all right now. After weeks on the old Gleaner, binful by binful, reelslats, sickle bar, auger, cylinder, straw-walker, straw-spreader, engine interweave vibrating the hands and wrists, the buttocks, thighs and feet. The mind empties out. Total trance, happier every time they unloaded on the go. Even getting along better with Malachi. Some burden removed. The wedding to be in the Methodist Church and Sorry to pick up Isadora Faire on his way back south from North Dakota. The scheme had worked goddamn. Marcus had a wife.

Haven't felt this goddam good since before finding out who the hell Marcus is in the first place. College degree. No plans. Windmill blades creaking rotation pump churning rattle and bangs. Spouting water, floating on his back two-tone brown face and arms, white chest and belly and legs farmer tan, morning sun. Hair drifting from the head among the moss. Alone in the universe. Just me and the waterdogs. A hemisphere, blue, one lone contrail eternity across, peaceful warm emptiness in the world.

Sorry pulled into the drive of the apartment house where Isadora Faire lived. Past the pool, the clubhouse. The barbecue grills. Late afternoon. Hot. Long drive, anticipation, excitement growing inverse to the distance, the scheme had worked. The city limits unbearable, broke out talking to himself. See Isadora Faire. Talk in the flesh. Marcus' wife from letters, the picture. At the door. Feeling very absurd. Pushed the doorbell. It'll be all right once we've met. Has to be. They're getting married. I'm the nephew. Whatever she knows, finds out, she knows. If she looks like the picture. Footsteps muffled behind the door, hand on the knob, stomach floats, breath, knees almost gone blond hair face.

"Hi." Looks hard at me. "Sorry. I can tell."

It is her! I mean really her! The nurse. "That's right."

"Come on in. How was the drive?"

Don't move. Can't really be her, get serious, an application in a computer goddamn standing right here in the door. "Not too bad."

Awkward silence. "It seems funny, like I know you." He looks away again wanting to run. "A long. Like. Well, from what I've heard people say, I guess you just fit the picture I have of you in my mind like the picture of your mother on the buffet at the farm. Come on in."

She looks hard at him in the dim hallway, beckons into the

light. She turns smoothly into the living room. *The nurse at the hospital.* Beckons him again. And he steps uncertain out of the corridor. *No doubt about it. It's her. Does she?* Holds back. *Make up your mind. Run or follow.*

She sits opposite a coffee table and chair. He follows. Sits in the chair. Looks around. She casts a breath. Smiles. "Can I get you something, Sorry? A beer? Some wine?"

"A beer. A beer would be great."

Watches her walk. Refrigerator door, poptop. Sorry looks around. Room empty. A couple of suitcases by the door. Surge of mirth and panic. Anxiety? Premonition? Jealousy? She saw the pictures. Heard the stories. Alone with Marcus at the farm. How many times. Unbelievable. Marcus. What would he say. Marcus. Reaching out to touch her. Sitting, a can of beer in front, sitting opposite. "Afraid all the glasses are packed." Sorry smiles, almost laughs, raises the can in salute, *she doesn't know me with hair.* And drains it half. He laughs. "Welcome to the family."

"Thank you. Nephew." Looks at him in toast, looks down at her feet. Pause. "Are you hungry?"

Elbows on knees, beer can, both hands between. She's about to laugh herself. *Does she know?* Looking for her eyes. "I suppose I could eat a little something."

Eyes to the kitchen. "I don't have a thing in the house. We'll have to go out somewhere."

"Sounds good to me."

Eye contact. He smiles. She smiles. "My uncle has a bar and grill in Mud Butte. It's a pretty drive out that way."

Leaning slumped back, *ain't this something, relax now.* "McMorold I'll bet."

"How did you know?"

Bolts upright spilling beer. "What!"

"That's him."

"You're kidding!"

"No. How did you know?"

"Goddamn." Scratches nose with middle finger of hand holding the beer can hiding his face behind. "I mean ain't that something. Small world. I. I stopped in there once. A few years ago. When we were pulling through on the harvest. That's all. A few years ago."

255

"It is a small world all right." Looks at him sharply.

Jumps up. "Sure is, you can say that again, small world, excuse me, where's the bathroom?"

"Through there to the right."

Steps in, locks the door. Cold sweat. Too much. Hand trembling slightly. What the hell you gonna do now. Looks in the mirror and laughs. She doesn't recognize, head shaved, dark sunken circles. But how long before she does? And McMorold will. Sits down on the toilet lid, chin resting in the palm of the hand. Got to come out sometime. Can't sit here forever. Crash out the window. Tell her it's a mistake, wrong house, I was looking for some other Isadora. But I can keep from going to Uncle McMorold's tavern. Can only push things so far.

Starts to the door, stops, back to flush the toilet, then one more grin into the mirror, and strides confident and ebullient back to Isadora Faire. "I tell you what. It's been a long day, and we got a long day tomorrow. Why don't we just go someplace close. I can imagine I'll suffer quite a sinking spell after I eat."

Looks for the eyes. "Okay. You have to meet Mother anyway. She won't be off till eleven. I know a place near here."

Eye contact again. Look at each other awhile. Laugh. "Well. Let's hit it."

They sat at a table near the piano, played by a short wavy gray-haired old man banging out old tunes with apparent introverted abandon. The place filled up quickly, men in casual suits, women chattering along. Junior Chamber of Commerce salesmen at local farm equipment dealers, plant supervisors at the Cargill elevator, young lawyers, businessmen and wives, and a few clusters of singles, out for a good time.

Sorry, wearing sunglasses now even in the dark restaurant, leaning over closer to Isadora Faire as the noise level rises. Trying to explain his view of Marcus. And having a little trouble at it. "You see, Marcus has spent his whole life struggling and doesn't know, notice that things are changing in the world. The small farmer is being pushed out by big business."

"Yes, he does. He talked about it a lot in his letters to me."

Letters. Goddam. "Well. Yeah. But he. I mean."

"What do you mean?" Looks at him grinning over her gin and tonic. "I almost think you don't want me to marry him." Playfully pushes him on the shoulder.

"No. I guess I'm just talking to myself."

"What are you going to do after the wedding, Sorry, now that you've graduated?"

"Oh, I don't know." *I don't know.* "College hasn't cleared up anything." *Letters. You to me to you.* "Just turned over more questions. Like a oneway plow churning up ants and grubs, wolf spiders swarming with million-legged young on the back. Stirring up dust covering your face so a row of teeth is all that's recognizable. Each round, each semester more."

"What do you mean?"

"I've been told the world's a simple proposition. But look. Confrontations on the high seas. Churches bombed. All kind of people giving wild speeches, people shot down everywhere you look. Canisters of poison enough for the entire universe sunk in the sea. Cause the metal won't rust out for five hundred years." *Letters, you to me not Marcus.* "What is the cause and what's the effect? I don't know, is the world losing its mind because I've lost mine, or is it me losing mine cause it's lost its?"

Sighs. "I know what you mean." Looks at him a long time. "You'll have to stay around the farm. I really like you."

Must have been crazy to ever think. "Who knows." *What the hell.* "I like you too, Isadora. I'm glad I." *Damn.* "I met you."

"Me too. Nephew."

What's going on? "I'm not going to call you Auntie."

"I'm not that old."

"But Marcus is." *Shouldn't have said.*

"You know he's twice the man half his age."

Damn. Getting out of hand. "Wait a minute, wait a minute."

Long pause. She looks at him smiling, almost laughing, leans in close. "Are you sure we've never met before, I swear I've known you. Somebody. You remind me of somebody."

Sorry looks down. Away. Drinks his beer. Looks over to the piano player jangling a song to completion. A group of young men come in, looking around in the dark. Silence falls a measure or two. Five of them, dressed in jeans, khakis, overalls, T-shirts, sweatshirts. The old man at the piano stares hostilely as they sit at the bar by the jukebox machine, back down at the keyboard. Sorry looks back at Isadora Faire looking at him in thought. Slaps his hand on the tabletop. "I know what. A song for my new aunt." Leaning over to the piano. "Heh, man. Play something we can sing."

The player rears back startled. Looks at Sorry. Sorry smiles, repeats the request. Short muscular arms place stubby-fingered hands on the keyboard, run a progression up the keys. He smiles wrinkling the high forehead sunburnt face around narrow deepset green eyes. "You know, ever since we won the war it's hard to find a song we all can sing."

Rearing back startled. "Tell me about it."

"Yep. Since then we've thought we could whip the world, and by God bout got away with thinking it. And now you'll not find a bigger bunch of spoiled sons of bitches on the face of this earth than the 'Mericans. You go to these plants around here, they talking about what we need to get the company going is some salesmen, some supersalesman. At the tractor plant, one of the tractor wheels has a stripped lug, they don't replace the lug, they throw the whole goddam wheel away, and think they're smart doing it. Over to the grain elevator when they have to put new cups in the legs, they just rip out all the elevator bolts and throw them away. Hell. Put in brand-new ones. There's always some supersalesmen to bring in some more. No stopping it. But I tell you we've worked her into a tizzy. Why, it's so bad. You want to know how bad things are today?"

"Let's hear it."

"If I get cold sitting around the house, I got to get up and walk. Walk. All the way down the hall and turn a little knob to get some heat. That's how bad things are today."

"That bad, huh."

"Why, the other day I went to the grocery store, the damn door didn't open for me until I was within three feet of it!"

"Three feet."

"That's how bad things are. And the last straw. I need to take a crap. Right here in this very restaurant, and I go to the bathroom. And the goddam toilet paper! Is the wrong color. Now that's how bad things are today."

"That's pretty bad all right. But let's see what we can do. You lead and I'll follow."

"Yep. The damn paper's the wrong color."

"Lead on, piano player."

"Okay." Launching into elaborate intro arpeggiations up and down the keys. "From this valley they say you are roaming." Sorry harmonizing. "I will miss your bright eyes and sweet smile."

Sorry stumbles mutters and hums his way. After the first verse and chorus the old man stops and looks at him. "I like your spirit, son, but we better get us anothern. How's this?"

Eases into "I Dream of Jeannie with the Light. Brown. Hair." Sorry lays a high tenor right on him, hangs in for a measure or two before reduced to humming again, and distracted by someone at the bar howling like a dog. The piano player snorts something under his breath, hits a quick transition into "When You And I Were Young, Maggie." Sorry shakes his head, they try "Down by the Old Mill Stream." Got it so good, do it one more time. Isadora growing uneasy. Gawking and giggling from the bar and other tables. But two old farmers join Sorry at the piano, divide bass and baritone between them and hit it again, ignoring for the time being the rude noises. The piano player hoots his approval, produces a song book from under the piano bench, and they work their way through a closely harmonized rendering of "The Whiffenpoof Song." Isadora applauds, but cannot outdo the yells and calls for a doctor, must be someone dying, from the bar. The quartet glare at the offenders briefly, but turn back to "Galway Bay" as the first quarter drops in the juke lighted up blue green and red, a long scaled dragon curling around the selection window breathing fire belching triple forte into the room she wore a itsie bitsie teenie weenie yellow polka dot bikini.

The old man slams his hands down on the keys goddam ignorant chuckleheads. Sorry looks from one to the other. Stalks over to the machine dragon breathing fire and rejects the button behind, stirring up loud complaining all around. He raises his hands and everyone strangely falls silent, looking at him pacing rapidly back and in front of the blue green red juke box. "We. Were singing. If you all want to, listen. Or better yet, join in. Please, at least, keep your loose change to yourselves and out of this machine."

"I've heard better sound coming from a dry bearing."

Starts to respond, thinks better of it, grins at the feller, a red-headed feller. Returns to the piano. The old man hits a chord. Sorry puts a hand on his shoulder, winks at Isadora.

She sits wondering what is going on. The taunts from the bar, the strong blond-headed boy. Man. Not much younger than. Oblivious to. Starting to sing again. "Sweet Adeline." Just wish I knew from where, where I've seen, who he reminds me of. Singing, surly crowd shouting insults, laughing, dropping money in the slot again punching buttons red green blue blurbing electric dragon music into the room drowning out the song.

I'm going to marry his uncle on a farm.

What have I. Strange. My own hometown gone violent strange, the blond stranger striding to the jukebox again dropping down behind as the jeaned sweatshirted redhead lunges, look out! reject, knocking against the wall, shoving chest to chest, shuffle standoff. Arms and necks flex tense hard breathing face to face. "Buddy, that was my goddam money you just wasted."

Staring silent, barmaid near panic rounds the bar as if to separate. I shout out, "Sorry, don't," piercing the silence knocking my drink over. He looks at me and smiles. The other hulk seems terrified momentarily. Sorry looks back at him, at the poor bargirl, dishtowel in hand. "Too bad to waste your money, friend." Reaching in his pocket, pulls out his wallet, fishes out a dollar bill, hands it to the girl. "Change this for me, and kindly give this feller his two bits back. And then me and my friends can get back to some serious singing."

She looks perplexed at the bill, at the man's sweatshirt, shrugs and returns to the register for the change. Sorry returns "Excuse me" past the feller to the piano.

I'm trembling, trying to sop up gin and tonic with the doily. My nephew. Surely he's not going to start. Singing. Singing. My God.

The whole quartet on the downbeat, "Wait Till the Sun Shines, Nellie." Such glee on the old piano man's face, banging away, crooning lead like he's never sung. The bargirl returns to the man in the sweatshirt still standing in front of the music machine eyeing the glowing dragon snorting flames. She hands him the quarter, brings the rest over and plunks it down in front of me.

The drop of the quarter in the slot. The close harmony of the quartet. Flashing blue green red dragon lights, the whirr of the electric-driven stylus, the clank of record withdrawal, Sorry's high tenor. Electric prerecord silence. A golden oldie. You ain't nothin but the quartet stops hound dog. Sorry looking over at the man at the dragon machine.

The redhead nods one time, lips curling down. Sorry turns to his singers, whispers something. I raise a hand as if to prevent. Sorry walking past the man to the bar, turning and smiling at the man, at the bargirl, at me, even waves. Then jumps up on the bar. Gasps and cries around the stools. The redhead backs away from the machine. And Sorry leaps. Hair streaming, shoulders raised. Legs and feet extended then tucking beneath at the apogee. Shoulders relaxed downward parabola floating hair, shirt rippling up over torso stomach muscles. Knees extending slightly. Body reclining, angling down. Toes rising, heels making contact with the selection window right below the dragon spitting flame. Legs kick straight down, Plexiglas giving, shatters, Elvis screaming electrical flashing, feet on the records through the records, sparks and smoke flying up around the waist disappearing in blinding light scarring retinas, smoke clogged, electrical burned rubber, plastic, terminal red dragon fire explosion reverberates to total darkness. Silence.

I sit numb. Blind. Eyes closed to shut out floating images green blue red in my brain. Silence. The chair scrapes beside me. I open my eyes. Slowly the glow of blond hair, smell sweat, electricity, melted chemical. Sorry grins in the darkness, hands me something across the wet tabletop. "I have slain the beast. I have the miscreant's tongue, m'lady. I have won your hand."

I look closely at the tangled plastic, light metal and wire. The arm and stylus from the dragon box.

What have I done. How the hell can I explain to Mother. He tore up what? He jumped from the bar, with both feet? And you're going to marry his uncle? What? Make up some story maybe. The dance floor collapsed, he stepped into an open manhole, the bruises abrasions contusion and lacerations are merely stigmata, nothing to worry about, that he's afflicted with periodically. And his uncle isn't crazy at all. I mean, he didn't even know him until a few years ago. You see his mother ran off with a. I mean she. He's had an unusual life in many respects and. Yes. He jumped from the bar with both feet and destroyed the jukebox. But Marcus is a kind gentle man, hardworking. Loves his farm. The land. I want to marry him. It's right. It will work, it has to. Doesn't it, Mother. Won't it, Mother?

How can you help me, Mama? Left alone to raise me by yourself. Left by the itinerant sign-painting womanizer. Big robust warm jolly mama. Throw back your head and laugh. All you ever wanted from life was a good time. And how many good times raising me working the graveyard shift at Regional? How many times since laughing happy I was conceived?

Mother.

Threw back her head and laughed. Large solid woman. White shoes, white stockings, white dress. "You did what? Bout time someone shut that thing down. Was it Les playing the piano?"

"Yes, Mama."

"Good o Les. I'll bet it did him a world a good to see that. How you feeling, son?"

"Well. My socks seem to be soaked with blood a little."

"Well, Isadora, honey, you'd better take care of this boy. I'll run the tub full of hot water. I declare. Jumped right on it, huh?"

"Yes, ma'am."

"Good Lord. I know Les liked that. You get in that tub, and I'll cook up something to eat."

Looked at Sorry and laughed as she turned to the bathroom to draw a tub of water.

Sorry tenderly removed the clothes. The jeans torn, singed. Looked over the legs and rump. Red black coagulated streams. A serious gash or two. Stepped into the water, stood ah-ohing, looking at the feet, the water turning red around ankles. Slowly settled down. Hot water stinging. Settled stretched. Still until it soothed. Leaned back closing the eyes to float.

Sudden rush cold across the face jerked up his head as Isadora Faire entered the room. Holding a syringe and ampule. Stood above him in the fog looking. His hands sudden impulse to clutch, relaxing forearm muscles sunbrown. Shoulders, pectoral abdominal red in hot blood-tinged water, flowing buoyant under lifting. Scrotum and penis. Looked. Thighs and knees. Scratches. One slice along the left knee. Skin gone from the right shin. Looked at the feet. She looked hot water and blood dilating nostrils. Long enamel tub standing white on curled clawed legs, wrought German spigot silver. Red water. Brown and red, blond hair. Dark curling floating. Hair. "Turn over."

Symmetric musculature. The spine. Buttock, bleeding, thighs, calves. She sits on the edge of the tub, trails fingertips in water, lightly touches the gluteus. The laceration. "You're all right."

"You think I'll live."

"You'll live. A suture or two and I'll give you a tetanus shot."

"I got medicine in the—"

"Hold still." Draws the vaccine, squirts, dabs alcohol, jabs the needle into the rump. "There you go."

"That was a hell of a tenor I was singing."

"Hell of a tenor. Where do you keep your clothes?"

"In the duffelbag in the back of the car."

She walked out through the house to the car. Opened the back door. Stopped. Stepped back and looked at it. Black. Chevrolet. Old. Reached into the back for the duffelbag and saw stainless steel under a blanket. Singing. My God. Pulled it aside. The guitar my God it can't be. It can't be. Old Chevy. It's him.

Stood there confused, disbelieving, believing it can't be it's him. Beat up my uncle. The hospital. Blond hair, singing, County Commissioner Krupp. Talking dark nightlit. About an old maid aunt. Children. Land. But how? Orphan? Could it be him. Beating up, running from the sheriff. Violent. Tonight. So shy, gentle singer. Thug.

And Marcus is his uncle. What will I do?

Stood with the duffelbag in one hand, guitar in the other fighting off tears and panic. Slowly turned toward the house, slowly up the stairs to the bathroom. Stood trembling before the door. Then pushed in with the duffelbag and guitar. Stood watching. Hot water, blood skin. Flaccid floating naked man lying in the tub. Wanted by the sheriff. Violent. Dangerous.

"Who are you anyway?" He looks from the guitar to her. "What are you doing here? Again."

Long pause. "I've come to get you. For my uncle. Marcus, to marry Marcus."

"But you beat up my Uncle McMorold. You're wanted for robbery, assault and battery. For property damage tonight. I should call the cops."

Rises up water shattering. Rests his hands on his knees. Constant dripping from the spigot plunking. "If that's what you want to do. But don't you want to hear my side of it? Before you decide I did wrong. I mean your uncle was challenging everyone, taking all their money. Fair and square. Well, he challenged me. And I beat him fair and square. But he wasn't going to give me the money. Now what am I supposed to do?" Pause. She looks uncertain at him, along the shoulders, arms hands, knees and thighs. "I mean, I'm at your mercy here. Do what you think is right. And remember, it was him that cracked my skull first with a cue."

Long pause. Hesitation. "What I want to know is what you're doing here now."

Smiles. "I'll admit when I sent the computer the." Stops.

She looks at him sharply, waiting for him to continue. He doesn't. "What did you say?"

"I . . ."

"About the computer."

He sinks back in the water.

She looks at him. Steps toward the tub. "You. You sent in to the computer. Marcus' name? You wrote all those letters!" Almost screaming, brandishing the guitar. "I ought to drown you in the goddam bathtub!"

Stomps her foot, Sorry flinches, bangs the guitar, metallic discord, on the floor, stomps out the door, back in, slamming it behind, grabs a bar of Ivory soap from the sink, hurls it splashing barely missing Sorry cowered in the tub, pulls down all the towels and washcloths, slams down the toilet lid and sits down hard, burying her face in her hands. Tense silence. Pulls yards of toilet paper, dabs the eyes. Then quiet. "I can't believe it. Goddamn you. You did it all, not Marcus. How could I be so dumb. What the hell am I to think now? What in the world is going on?"

Sits. Water vapor swirling quietly around the light above the clouded mirror. Rhythmic dripping. Water rustling in the tub. Sorry finally pulls the plug. Stands stiffly. Takes a towel from the floor, begins gingerly around the lacerations and abrasions. She sits looking at him. Sniffing. Eyes meet. "I guess it's not too late to call the whole thing off. Wouldn't blame you none if you did. You could explain it all to your mother, your friends. Your boss at the hospital. But before you do, Isadora, remember. I wasn't there when you met Marcus on the farm. All those visits. I had nothing to do with that."

Watches him dry. Finally gets up, opens the medicine cabinet, takes out a bottle of iodine, holds it in her hand a moment. Then sets it on the basin and leaves.

Sorry walked next morning uncertain, sore, down to breakfast. Sweating. Isadora's mother singing in the kitchen, bustled out, hugged him. "Sit down honey, I'll have ham and eggs ready in a jiffy. Here's some juice. This is the big day. Isadora going off to get married. Never thought I'd see the day. Good Lord. Going to be a hot one too. Already bout ninety out. Isadora'll be right here, you just make yourself at home, Sorry, and we'll have breakfast before you all leave. Mighty hot day for traveling I can tell you that. Mighty hot."

She went off singing into the kitchen. Sorry sat, drank the juice. At least the mother still thinks things are normal. Footsteps on the porch. The front door opens. Isadora Faire carrying two suitcases. Wearing a sleeveless short dress. Moving smoothly through the living room. Legs and hips, breasts, hair. Glowing slight perspiration. Looks sternly at Sorry. "I'm ready."

He swallows, nods. The platter of eggs, ham, tomatoes is carried in. They eat in silence, only Isadora's mother talking. Recounting the whirlwind romance, the handsome signpainter. The birth of Isadora.

Tears finally came as Sorry carried the suitcases out to the car. Hugging and kissing, promising letters, visits. "Mama, we'll see eath other in a week at the wedding."

"Of course. I almost forgot. Sorry, I have something for the reception I want you to take in your car. A case of champagne. For the wedding night. Here in the garage."

Sorry and Isadora look at each other for the first time. "Champagne. Oh. Well. That's very nice."

Put the wine in the car, and they were on their way. Hot. Silent. Windy trip heading south.

The first hundred miles not a word. Isadora Faire staring straight out the window. Wind tossing hair about the back of her head. Sorry whistling to himself, singing inaudible tunes. Waiting for someone to talk.

Highway rippling heatwave mirages, dust billowing out of the ditches. Trucks laden with combines, pickups pulling trailers sway swerving, fighting headwind. Sky blue brown over stubbled fields. Heat. Dust.

The second hundred miles. Rings of mud on necks and forehead. Isadora Faire falls into troubled sleep. Sorry observes cautiously. Trying to think of something to say.

Lunch in a small town roadside hamburger joint. Thermometer

nailed to the awning post over the sidewalk at the local bank 105°. Clouds of dust gusting by the plate-glass window rattling. Sorry looks at Isadora Faire. Her eyes avoiding. Eating without tasting greasy bunned burger, lettuce tomato pickles grilled onions, french fried potatoes. Chocolate malt. Surreptitious glances at Sorry. He finishes off his cheeseburger, wipes sweat from his eyes with a napkin. Leans back in the booth, clears his voice. "You know, Isadora, this sure is strange."

Jarred by the sudden voice. "What."

"This whole thing is strange."

"Oh."

"Your uncle, my uncle, you and me, all tied together by a computer."

Looks at him for the first time directly. "You really are the guy on my ward bothering the commissioner with your guitar."

"Yep. That was me."

"Damn. That's. That's more than strange."

"It's a small world."

"That's not the half of it."

"So why are you mad at me?"

"Why am I mad at you! Beat up my uncle! You court me under false pretenses! You. Confuse everything. You."

"But nothing's false. I just helped Marcus out. You met him, you're going to marry Marcus. My letters are no more false than the computer introduction you sent off for. At least a human being wrote them."

"But don't you see I don't know if it's. I just don't know."

Flops the hamburger crescent on the plate, rubs her cheekbone, looks out the window. The empty street. Sorry doodles a french fry in ketchup. Swallows it. Another. Looks at her. She turns. A grimace, almost smile. Sorry wads a napkin, set shot across the table into her empty malt glass. "Come on, Isadora. A little random chaos can't get you down. I could tell you about random chaos. It takes on a pattern. In fact, I've seen so much that this seems normal to me."

"Well, it doesn't to me."

"What do you think all those computer riffs are you worked with in the hospital? The computer finds patterns in the chaos of data, statistics, correlations, and people make decisions accordingly. The Datamate computer did the same thing, and what's more there seems to be a big computer in the sky, the ultimate computer, omniprogrammed, doing the same thing with us poor units of measure condemned to live out our lives within its parameters. Take that truck driver over there eating his hot roast beef sandwich. Think of the mind-boggling coincidences, the string of haphazard events that led to our being in this roadside greasy spoon at the same time. Any slight change in any of the chain and we wouldn't be here together. If he would have overslept, if I hadn't stopped for gas five miles back, if his parents hadn't moved from Arkansas when he was six because the house burned down when the dog knocked over the kerosene lamp chasing the cat they'd found half drowned in a gunnysack, if you hadn't sent in your name to the computer, if I hadn't started shooting snooker with Sapulpa Slim, if my mother hadn't had a flat near El Reno, Oklahoma, or the man from whose truck the nail had fallen's mother hadn't decided to marry Jake instead of Manard, if Jakes's great-great-grandmother would have had a headache that night. It's a goddam miracle our path happens to cross with that truck driver, and his crosses with the cow he's eating now. Except we don't think anything of it. Once the miracle happens, it's just another ordinary day."

She looks at him a moment. Snorts a noncommittal smile. "You know I think you are definitely crazy. No doubt about it."

"Now finish your hamburger and let's get on down the line. Auntie."

The next thermometer they passed said 109°. The horizon rolling, quivered, disintegrating, and recombined. They talked slowly. Tension broken. Hot and wet. Clothes twisted about their bodies. Until the car sputtered and died coming into McCook, Nebraska.

And rolled up the drive of an old motel.

Sorry looked lethargically at her. Shrugged slowly just-what-we-goddamn-need. Got out and circled to the hood, raised it, came back, tried to start it, nothing. Went back, had her try it while he checked the sparkplug wires for fire. None. Took off the distributor cap and inspected it. Cracked. Told her he'd be back, went into the motel office to phone. Isadora Faire sat. Hot. Emotionless until he returned. Opened the door, slid in behind the wheel. "Welp. Looks like we're out of luck. A distributor cap for a '31 Chevy isn't the most common item around. The only place that might have one is closed for the day."

"Uh-huh."

"So."

"So."

"So. Looks like we're stuck. Looks like we've two choices. The mattress in the back, or this old motel. I suspect a cool shower wouldn't hurt either of us."

"Old motel it is."

"And I'll tell you what. We'll continue the interrupted celebration of last night. I've got my guitar to sing you a song."

"Sounds good. I guess I can get used to a nephew who beats up uncles and destroys jukeboxes."

"You know I can't help it."

"Sure you can't."

Walked loose, limber, to her room. Knocked, and entered. The air warm heavy against the face, water vapor, aroma. She stood in purple and scarlet. Gold earrings, a green jasper ring. A string of pearls across the clavicle and breast. Knees calves ankles open-sided low-heeled square-toed scarlet shoes. Two gold cups on the dressing table, champagne in a plastic tub.

Suddenly Sorry didn't know what to do. Stood a moment at the door looking at her. Smiled a compliment and sat on the bed. The TV silently radiating smoke, Buddhist monks burning a village, gunfire at a Georgia filling station, shotgun and a car. Isadora gets up and turns it off. She walks about the room closing suitcases and cosmetic kits. Disposing of wadded Kleenex. Picks up the cups. "Have always saved these for a special occasion. My mother says they belonged to her grandmother. Since Marcus, as we both know, will not allow the champagne on the place. I guess this will qualify."

Hands him a bottle from the tub. He carefully peels the foil around the neck, untwists the wire with the left hand, holding the cork with the thumb of the right, eases the cork out and pours champagne into the golden cup held in her hand. Long stem burnished vines, leaves clusters of grape wrought circling the rim. Green gold foaming wine, her wrist, ring, looks up at her face. A little afraid. Fills the other cup, replaces the bottle in ice. Lifts the wine. "To. To the family."

"To us."

"To you. And Marcus."

"Marcus."

Downs the wine, "Hey that's just what a man needs after a hot day on the road." She fills the cups again. He sits on the bed, picks up the guitar. Begins picking out a quiet melody. Sipping champagne. She refills, sits back in the chair in the far corner of the room, kicks off the shoes, tucks her legs up under. He plays. Steel strings, stainless steel, bronze resonator resounding articulation reverberating overtones, undertones. Hissing zipping fingers along the wrapped steel, pinging frets, fingernails, slow rhythm building in the room. Evening sun slanting through, double-image shadow on the wall, rising larger toward the ceiling. Glowing darkening air. Diffusing steel-body, gold cup iridescence.

She sits scarlet, deeper purple. Moving to pour more wine. Opens another bottle. Listening. Watching. Dusk fills up the room gone dark. Backlit night light, heat lightning along the horizon. He played. And started to sing. Knowing what would happen next.

> *Night wind rising dark sun sinking*
> *rolling folding grass and land,*
> *flowed before me flowing after*
> *like the grain flow through my hand.*
> *Amber golden lonesome woman*
> *rolling thunder where you stand,*
> *slowly holding morning after*
> *like the rain flow through my hand.*
> *Random river muddy water*
> *washing traces from the land,*
> *ever changing prairie woman*
> *like the pain flow through my hand.*

No. It can't. Happen. Silent, dark. Isadora. Marry Marcus. Can't don't. Put the guitar on the floor. Marcus Isadora uncle and wife. Can't don't. Get up uncertain across the dark vast little room. Silent breathing louder, smell her body, hair, her dress. Warm. Dark. Perspiring. Eddies across the forehead, nostrils, mouth. Silent pounding temples, legs weak, trembling can't don't. Kneel down before her. Knees thighs. Lean and kiss soft down tickling hair. Warm moist fragrance on the face. Can't don't. Lay hands caressing muscle warm skin, cloth, dress hem, hips silk belly rib cage sighing. Can't don't.

Sorry.

Isadora.

Don't. Can't.

Take off the dress.

Don't.

Look pleading at him on his knees, dress pushed back across his arms, hands warm wet beneath the breasts. Marcus.

Can't.

Slowly pull the dress over her head, from the arms floating to the floor. His tongue. Her hands in his hair. His hands cupping breasts nipples. Kiss. Shoulders neck and hair, earlobes cheekbones and chin. Kiss the throat, the open mouth muffling.

Sorry don't.

Pull her down. Trembling window light along long body stomach tensing. Hand. Fingertips beneath elastic soft resilient sweating hip to hip to the mound of tangled pubic hair wet warm supple, can't don't whisper in the room.

Sorry. Take off your clothes.

Isadora Whitehands
Learns Who She Isn't

I SADORA Whitehands stood at the edge of the clearing by the trees. She was the last person I ever thought I'd see. Born, grew up in a big mansion, double veranda porch east, south and west, east of the Grand River. Mighty nice house, built before the Civil War. Oak, pecan. She never would hurt for anything it looked like. Her little brother Gordon always sort of a bad ass, but she seemed well on her way with no trouble. How could she miss. Her daddy rich, a big executive of an oil company. One of those white Indians, an executive of the tribe. In on all those schemes to take the Cherokee's money and use it for the white people of northeastern Oklahoma. He wasn't a grafter, one of those who knows someone in the County Assessor's office, get them to take some full blood's land off the restricted list and put it on the tax rolls, man doesn't even know taxes are owed, probably wouldn't pay even if he knew, doesn't know until the grafter comes in, about three years later, and gets the land for back taxes. He wasn't one of those. Who'd go to court and get some Indian declared incompetent and have his secretary named legal guardian in order to sell the land to pay for the man's burying expenses, even though he's as spry as a coyote pup. But her dad was a member of the Cherokee establishment. Part of the way things are. The county clerks who'll do the midnight work on the books, the Bureau of Indian Affairs officials who don't know what's going on or give a shit, don't even understand or speak Cherokee, although Isadora Whitehands and Gordon both do. Part of the people in charge, getting the laws passed favoring white people and hurting the settlement folk.

He was in on planning and building Tsa La Gi, the Cherokee village tourist park, the monkey farm, supposed to give jobs, restore pride, as if lack of pride was a problem. What it did was give minimum wage work, forty-five dancers, during the time of year when people didn't need work anyway, what with the harvest and all, and bring in millions of dollars to the white community from the tourists, bring in white tourists to gawk at debased ceremonies, tromp all over taking photographs. Throwing shit on the ground.

I've seen how this stuff works.

I used to work for the general consul of the Cherokee Nation over to Fort Gibson. Fat southern-talking red-faced white man. But he's Cherokee according to United States law. His daddy got his name on the Too-Late roll when he was a baby, before they closed it out in 1907. I was one of his assistants. The summer before I went to the University of Tulsa on the basketball scholarship. Used to run errands for him and drive him around in the official car. Know how it works. I remember one time me and John Tallchief were both in the office when a young white man and his wife came in. Interested in studying us, lots of people wanting to study. This man and woman were talking to him about what they were doing, it was noontime, and they send me out to get a bucket of Kentucky Fried Chicken and some Cokes. And when I get back the general consul of the Cherokee Nation, tucking his napkin under his double chin, tells these white people to take all the white meat they want. These boys can make do with the dark.

I don't have much use for the tribal government. And they don't have much use for me. Only when the War on Poverty was declared, and they found out all us out in the settlements was worth money to them. They got interested. And Isadora Whitehands' daddy was one of them. Come from a long line.

Sort of funny to think about it. Me and her and Gordon were best friends, summers, when my Aunt Ruth took care of them. That was back when we used to live in the log cabin at Linder Bend, the one with the shotgun hole in the floor, see the chickens under the house through it, before the Army Corps of Engineers flooded the place out with Tenkiller Lake. Dad worked on the road crew and mama in the cannery. We'd hitch a ride with Aunt Ruth's brother-in-law in that old '41 Ford pickup he used to drive, and two of his cousins who worked at the cannery, and they'd drop me and Aunt Ruth off at the mansion. Did that every summer till I was seven or eight, old enough to go with Mama's aunt's family picking. We'd do strawberries, peas, beans, tomatoes, huckleberries. But me and her and Gordon had a hell of a time back then. Talked Cherokee all the time, and you talk about adventures. The stables and horses, barn, exploring the creek that ran through their land, the pasture with Hereford cows and that big ol bull named Bulldog. The big old house on rainy days, prowling hide and seek through the attic and cellars.

When I started doing the harvest I didn't hang out too much with her anymore of course. Spent most of my time in the settlements. Went to college a semester, but I didn't like it. Came back home. Take care of Dad, now that he can't work, messed up his back building a road over by Pryor. I hunt and fish. Get by. Not like it used to be. Guess it's part of growing up, but more to it than that. Ever since they flooded Linder Bend it seems like I've lost my place.

But we get by. Dad says there's still as many full bloods and settlements now as before when the Europeans first come. Dad and the old men still travel round from settlement to settlement visiting each other, use tobacco, sit out all night talking about the world and how it's going, observing, swapping views and arguing strategy. Talk about the Prophecy, looking for a sign. That the water bucket is empty, the Cherokee at the rock bottom, from where we will rise again.

But like I was saying. I spend most of my time in the settlements, and the last person I ever thought I'd see, hadn't thought about her in years, to see Isadora Whitehands at a stomp dance down at South Greasy. Saw her across the clearing and recognized her right off. Ran over, excited to see her, but just as I got there, before she turned, I stopped to look at her, tall, brown, long black hair down her back. My mouth open to talk, and nothing. I'm standing in jeans and beat-up boots and flannel hunting shirt, a six-pack of beer under my arm in a paper sack, hadn't combed my hair for a day or two, and nothing to say to her.

She turned to me. And grabbed my arm. "Richard Chewey!" She laughed.

"Isadora Whitehands." He laughed.

"What are you doing here?"

"I belong here."

Her hand drops from the shoulder, looks down at the ground, back up. "It's sure good to see you, you, you're. I knew who you were right off."

"Me too."

Stand there. Kids again. She starts to smile again. "It's been a long time, hasn't it?"

"Sure has. How's Gordon?"

"Hasn't changed a bit! Just grown up is all."

"We've all sure done that. How about your folks?"

Pause. "They died. Were killed in a plane wreck, I . . ."

"Oh. I'm sorry to. I guess I had heard that, just slipped my mind I . . ."

"That's." Long pause. "How's Aunt Ruth doing?"

"She's doing good. Can't get around so much anymore, but her mind and tongue is as sharp as ever."

Laughter from the grassy rise, drums and rattles. "How are you doing, Chewey?"

"I get by." Looks at her. Begins to grin. "You're looking mighty good. Let's go dance."

Looks over her shoulder at the dancers lining up, back at him, her feet. "Let's, let's go somewhere, sit and talk. We've got some talking to do, some time to catch up on."

Down at the six-pack. "Sure." Holds it up. "Like a beer?"

"Great. Where can we go?"

"Follow me."

He leads off the clearing into the woods. Blackjack oak, hickory. Along a path, screaming insects falling silent before, cranking up behind, dust, flinty ledges, loose shards. Spitting, wiping spider webs from the dark. The woods layered in the nostrils. "Watch your step." Out to solid rock, an outcrop, still sun-warm, perspiration clinging to the faces, a humid film suddenly cooled into the open air, South Greasy Creek thirty feet below and across the floodplain and rise.

Smell wet stone, fish and rotting wood. Dusty night sky, dry yellow moon and stars. They stand and look. Chewey takes off the flannel shirt. Folds it on the ground, haunches beside it. Bats flop across humid moonlight above tepid water, frog calls. Isadora Whitehands stands. Nighthawks. Chewey pops the top of a beer, a long pull, wipes his mouth with the back of his hand. "Like a beer?"

Looks over at him quickly. "Sure."

"Sit here, on the shirt."

Sits. Takes the can, drinks. Folds her arms around the legs, chin on knees. Watch. Listen. Slaps her neck. "Damn mosquitoes!"

"They are a little bad here. Look out, I got some fly dope in that shirt pocket." She shifts over onto one hip. He reaches under, removes a small bottle with a cork stopper. "This'll do the trick." Dabs some, touches, hesitates, rubs it along her arms, ankles and feet. Tips of fingers on the forehead. "Turn around." Lifts long heavy hair, hesitates again. A drop on each shoulder, the nape of the neck, slight tremor through the back beaded billion glowing movement of light, around the shoulder blades, hair drifting over the fingers. "That ought to do it." Sits back down, smears his arms and neck, chest and back. Sticks the cork back in, puts the bottle in his pants pocket. Finishes off the beer. Opens another. "How's the mosquitoes?"

"Hightailed it out of here."

"What'd I tell you." Thick air stirs drumming, chants and bells over the trees, fades into the drone. "It's pretty hard to beat this for a spot."

"Can't beat it with a stick."

"Dad and I come here a lot. Sit. Talk, about the fish and the animals. Watch the sun come up. Tomorrow it'll be right over that black walnut, see the one on the ridge over there?"

"Uh-huh." She pulls another beer from the plastic loop. Pops the top. Drops the tab into the empty can and shoves it into the sack. Drinks. "What you been doing all these years, Chewey? How long has it been?"

"It's been a long time." Looks away from her. Out over the creek. Toward the east, the walnut tree on the horizon. "I been getting by. I hunt. Take care of Dad."

"You hunt?"

"Yeah. Deer mostly."

"Never figured you for a sportsman."

"I don't hunt for sport."

"Just kidding."

"I keep a lot of people in meat. Eating beans, salt pork, potatoes and pan gravy can get a little old, a little deer meat tastes mighty good now and again. Dad and I got to talking about it the other day, figgered out I take more than a ton a dressed meat a year."

"A ton! That's a lot of protein."

"Sure is. Dad gets the first cut, the tongue and liver and loin. He gives some of that to Uncle Castle and Aunt Ruth, Uncle William, and they give out a little of that to neighbors. My sis over to Bull Hollow gets a joint, shares it with her friends, then my brother down at Blackgum Mountain. Whatever's left I take to Smileyburg Baitshop, so anyone wants some meat can come by and pick it up."

"Don't you keep any?"

"I get my share, invited to supper a lot."

"Why don't you sell it?"

Looks hard at her, laughs through his nose. "I guess I could." Looks away, up at the sky.

"I guess that was a dumb thing to say."

"Oh, not so dumb." He looks back at her. Smiles. "In fact, I used to do that. Whenever I'd bag a deer I'd sell it to some white man for twenty bucks or so, me and some of my friends go out drinking. And usually get into a whole lot of trouble."

"Why did you stop?"

"I still can drink and get into trouble. But I don't sell no deer to the white man anymore. I lost my power. Lost my magic. Ordinarily I'm a hell of a shot."

"I do remember you inflicted a lot of trouble with your slingshot."

"Yeah. That's right. Well, I was still that good with a rifle, shit, I couldn't miss. Anytime my buddies and I wanted a good time. Just get me a deer anytime and sell it to the white man. Dad kept telling me I was messing up, that the deer was put here for food for the Cherokee, not to sell to the white man for drinking money. But I didn't pay him no attention. One day I was out hunting, been stalking a big old seven-point buck all morning, worked my way downwind, knew he was up at the edge of the woods on the ridge. Worked my way along the creek around, climbed up the bank, I mean I was good, no one in God's creation could of heard me coming, not a single pebble fall. Sometimes my mind the only thing holding me on that cliff. Breathing nice and slow, heartbeat soft and regular. And I come over that ledge and he rose up and looked at me, right in the eye, and I fired. And missed! Buck just stood there looking. I fired two three more times. And then he sauntered off like I'd just spoiled his view or something. Well, I didn't think too much about it. Till the next time I'm out, and damn if it didn't happen again. I mean the feller is so close I could of brought him down with a rock! I fired and couldn't hit him no way. I told Dad about it. And he said I might as well hang up my rifle, I'd lost my power. Cause I was selling meat to the white man. He said it was a sign. You should always try to live right, follow the White Path, not to be confused with white people's ways, follow the White Path, and to look for signs you were straying from it. And I was straying. Hang up my gun."

"And you did?"

"I hung her up. I knew he was right. It was no use. The deer didn't want to die for me. Didn't hunt for over a year." Reaches over the rock, hooks the six-pack by a loop and drags it toward him. Peels one. "One day Dad said he thought I might be straightened out. He'd try to purify me, get my power back. With remade tobacco. Some potent stuff he said. Grew it out back of the house, burned off the patch where he was going to plant it with some lightning-struck wood, on a day a thunderstorm was coming up. Plenty of thunder. He took some of this ancient tobacco he calls it, got up at dawn, chanting, down to the creek running east below the house. Held it up to the sun, still singing, then chewed it, plenty of saliva, and he spits it into his left hand, blows on it seven times and starts chanting again while he's kneading it round and round counterclockwise with the four fingers of his right hand. Till he sings the song to the powerful wizards four times. I was watching from the window. Wasn't supposed to be there. He was just remaking the tobacco he was going to use. Few days later at dawn we both get up. I'm a little skeptical of the whole thing, but what the hell, I'll try anything, even going down to the water. I got my rifle with me, Dad's chanting again, builds a fire on the bank, chants to the east, north, west and south while the fire burns down. Then he rakes up the ashes into a mound, takes some of the remade tobacco. Puts it in his mouth, chews it, spits it into his left hand, rubs it with the fingers of his right, rubs it on the barrel and stock of my rifle. Starts singing again, rubs it on my breast, forehead, blows on the rifle, blows on me. And I'm starting, I don't know how to say it, I mean it's getting real serious, getting exciting, like something dangerous might happen. The sun turning the east thin red golden, Dad singing, birds stirring. He takes some tobacco dust, sprinkles it over the mound of ashes, it falls to the southeast bursts into flames. Dad starts chanting again, gives me a pinch of tobacco to eat. Tells me go to the southeast, I'll bag big game today. Well. That's just where I was thinking of going. And sure enough, wasn't out an hour when I spied a big buck a hundred yards away. I knocked him down with a single shot. And been raising meat for the Cherokee ever since."

Long silence. The trees stir, long-eared owl, drum frogs, insects. He hunkers on the flint ledge, pitches a pebble to the water. Turns to look at her. She looks at him. Richard Chewey, grown. From summers. Gone. *Pungent tunnels, hidden chambers in new-baled hot prairie hay. The barn. Chewey. Gordon. In the house, something suddenly gone from the green of the trees along the creek, the air closer to the windows. A hush anticipation. A killdeer calls. Listen, stark insistent where the rain will be. Chewey. Gordon. The walls, the pictures, distant. Quiet crouching below the sill. The curtains loom uncertain light. Childhood afternoons. She was afraid.*

Mother always told me and my brother Gordon we should be proud of our Indian heritage. How great a man our great-great-grandfather Elias Boudinot was. How important our dad. How much money he'd made, come up from nothing. How the leaders of the community would come when they needed advice. But she always said it in a way, I realized later, made me think Indian heritage was something to be ashamed of really, praising the things that were closest to what the white people do. The portraits of solemn men and women in high collars, tails, frilly lace and bodice. Indian heritage was something you read about in books, what a

278

great tribe we were to be smart enough to overcome it and turn white. It was something we used to be. Something past. And best not to look at it too close.

And all the time I was growing up I never connected it with what I saw all around me, with Aunt Ruth, who really raised me, with Richard Chewey and the things we did together. It never occurred to me I was speaking two languages. One for a proper world, the real world I thought, and one fantasy fun world, exploring and play. Aunt Ruth taught us all the dances, the ceremonies, songs and incantations, and we learned them as games, like we did at school, square dances, polkas, Greek, Mexican hat dances, songs from *America Sings*. Nursery and children's rhymes. Hardly ever saw our parents. So I never connected what they said with our growing up. Would have to go away from it, when I went to the University of Kansas. And suddenly things began to connect.

I was like any other freshman girl in 1960. Big-eyed, raring to go. All the sororities courting me during rush week. Pledged Chi Omega, girls of all the best families.

But after the first excitement wore off, after enrollment, the first date, first big party with the Phi Delts, after answering the same questions over and over again, some sincere, some veiled hostility, and all naïve, I began to think. To have to think. About myself.

At first I thought, if I thought at all in broader terms, I thought it was just the normal thing. First time away from home, growing into womanhood at a crucial time. The same as all my sisters in the house. How far to go. With whom. And why, why any of this, the books and school. The loneliness. And Mother's answers didn't seem to work, especially for questions I couldn't even say, coming across dark beer bottled tables, fraternity basement noisy rock and roll. Pride. Dignity. But when I looked, talked in rooms crowded cheap warm wine and cigarette smoke and teddy bears, day-old perfume and powder, hair spray cans. Listened to the others and could not talk to them. Could not say what I. I knew, realized, I was not the same. I was forced, being forced by everyone around. To be Cherokee.

Little by little. I had to respond. To become what I was but had never been. Conscious of myself, to play myself, put on a mask everyday, cause no one would let me forget. Could finally see it in all the eyes. I had to be a parody of myself. A shell about an emptiness. That needed to be filled.

I walked a lot alone around the campus, didn't primp as much, my hair hung down from a leather headband. Got out my buckskin dress and moccasins. Cut classes more, hung out in off-limit cafes. Sullen, silent. The sisters whisper, giggle, catty conversation when I pass. I am not what they think.

And I began to read.

One night, hot spring evening, my junior year. I'd moved out of the sorority house the semester before. I was out walking. Heading downtown to a little diner where you could get breakfast twenty-four hours a day, just wandering really, thinking. Troubled. Grades falling, had a big paper due and hadn't done a thing on it. Feeling out of place, isolated, the whole year, and with the warmer weather was starting to fester more and stink. Walking down the street, I had the dumb feeling it was all with me. I was the one not right, a vague sense of rhythm, blue and flashing, I had to do something, make up my mind, I mean it couldn't, regular interlacing blue light rotation, couldn't go on like this, the street, the school, me hanging from my bones, sordid, heavy. The lights going around from the several police cars in the street. And a crowd of people. On the other side a block ahead.

I cross over to see. People were mumbling, a louder uncertain curse or two at the police standing, nightsticks around the cars, but mostly almost reverent silence. Passive. Handcuffed men in the back seat. Black men. Blue sharp rotating light. Listen to the talk. A sit-in. Had come to the bar and the bartender wouldn't serve them, they wouldn't leave. The police, the blue orbiting, reflecting the window, windshields, neon lights. Red. And blue. And they, two policemen, bring out a woman. She walks between, each holding her by the elbow, light-skinned, but dark brown red by the police, deepset dark eyes catching playing blue light, black sleek hair. Deepset dark eyes find mine through the crowd. I know her, she knows me. In the same poly sci class. Had been aware of each other from the first, never spoken, just aware, I don't know why. But her eyes seek mine. And she pulls her right arm free, looking me in the eye, and a raised clenched fist. Pulled back down and hustled into the car.

The crowd stands long after the cops are gone. The bartender tries to shoo them away. Finally closes the place up. Hot night. Moths and beetles rotate about the lamppost light. The neon dies. I wonder why.

Something has happened. An excitement. I move quickly back along the sidewalk, I don't know why, but think I will, up Ninth Street to Tennessee. Blue light, heat lightning scatters the leaves of trees. To Thirteenth Street and up the red brick hill. Some memory. Some emotion from a dream you can't remember suddenly taking form. An awareness was all. We'd always known when the other was there.

The next day Gordon called to tell me Mom and Dad had been killed.

Gordon and I had some serious thinking to do. Cause the lawyers were there before we even had caskets in the ground. The first thing I decided was to drop out of school for a while at least. Nothing made any sense now, the things I was just beginning to work through were suddenly totally destroyed by a set of high-tension wires near the end of a fog-bound airstrip in northern Missouri. Before I had anything at all to replace them with. Left me a shapeless void.

And Mom and Dad's things were not in order before they went.

We had to sell the house we grew up in to pay the inheritance tax, but managed to keep the ranch in Adair County Gordon had been working. I decided to move in. And go to work.

It was the first time back there for me in six years or more. We drove off the main road, angling over the rough gravel. Evening. Long light. The pasture grass burned white by dog-day sun. The broadleaf fence row, the trees intense green. Stark, spare, austere. Indifferent beauty. A golden September pollen gauze held silent, soothing in the heat. We stood in the drive. Just stood there. Turned, tears streaming down the cheeks and Gordon hugged me. We hugged each other. At least we had a place.

I moved about restless. Lonely. Grateful for the physical exertion. My thoughts began to form, to crystallize around the shape of the river bottom, the massive flux of clouds and light, the flight of crows, movement of the cows, red, yellow cast of autumn leaves, blue ghosts of trees caught among the living on the ridge.

I began to drive the teeth-jarring back roads to the settlements.

Looking. I wasn't sure for what, just sure somehow it was in these flint-choked hills, looking, until one day I came upon Tenkiller Lake. I stopped the pickup, walked down to the edge. There was a family fishing off a ledge in one of the back waters thick with dead trees. A mess of bluegill and some bass. We talked awhile. Said this was a good place to fish. Right close to where they used to live, bout forty yards out and forty foot under. Linder Bend. And all of a sudden I knew what I was looking for. It was Richard Chewey I had to see.

It was clear to me I would see him again. Hadn't thought of him in years. But I realized I'd known all along—the last day he left the house with Aunt Ruth when we were eight years old—we would see each other again. Aunt Ruth kept telling me all about what he was doing. I even saw him play basketball in high school once, at the state tournament, but none of it really meant anything to me until that empty day looking out over the opaque wind-rilled green water of Tenkiller to the sun-bleached treetops of where Linder Bend used to be. I knew Chewey had been where I was now. And I knew I would see him again.

Scared to death the night I went to South Greasy to the stomp dance. Pulled the pickup in behind the other cars parked along the road. Had wanted Gordon to come along with me, but I knew that wouldn't work, I had to do it alone. Got out and walked through the woods toward the sound of people, the firelight. Could hear the singing. And recognized the songs. I stood at the edge of the clearing, and it was as if. I mean I knew the songs and the dances, but had never really seen them before. The lines of dancers, the voices mixing, the dust. I mean, what had always been a game, been with me all these years, took on form and became frightening and real. I'd known it all my life, longer than all my life, Gordon, Chewey and me. And Aunt Ruth, stories she had told, the smell of her, the sound, all extend through the curving space between the fires, the trees and me. An awareness was all. A sudden convulsion of the lungs, a shiver along the fingers to the feet. And when I turned, he was standing there.

The whole world jumbled up on me. Didn't know what. Like a kid again, like I'd never been, never understood. An uncertain terror shaking, threatening me. And calm. At the same time. The sweet physical yearning. Like my brother. For Richard Chewey.

The emptiness was filling so fast it. I couldn't keep up. We talked for a while over South Greasy Creek. I didn't want to come back to the clearing clouded dust and shouts, laughter, song bells and rattle. I knew the songs, I knew the dances, but. I couldn't. More beer. We switched to sweet red, had to lose myself, dissolve into the night, the group. I had to get drunk before I could sing. And join the line. Stumbling at first, more than a little drunk, memory a little slow, all those years between. Moving unison, chanting. Watching motion, thick sound merging, pulling me out, pulling me in, forgetting to remember swept up one mind one. For the first time in my life a feeling of festival, celebration and ceremony. Letting go, excited fear feeling no more alone. Caught up. No more. Feeling nothing. Just rhythm earth trees and sky. Just Cherokee was all there was.

Woke up in harsh sun tangled sheets. Richard Chewey sitting at a table across unsteady distance, a stained coffee mug in his hand. Sour mouth and smell wadded bedclothes in the corner. A room. A house. One wall not painted yet, a new house, LOF stickers still on the window glass in the sun hurting my head, entire body ringing the pulse of the heart and vessels. One eye stuck shut. "Did I have a good time?"

"You threw up in bed."

"No. I didn't, you made that up, I don't remember I." Looks to the corner pile.

"You still had a good time."

"I'm glad of that. I'd hate to think. I'm gonna die and not have had a good time." Looks around with one eye. "Where you been all these years, Chewey? Where the hell are we now?"

"This is Dad's new house. A project of our tribal government."

"Where's your dad?"

"Visiting an old friend at Burnt Cabin. Be pulling in in a couple of days with the latest word on the Prophecy."

She swings the feet onto the floor, tries to focus both eyes on the coffee, then the hand, the arm, shoulder. On the face across the room. "What do we do now?"

Blows across the mug. Takes a sip. Another. Puts the mug back on the table. Looks at her. A slow noncommittal smile. "The White Path. You got to look out for the sign."

Looks at him. He laughs. Fragments of the night falling in some sort of sequence. Settles back down on the bed, on her side, still looking. Tries to smile but it hurts. Takes awhile for her to realize that they are speaking Cherokee.

We went wild there for about four weeks. Roaring around the countryside on a Harley Hog. Wonder we weren't both killed. In all sorts of ways. One night a high-strung cable took us both off coming into a parking lot. But not going too fast, cut the palm of my left hand hitting the ground three-point landing. Chewey caught the cable, just a big welt across his chest. And a sore neck. Few dents and scratches on the Hog.

Gordon and I baling hay all day, or plowing, moving livestock from one pasture to another. Sometimes Chewey would help, sometimes he'd be out hunting. But hardly a day went by we didn't end up on the motorcycle.

One night we were in the little crossroads store out by Locust Grove. A bunch of us talking, drinking beer. And the county sheriff pulls up and comes in. Everyone goes quiet. Looks down. Waiting to see if he'd take anyone away. Anyone he wants. Chewey is distant from me all of a sudden, been quiet joking and talking the minute before. And now he had closed me out. Him. Everyone in the place. Seething anger. Chilling. And I feel it growing up in me too. Anger so great it isolates. The sheriff jokes a little about the beer. Then leaves. I look around at the faces. At Chewey. That is too angry to be, I thought when I saw it, felt it. Then and later. Whenever the law was around, and sometimes even reading, a book, a letter from a lawyer. Could feel it in me, see it in Chewey. That is too angry to be. And I slowly realized Chewey would be leaving soon.

It was a cold day. Colder than I thought. The January blizzard. Hadn't seen Chewey in a couple of months. Don't ride so much around on motorcycles in weather like this. The storm hadn't hit yet, but wind and purple red sunset told you it was due. I'm coming in from milking when Tallchief lets Chewey off in the drive. We walk toward each other. He's got his G.I. jacket, hands stuck in his pockets. I've got a bucket of milk. We stand, both hunched against the wind looking south. Chewey takes his hand out of the right pocket and wipes it across his nose and mouth. Blows through his fist, sticks his hand back into the pocket. "Dad died last week."

Silence. "Went out last Sunday morning. Came back about a half-hour later, I thought he'd forgotten something. Came in told me he was dying. His heart. Told me where all the papers were. And died."

She sets down the milk from her right hand, claps a couple of times, rubs the palms together, picks up the bucket with the left. "Let's go make a fire in the summer kitchen."

He walks with her, her right arm resting in the crook of his left elbow, to the summer kitchen. Stands looking out the north window. She loads the stove. Lights the old newspaper. Finally the wood pops, wind and heat roar in the stove pipe. And she closes the grate. Sits on the bunk. A smoky thermocline wavers in the air and curls.

Chewey stands at the north window. "Tallchief stopped by tonight to tell me that in order to get the house built with the tribal government's plan, they had to take the land off the restricted list. Now Dad's dead, they can start collecting taxes. And with the house, they'll be high."

She sits. Milk bucket at her feet. Waits for the heat to expand. Cold draft from the cracks around the window. "Maybe there's something to. Maybe talk to a. A lawyer." Falls silent. Very cold.

He stands at the north window. Then moves to the stove, opens the damper, the grate. Adjusts the wood. Closes the stove, resets the damper. Walks over and sits on the bunk.

We spent the night in the summer kitchen. And the next morning Chewey left.

I had plenty of things to think about. I'd grown up in the old house with my parents and brother, raised by Aunt Ruth, gone to college, started to question and read, Mom and Dad killed, dropped out of college, known Chewey and all this as boy and man. Returned to land that great-great-grandad Elias Boudinot had. And now this.

But finally, I thought, I have time. To think it all out. Things will slow down a little now.

Shows you have naïve I still was. You never know when a blond-haired stranger's going to drive up and complicate things with a steel-bodied guitar and a song. It's a bad feeling when you become a stranger in your own world. Look at it and see.

Mackey Wants to Tell

Yet used to it. Being the town joke. Because you're small in size. And they think you're small every way. The sad thing, you become what they think. Had to drop out of school cause they wouldn't tolerate the difference. Couldn't get decent work more than pushing a broom down at the Mercantile, or over at the Bar and Grill. Or the barbershop. So they let me sleep in the feed shed, give me enough for food. And you start joking back. Your stock answers about the weather down here and up there. Accepting the nickel for a bottle of pop when grown-ups start talking about off-color things. You start acting like a child.

And they take away the parents too. I mean, I had a mother and father. Upstanding citizens of the community, but no one acted like I was theirs, except veiled signs of pity for having such a cross to bear. And now, even though they're remembered with fond memory, no one allows me to be their son. It's like I've been an orphan all my life, as well as a dwarf.

Well, that all changed when the shortest man in town met the tallest, the biggest in spirit. When I started working for Marcus Baldwin. It was back in the spring of '38. I was walking down the sidewalk, going from sitting around the cream shed down to the grain elevator where I expected to sit around on a can of grease for the rest of the afternoon playing cribbage with Henry Lyle since the harvest wasn't in full swing yet. Anyway, as I passed by the blacksmith shop I notice a horseshoe laying in the dust. I glance over into the darkness of the place, see Blackjack Hennessey at the anvil and a few of the town loafers standing around idling the day away swapping yarns and watching Blackjack shoe a horse. And I see Marcus. Definitely no idler. Well, I reach down to pick up the horseshoe and nearly blister my fingers it's so hot, throw it back down blowing and licking the burns. And everybody inside busts out laughing. Everybody but Marcus, and Blackjack Hennessey deadpan pumping the billows glowing coals a couple of times. "What's the matter, Mackey?" Spits cracking steam into the coals. "Burn your hand?"

I stop licking my fingers, look at the loafers laughing, clenching my jaw, back to Hennessey. "Nope." Fold my arms behind the back. "It just don't take me very damn long to look at a horseshoe."

And I walk on across the street. As I'm passing the Mercantile I hear someone calling my name behind me. Expecting it to be someone still kidding about the horseshoe, I don't even turn around until a big hand turns me around I gaze up into the sky and Marcus Baldwin's face.

"Mackey. I guess I've always sort of thought you weren't much good for anything the way everybody else does. Now here I am. The harvest coming up, just buried Mom, short of help, me and Blanche. A man shouldn't look down on another man. But rather let him labour, working with his hands the thing which is good, that he may have to give to him that needeth. Mackey. How'd you like to work for me?"

Look up at him suspiciously. "Is this some kind of joke, Mr. Baldwin?"

A broad sweeping gesture with his hands. "The harvest truly is plenteous."

Slowly grinning, then laughing. "But the labourers are few." And I've worked for him ever since.

Marcus isn't a talkative man, but over the years he's told me many things. Told me how he feels about things he's never told another living soul. Driving down to Anadarko to pick up a load of hay. Touring the place in the pickup before the sun goes down. Waiting out a rainstorm in the machine shed. Almost as if I wasn't there, he talks. Not often. But once he gets started he can tell some stories. I've seen him go to the cemetery ever year after harvest standing at his mother's grave, the way he keeps the southwest bedroom clean. It adds up over the years. So I'm the only one in all this world who really knows him, knows about Blanchefleur, how he feels guilty, how somehow he's to blame. And I know he wanted a wife and kids. He told me lots of things. Not in so many words. But it all adds up. And I know for all his silent strength he's a lonely man, because I understand loneliness. And I know that I was all he had.

Until Sorry came.

And it's not because he's tall and strong and young. I suppose most people would think that. But he just doesn't belong here. He's a stranger. Anyone can tell he and Marcus don't really have a thing in common. I watch them all the time. Not like me, who's been here all these years, working the land right alongside Marcus, through the good and the bad. I can understand Marcus wanting to hold on to him, his only living relative, the son of his sister. But it's not fair to me. I mean this farm is the only home I've had since my parents died, Marcus the only people. And when somebody else just walks in and takes over, moves right in. It makes you mad. And it's not just me. Malachi feels the same way I know. I can tell. I watch and see.

But I guess it really isn't fair to hold it against Sorry. He can't help what he is. But he's done nothing but stir things up around here since he's come. And I don't know what's going to happen now Marcus has married that woman. I don't know. Don't know what Sorry's up to. But it's no good.

And I guess I really owe it to Marcus to tell him what Mackey saw down by the swimming hole the other night. I saw it sure. I did.

It was a hot night. Must of still been ninety at midnight. Couldn't sleep, tangled sheets and sweat, got up and went to the porch by the well. From every side the friction, grass and wires and trees dragging through the mass of hot air flowing slowly across the

288

land. Night birds, owls and nighthawks. Hound dog bay and call along the creek, whiteface Hereford bull snort and bellow butting against a bois d'arc corner post. Fence row, phone line, and the metal twang of distant guitar music. Mackey sitting rocking on the porch, ivy rattling on the well, petunia blossoms tossing back, rocking staring at the gibbous moon and clouds. Saw her, Blanchefleur, Isadora. Flowing white gown across the barnyard and down the lane. A clump of silence moving through crickets and katydids in the hedges, the frogs toward the creek. I stop still. A lace curtain lapping at an upstairs window. Hot. Slide from the chair to the porch, look out over the yard to the east pasture, back up to the window, move off the porch down the walk to the front gate, out into the drive. Heat rising from the hard baked red roadway. Walk east to the pasture gate. Crawl between the barbed wire along the ruts to a cowpath, through the draw toward the swimming hole. Voices garbled from the other side. Mackey climbs up on an outcrop and sits.

White cloth and hair. Penumbra below the hully gully. Glowing in shadows, movements, words. Sorry and Isadora Faire. She sits upon a blanket, he paces shirtless back along the bank grass sloping down to the dark green smooth water surface reflecting, undulating the moon through branches opposite elms and coffeebean. Scoops up a flat stone and skips it patpatpat across disintegrating moon ripples.

Mackey squats and watches, rocking slowly, staring at the light. Staring through the man, blond, slapping arms along his side, voice anxious agitated lost in the slow channel of air around the sweating torso, liquid light. Rocking. Don't hear the sobs. Staring through, Mackey swaying back and forth. The light, white cloth gown, his hands on her cheeks, along her sides, her hands and arms white light in shadow rising over her hair. White cloth flowing over naked body lift the hair falling rippling back along her face and shoulders. Floating in the air down the slope to grass by the water. He wipes her eyes. Pushes her back on the blanket, kissing neck breasts belly. Don't hear the sobbing. Mackey hanging on his sharp skeleton, horror beating wings, swaying back and forth. I don't see her hands on his head, her legs white shadows, calves and ankles and feet across. Don't hear the screaming locusts, beetles, frogs. Only white, only greenyellow fireflies, floating moon shimmer and sweat, clinging pajama cloth white, rising, thrust out, rocking, don't see, don't hear, rocking, hopping hands heavy damp toads after rain. Staring through hot viscid splattering on the shale.

And I rock there loosely, sweat trickling, filling up the eyes. And watch him take his uncle's wife.

Mackey and Marcus carried crates of eggs from the cellar and loaded them in the back of the pickup. Mackey closed the tailgate as Marcus went in the back porch to pick up the ledger, leave instructions and tell Isadora goodbye. They both climbed in and headed off toward Oklahoma City.

This would be the day to talk.

Mackey sat silently gazing at red dust covering the dash. Waiting for the time. Marcus turned on the radio for the noon news and weather, the farm market report. Traffic gathered around the pickup, heat rising. A steel guitar and fiddle from the radio and Marcus snapped it off. Mackey looked over out of the corner of his eyes, up into the vault of the cab, smoke massive gray workshirt, billed cap and pipe. Would have to speak. Looked back at the dust, the dash, sitting on the edge of the seat, straining to see over, to look at the skyline haze dull red brown, the trucks, trailers, pigs cows chickens to market to slaughter. Smells concrete, manure, exhaust. Gasoline tankers black billowing hot diesel blast against the face. Chunks of tire tread along the highway. Roaring rattle banging. Past a double-decker cattle truck foul rotting animal waste soybean decaying stench constricting nostrils and lungs, plaintive cries complaint, nervous urine. Slowly past, a yearling cramped neck face against the aluminum siding staring back. At Mackey riding past. Stoic fixing stare eye to eye until reflected sun from the pickup window jiggled across, pushing the kinked neck in, sudden kicking shifting back around over the shit-smeared rump in front. Mackey quickly looked back to the dash, to the dust.

What to say.

Raised a finger, slowly traced a stick figure in the dust. A man. Then a woman. Looked over to Marcus, rubbed out the drawings. Looked back out the window, up at treetops and oscillating high-lines between pole top crosstrees. Sun. Heat. Must tell him.

Slid back into the seat on hot vinyl covers. Trembling engine road vibrations. Got to say it Marcus, Sorry Isadora. Tires rhythmic thumping. Marcus, how could they?

Head sank suddenly jerked back up, blinked. His chin reflected in the windshield, sunwash white hot where eyes should be. Treachery Marcus. And slouched sideways asleep. His head in Marcus' lap.

"Come on, Mackey, let's hustle."

Blink up sweaty grog face pushed out of shape. Tongue mouth nasal passages lined with mucid highway. Blinked again, rubbed the eyes, recognized the pickup cab, Marcus, the back of the IGA store. Groaned hollow depression. From. From Sorry Isadora. Have to.

"Let's go."

Mackey dropped out of the cab, circled around to the tailgate, unhooked his side, Marcus let it creak bang down. A stockboy came out, leaned his broom against the door, pulled off a crate and carried it in. Mackey wrestled one to the edge, Marcus carried it in, Mackey pulled another, struggled it off and set it down in the doorway, nudging the broom cracking down over a row of a dozen eggs. Perfect crease along the big end of the egg shells. The stockboy returns. Marcus. Look at the eggs, Marcus at Mackey. "Can't be handling eggs like you were fighting tigers, Mackey."

Mackey picks up the broom silently. Marcus picks up one egg, peels the cracked shell off, lifts it to his mouth and drains it. The stockboy blanches, eyes widen. Marcus picks up another one. "Can't let good eggs go to waste."

Peels the shell, drains it. Wipes ectoplasm from his chin. Picks up another one. The stockboy's lip quivers watching the head toss back, Adam's apple bob, the empty shell discarded in the trash container. Mackey leans against the pickup watching the fourth egg slurp down, Marcus smiles, offers the fifth to the stockboy who swallows hard, then runs off into the back of the store. Marcus offers it to Mackey, he declines. Marcus pours it down. The stockboy, pale queasy, returns to see the eighth and ninth go, is offered the tenth, disappears into the store again. Marcus shrugs, and finishes off the last three eggs. "Well, Mackey, we're not going to get these delivered standing around."

The pickup pulled from concrete sweltering heat to the dirt

road sudden cool quiet silent trees. Mackey stuck his head into the wind. Would have to tell him now. "Marcus."

"Um."

Still looking out the window. "I. You better." Looks over at him, eyes on the road. "You better keep an eye on Sorry."

"On Sorry? What for?" Calm.

"You don't. I mean, you haven't." Looking out the window. "We don't really know much about him. What kind of a."

Pause. Watching the road. "He's Blanche's son."

"But what do you—"

"Why should I, do you think I should keep an eye on him?"

Looks at Marcus, down at his hands, dark shadow grassy bank swimming hole blanket white. Legs arms breast. White hair and sweat. "Him and. And Isadora."

Marcus brakes the pickup to a stop. The dust wake settles over. Without looking at Mackey, he takes out his pipe from his shirt pocket, the can of Prince Albert from the dash, stuffs the pipe. Lights it. Leans back in the seat. Puffs a few times. "Mackey. How long have you been working for me?"

Still staring through his hands. Slightly rocking. "Over twenty-five years, Marcus."

"Haven't I always treated you right?"

"Yes."

"Now what have I done that would make you want to go and say a thing like that?"

Mackey doesn't answer. Marcus puffs a few more times on the pipe. Starts the engine and pulls back out on the road. Mackey looks over at him. Looking ahead. But not at the road.

Isadora Faire
Wonders What She's Done

ISADORA Faire stands by the tractor and plow, on the high terrace of the hill east of the house. Can see across the trees of the creek channel, ponds and swimming hole, the windbreaker lane to the barn, roof shingles, brass nodules gleam peaks of lightning rods. The house among the elm, west mulberry row, chicken houses, granary along the bois d'arc to the machine shed. Heat distortions, red shale road, highwires, barbed wire, Johnson grass. Birds shift and call. Thick aroma of sod, soil turned shear furrow polished surface, moisture driven with the sun. Grub worms. Wolf spiders. Ladybugs potato bugs. Ants, granddaddy longlegs bristle stubble yellow white gray dusted through red clodded earth. Wind. Lifts her hair and drop upon the neck and shoulders. Should feel good. Engine oil and gasoline, cowling, fender metal, ticking as it cools. Should feel good.

It's been a year.

She returns to the tractor, the burlap gallon jug with lemon slices. Hooks her finger in the loop and rests the weight, cool evaporation, in the elbow crook, sundark dust red arm, to drink, spills water around the chin, down the neck, breastbone between her breasts. Feel good. It's been a year.

She inspects the plow, climbs back up into the hot steel spring seat, heat through jeans on the backs of her thighs, rewraps her hair and starts the engine. Sits there, easy loping idle. Then sets the throttle, engages the clutch, starts off to finish up the field.

She pulls the tractor into the machine shed beside the combine, disconnects the plow. Walks slowly between the granary and chicken houses, through the back gate to the house. Alone. Marcus, Sorry and Mackey gone to Yukon. Removes her clothes standing on the cellar mound in the east yard. Gets the hose and red ring sprinkler. Turns it on and stands, washing alluvial dust from arms and shoulders, farmer tan, from her face. Walks around the house to the west yard to get a towel from the line, spread it out in the sun to lie on and dry by the honeysuckle clumps on the west hog wire. Wasps, humming moths and bees. She takes a loose cotton dress from the line, pulls it over her head, goes into the kitchen through the back porch to start supper. Then up to her room.

She picks up the calendar and starts to write. Stops, pencil to her mouth staring out the window, moving treetops. Puts down the pencil, thumbs through the pages.

Should feel good.

It's been a year.

Sept. 1. 1964. Tuesday. The worst dust storm I've seen for a while. It's cooler now, wind in the northwest. Strange beginning to a strange new life. Already invited to W.S.C.S. (Women's Society of Christian Service) at Mattie Harris'. The house real dusty. Marcus showed me about the pullets. Looking very good, have to get them in the hen house soon, he says.

Sept. 2. Wednesday. Marcus and I took eggs to the city. Lot of fun. Cooler but no rain. Went to official board meeting at the church.

Sept. 5. Saturday. Two men out from the city to work on the pump in the well under the house. Stayed for dinner. Got it all fixed but a small part.

Sept. 7. Monday. Marcus and Mackey went to Oklahoma City for the pump part. First time alone on the farm with Sorry. We didn't see each other much. We're doing good.

Sept. 8. Tuesday. W.S.C.S. meeting.

Sept. 9. Wednesday. Took eggs. Went to choir practice. Got two pullet eggs today!

Sept. 10. Thursday. Worked in the middle hen house all day. Malachi and Viola helped. Moved in feeders and waterers. Got the pullets all fixed for winter. Very tired, but went to the schoolhouse for fun night with Viola. Marcus stayed home.

Sept. 12. Saturday. Sprayed and vaccinated calves. Irene brought eggs. We buy from her and others, take to city to sell. Egg business seems to be mine now. Baked my first bread. Marcus loved it. Like it used to be before.

Sept. 14. Monday. Cleaned the nests in the east and west hen houses.

Sept. 15. Tuesday. Washed and cleaned last hen house, still have some whitewashing to do. Rained half-inch last night. Ninety-eight degrees today. Mighty close in the hen house.

Sept. 17. Thursday. Record breaker. Ninety-nine degrees. Marcus and Sorry went to Shawnee for a hundred bales of hay. Mackey stayed. Very strange. Went off to the ponds to fish, only back for lunch, hardly said a word. Did catch some awful good bluegill and a couple of bass. Baked a cake for Will Rogers Hospital. That's a switch.

Sept. 18. Friday. Went to W.S.C.S. meeting in Oklahoma City, and to Rainbow in town at night.

Sept. 28. Monday. W.C.T.U. meeting with Viola. Women's Christian Temperance Union. Lots of meetings. Not sure, but think I should feel a little hypocritical. Adjusting to things. I think.

Oct. 1. Thursday. Farm Bureau business meeting at Banner School House. Served cake and ice cream.

Oct. 12. Monday. Annual meeting of Farm Bureau in El Reno.

Oct. 28. Wednesday. Marcus and Mackey working on the ponds, wanted Sorry and me to take the eggs. I don't think I'm ready for that. Said I didn't feel good. Malachi went.

Nov. 2. Monday. Marcus and Sorry still digging in the dirt. W.C.T.U. with Viola, working on a meeting, bringing the discussion groups up to date (trying to). Kind of fun.

Dec. 2. Wednesday. Egg day. Marcus and Mackey gone to Okarche for hay. Just me and Sorry. We did all right. Didn't talk much, both trying hard. Foggy, damp, cold.

Dec. 20. Sunday. Cow broke her leg in the east pasture. Had to butcher her. Life is real, life is earnest. Rain. Cold. Forty degrees.

Dec. 21. Monday. Viola, Irene and I went shopping in Oklahoma City. I'd forgotten what crowds were like. Marcus took the beef to the locker and eggs to store. Have to take the rest to the other customers tomorrow. Twenty-six degrees.

Dec. 25. Friday. First Christmas on the farm. Big meal. Mama came down, Keeper and Hank. Good time. Sorry seemed in a bad mood. I don't know. To tell the truth, I am too.

Jan. 1. 1965. Friday. Cold twenty-four degrees. We finished cleaning the hen houses. I nearly froze.

Jan. 6. Wednesday. Sleet, rain, then froze on the roads, slick as glass. Went to El Reno to get car tags and on to Oklahoma City to deliver the eggs. Were glad to get home.

Jan. 8. Friday. Too bad to go to Irene's birthday, roads so slick. Worked on income tax reports. The sun came out and was a real nice day overhead.

Jan. 9. Saturday. Cold. Roads still bad, but thawed some. Went to El Reno afternoon to Farm Bureau board meeting. Mopped the kitchen.

Jan. 10. Sunday. Sun is shining still cold and snow on the ground. Started to Simpson's golden wedding got stuck and had to walk home.

Jan. 23. Saturday. Went to El Reno, Chickasha, Verden. Nice day. Didn't get home till late. I didn't feel too good. Sorry hung around the house.

Feb. 1. Monday. Went to the County Farm Bureau meeting with Malachi and Viola. Marcus' first public meeting presiding as president. He did just fine.

Feb. 10. Wednesday. Sorry and Mackey took the eggs. Marcus and I started painting the doors and windows on the garage. Churned three and a half pounds of butter for the locker. Marcus to a soil conservation meeting at night in El Reno. I am very lonely now. Don't know why. Or maybe I do.

Feb. 13. Saturday. Cleaned house, painted garage windows, south door. Moved cows to pasture on east wheat field. Went to the Yukon Methodist Men's Club annual ground hog supper (postponed from last week because of ice storm). All you can eat, served *1,800* people, sausage, kraut, ribs, potatoes, gravy, apple butter, biscuits, butter, coffee and milk. Very good. Sorry gave me a valentine.

Feb. 20. Saturday. Barbershop quartet show at the Municipal Auditorium in Oklahoma City. Marcus didn't want to go, been trimming trees all day down by the bridge. Just me and Sorry. Very nervous about it, but we had a good time. Didn't think I'd like barbershop singing, but I did. Sorry seemed like his old self. First good time I've had in a while. Maybe things finally working out.

Feb. 21. Sunday. The first calf! Old Roany. I was breathless. Beautiful. As exciting a birth as the first human I did.

Feb. 27. Saturday. Marcus and I went to Cleveland, Ohio, for a convention of soil conservationists. Just got back. The honeymoon we never had almost. Things working out I think.

March 10. Wednesday. Real windy, dusty. Took eggs, came back by Bethany to pick up meat from the locker. Very depressed lately. Must be the winter and the dust.

March 22. Monday. Cold! Twenty-four degrees. Where is the spring? Went after the chicks. I love them. Gooder's health is failing fast. Marcus had to take him to the hospital. I'm worried about Sorry.

March 24. Wednesday. Took eggs and taking a cold. Don't feel good! Don't feel good!!! Do as little as possible, just work with the chicks in their brooder, warm and secure out in the garage. Do they know? Went to choir practice, it rained and I didn't stay long.

April 2. Friday. Green bugs in the wheat. Marcus, Mackey and Sorry to a soil judging contest in El Reno. I stayed home. Didn't do a damn thing.

April 6. Tuesday. Had to go to Oklahoma City to see about a rest home for Gooder. Not exactly something to cheer you up. Chicken work in the afternoon. Windy, dusty. Warm. Chicks doing fine. I think Sorry's thinking about taking off.

April 7. Wednesday. Egg day. Finally rain to settle the dust.

April 8. Thursday. Rain.

April 9. Friday. Dressed a hen. Marcus to a soil conservation meeting in Yukon and I got my hair cut. Rain. Got stuck coming back, had to go get the tractor to drag us out of the ditch.

April 10. Saturday. Rain!

April 11. Sunday. Rain!! Can't go anywhere. Muddy roads. Feeling very bad. Sorry's starting to hate me, I think.

April 12. Monday. Finally! Fantastic seventy-five degrees, sun, still, everything green and good. Supposed to get hotter tomorrow.

April 13. Tuesday. Goddamn! Goddamn! How could it happen, how could I do it!!! Such a goddam hot day and the night so beautiful. I don't want it to be this way.

May 20. Thursday. Hailstorm last night. Damaged a lot of wheat. Blanchefleur's room. Very strange. I don't know what's going on. He seems so sad and vulnerable sometimes, needs someone. But why do I do it. Sometimes I think I have some urge not to change my life but destroy it, escape. Don't know to where.

May 21. Friday. Mowed twenty-seven acres of wheat for hay. Just me all by myself. It was fun. Billy Paul to help bale it.

May 28. Friday. Finished up the baling for the time being today. Billy Paul, Sorry and a crew of high school kids. Sorry looked great. 750 bales, about half of it, 250 put in the barn, and the boys have to go to National Guard. Sorry said he didn't even have a draft card.

May 31. Monday. Rain. Had to turn the bales left in the field to dry.

June 1. Tuesday. Rain. Turn the bales.

June 2. Wednesday. Rain. Just going to have to plow them under. Small loss considering many lost everything. Egg day. I shouldn't feel as happy as I do. What's going to happen? Can't tell what Marcus is thinking.

June 11. Friday. Gooder died today. Viola and I went to Yukon and got the casket, made arrangements. Harvest started. Billy Paul and Bob with us for dinner and supper. They'll all be heading north in a few days. Maybe I can think things out. Scared. Just me and Marcus and Mackey. Maybe go spend some time with Mama.

June 15. Tuesday. Finished cutting. Not too good, green bugs and hail damage. Seventeen bushel to the acre. Sorry left with the crew this morning. I'm tired. Funeral. Dressed 16 fryers the last three nights.

June 17. Thursday. Marcus and Mackey went to Okarche to get oats for the chickens. Started mowing the roadsides and cleaning out fence rows when they got back. Ninety-nine degrees. While

*they were gone I just sat naked in the yard in the shade of the
elm drinking lemonade. Slight breeze. Calm. Miss him. I've got
to figure something out.*

*August 13. Friday. Spider Leddy came by today to cull the hens. A
hundred and seven degrees. Lost some hens from overheat. We
got real tired ourselves. Spider stayed for lunch. Dressed three
hens.*

*August 14. Saturday. Mackey and Marcus took the culls to Ok-
lahoma City. I dressed four fryers. I'm going to be learning to
plow soon. Malachi called from North Dakota last night. The
crew will be back in about a week.*

Isadora Faire put the calender back into the drawer. A year. Just
goes to show you never know what anything is really going to be.
How could you when you think. I mean how could something that
seemed so ridiculous one time, then reasonable, after all the visits to
the farm, Marcus so, how could it turn out so, so. How could it
happen. Mama never told me about these things. How could she.
Her marriage certainly was no example. At least when I went into
nursing it was something she knew something about. But even then
I had to find out myself, even expecting some things, the reality of it
is so intense it still sneaks up on you.

There's no way to really be ready for the first person you see
die. Before you grow cold. And it seems it's always one you like,
not one of the sons of bitches that treat you like a slave, they never
seem to die, always someone gentle, soft eyes, tender wisp of human. Maybe something to do with the nearness of death. Maybe
everyone at that edge is, if not. Anyone about to die will draw you
in. Because they know. You know. The chill. Awe. The eyes go
dull, cold things. When you look, it looks the same, same fingers,
knuckles, backs of hands, wrist lined with hair, nose and mouth.
Still warm and supple. But you know the instant you come in the
room. Something is gone, intangible, spirit, breath. Life.

And that's only the beginning. You have to fill out reports, get
the orderlies, the doctor, get the body out of the bed, someone
waiting for the space, time's money, and roll it away. To the
morgue. Whistling while you work, to yourself of course, keep the
old spirits up. Not a kid anymore, seen bodies before, right? Roll it

down the hall, would have to be midnight, kind of a funeral march, even imagine Chopin somehow interweaving the Musak. Do anything to avoid the reality, I mean you have to, pushing it toward the elevator at the end of the corridor, long way off, should be, long way, getting closer. Maybe someone else will, but no, alone. You've got to do it alone as the doors slide closed, and it's you and death. You know elevators are weird anyway, right? Even when the people in them are alive and your friends. Conversations stop when the doors close and not another word until they open, and midsentence the discussion continues where it left off. Claustrophobic. So I'm in there with death, fighting with the mind, you know, like walking down the dark street when you're a little girl and a sudden panic comes over, no reason, you break out running in absolute terror. Well, there's no place to run in the elevator, and I'm not a little girl, but there's plenty of goddam reason cause the body just gave out a mournful sigh, opens his goddam eyes and sits up on the stretcher! Now I know, that is I've read all about spontaneous muscle contractions, but who the hell is thinking about textbooks! Who's thinking about anything in this aluminum neon sepulcher spouting happy days are here again over hidden loudspeakers on its way down to Hades, I'm going absolutely strange with fright pushing with my heels into the opposite corner from this almost blue. Man? Blinking blank eyeballs and making lewd gestures at me!

But that was easy to get used to compared to some of the other things. Things you never, at least I never got used to. Like the politics, or the educational value of who would live or die, whose vital signs would or wouldn't be maintained because someone did or didn't find it interesting or challenging, wanted to experiment, had something to learn or at least publish from it or considered death a failure and would never give it up. I could never get used to that. Never could.

Birth. Death. You can get used to that.

And adultery.

All the time I thought it was a dusty word you looked up in the dictionary, high school English. Not something you do on the farm. Boy oh boy you never know how things will turn out. Can't even think straight about it. What am I going to do?

It's been over a year now. Nebraska, hot, the Chevy. I should have known, I guess I knew, we shouldn't have stopped at the motel, drunk the wine, but we had to stop, he is, was going to be my. I knew, but couldn't stop it, didn't want to stop. First time I saw him. But I knew it was crazy, last nostalgic binge, before the world, just as crazy, I mean me, a farmer's wife tending chickens plowing fields mending fence. Already strange enough I guess. Seemed like a fantasy. How could I convince myself it was real, Marcus, the farm, the crazy story with the computer. The blond-headed supple Sorry and guitar. Two bottles of champagne. It was real. I could understand. Goddamn why did I do it? How could I when I knew I would.

Wake up. Harsh sun, McCook, Nebraska, motel sheets throbbing headache roiled through stainless steel etched intricate light and design. Gold cups, one tumbled, worn green linoleum, and empty sun-shot green champagne bottles. Glaring. Sudden realization sweeping confusion. Panic dread despair. Aroma thick heavy. Struggling against inertia. What have we, overwhelming, we have, looking, resisting the image, Sorry, face eyes, matted hair, resisting Marcus standing in the sun wiping perspiration with a foresleeve above, towering over, shadowing sloping land. Marcus. Can't push it back. The sun on the guitar, the cups, the bottles, the purple and red dress strewn among Levi's and socks. The smell. The bed tangled across his buttock, my knees.

He turned languid scrotum stirring engorging dried seminal vaginal fluid. Blinked comprehending but almost with a smile, a grimace. Beaten him. This time.

Rolled away leaving her alone, Marcus standing silent, blocking out the mind.

Her hand begins to shake. Trembles queasy stomach, sweat. And sank back on the bed staring at the motel ceiling afraid to move to touch his back, to call him back and ask, to cry, to deny what we have done.

And cannot go back.

The sun climbing. Already in his hair. Crowd out the moment. Unfolding. Someone bangs vacuum sweepers along the corridors. Eggs frying in a kitchen. Someone unlocks the place with a distributor cap for a '31 Chevy. The chickens fed. A preacher looks over his calendar. Unfolding. As Isadora Faire swings dizzy cold feet sweating to a worn linoleum. Not looking, but he is there, at

Sorry. Blood pounding. She walks to the shower, turns it hot and lets it splash, lets the body drain. Sorry. Thighs and hips, rib cage. And smile.

Sorry.

Water streams over the face gargling, clearing. Marcus. Water hot pounding nipples trickling loins, soaping labia buttocks ass thighs red splashing water. Sorry. Marcus.

Oh goddamn.

Clanked off the shower, throws back the plastic curtain. Sorry stands naked in the foggy bathroom. She doesn't know, look away, stare, a naked man, Sorry, Marcus. What. She steps out, hesitant, grabs him around the waist, wet skin body steaming together, smells hair, sweat. Still on him. This is crazy don't.

"I love you, Isadora."

Looks up blinking smile welling tears. "We better. Let me, why don't you. We better talk."

"I love you."

She walks over and wraps a towel around her, sits on the toilet seat. "I think we've got more practical things to talk about."

Sits on the edge of the tub, naked, condensation. "Yeah. I guess you're right." Clasps hands between the knees staring at his feet on the floor wiggling the toes. "Yeah." Looks over at her, she looks away, he looks back to the floor, up at the fogged mirror, laughs back at his feet. "What do we do now? I take you away from Marcus? Come live with me, share my life?" Looks toward the door. "The fucking world is too crazy."

"We've got to do something, Sorry."

"No doubt about that."

"What do you want to do?"

Turning hesitant back to her. "I want you."

"So?"

"So hell! How can I take. I mean, what do I do, go ask Marcus for your hand? Hey, Marcus, I've fucked your wife."

"I'm not his." Explodes sobbing, bent over face in hands and thighs drops the towel.

Sorry immobile tenses a moment, then moves over, tentatively crouching, touch her back. "Isadora. I." Face collapses tears choking off.

She finally looks up. "Sorry. How could we do this. To Marcus. How could I. I love Marcus. Too. I think. In a way. I mean I thought I. But. I."

Sorry sits back against the tub, picks at terry-cloth naps of shower mat. "Do you think. Should we."

Looks at him a long time. "No."

Pause. "It would be stupid. For us to try, wouldn't it. You've got to have something to offer to. I mean a home, life, family. A plan. Something." Survey the ceiling. "The craziest thing I can imagine right now is settling down and raising a family. It's crazy to have kids. Something must be wrong with that somewhere. I want to feel, like I did for a few hours. With you. Feel part of—I don't know. But mostly I feel alone. Can't think of the past, I can't think of the future." They sit not looking. Isadora wraps the towel back around herself. Stands. Look at each other. She walks to the other room, starts gathering up her clothes. Sits on the bed. Knees spread, feet tucked up together. Staring at a bruise on the inside of the right knee. Sorry comes in, stands at the foot watching her hand trace ripples in the sheet. "I guess we've really fucked up, haven't we? Marcus. You."

Pause. "No. It was all a . . . dream. You can't feel guilty about fantasies. Gives pleasure remembering them in the morning. And we all go on about our business in the world."

Looks at her. Walks to where his clothes are. Starts putting them on. "You know." Pulls on one leg of the trousers. "I think there's a flaw in that somewhere."

Watches him pull on the other. "Can't be. Or we're all in trouble."

Big trouble. I was unsure about marrying Marcus before. What was I going to do now. But what else could I do. You step out in the middle of a mud puddle, nothing else to do but slosh on through to the other side. One thing was clear. I loved the farm. And thought I could stay away from Sorry, we could stay away from each other. After the wedding.

What an event! Hot sweating white wooden frame Methodist Church, open beam ceiling, wooden pews and red carpet leading to the pulpit. The large railroad-tie cross and choir loft. Peaked slender windows distort the grass expanse, let globules, molten amber and green, slant parallel restless motes across the congregation. Perspiration streaming down Marcus' face, pale, only time I've ever seen him weak, Sorry, the best man. Viola the matron of honor. It was crazy. Every woman in town standing there, why were they standing? Must of been sitting in the pews, overhead broad-blade fans slowly beat the stifling air and dry red dust. Sorry silent. Couldn't tell if he was laughing, crying, if he was going to shout out when anyone with any reason why was beckoned, whether I was going to shout out, run out, but no one could do anything in this heat but go on through with it. Stolid gentle hard-as-nails pioneer women checking me out, the young mail-order bride come to town to marry Marcus Baldwin.

We tried to stay away, thought we could do it. I knew I was just a substitute to Sorry for whatever he was looking for. But. The quarters are mighty close down on the farm. Working together, scooping out the granary, sweat, side by side, smell each other's closeness. Carrying crates of eggs to the cellar, pass on narrow dank webby stairs, a breast, a hand brush past. Naked sundown at the swimming hole, see him, standing on the grassy rise. Watching.

If only Marcus would have, almost ashamed to say it, been better. I mean I understand, he's older, hard lonely life, what do you expect. Give him time to learn how to relate to a woman, to me, sexually. I think I wanted him that night in the cellar and he could tell it and he wanted me and it scared him. Scared me a little bit. I'm the first woman he's ever slept with. He'll learn it's more than Christian duty or mandate from his mother. In time. Definite signs of possibilities. But. We didn't seem to have the time.

Everything, the work, the land, the farm an extended home. We both work at home, we both are breadwinners, a unit, a community within a larger community, Mackey, Viola and Malachi. The town. I love it. Never felt so, I mean this makes sense to me. I can see immediate connections of what I do. I fry a hen, I wring her neck myself. Chase her across the yard and snag her leg with the wire hook, grab her by the head, first time was terrible. Too timid, whipped her around too slow, horrible, would, couldn't snap her neck, getting longer and longer, till I realized you've got to be serious about it. Decisive. You've got to *kill* the chicken. Violent. Snap of the wrist. And the headless dance splattering blood across the drive. But I do it. I tend the chickens, run a business with the eggs I fry. The radishes, lettuce, cucumbers, tomatoes, potatoes, summer squash, green beans, bell peppers, onions, chard, corn, cabbage, carrots, peaches, apples and dewberry cobbler. I helped do that, produce that with my own two hands, dug, sweated, planned, fought drought, crows, plagues of locusts and cutworm infestations to put it on the table. Marcus and me. I know, as I didn't when I was little, what my grandmother meant when she said to understand creation you've got to live close to the earth.

But we didn't have time. Not with me, not with Sorry. How could I have had time. Marcus. How could I have?

I'm weeding the flower bed at the southeast corner of the house. Hot April afternoon after days of rain. Shorts and halter top. A shadow falls across my hands. I look up into the sun eclipsed by his head, hair corona. Shirtless. Shoulders shimmer, bend of breast and stomach muscles, groove along the belly. Looking at me. "I got to talk to you."

"What about?"

"I'll be down at the swimming hole tonight."

"But."

"I'll play the song to let you know."

"No, Sorry, I don't."

"I'll play the song."

He lifts the wooden water bucket from the well, tips it to his mouth to drink. Puts it back down and walks away.

My life about to change. Again.

I lie awake, Marcus asleep for hours, waiting. No will to resist. The heat. Marcus snoring, the thought, the memory live, dark bedroom, steel-bodied music drifting garbled through the trees tossing moon shadows about the walls. I had to, couldn't, resist.

And I'm still going. Awake in the room, Blanchefleur's room. Feel no guilt, no shame. Even love Marcus still, even. The excitement. Intrigue, queasy thrill of, is it incest, events beyond control, love more intense than.

If Marcus would have only done something, said something, objected when I moved to Blanchefleur's room, flimsy excuse of insomnia. Said no, said please don't, said something. Something would have had to happen. I couldn't go on, two men, sneaking from Marcus' bed to. It's so easy now to go on. Like this is the way it's supposed to be.

But how long?

Isadora Faire picks the calendar back up, the pencil. Looks around Blanchefleur's room. Starts to write something. Stops. Scratches it out. And goes downstairs. Leaves the back porch, through the back gate to the chicken houses. Picks up a bucket slung over her right arm. To gather eggs. Warm close humid poultry. From cubicle to cubicle. Carries the eggs to the back porch. Washes them in a large porcelain bowl, soda and water, one at a time. Down, feathers, straw stuck chicken droppings. Lines them on towels on top of the old buffet. Rows of eggs already washed. Gets out the candler, metal cylinder, closed except for a round hole a little smaller than an egg diameter in one end. Places it beside the balance scale, spoon platform egg shape, arc indicator, small, medium, large, extra large. Plugs the candler in, turns on the light inside. Takes the cracked eggs into the kitchen, to put in the refrigerator, checked on the potroast in the oven, looked at the clock ticking through the door to the living room. Went back singing to the porch, began to candle the eggs. Potroast, potatoes filling the narrow porch. Afternoon chickens and trees. Light. Caught perspiration along her face as she moves, turns. One egg at a time, small end first, translucent against the candler yellow orange, tips of the fingers luminescent red, looking for blood spot shadows, laying them aside, weighing the clear ones and putting them in the proper crate on gray press-formed fiberboard separators. Six by six three dozen. One layer at a time, five layers to a side, fifteen dozen per side, thirty per crate.

Egg after egg.

She put away the last dozen from the towel, carried the porcelain bowl to the back door propped on the hip, pushed open the screen and poured the water along the petunias and morning glories bordering the east walk. Put up the candler, the scale in the left compartment of the buffet, wiped water from the top, gathered the towels and hung them on the line in the west yard to dry. She went around the west drive to the mailbox, across the front to the east drive to the second box. *Daily Oklahoman, Oklahoma Farmer.* A letter from her mother. Returned to the kitchen to take the pot roast from the oven, put the green beans and bacon on. Make gravy. Mash potatoes. Steep the tea.

And wait.

After supper Sorry and Mackey washed the dishes. Marcus read the Bible, watched the news and weather. Isadora Faire went up to her room, Blanchefleur's room, sat on the bed. Tired. Stretched the muscles low sweet warm aching, moved to the dark oak dressing table. Blanchefleur. Began brushing her hair. Blue curtains stirring, blue bedstead, blue flowers on white wallpaper. Everything the same, the way it was. She didn't, couldn't change it.

Felt, heard the footfall on the stairs. Marcus. Appears distorted in the mirror, stands in the door, looking. She keeps on brushing, weak smile through the mirror, mottled tarnish at the edge. "Marcus. How did it go today?"

"We got most of the errands run." Comes into the room, never has, to the chair at the foot of the bed. Blue. "Chicken feed, barbed wire and staples so we can get started mending fence, some posts need replacing."

"I finished the east field."

"I saw it." Sitting, looking at her dim reflection. The brush stroking hair. "We'll be cleaning trash from the hedgerows tomorrow, couple of days. Think you can plow mornings? The west place?"

"Sure." Never come in before, sit. Watching. *Does he?* "Did you get the can of grease?"

"It's in the machine shed."

Will he say. Ask. Can I? "Good. Plow between the terraces? Contour, anything different than I've been doing?" *Oh, Marcus, I'm.*

"Just be careful in the northeast corner where it slopes down toward the creek. It's a little steep there, gumbo, she could rear up on you if you don't watch it." Falls silent. Still looking hard. "Been meaning to do some work in that corner when we get the time. Heavy runoff there when it rains. Losing too much topsoil the last couple."

Marcus, sleeves rolled up, dark brown dim dressing table reflection, arms, sun-bleached hair catching light, muscles working his hands, vessels standing out, turning his pipe in his fingers, immobile face pale forehead dark cheeks, broad shoulders, a big man, *Marcus, I wish, I.* "I'll watch out for it. It's pretty dry." *Marcus, I.* "Shouldn't be too much trouble. . . . I'm getting pretty good at it."

Long silence. Watching her brush her hair. Wheat stubble yellow in the light, the blue. Blanchefleur. "How are the chickens holding up in the heat?"

"Good. Got over a hundred eggs today. Marcus, I." Stops.

"What?"

"Nothing. I just think. Think they're laying well. I'm doing pretty good. With them. I like it, you know."

"Was reading in the *Oklahoma Farmer* that came today. Some people down at Stillwater claim if you wash your eggs they rot quicker."

"Why's that?"

"Seems it washes off a natural wax on the shell, makes them porous, bacteria and the like gets through easier."

"We lose quite a few when it's hot."

"They say to clean them with a very fine emery cloth."

Marcus, what. "I'll have to try it."

"I'll get some tomorrow in town." Takes out the can of Prince Albert. Stuffs the pipe looking about the room, the ceiling, window casings. At Blanchefleur's things hanging on the walls. A kitchen match from the shirt pocket, strikes it on the pants leg, suctions flame billowing smoke blue gray hanging among the blue. Looks at her. "How you getting along with Sorry?"

Isadora stops the brush. Looks. Through the smoke, the old mirror warp, was it smoke, humid air, hot air flash cross the forehead, clouding his voice. "What do you mean?" *My voice.*

"Just wondering. If you'd noticed anything. He seems to be acting strange lately."

Stroking. "What. How do you mean?"

Looking, but not. "It's probably. Doesn't mean anything. Ever since the, the wedding. He's been. Well, I don't know."

Puts down the brush. Turns. The real eyes. "I couldn't really tell." Can't. Look away. "I've only known him. Since the wedding. Couldn't say if he's changed or not."

Another match to the bowl of the pipe. "He always has been sort of a different acter. But he seems. I don't know, I guess I haven't known him long myself. I was just thinking maybe he might of talked to you."

She turns back to the mirror. Wipes the palms of her hands, picks up the brush, puts it back down, dabs sweat from the eyes with Kleenex. "No." Clears her throat constricts. "I. He hasn't."

"Uh-huh." Looks at his cracked hightop shoes. Red dirt, caked around the soles, shoestrings short and knotted. Grommets and clasps. "Well. Maybe you."

"Marcus."

"Uh-huh."

"I'll try. See if I. I mean, if I find anything."

"It's probably nothing, just my. He's. But if you talk to him."

"Sure."

He looks around the room. Back at the mirror, Isadora hiding her face in cold cream. "Guess I better hit the hay." Sits awhile longer. "See you." Stands up. "In the morning." A few steps, behind her on the stool, walks to the door.

"Marcus." He stops. "I." *Nothing to.* "Goodnight, Marcus."

Looks at her. "Night."

She hears him down the hall. Removes the cold cream without looking. Turns off the light, takes off her clothes. Stands in the dark. Smells him still. Clean. Sharp. Prince Albert trace sun and perspiration.

Then falls on Blanchefleur's bed.

And cries.

Isadora Whitehands
Gives an Oration

G_{HA}!

I sit on the bluff above the creek and look. And can almost feel what it was like. Before the highway, the telephone poles and fences, before the town. Before great-great-granddad Elias Boudinot settled on the Illinois and Uncle Stand Watie with the store down on Honey Creek where the concrete bridge is now. Before the Indian Wars and Cherokee removal filled Oklahoma with strangers. Before the white man came and Thunder was our friend.

(July 19, the Redbird Smith place, six miles northeast of Vian, Oklahoma. The seven Cherokee clans have gathered, danced, sung, eaten. And now Isadora Whitehands stands before them at the edge of the clearing. Nervous. Excited. Her first ritual oration, where the ancestors have spoken. Prologue. For as long as there has been a people. She has done her preparation in libraries, in papers rescued from her parents' attic, stood alone out in the pasture. Practiced. Revised. Chanted. Pauses. Swallows. Looking out at the people sitting semicircle, standing, lying on blankets on the grass. Babies crawl, children shout. Sorry and Gordon Starvingdog on one side, Wendall Sorethumb and his brother at the outer edge of the crowd. She folds her arms across her breast, dark eyes fixing, speaks.)

Can almost feel the hills. Treeless prairie knee-deep, and black-jack oak along the valleys. Rabbits, pheasants, turkey. Foxes, bear, wolves, wildcats, panthers. Deer, elk and buffalo.

The grass will never cover the treachery, betrayal. The murder. And I wonder what it really means to me. Look down at my hand, back out across the land and try to see.

Georgia. July. 1837. Elias Boudinot, his wife and young son Elias Cornelius. Settle up with the white men taking over their home. After the long exhausting struggle to save the ancestral forest, the bitter feuding, faction against faction. They load up the carriages. The horses snort and stamp the earth, crows filter through the shagbark hickory and loplolly pine. They look at what they will never see again. And leave. Exile. One year before the Trail of Tears.

They travel thirty miles north from Creek Path through Alabama, into Tennessee to Nashville, on the Cumberland River. Frontier town. Warped weathered boarded walks around the muddy square, summer mist saturates unsteady air on top of the river bluff. They leave the horses to be shod and ride out to the Hermitage to make a social call on Andrew Jackson.

Think of it. Cherokee fought alongside of him, would've never defeated the Creeks without Major Ridge's warriors, would've never been President. And he wouldn't lift a finger to save the Cherokee lands.

But still they go to visit Andrew Jackson.

Then continue their journey. North through Kentucky, cross the Ohio River at Berry's Ferry to Gloconda. Then west across southern Illinois to the Mississippi. Flat blackland plains give way to stagnant bogs and marshlands, swamps. They take the river ferry across to Cape Girardeau, Missouri. Cross the river bluff hills onto the Ozark plateau, rolling grassy hilltops, overgrown valleys, creeks and rivers. Forest. And then out onto the prairie again. Seven weeks cross-country to the Oklahoma District. The Cherokee Nation West.

And it has led to this.

But how had it happened? What tortuous weave of treachery and betrayal would set two Cherokee statesmen, Elias Boudinot and Chief John Ross, both bent on the same task of national salvation, set these two in mortal opposition? How do you think of such a thing? What good to try to think of it? Of the proud Cherokee hunters, warriors who had fought on the side of the British in the Revolutionary War to defend our Georgia and North Carolina homeland, to push the white man back into the ocean. We were an independent nation in the Peace of 1783, and kept fighting until the U.S. Government sought an end to hostilities and we signed the Treaty of Hopewell in 1785. Put under the protection of the United States. *Gha!* Like foxes guard the chicken house.

In 1793 the cotton gin was invented. And the Creeks were defeated, and ceded the last of their land to the south. The white cotton growers could now focus all their attention to driving the Cherokee west of the Mississippi. The Cherokee people were divided, confused. Rights, lands and lives slowly treated away. And they started to move west into the Oklahoma District. In March of 1820 President Monroe asked Congress to extinguish the Indian title to the land.

It was then that Chief John Ross and Elias Boudinot, along with his brother Stand Watie, Major Ridge and John Ridge, stepped forward to try to snatch the nation from ruin. They wrote the blood law forbidding the sale of Cherokee land under penalty of death. They would not give up another foot. They would prove our ability to live as a civilized people. A Cherokee National Constitution was adopted. Elias Boudinot founded the *Cherokee Phoenix,* number one, volume one, February 21, 1828, printed both in English and the Cherokee syllabary.

But civilization doesn't stop the invasion. Gold was discovered in the northwest corner of Georgia in 1829 and three thousand miners swarm into the Cherokee lands. Georgia declared all laws and regulations of any kind whatever, made, passed, or enacted by the Cherokee Indians to be null and void and of no effect, as if the same had never existed. The United States Congress made it unlawful for the Cherokee council to meet. Except to cede land. White men took over homes and farms with impunity. There was no remedy. The Cherokee had never existed.

There were those who wanted to take up arms, the only language white men understand. But Elias Boudinot and Chief John Ross maintained a civilized nation does not resort to force. We will pursue our cause in the courts of the land. And when John Marshall's Supreme Court ruled in 1832 that the Cherokee Nation was a distinct community where the laws of Georgia have no force, Elias Boudinot and Major Ridge and Chief John Ross and all the Cherokee people thought their long-sought victory was won. They had an ally, Andrew Jackson, an old comrade in the White House, they thought. But all Old Hickory could say for his Indian friends was: It's Marshall's decision, let him enforce it.

Chief John Ross was undaunted by Andrew Jackson's refusal to intercede on the Cherokee behalf. Encouraged by the Court's ruling, he wanted to continue the fight to keep the ancestral homeland. But Chief Justice Marshall also said: "If it be true that the Cherokee Nation have rights, this is not the tribunal in which those rights are to be asserted. If it be true that wrongs have been inflicted and that still greater are to be apprehended, this is not the tribunal which can redress the past or prevent the future."

Elias Boudinot understood. The struggle was over. The land was lost. He formed a treaty party with Major Ridge, John Ridge and Stand Watie. Think what inner turmoil, indignation and suppressed rage he travels with to Washington. To make the best deal possible for land that was no longer ours. Chief John Ross called him traitor. Waged a desperate campaign against him. Went to Washington and was ignored by government officials. Could not prevent Elias Boudinot from negotiating an agreement: $5,000,000 and land in the Oklahoma District.

Elias Boudinot understood. And knew when he signed the Treaty of Cession on December 29, 1835, he had signed his death warrant. By the blood law he himself had helped to frame.

Chief John Ross said: "Because of Elias Boudinot's treaty, we have been made to drink the bitter cup of humiliation; treated like dogs; our lives, our liberties, the sport of white men; the graves of our fathers torn from us, until driven from river to river, from forest to forest, rolled back nation upon nation, we find ourselves

313

fugitives, vagrants and strangers in our own country, and can only look forward to being driven at the point of the bayonet into the Western Ocean."

Chief John Ross resisted still. On May 10, 1838, General Winfield Scott issued a proclamation: The Cherokee had one month to get off the land. 17,000 people refused to move.

Scott sent the army in: 3,000 regulars, 4,000 volunteers. Families surprised at dinner, bayonets, clubs, rifle butts, driven from the table into the night, miles to the stockades. Frenzied lawless bands followed on the army's heels stealing livestock, looting houses and farms. Search out the ancestors' graves to strew their bones and vestments over the sacred ground for silver trinkets. Women dragged screaming from the spinning wheel. Perhaps allowed to feed the chickens one more time before they become white men's chickens. Or stripped naked, mauled and pawed unsteady light of the flaming cabin, children run off into the woods, mother begging to go find them, take them with her, but herded with the rest, soldiers whooping hollering, driven like cattle, through rivers, can't even remove the shoes, across fields through briar into the pens. A deaf mute ordered to turn right wanders left his head shattered by the volunteer's musket ball. Twenty-five days. Every shack and cave searched. The Cherokee rounded up. Imprisoned in stockades. Loaded into double-decked keelboats at Ross' Landing on the Tennessee River. And hauled downstream to the Ohio River at Paducah, Kentucky, downstream to the Mississippi River, downstream to the Arkansas River at Montgomery's Point, Mississippi. And up the Arkansas, brown-yellow water full of sandbars, snags and submerged rotting trunks, meandering intense green brush tangled vines and trees. Summer sultry river air to Fort Smith, Arkansas. Then overland into the Cherokee Nation West.

Heat and drought.

Sickness and heartbreak.

Death.

Chief Ross finally knew he had lost. Yet he managed to win a postponement of the removal until October, when the weather would be cooler: 13,000 wait in stifling concentration camps. Measles. Whooping cough. Pleurisy. Bilious fever. Until autumn finally comes on cruel wet and cold. They are loaded into wagons, ride horseback and oxen. Or walk: 645 wagons, 5,000 horses. Cross to the north side of Hiwassee Creek above Gunstocker Creek, cross the Tennessee River at Tucker's Ferry above Jolly's Island at the mouth of the Hiwassee south of Pikeville. Through McMinnville to Nashville. Cross the Cumberland River to Hopkinsville, Kentucky, the Ohio River near the mouth of the Cumberland, through southern Illinois, winter bitter sleet and snow. Cross the Mississippi to Cape Girardeau and Green's Ferry, Missouri. By midwinter all the game has been killed along the southern route and the trail has to be pushed farther north through Springfield, Missouri. Ten miles a day. Rivers clogged ice. Wind. Freezing rain. Frostbite, influenza and pneumonia. Heartbreak. Death. Every night ten to twenty brothers, sisters, children, friends turned into the frozen ground. Over 4,000 die before the winter, the trail of tears traveled to its end.

The moans and the crying constant in their ears. Hear it still! Bitterness. Like they never smile, they never laugh a lifetime long.

Those who held out till the last and suffered the consequences did not intend to submit to the government of Chief John Brown, of those who had come early of their own free choice, who had abandoned the homeland east without a fight, who sold out the homeland east for promises of money and of land.

A council was called at Takatoka to try to resolve the differences. The Ridges, Stand Watie and Elias Boudinot came as observers, wanting to stay out of tribal politics, but left the same day they got there when they saw the resentment among the Ross men who felt betrayed, whose wives, children, parents had died along the trail.

The council broke up without settling anything. Rumors. Standing between the entrance way of the two cabins. Major Ridge. John Ridge and Elias Boudinot, talking to Chief John Brown. *It's their doing that the council failed, sabotaged the council for their ends. To sell us out again.*

A secret conclave was called. The seven clans. Talked or sat quietly in the council house around the fire. Smoke rise and fall upon the floor, drift and rise again. Shift. They sat solemn. Used tobacco. And tempers flare. Rage. *All! the death. All! the suffering. John Ridge, Major Ridge, Elias Boudinot, Stand Watie. Did not suffer! We saw it all! They must be tried! Treason! They must be! Gha!* Judges from the clans of each. Three men from the clan of every traitor called. To pass judgment upon them and their crime by the blood law of October 24, 1829. *Death!*

A hat was filled with numbers, one for every man there. Twelve numbers with an *X* affixed. Each one stepped forward to draw his lot. Twelve *X*'s. The twelve executioners drawn.

Cool pale light morning light hanging fog in branches of blackjack. Horses snorting, hooves on compost forest floor, whispers. Three dismount, walk silently to the house. Enter, silently move from room to room. The children. The guests. The mother. John Ridge asleep. A pistol placed at his temple, the hand tenses and the hammer slams shut. It does not fire. Ridge wakes, focuses, tries to jump, is dragged from the bed, shouts, scuffling waking others, the wife, the children, dragged from his room through the house to the yard, murderers screaming so as not to hear. His wife knocked to the floor where she can only watch. A man on each arm, a man on his chest. The knife flashing dull morning light, plunging twenty-five, twenty-six, and the final slash splatter blood across the throat. The helpless lump thrown up in the air. And trampled single-file. Can only watch the final words drown in gurgling blood. As they disappear indistinct in trees and shouts and horses down the road.

Major Ridge observed the trees. The Line Road to Arkansas. His horse lapping at White Rock Creek. They erupted startled flights of birds fire smoke exploded leaves and twigs. The horse screams out, rearing back panic, drops Ridge to the water flowing blood sparked and clamored cross the sandstone ford.

Elias Boudinot discussed his house with the carpenters at their work. His little boy, Elias Cornelius, watched from the open window of the summer kitchen. Four men approached and asked if Boudinot had charge of the public medicine. He did. They needed medicine for the grandmother and two uncles. He started for the mission. The man behind unsheathed the knife and plunged it in his back. He called surprise and fell. Another man drew a tomahawk and split the skull seven times.

Only Stand Watie escaped. When a Choctaw brought the news. Standing by the sugar barrel loudly bargaining the price, under his breath he told what he had seen. Before Stand Watie rode off to Arkansas, to exile from his home, he stopped by his brother's house. The winding sheet stained and dripping blood upon the wooden floor. Threw back the shroud. And swore his vengeance.

And it has led to this.

John Ross was elected principal chief. A constitution approved. Another newspaper, the *Cherokee Advocate*. By 1859 there are 21,000 Cherokee, 1,000 whites, 4,000 blacks. There are 102,500 acres under cultivation, 240,000 head of cattle, 20,000 horses and mules, 16,000 hogs and 5,000 sheep. The farmers get thirty-five bushel to the acre of corn, thirty bushel of oats and twelve of wheat.

By 1857 there are thirty public schools with 1,500 pupils, an all-Cherokee staff in a system better than Arkansas and Missouri. Seminaries for men and women open in Park Hill, brick churches. Tahlequah, the capital, and Park Hill, the cultural and industrial center. Streets laid out, lots sold. The Supreme Court building put up in Tahlequah, town square headquarters for the council and Chief Ross. A two-story brick hotel built by Mormons stopping on their way west. Business booms in '48 and '49 supplying boots, saddles, picks, axes, clothes, horseshoes and gold pans to prospectors headed for the gold fields of California. By '51 there are eight stores, two dentists, one lawyer, a Masonic Temple and by '52 plans for a national jail.

Chief Ross tours the nation and addresses the delegates to the National Council on what he has seen: "Cherokee neighborhoods show marked improvement, and furnish a sure indication of the susceptibility of all classes among the Cherokee people for thorough civilization. It now becomes the duty of our National Council to sustain and strengthen our institutions and to guard against every untoward encroachment."

Susceptibility for thorough civilization.

When the Civil War breaks out, Chief Ross wants to stay neutral. But the Choctaw and Chickasaw lean to the South. The Osage, Shawnee and Seneca sign treaties with the Confederacy. Elias Boudinot's son, Elias Cornelius, and Stand Watie see their chance for revenge. Come from exile in Arkansas to organize guerrillas, a chapter of the Southern Rights Party, the Knights of the Golden Circle, to fight for the southern cause against Chief John

Ross. A Baptist missionary reorganizes the Keetoowah, the ancient and secret Cherokee Nighthawk Society, to fight for the abolitionist cause. The North and the South supply arms and open warfare breaks out.

Chief Ross is isolated. The Battle of Bull Run: lost by the Union. The Battle of Wilson Creek: lost by the Union. Stand Watie the South's commander, now a Confederate hero. It seems clear the North is losing the war. Chief Ross said: "We are in the situation of a man standing alone upon a low, naked spot of ground, with water rising rapidly all around him. He sees the danger but does not know what to do. If he remains where he is, his only alternative is to be swept away and perish. The tide carries by him, in its mad course, a drifting log. It, perchance, comes within reach of him. By refusing it, he is a doomed man. By seizing hold of it he has a chance for his life. He can but perish in the effort, and may be able to keep his head above water until rescued, or drift to where he can help himself."

Ross signs a treaty putting the Cherokee on the side of the Confederacy and goes into exile in the East while the Cherokee Nation is destroyed. Again.

Stand Watie surrenders June 23, 1865. The last Southern general to give up his sword.

The Union moves to put all the rebellious tribes under one government. Chief Ross, old and dying, returns from exile to oppose. The railroad lobbyists settle in Fort Smith, use Elias Cornelius Boudinot and Stand Watie to accuse Ross of treason and rebellion against the United States and the Cherokee people. White courts and military posts are established within the nation, right of way given to the railroads.

Chief Ross dies August 1, 1866.

And the railroads begin laying track.

Retreat into the flinty back hills, oak-hickory forests of northeast Oklahoma. Chief Redbird Smith revives the secret Keetowah society. Full blood, holed up in log cabins, shacks. Seasonal jobs. Strawberries in May, beans in July, pick cotton and gather pecans in August and September. We gather now twice a year here at the Redbird Smith place, today, July 19, to celebrate his birthday. And the Green Corn Busk in September. From Flute Springs, Chalk

Bluff, Goat Cliff, Pumpkin Hollow, from the haunted remains of the Cherokee Nation West. To keep the rituals. Ball play, stalk shoot, oration, feast. And dance. To guard the sacred Wampum Belt. To keep alive in the council houses with seven ritual woods, the seven clans, *Ani:gha:wi, Ani:tsi:sghwa, Ani:wahhya, Ani:wo:di, Ani:saho:ni, Ani:godage:wi, Ani:gilo:hi,* the eternal fire of the Cherokee.

And to think of what it means.

How do you decide such a thing? Would it have been just as well to fight it out in Georgia, North Carolina, Tennessee, like Tsali did. Awakened in the night by his kinswoman's screams to see her dragged by the hair by one of General Scott's men, trousers hanging open bobbing hard-on for the bushes. See her struggle to her feet. See the hatchet in her hand, the brains and blood splatter her disheveled clothes. The soldier's buddy tries her from behind, she spins, removes his nose with the first, and then the eyes. Would it have been just as well, like Tsali did, to take the hatchet from the woman's hand and go with her into the Smoky Mountains of North Carolina, to the *Ani:gilo:hi,* and fight a three-year guerrilla war? He finally turns himself in for the murder of the two soldiers, gives up his life in front of a firing squad of his clan in exchange for the right of his people to stay, the Qualla Boundary Cherokee, in the mother mountain forests.

Is it betrayal that Chief John Ross placed so much trust in the laws of the Federal Government, in nonviolent resistance, misled the people into thinking they would not have to give up the land, left them false-hoping, unprepared for what was to be?

Is Elias Boudinot a traitor because he accepted when time and death was all that was offered?

And what does his death mean when his brother Stand Watie fights for the Confederates in the Civil War? And his son, Elias Cornelius, is a delegate for the Confederate Congress? Works for the Texas Railroad, the states of Kansas and Missouri, writes articles to open the Oklahoma District up?

What does it mean to all of us that the ancestors did these things? That we are divided and set against one another. That our heritage is destroyed.

It seems empty sometimes. Watching a cancer grow. The animals leave. The rivers turn. The air.

Can only watch with dull eyes. Sit on a bluff above the creek and look. Think about how it was. Could have been.

And how it is to be.

Uhí:soʔdí.

Endure.

Marcus Has to Know

MARCUS stood at the northeast corner of the machine shed and looked. Sorry and Isadora Faire, laughing, from the back porch to the pickup. Malachi's pickup comes from behind the granary, stops. Heard voices, a door slam, the pickup start, gears mesh and Sorry and Isadora head for Yukon. Watched the dust trail over the hill east.

As Malachi gets out. Hands in pockets, starts walking down the drive between the chicken houses and the granary toward the machine shed. Marcus moved back along the north side to the fence row, picked up the scythe and started chopping sunflower, devil's claw and jimsonweed, kicking hedge apples into the ditch. Malachi comes around the corner. "Morning, Marcus."

Still chopping. "Morning."

Standing with hands still in pockets, "Gonna be a nice day, looks like."

"Yep."

"I'm going into El Reno to pick up our Maytag's being repaired. Want me to get those roofing nails we need for the barn?"

Flinging severed stalks, milkweed juice, grass. "Sorry and Isadora. Are going to get. Them in Yukon."

Stands. Breathing new-cut vegetation. "Marcus. How long have we known each other?"

Stops. Turns to look. "Since 1945." Resumes scything. "Why?"

"You know I've always sort of considered you like a brother. The brother I never had. You're the one give Daddy the job as caretaker at the Methodist Church when he come through down and out during the war."

"He had experience. Keeping up buildings."

"You're the one sent the telegram to California when he died, and let Viola and me stay on the Smith place after the funeral until we got settled and could afford some rent. Got Viola the job cooking at the hotel before it burned down."

Stops again. "Malachi. You got something to say? If not, as much as I enjoy reminiscing with you, I got a long fence row to clear here." Look at each other. Marcus turns again and continues, faster stroke, slinging plants, cleaved hedge apples a little dirt now and then higher into the air. Malachi strokes his beard, still standing. Marcus stops, turns. "What's on your mind, Malachi?"

"I was just wondering. About Sorry and. About."

"What about Sorry?"

"If he's made up his mind what he's going to do. Now he's been out of college awhile."

Back to the fence row, bind weed, thistle, volunteer maize. "He lives here. On this farm."

"I know he's supposed to be your sister's boy, but . . ."

Scythe midair motionless. "But what?"

"But."

Leans the scythe against the barbed wire. Walks to where Malachi stands hands back in the pockets of his coveralls. "What are you trying to say, Malachi?"

Stand there face to face, Malachi looking then to his feet, back to Marcus' face, up to the sun in the tops of the hedge row, cardinal clutters past. Malachi backs off a step or two. "Nothing. I'll see you when I get back from El Reno." Turns, walks to the northeast corner of the machine shed. Stops. Marcus still standing. Takes a few steps back toward him. "Marcus. Maybe it would be better. For all of us. If he left."

Marcus watched him stand there a second at the corner of the machine shed. Then Malachi turned, disappeared back down the drive. Marcus heard the pickup start. Fade beyond the house. Watched the dust trail over the hill east. Stood there. Watched and listened.

Returned to the fence row. Picked up the scythe. And chopped it down snap! Broken. Slams down the handle, storms past the machine shed, across the edge of the wheat field behind the chicken houses past the old toilet over the terrace to the back of the barn where Mackey is trimming grass. Mackey looks up startled, sudden energy thudding down from the sky, no question about it, fear throwing him back against the planks, Marcus is mad, no question this was it, yanked from his cowering, thrown into the air and pinned descending, bam against the barn face to face with Marcus. First time face to face. Suddenly calm, for the first time, Marcus seethed quietly breathing hard. Mackey staring through, legs dangling listless. Marcus finally blinks, slides him down the wall to the ground, turns and walks away a few steps up the slope of the terrace, faces Mackey still staring through.

"Mackey. What do you know about Isadora and Sorry?" Mackey begins to nod, to rock back and forth, hardly noticeable, the head, then slightly in the shoulders. "Come on. Tell me what you think you know." Silence. "Mackey!" Strides down the terrace and kicks the wall right next to Mackey's head. "Mackey!" Didn't even blink, not a flinch. "I'm not just talking to hear my teeth rattle, goddamn you!"

Marcus shrinks back, goes down on his haunches, head bowed, Breathing. Slowly. Looks back up. Quiet.

"What do you want to tell me, Mackey?"

Eyes focusing on Marcus' face, sun sheen forehead perspiration. "Marcus. Tell them you're going to. To Tulsa or somewhere. Won't be back until. Tell them you'll be spending the night, but instead go to the shale bank west of the swimming hole and wait till dark. You'll see what I'm talking about."

Marcus pulled the pickup into the pasture south of the road over the hill from the swimming hole, rocking and bouncing over the ruts from the trail into a stand of persimmon trees. Crows loped from the tops cawing warning. Cut the engine and sat. A long wait till dark. Reached into the glove compartment for the box of .22 longs, pulled the .22 from behind the seat and loaded it thoughtfully. Climbed out and stood. Calm. Only now and then a breeze stirring. Sunrays slanting across the slope of buffalo grass and broom weed into the edge of the trees, shale gullying denser toward the creek. Full moon tonight. High clear sky. He ambled over to the persimmons and shook down a handful. Subtle interweaving bird calls, insect modulations. Sucked the sweet tart clenching meat pulp. A sudden surge of air in elm crowns along the main channel of the creek, alfalfa from the field to the southwest, insects and birds fall quiet, waves dissipate across the canopy. An instant silent anticipation. A katydid trill, answer, call, swell across the silence.

Marcus stood a long time to watch and listen.

How little he'd ever stood and listened. Just work. No time to contemplate, stand in awe and wonder.

Finished the last persimmon. Changing light. Darkness building under branches, in draws beneath fallow green pulsing leaves. Waited till grays and blues blended. And a red golden flat rippling moon rose enormous over the falling land.

Picked up the rifle and began to walk. Slowly. Stopping often to listen. Circling south and down into the woods along the watershed, then north, carefully, quietly picking his way along the red shale banks and cliffs, outcroppings, wild grape and thorn bramble memory rising thirty years, forty. From little boy, the same .22 stalking possum, coon. Slipping in under this tree crow roost with a .410 crawling low eerie rustling opaque black umbrella, close thick crow droppings, molty quivering hushed movement, thick air heavy with the smell. The .410 held arm's-length vertical, butt resting on leaves. The sharp report acrid blinding explosion rending the night, panic screams and flight above frenzied feathers, bloodied bodies wings flopping, twitching to the ground. The ecstatic victory dance, shotgun pumping rhythmic above the head in both hands. The knoll lined with carcasses. The man Marcus looking now across the empty hill. The moon. Dark line of the trees upstream. Leading on. The man Marcus. Caught up. Suddenly sinks down and cries. Alone.

Water gurgled through narrow shale juttings into tepid backwater, quiet flowing planes, in steps, rilled gridded continuous moonstruck steps, long gradual, turning switchback, pools, cutbank, absolute course, inevitable immaculate, swimming hole to here. From little boy to here.

Picked up the rifle and walked.

Serene again.

Gliding steps caught up.

Leading on.

To the bridge.

He ducked between the wires of the fence, waded beneath. Red concrete abutments echo tight about the ears. Stood listening for a sign. Nothing. The water flows. Nobody there. Carefully made his way below the dam along the rise to the shale hill thirty yards above the swimming hole.

Climbed up.

And sat.

Sorry came down the road and through the gate. For some reason. Didn't think about it until he saw moon on metal atop the shale ridge in front.

He stopped curious. Then recognized Marcus. Suddenly weak and cold. Attempting to blot him away with explanations. Then calm acceptance, nothing to do, to say. This is it. Too late to run, to find Isadora to warn her not to come. Already on the path, down the lane by the pool. And Marcus already has seen. Her. Me? Too late to run.

Walk on now, Isadora down the spillway of the big pond, doesn't see him, me. Doesn't know yet. Glint of moon on. Metal. Barrel. .22 rifle. What had you imagined it would be. What were you to say. What to say, to do, walking down the slope toward her standing now at the water waiting for. Something, got to do. Call out, and hope she. "Isadora!" She looks up startled. *Anytime now a .22 slug crash the brainpan.* "Isadora. I know it sounds crazy to have you meet me down here to talk about Marcus." *She has to know something's wrong, standing yelling at her thirty yards away.* "About my problem with Marcus." *Come on, woman, figure it out.* "I'm glad you came even though it might sound silly meeting here at night. But it's a nice spot." *Keep talking till she has to know.* "Especially with the moon so bright, you don't even need light to see

325

things." *Don't move.* "I come down here walking a lot by myself when something's on my mind." *Let's see what happens.* "And I've been thinking of Marcus lately."

Confused. Hesitant. Eyes darting back and forth. "Yes. Well. What is going on? I mean, what do you want to talk to me about, about Marcus?"

"You don't mind me talking to you about him? After all we hardly know each other." *She's got it.* Walk a little, knees weak, closer. "You don't think I'm. I'm. This is a little strange, I guess."

"Well, Sorry. I'm glad you wanted to talk." Clears throat. "It's time we got to know each other better. And Marcus has even talked to me. About you. He's a little worried himself."

Sees her lip tremble. "Oh, really."

"Yes. And I've worried a little too. That we, you two don't seem to get along better. I came down here because as it turns out Marcus has asked me about you, to find out what's bothering you."

Long pause. They both start at the same time, then Sorry. "I don't know. We don't hit it off the way we should. He's near." Slight motion with the eyes and head toward the shale bluff. "But he seems so far away sometimes. We just don't seem to be able to talk to each other." Stand silent. In thought. Suddenly. "Sometimes I think he blames me for Blanchefleur's death."

Eyes large dark dart afraid from the shale bluff to Sorry's face. "You what? Sorry. How could you say, what makes you think such a thing?"

Excitement in the voice, louder. "I think it's true. Why else would he be so hard?" Almost turns his head to the bluff. "I came to live here to get to know him, my only relative, love him, and he acts as if nothing has happened."

"That's not true. Marcus can be very kind and gentle. I told you he's worried about you. Really. You've just got to get to know him. We. That's the most ridiculous thing I've ever heard, he blames you for—"

"Well then, maybe I blame him!"

Silence. Uncertain. "What?"

"Yes, I blame him for running her off, for not thinking of anything but work. For his arrogance, self-centered, pious—Why did she run off from him? I think I know. If he—"

Hands up to her face. "How can you say such—"

"He has to work, build for the future, it's like everything he does, if he only understood more than that. He worked for my mother, but ran her off, he's building and developing the farm. Progress! He's proud of the creeping skyline, the developers buying up the land, making it so expensive you can't afford to farm it, he's going to end up destroying what he's working for. Yeah. I blame him. He runs people off. His father, his sister, my father, and I'll be next, and he'll be left with nothing but the smog from Oklahoma City and jam-packed cheap houses and apartments crowding in on all sides. That's what his future's going to be!"

Confused. Angry. Scared. "Sorry. You're wrong. He's. We . . ."

"You just defend him because you love. Him. Admit it, you." Stops abruptly. Realizing. Stammering. "You. I mean. Naturally, you love him, and . . ."

Long silence. "Sorry. I." Eyes filling. Voice thick. "I don't know what to say just now. I think I'd better be."

She turns and runs up the slope. He watches her along the edge of the big pond, disappear into the lane. Stands trembling now. Cold. In hot moon.

Marcus. The .22.

Stands waiting. For the slug to blot it out. To end it. Got to end. Marcus and Isadora. Together in the room. The bed. Loves him. He's won again.

Stands there until it feels absurd.

And leaves.

Marcus, gripping the rifle sweating in his hands, looked down. Tried to pray a foreign prayer. Blue white moon deep vast across the sky, the pasture. Empty. Alone. Forgive. The words. Would not. The sky and pasture. Would not hear. Could not speak. Blanchefleur. Isadora. Sorry. Silence.

And could not speak the word.

327

Sorry Takes His Leave

EVENING. Thunderheads, sturdy, slow, changing with the light. Rolling dark and purple gray, rippling restless electric discharge, red blue fitful white. Inexorable movement along the southwest horizon. Silent. Domes thrust 40,000 feet suffuse vermillion transparent to the intense white of the slanted sun. The moon. And Venus. Chattering irrigation heads reverberating up and down the metal pipes, sputtering rhythmic dissolution harmonic circular water spray pounding earth, splashing leaves and branches, tomatoes, lettuce, chard, dewberry bushes, the peach and apple trees. Woven along the field receding repetitions, uneven, to the distant pump pulsing muted from the northern ponds. Prisms. Floating mist. A desultory wind makes its way across.

Sorry, shirtless, beltless trousers rolled to the knees, stands wet and bootless leaning on a long-handled shovel. It grows dark around him. Mammatocumulus, heat lightning behind the black foliage of the house. The only light from the kitchen window.

He started walking along the pipe, squishing mud between the toes, ducking under and around the sprinklers, to the pump to shut it down. Stepped ankle-deep cold pond water, frogs squawk plop grow silent around, glutinous mud beneath the willow trees, trailing tendrils in the mud-red water. Sorry looks back over the dam to the house.

Stands entranced. A long time. The swimming hole, Isadora, Marcus in the moon. Since her touch, the smell, since, damn, a long time. And time.

Can't stay here anymore. I'm the one, messing up, being pushed, pushing to. To what? What for? I don't get along, she loves him, said so and hasn't returned to the swimming hole. Hasn't returned to his bed, just sleeps alone and waits. We wait. For what? Do nothing but want. To. Just want. Her. Just want her again. Tonight.

Evaporation chills shudder through the shoulders and back. Black purple clouds filling up the sky from the south overtake the sickle moon. Darkness, cold. The pond falls silent. A rapid tremble flexing dark across the water, willows flail and slap. Sorry slips up the Bermuda grass to the top of the dam and looks around, sunflowers toss, the sky gone low and dark, the house feeble yellow light across wet furrows along the irrigation pipe. He shivers. Crouches back down to the water, washes his feet across the mud. Then follows the pipe back to the truck garden. He puts on his boots and slings the shirt and belt across the shoulder.

Walks through the orchard to the lane. Stops at the little pond to wait.

Two lights remain.

Upstairs southeast corner goes out. Marcus. Then Blanchefleur, Isadora's room.

And Sorry begins to move again to the house.

Pulls back the double-loop spring latch slowly squeaks open the gate, swings it shut. The house blue enormous dark windows. Silent lightning interplay distant rumble rolling cold sky. The fence, the wires, the crowns of trees, the wind. Sorry moves quickly from the trees by the gate across the open walk to the back porch, enters, through the kitchen, dark, doesn't see the table, doesn't see the rocking chair, rocking slowly in the living room, to the stairs. The staircase sightless dark pushes on the eyes. Sudden snoring welling up. Hesitates. Stands pounding on the stairs, the distance, the creaking house. Then bolts, swings round the banister along the landing, toward the door, Marcus, ajar, then right, no pressure no resistance, the door to Isadora. Tonight. Swings open and closed and stands. Breathing. Final breath and whisper from the bed. The final distance. Got to. Got to go, to do, but now. Nothing. To say. Nothing to be, to do but dark and distance reaching out to her. Until morning comes.

He kneels by the bed. She looks at him. "Sorry. What are you?"

"I had to."

"But Marcus—"

"Shhh."

Cloth rustles, the belt buckle clangs upon the floor, a boot thumps, every breath shaking the house. Takes off his trousers very carefully and slow. The bedsprings scream, the snoring stops, he freezes one foot off the floor. Until the snoring starts again. The bed is warm. She turns away. He pulls her buttock to his belly. Lie there. Kiss her back between the shoulder blades. Whispers, motionless, only the hand from ankle, shin to knee and thigh along the hipbone, tastes the salt on her cheek along her nose, her mouth. Her hands in his hair, the tears. They lie there. Warm, wet, wipes his eyes on her breast, her stomach wet. Lie there. Don't move. She lies on him, face between the shoulder and the neck. The tears run down.

The dark.

The hands. Soft. Whispers. Breath. A long time silent gentle darkness, wet with crying.

Until the room begins to fade and jumble, slip distortion knead the sweat the tears and bed and body. The clouds heavy hanging dreams across and down the weight the touch the night. To semi-sleep. Until morning comes.

Mackey stands on a chair before the stove. Frying eggs. Marcus out in the yard, check the thermometer, assess the sky. Sorry moves slowly through the door from the living room, stands stretching, rubs the eyes. Mackey looks. Right at him, they look at each other till Sorry looks away, turns round, retreats, reappears with shirt and boots in hand, grabs an apple from the counter by the banana cookie jar. "I'm heading on to the truck garden, Mackey."

Mumbling out the back porch past Marcus coming in.

Isadora comes down the stairs, through the northwest down-stairs bedroom to the bath. Washes her face with cold water, brushes teeth, combs the hair. Leaves through the back porch door past the upright freezer, the buffet and bunk into the kitchen behind Marcus sitting at the head of the table listening to the morning market report. She looks at the coffee pot among the apples, not perking yet, and sits.

"How'd you sleep?"

"Huh?" Mackey turns to see.

"How'd you sleep. Fine cool night."

"Not. Not too well. For some reason."

Mackey bangs the skillet across the burner, carries oatmeal to the table. Isadora staring in the coffee cup, heavy white stoneware stained, a crack across the lip. The coffee perks. She gets up and pours a cup. "No eggs for me, Mackey."

He serves up Marcus, brings his own plate to the table, climbs up on the chair he'd been standing on. Looking from face to face. Eating in silence for a while.

"Mackey and I'll be cleaning up and burning brush up in the north pasture this morning. From around the north watershed and ponds."

"Um."

"Bout time we cleaned out the chicken houses."

"Um."

Mackey slowly eating oatmeal, a big spoon clutched. Looking hard from face to face. Tense silence. Isadora not looking up from coffee, black, bubbles, aromatic from the cup. Occasional nervous exhausted sips.

Marcus wipes the yellow from his plate with bread. Mackey collects the dishes and stacks them by the sink. Marcus takes the toothpick from over the ear. Looks at Isadora. She's not looking. Then stands. "Mighty fine breakfast, Mackey. Let's hit it."

And leaves her sitting at the table.

Mackey follows close on Marcus' heels. Pumping gas into the pickup, Marcus turns and stumbles over him. "Mackey. What's got into you. Have you got the axes from the machine shed?"

"No, Marcus."

"Well, hustle."

"I. Okay."

Marcus checks the oil. Wipes dust from the engine. Doesn't notice distant two-stroke engines along the county road. Mackey tosses the axes on behind and they head out to the north pasture. Mackey fretting with the cuff of his shirt.

They get out at the brushpile. Mackey stands. Marcus gets a can of gas from beneath the deadwood in the back, splashes on the wood, doesn't notice rising dust in the southeast, the engines. Sees Mackey stand and fret, do nothing but watch from the tailgate. Takes a kitchen match from his shirt pocket. "Stand back, Mackey."

"Marcus."

"What?"

"You got to stop Sorry and Isadora."

Marcus strikes the match on his pants leg. Holds it for a second. Looks at Mackey. Pitches the match. The brush explodes percussive combustion blasting blue white oil smoke curling, waft, hanging in the early air. Chrome exhaust pipes, knobby tires sun-flamed extension tubes, heterochromous teardrop tanks Harley Hog, Yamaha, Suzuki, Kawasaki, Honda, Ducati, Indian, churning up the shale bank south of the road by the swimming hole spinning grab throwing red shale dust mingling admixture expended lubricants, carbon monoxide, sulfur dioxide and water vapor.

The Oklahoma City Leaping Lepers.

Grease-stained dust-impacted blue jeans and jackboot hobnail. Leather jacket, jean jacket, Vietnam infantry jacket embroidered red orange blue skull in crash helmet. Sunburnt asymmetric bearded long-haired bikers. Toothless grinning. Earring. Nose ring. Tattooed. Scarred. And big-buttock loose-breasted women on behind. Tearing up the shale bank, catapulting follow the leader, ripping out pasture grass. Billowing autumn sky, drifting north.

Marcus and Mackey, fire-bleached faces anxious agitated, circle around dead twigs, branches, trunks. Underbrush and scraps. Elm, bois d'arc, cottonwood deadwood burning crack popping swirls smoke and flames throwing up sparks and glowing skeleton leaves. They toss debris from the pickup bed, voices strained against the fire.

"Mackey, I told you never bother me with that again."

"But, Marcus, just come and—"

"Like last time, have me like a bonehead fool in the middle of the night."

"Wasn't Sorry out late last night moving the irrigation down at the truck garden?"

"So what."

"And Isa—your wife slept in Blanche's room."

"Mackey, I'm warning you if you don't mind your—"

"Just come and look, I can show you red mud tracks up the stairs right to her room."

A ball of fire explodes the central frame of trunks and branches, showering smoke and embers, driving them back behind the pickup. Eyes constricting, acid bite watering. Marcus looks up wiping tears and sees the dust cloud to the south, hears beneath the fire searing hisses cracking oxidation throb of engine rev and back-off.

"Just come and look, Marcus. Tracks right to her room."

"Mackey. I don't know about you."

Still looking toward the dust. Distracted now on all sides, Mackey, the fire, the red cloud drifting from the south. Paces back and forth along the pickup, intense heat driving them further back. Marcus examining the southern sky, Mackey coming around the pickup. "Marcus."

"Shhh!"

"Marcus, better move the pickup, the lenses on the sidelights are starting to melt, it's too close."

Marcus jumps into the cab. "Watch the fire. I gotta check out those motorcycles. Hoodlums from the city on motorcycles." Bounces out the gate and south down the road west of the house, pulls up the drive, find Sorry, motorcycles. No. Not motorcycles. Marcus jumps out and heads onto the back porch, know he's not, "Sorry!" the kitchen. Of course. The kitchen, caught them there before, blocking up the door, seen them at the kitchen sink laughing together, touch. Her head thrown back and him looking, knowing smile. How could she. Mackey the living room, bolts up the stairs to see.

Footprints.

Red mud. Up the stairs along the landing to Blanchefleur. In the room. A glint of brass beneath the bed. A buckle. Rodeo champion.

Marcus bellows out "Sorry!" and plunges down the stairs knocking over kitchen chairs on the way out into the back yard yelling "Sorry! Isadora!" Two-stroke engines throbbing louder.

Isadora appears in the west door of the chicken houses, sees him. And it's clear. *What did you expect? Hurt and angry because. You. He loves you.* Look at each other, her eyes fill, she knows. *Too late?* He lunges for her, she ducks back in among a ripple of hens as Marcus crashes the door. Isadora in the northeast corner. Behind the roosts in front of the long row of wooden laying cubicles. Marcus at the southwest door by the feed trough and watering can. Thick warm soft aroma, chicken droppings, feathers. Low pluck pluckpluck pluck chickens settling back down. Marcus breathing hard, trembling. Isadora, a bucket of eggs around her arm. An egg down-stuck in her hand. Marcus steps a few feet through straw and milling chickens a hen squats and hunching her wings, he flips her aside with his toe. "You. You harlot, whore of Babylon. You . . . "

"Marcus. I . . . " *He loves me. Angry. Trapped.*

Trapped. The door to the next chicken house on the other side of the roost. Marcus starts for her again, she throws the egg, crack, ducks crawling under the roost scattering fowl flapping flurry feathers and straw, through the door into the middle house, Marcus burrowing under after. She grabs the outside door, can't get the latch, jumps clear of Marcus around the middle roosts upsetting feed troughs air full of churning flutter along the cubicles on the north wall, cackling swarms panicking hens. She throws another egg missing, "Marcus, wait. Stop. Let me . . . " Marcus grabs around the corner stop her, teach her, get a hold of slipping chicky-doo a rack of cubicles tumbling dumps chickens eggs and straw to the floor as Isadora escapes into the third coop behind a herd of flying chickens run in circles scream and shouting. Marcus has to backtrack and down the center aisle fighting air thick with flapping birds. By the time he makes the door Isadora is out onto the drive, bucket of eggs, sprinting around the house to the east as Sorry leaves the barnyard coming from the truck garden. To find Marcus. About the motorcycles.

Marcus sees him. Bellows.

Sorry looks at Isadora heading down the drive toward the road. Back at Marcus. *This is it. No doubt about it.*

He decides to go wide, Marcus a big man, good reflexes. Number 18 has great quickness, ability to change direction. Marcus' lateral speed turns the play inside, Sorry cuts back, a quick juke. Can't take him one on one and is around heading for the porch roar of the. Roar of the motorcycle engines. Sorry crashes through the house upstairs for the keys to the '31 Chevy. Trapped behind the line. Marcus blocking up the middle, plugging up the stairs, Sorry instinctive feel for the holes, makes for Blanchefleur's room, locks the door, out the window, roaring, engines roaring outside on the roof of the front porch, *always through windows,* engines. Motorcycles.

Isadora surrounded, exhausted, weeping on the south road down the drive.

Marcus kicking the door. Stops. Heads to his bedroom window. Sees the Lepers, Isadora on the road. Toothless scraggly bearded pimples scabby knuckles revving, battery acid holes in jeans, blasts blue smoke surrounding Isadora in dust on the road. "Come on, farmer's daughter, we heard about you, you want to go for a little ride, baby. Ooowee! We'll take you for a little ride."

Marcus charges back down the stairs, outside and down the east drive. Yelling. "Take her! Take the whore. You can have her."

Sorry swings from the roof, leaps into the Chevy and aims her around the house falling off the steep west drive out on the road, drifts the corner east toward the mess of motorcycles, throws her into a power slide scattering bikers ever way, only Isadora left two feet from the Chevy coming to rest sideways in the road. She jumps in, Sorry guns it backwards, tires spinning, one last glimpse, Marcus leaping up onto the red shale wall of the rock garden *bad blood* to watch them *bad blood for generations* reverse down the road west.

Motorcycles swarm wheelies after them, gears shift grinding acceleration forward around the corner. Heading north past the house, the pasture, the towering bonfire and Mackey silently turns to watch.

The Leper leader Harley pulls alongside shouting obscure obscenities, Sorry swerves, Harley reflex evasion sends the wheels out from under him, spiraling on his side, flying churn through motorcycles scattering into ditches, flung up over the fence, in a tangled chain reaction slide.

Nothing but dust in the rearview mirror. Sorry accelerates on over the road up a long hill, dropping down along a creek channel, cross a booming flat railless wooden spring bridge, S-curve through undulant red shale hills, sandplums, another rise, flat pasture, and down along the creek again dense trees crowding the road. Four miles. Turns east where the road ends. Across the trestle bridge, rumbling cross-laid wooden bed and parallel two-by-twelves. Then pulls off the road, down a path through a wash in the bluff into the trees above the creek. Down over a sudden drop between red shale banks. Onto a flat shale stratum by the water. And stops.

Looks over at Isadora. Still holding the bucket of eggs in her lap.

They sit silently listening.

Waiting.

For what?

Nothing. This is it. All over, no more, nothing to do, moonlit on the shale hill above the swimming hole, tried to stay away from each other again. Couldn't do it. Seeing. Watching each other move. In the kitchen. In the barnyard. In the fields. Hearing at night between the walls, standing alone together washing dishes at the sink. Nothing but you. Your face, nose, ears, lips teeth and tongue. Voice. Walk. Nothing but. You. "I had to come, Isadora. Come see you again. To be with you."

She looks up from the eggs. "I'm. I should have. I guess I didn't kick you out, did I?"

Slides over to him, trembling. He strokes her hair, to soothe, to say something, but nothing comes. "It doesn't make sense, Isadora. What you hear about love. Where do you find a place for it. Soil to grow in. Seed aren't worth anything without dirt, water, fertilizer. But the only thing we've got is plenty of bullshit. And I. It's so damn frustrating. I sometimes see, like a dream right before you fall asleep, I see clear, I understand, and reach out. But when I wake up there's nothing in my hands."

Fall silent. Sit for a while. Isadora slowly calm. "What are we going to do now?"

"Damn. All we ever do is wonder what we're going to do now. Next. One mess to the next. We're going to spend the night here, that's what. In the 0 '31 Chevy, my dad's Chevy, in the back seat mattress where more than likely I was conceived on Marcus' sister, going to spend the night naked with Marcus' wife. And, and eat eggs. And then in the morning we'll wonder what the hell we're going to do next. In fact I know what we're going to do. We're going to live in these woods. Right here. Goddamn. Make us a home."

"Prop the car up on cinderblocks."

"Right."

"Put in a garden. Get a dog. Make bows and arrows to hunt with."

"Right. You're mine now. I won you fair and square. Marcus gave you away. To the Lepers, said they could have you, and I took you, rescued you. You're mine now."

"Law of salvage."

"Yeah. Finders keepers." Trails off into silence. "Damn. What are we going to do?"

Sit listening to the creek.

"You know, Sorry. Always known what we're going to have to do. One of us is going to have to leave."

"One of us?"

"Because you're right. You. We don't have a place. Because love. Isn't a cause. It's an effect, it doesn't make things happen. Things make it happen, and we don't have. Those things. All we've had, like I said from the very first, is fantasy. If I left with you we would collapse within a month. The fantasy is so strong because it makes clear how much we lack, you know, what we don't have. We. I've been sidetracked. Don't get me wrong. A fantasy love has a lot to be said for it, the best kind even, for the short run. But the run is longer than that." Pause. The movement of branches through the windshield. "You know, what I really want, I really believe, I'll find on the farm. I didn't even know it before, not for sure. With Marcus. For all his old-fashioned ways and faults, Marcus treats me like he treats everybody else. He's used to having strong women around."

"But he ran you off. How can you . . ."

"I think I can. He lost control today. Because of me. I can. I know Marcus a little bit better now. The trouble people have dealing with him can be seen more ways than one. He runs people off. Or people run away. No one has ever stood up to him. Well. I want to stay, and I am going to stay. And you know what? That's all it's going to take. I hope. I think. Some resolve."

"But don't you see."

"All we need is some time. It won't be easy, it may be hell. But I've got to do it, cause one thing's certain. Running won't."

"But you . . ."

"Don't talk me out of it."

Sit. Not looking at each other a long time. She twists the green jasper ring from her finger. "Here. Take this. To remember. It belonged to my grandmother."

Looks at the ring. Pause. Rubs the tip of his nose. "Then he's. I've lost. Everything."

"You've got everything to find."

Keeper Sells the Farm

Robert Keeper rubbed a gnarled hand across the face. Not light yet. Saw profile hand *coming out chute number two pulling leather no ride.* Untangled the muggy sheet, swung heavy feet to the linoleum. Stale cigarette butts, cold coffee cup, letters by the faint phosphorescent alarm clock ticking *jolting eight seconds gnashing teeth snorting* picked up the clock to see, 5:30. Not light yet. Getting on, getting on toward fall, winter. Rubbed sweat from his eyes. But sure don't seem like. Put the clock back on the nightstand. The picture framed shadows. Sorry with a 4-H calf. Rose from the edge of the bed, popping bones, creaking floor to the closet. All color gray. The red, gold, silver green embroidery on blue. The shirt. Blanchefleur wore. Still hanging, the day. Pale. Alone. Took out a Sears shirt. Buttoned it slowly, picked up trousers hung over the chair back, lift up one foot, balanced, back to the floor, up again and through the leg, then the other. Pulled up the pants, stood spread-legged tucking in the shirt, snapped the waistband, zippered the fly, buckled the belt. Bronze. Saddle Bronc Champion. Gathered loose change, pocketknife, fingernail clippers, wallet from the bureau top. Found the boots in the dark corner, still dark, shorter days, next to the wall. Fished around in the top drawer for a pair of socks with no hole in the toes. Moved slowly to the door into the kitchen.

A blue glow propane flame beneath the gray porcelain coffee pot. Soft percolation. Aroma. And Hank a black hole against the windows where he sat and waited. "Morning, Keeper. Coffee's almost ready."

Sitting at the table, pulling on socks and boots. "How'd you sleep, Hank?"

"Pretty sultry night."

"Sure was."

Gets up, walks to the sink, rinses a tin cup, shakes it a few times to the stove, pours coffee. Stands at the stove awhile. Finally moves back to the table. "How are things looking?"

"Pretty good. Soon as it's light I'm gonna get on the ol tractor, get her tuned up fore people start showing up."

They fall silent, each intent on the coffee cup.

"What time did the auctioneer say he'd be here?"

Sorry drove down the highway, fifth of whiskey cradled between the legs, green jasper ring on the little finger. Things not working out.

Only thing to do is move on. After four days sleeping alone in the woods by the creek, four days since Isadora walked back down the road to him, sleeping alone in the back seat of the Chevy. Waiting. For what? Move on. In the dark, toward dawn. Past the farm. To the swimming hole where, the shale bluff. Sit in the dark, steel-bodied guitar, and play the signal song. Did she hear? And move on.

And take another pull from the bottle. Surging fingertips and brain. Isadora. Rolling shale hills bluffs and valleys giving way to flattening plains shortgrass. Don't think of her. The hands cowboy hands on the steering wheel, black dash gray velvet lining saturated red dust. Steel-bodied guitar on the back mattress, taking Marcus' woman away, Blanchefleur, Isadora. Restless homeless lonely cowboy. Sorry shook his head, looked at the hands, the legs, stretched feet on the accelerator, beside the clutch pedal. Roger Lyons. Looked into the rearview mirror leaning forward close. A face. His face afterall.

Rested back in the seat. The engine smooth gliding highway. The land. He looked. Born here. Grew up. Played football All-State number 18, salutatorian. Plowed, sowed seed, cut wheat.

Why feel like such a fraud?

Home. My home after all, maybe crazy to ever leave in the first place. Hank and Dad. Can trust them, easygoing, cowshit on the boots, idle talk on the porch watching the sun go down. Like always. The feeling coming over the road. Zing. Home.

I was coming home.

The Chevy rumbled off the blacktop onto the sandy section line, swerving a controlled fishtail accelerating dusty wake. Warm fall morning. Cottonwoods dull green touched yellow along creek beds. Cows turning to watch. Sorry, hair twisting flying around the face, impassive. Exhausted. Alone. Fence posts clattering by. Crest a hill, there it is! Foreground windmill churning, pumping, long rusty pipe to galvanized tank. Moss circling the edge hanging, brim dipping trickle, a meandering path through bare trodden ground, past the concave salt lick into buffalo grass falling away to the far section line corner. Hedgerow. Trees. A red barn. A silo. Modular structures, outbuildings. The house. The farm.

And cars. Lots of cars and pickups parked in front, along the road.

Sorry drove on to the corner, turned north for the farm, not really thinking, wondering what, but wondering what was going on, should have called before. Been a while since. A long time actually.

Pulled off the road in front of the house. Lots of people here for some reason. Got out, stretched, feeling strangely good, home, but. Why the crowd. Sounds from the barn. Walked around the back of the house to see.

Combine, tractor, springtooth one-way disk drill hay rake cream separator. Tables full of Mason jars. Dishes. Crocks. Chicken feeders brooder. Corn knives scoop shovels spades sledgehammers crowbars. Axes. Saws. People milling strolling through, looking over, laughing, talk.

An auction. What is going on. The auctioneer steps up, the

crowd gathers. "Next item. A 1940 International Harvester tractor. Fine machine." Hank comes from out of the barn with the crank. "Tell you what I'm gonna do. This ol rip is the finest machine ever to pull a plow. And if she don't start on the first quarter-turn, I'm gonna give her away to whoever wants her."

Inserts the crank, walks around to set the choke and throttle, returns to the crank, motions for quiet, spits on the palms of his hands, leans over resting left hand on the grill, grabbing crank handle with the right, plants both boots, gives a gentle quarter-jerk revolution and she's tying every bundle, running purring quiet contented not missing a lick.

"Who's gonnagimme two hundred dollars, twohunner twohunner, gimme two fifty."

Sorry walks back to the front porch. The drive. The whiskey. The. To sit down. Exhausted where he stands.

Hank sat silently rolling a cigarette. Keeper seemed embarrassed, apologetic, ashamed. Explaining. How he'd meant to write, but. "But one thing. Led to another. Lots of hassles, pretty busy you know. But anyways, now you're here we can, I mean there's no need to write." Sorry listening passive. "That we've sold the farm." Hank rises, strikes a kitchen match on a post. "You see, these lawyers from Denver come down to talk to us, representing a feller up in Colorado." Porch. Elm tree in the yard, old tire hanging from a frazzled rope. The mailbox on a two-by-four in a milk can. Smell the cedars crowding the steps. Goatheads along the edges. Home. "Well, they offered over a thousand dollars an acre for the old place. I mean a man can hardly afford to farm at prices like that. What with the taxes. And Hank and I ain't getting any younger, we figgered, what with you. I mean. The equipment all getting old, need to replace it soon. A new tractor goes for $60,000 nowdays." Looking around the porch for help. Wanting to stop. "Besides. More to life than."

Hank gets back up to flick ashes. Look down at my fingernails. The ring. Sorry looks up at Keeper. "What are you gonna do?"

"I figger some of the money is yours. I mean I always figgered you. Some of the money's yours."

"What are you gonna do, Dad?"

"We got, Hank and me, we got a house, nice little place in

342

town. Relax. Take it easy. There's more to life than trying to keep from starving out on a farm. We'll sit on the porch like city folk, loafing and lying. Won't we, Hank?" Pause. "Might even go back to riding rodeo." Silence on the porch. Keeper looking from face to face. "Hell yes. Why not. More to life. Hell. Why not."

Sit numb through the afternoon. Evasive greetings to those who pass. "Sorry, how you doing, son." From high school. Old friends. Use to plow for, buck bales with. Looked out across the road and pasture, the windmill a mile shimmering autumn heat. Born here. Grew up. Home. The rhythmic cant of the auctioneer from the barn. Going once. Part of me. Going twice. My own sweat and body. Going three times and.

Gone.

Sorry Goes Crazy

STRETCHED out along the highway. Down the long incline, the narrow steel truss bridge, the long rise beyond. A couple of miles of thin squirming asphalt, telephone poles, fence posts, road signs, white stripe, yellow no passing line at the bridge, the top of the distant hill rippling thermoclines, exhaust fumes of the Wiley outfit out of Texas.

Sorry brought up the rear. In the oldest, slowest, an old green six-cylinder ton-and-a-half Ford with a Massey 95. Bogging down as he crested, looked ahead, could see the twelve trucks piggy-backed combines and header trailers. The newest almost over the hump, the five twenty-foot house trailers pitch and weave behind the pickups, the cross wind, the rolls and frost heaves of the road bed. He shifted axles, double-clutching, over the top through the gears, picking up speed to run the next. Hand throttle full-tilt, unzipped his pants, opened the door pushed against the pressure stepped out on the running board, holding on to the wheel with the right pulled out the dick with the left, leaning away at the hips as far as he can, head turned, thrown back out of the backwash of air to piss. Can't stop now, takes too damn long to get this baby up a head of steam. Climbs back in to see the lightning across the horizon, no cutting tomorrow looks like, to see the White cab-over diesel semi hauling ass down the other side of the hill toward him billowing black plumes drifting smoke for the narrow bridge at the bottom. Quick calculation. Estimated time of arrival, $T = D/R$, acceleration equals f double prime, the White will hit the north end of the bridge exactly coincidental with the Ford's arrival south. Instantaneous rate of change, f prime, more or less equal for both rigs. Eighty miles per hour. Put on the brakes? Hell no. Too damn long, never get up the other side, width of bridge minus the quantity width of Ford plus width of the White diesel, equals, give or take a foot or two, positive six inches. Keeps the hammer down. White does too. Picking up speed. The diesel's air horn bellows, Sorry easing her over toward the shoulder as far as, got three inches to spare on either side, plenty of goddamn, bridge surface not the smoothest I've ever, correct for fucking windage, southwest at thirty-five mile per, gust to, will suck toward the trailer past the tractor wake blowing out, not much tolerance for course corrections too late to goddam worry, steady as she, wish the ol Ford's steering was a tad tighter motherfuck WHOMP shatter glass flying shook violent back and forth scattering consciousness sound falls back blasting off the north end of the bridge. The ass end of the semi disappearing in the rearview mirror. If there'd been a rearview mirror on the left side, the right hand mirror gone too, both clipped. The semi got the left, the bridge truss the right, just the glass splinters reflecting on the front seat and jeans. And the Ford moans and hunkers on up the rise. Hot damn baby all right! Sure as shooting, rain tonight, no cutting tomorrow. All goddam right with me I could use the rest.

Sorry pulls into Bird City a mile behind the next slowest truck. Tools along U.S. 36 looking for the place to pull in, the empty lots all packed full, a cold slow rain settling in. Trying to see where his buddy ahead pulled off through the sprinkled dust, road grime, saw the familiar Ford, the GMC, how bout that! Marcus' crew in town. Bob, Billy Paul. Hand on the steering wheel green jasper ring. Be good to see those two again. Been a long time.

Sorry pulled in alongside the last Wiley truck clear outside of

town. Old man Wiley saunters up, wad of Redman chewing tobacco in his cheek. "How's she striking, Sorry?"

"Can't complain. Did have a little problem with my rearview
mirrors though."

Inspects the severed metal braces. "Goddamn, Sorry. What the
hell happened to the sons of bitches?"

"Well. Turned out there was just not enough room on that
narrow bridge over the North Fork of the Smoky Hill for that semi,
me and the mirrors all at the same time."

"Now, Sorry, I don't recollect no narrow bridge on the North
Fork."

"It could of been the South Fork, I'll admit I didn't have time
to reread the sign."

"You're just gonna have to be more careful, son."

"How long I been driving for you?"

"This is the third harvest, ain't it? You first come on the year
the cyclone tipped over the cook trailer between Sitka and Hoxie,
wasn't it?"

"Yep. How much damage I done this old Ford in them years?"

"Well, let's see, Sorry. Hell. Those mirrors gonna set me back
eight, ten bucks apiece. Add that in, guess that makes about sixteen
to twenty bucks. But that's not what I mean. I mean about knowing
where you are." Spits long arc into the ditch. "Man be in a hell of a
shape to cash it in and not even know where he was."

"Yeah. I guess you're right about that. You think anybody is
interested in going into town tonight after supper? Sure don't look
like we're gonna be doing any cutting tomorrow."

"I imagine a man could find somebody." Spits. "If he looked
hard enough."

Sorry knew right where to look.

Billy Paul, St. Louis Cardinals cap pushed back on his head,
over at the number two snooker table. Bob, left foot propped on
the brass rail, in the middle of a bunch of loud laughing harvest
hands, beer glass in the fingerless gap gesticulating through hovering strata of smoke. Sorry walks up behind him. "Hey, buddy, you
don't by any chance happen to have a copy of the periodic tables on
you, do you?"

"Well, goddamn! Sorry. How the hell are you?"

"Not too bad, how bout yourself?"

"I guess I'll make it, scuse me, fellas." Walking over to the snooker table. "Hey, Billy Paul, put down that cue stick, boy, look who's here."

Shaking hands. "Sorry! Sure glad to see you, how the hell are you?"

"I guess I'll make it, how bout yourself?"

"Not too bad. You think you'll make it, huh? You're just the man I need to see. What do you think? Will that 5-ball go in the side pocket between them two red ones?"

"Mighty thin cut."

"It'll do her though, won't it?"

"You'd have a leave on that red and the 7 that ain't half bad."

"Hell yes."

"Course if you miss, your man's gonna have that good leave."

Chalks his cue, kisses her right in. "How bout that?"

"Not too bad. I think you're learning a thing or two. Bob and I'll be over in the corner booth soon as you finish taking this feller's money."

They sit. Bob pulls out a pint of bourbon in a brown paper sack, takes a hit, face skewed about the lip, chases with his beer, passes it over to Sorry. "What you been up to? Haven't seen you, let's see, been at least two, three years. Alliance, Nebraska, that time it come the big storm we trying to get home drunk. Billy Paul got up to piss and the tarp dumped twenty gallon of water on us."

"That's right. I been doing all right."

"You look pretty good. Little unfocused about the eyes maybe."

"You always said I should make things simple." Takes another swig, chases with beer. "Well, I can't make it much simpler than it is now. Just me, my steel-bodied guitar and the old '31 Chevy."

"Yeah? But if I know you, you somehow got that complicated too. Whatcha doing for money? I mean, besides this ritual summer madness."

"I work odd jobs. Travel around."

"Like what?"

"Well, there was the time I was the chief burger fryer at the Griff's Burger in Lawrence, Kansas."

"That sounds like an odd job all right."

"Wasn't half bad."

"All bad I'll bet." Another swig.

"It had its moments. I'd come on duty at eleven in the morning, right before the big rush, get everything ready. Had my stainless steel prep table to the right, the 24-by-24 grill, the gallon bucket of chopped onions and cross-cut industrial dills, the deep fat wells on the left for the french fries. The patties in the deep freezer behind, 2½ by 2½, 960 to a box, so 81 patties, a 9-by-9 matrix on the grill, got the buns all lined up on the prep table, the cheese squares, all precut individually wrapped, at the top, ratio of about two to one, cheeseburgers to regular, which means each grill load will be 54 to 27." Takes a shot, a gulp of beer. "First you slap on the meat. Plenty of time. First time through cause there's nothing to bag and the buns already laid out. Get the frozen potatoes, dump a batch in each basket, drop into the fat. You see these things cost eleven cents each, thirteen for cheese, so the pace is gonna get hectic, peak about 12:47, then trail off, bell-shaped curve, and the prep process itself accelerates to a crescendo. After the fries are down, pick up the pace to open the buns, presplit but still requiring a certain high-speed delicacy of touch, then the spatula, first string of orders coming into the girl at the window, turn all the patties, starting with the first one down, usually the bottom right to left, then up to the next rank left to right and so on zigzag to the top. But for variety sometimes top to bottom, or even spiral one way or the other around the grill, get them all flipped and symmetry restored, you place the cheese, top, bottom, left two-thirds or right, spoon on the chopped onions, actually fingers better, but violation of the health code. Finger on the onions, place getting plenty steamed and greasy by now, sweat starting to pearl and river, toss the onions onto the sizzling pile, grab your pickles, put them on the bun bottom on the prep table, one section per, time to get serious now. Get your toe hooked"—a pull of bourbon—"on the leg of the prep table"—on his feet, toe hooked, legs spread, knees loose, hands and forearms parallel in front—"and you pivot. Six at a time. Three in each hand moving the bun tops over to the grill, check the bags. Ready. In rhythm, toe hooked, pivoting, spatula in the right, scooping them up, three at a time, pivoting man, anchored with the toe, till the grill's cleared. Pull up the fry baskets. Scrape the grill clean, another matrix of meat, gob of french fries, bag the burgers, blue bag regular, red bag cheese, bag the fries, place the next raft of buns, toss everything bagged under the ultraviolet and you're off on the repeat cycle. Two, three hours straight on a busy day." Comes up from the grill. Drains the bottle and the beer. "Naw, the job wasn't half bad sometimes." Sits.

Bob uncorks another whiskey. "And the best thing about it was that you knew you wouldn't be doing it very long I'll bet."

"There's sure something to that. Gimme a snort." Bottle passes. More beer ordered. "Then there was the time I was a midnight watchman. That was really something. Took me two months to get used to the schedule, midnight till eight in the morning, only getting about four hours a night sleep. That was up in Michigan, Ann Arbor. Now there's a town for you. Only place I been where the beggars hand you a joint as a receipt for the quarter you give them. Man, I been around the last few years. Worked in a fiberglass factory for a while, soybean crushing mill in Wichita. Even delivered the *Kansas City Star*, me and my old '31 Chevy, three-thirty every morning. Shit, Bob, I can't make it much simpler than that."

"And?"

"Same old crap."

"I don't know what I'm gonna do with you, Sorry, I try to teach you the goddam secret of life and you do nothing but fuck up."

Looks at him awhile. Breaks out laughing. "You old crazy two-fingered, one-lunged bastard. It sure is good to see you again." Falls silent. Another drink. Another. "How's Marcus doing?"

"Same old Marcus."

Another. "Isadora?"

"Doing real good."

Look around the bar. Finish off the bottle. "Tell her you saw me."

Winks. "Sure thing. Real careful." *Like he understood.*

Guess maybe he does. "How's she look?"

Fishes out another pint bottle, slides it across the tabletop spinning, stops pointing neck. "Open this up you crazy like a bull got in the jimsonweed."

I guess I was getting a little crazy. And started thinking of ways to get back and see her. I had to see her, touch her. Be with her again. I

349

thought of sneaking in at night with the guitar and singing our signal song to meet down at the swimming hole. But knew Marcus would kill me sure. But what the hell. I had a plan.

You see I had my old college buddy Honest John and his woman Lynda. He taught English at some small college near Pittsburgh for awhile. Union organizing, got fired. He'd become sort of a craftsman. She was a yogini, had a studio overlooking the Monroe County Courthouse in Indiana. During the summer they traveled around in a VW bus selling jewelry, rings, earrings, bracelets, belt buckles, floating butterflies, quilts, stuff like that made out of silver wire, brass, stones and scrap cloth. I ran into them out in southern California.

I picked up a little spending money now and then as a street singer. Actually a little more than spending money. You can make quite a bit if you halfway know what you're doing. I almost headed off to Europe with a couple of musicians. They could make enough in northern Europe, Germany, Holland, Scandinavia, to live the winter in the south. Greece or Italy. You see the secret of singing in the street is knowing where to stand. Someplace quiet and with people walking by who've been shopping. That's the trick, striking the balance between where people are and noise isn't. A nice little equation, which deteriorates at both ends. Sometimes you can get more sound and more people, or less noise and fewer people and it will yield the same money. But no noise and no people and all people and all noise won't catch it, and too many people with quiet breaks down the equation too, cause they've no place to stand and listen. All noise and no people is just a theoretical possibility.

You've also got to know what songs to sing, tailor them to the audience. What you sing at shopping malls got to be different than on a campus, which also dictates what you wear. You can't be singing protest songs wearing this-could-be-my-own-runaway-son's clothes, or old favorite ballads looking like a drug-crazed hippie. Probably my biggest asset is my guitar. To sing out on the street you need something that is loud and unusual, and the steel-body fits that to a T. Banjos are also good, and fiddles. Most important to your long-term survival is knowing how to deal with the police. Cause the police sure gonna deal with you. In fact, you don't even have to be singing if you have long hair and drive a '31 Chevy to deal with the police. They pull you over two or three times a week just to see how you're doing.

Which gets me back to Honest John and Lynda. One day out in California, we were working a pitch together, checking out whether we'd each make more that way. Synergistic, you know. And the police busted us. Now the first thing you learn is to travel clean, so we expected the usual hassle and then have to move on. Which was enough to piss us off, cause we were in a good location, near the beach, pulling in all sorts of bread, but like I say, you got to be able to handle things like this. But these cats were serious.

Two cars whip up either side of us. My friends had their wares laid out on a blanket beside the bus, and I was sitting on my stool, the old milking stool used to be back home in the barn, really getting with it. One of them days, sun shining, calm, mild. Just grabbing into the strings pulling music out, flowing from the tips of the fingers, the wrists, arms, shoulders, back and legs and feet. Singing some Roger Lyons stuff from the notebooks. Floating. My first impression was of two large dark blue figures. I think one's coming to throw some money in my hat and the other to look at jewelry. Always try to make eye contact with the patrons, even when I'm carried away, and damn if it wasn't the ugliest cop you'd ever want to see towering over, making it very clear he didn't care one bit for my ecstasy. I try the innocent approach, smiling and playing on, but he reaches down a ham-sized fist grabbing the guitar neck, choking off a brilliantly articulated A7, and bringing me up off my stool. And I see the sucker's got his pistol drawn in the other hand, and I've no alternative but to stick em up. Feeling pretty ridiculous at this point, when I notice Honest John and Lynda spread-legged leaning up against the side of the bus, the other cop walking right over the blanket, crunching earrings, scattering money frisking them. It seems clear all of a sudden that they're not just going to ask us to move on.

The cop kicks my left foot out from under slamming me up against the rear end of the VW, and hands flying all over, not missing an inch. I'm trembling cold. Cold. What happened to the sun? I'm just trembling, seeing for the first time the third man standing with a Winchester pump-action shotgun at the hip angled up right at my head. I mean these cats are serious.

The initial turmoil dies, the cops standing back. Admiring their work, shoving back the crowd that's gathering. I look over to Honest John wondering if I'm looking quite as shaken as him, trying to decide what the hell is going on, waiting for the explanation.

As they're slapping the cuffs on us, I manage a weak "What's going on, man, isn't this a little severe for peddling without a license?" and the cop jerks my arms behind. "You're in a heap a trouble, boy."

Lynda breaks out laughing, I always admire someone can keep a sense of humor, and we're herded into the back seat of one of the black and whites, still shaking her head, the laugh more a melancholy chortle now, and slam the door. The heat is back. Windows rolled up, sun shining through glass. We begin to sweat. And they begin to search the Chevy and the bus.

They are very thorough. Pull out all the duffelbags, rucksacks, bedrolls, dop kits. Go through, shaking, turning inside out. Take off the door panels, empty the ashtrays and glove compartments. Taking their time. Squishing through jars of cold cream, Vaseline. Slitting open tubes of toothpaste. And we're sweating. Watching it all through suntint safety glass, arms and hands cramped behind. Silent. Not talking, thinking. Passed through a door, one way, and didn't know where the exit was gonna be. Seemed comfortable now, stultifying heat. Muted distant sounds. At least nothing was moving. Except the sweat running down.

They get out a little vacuum sweeper. Take out the floormats and sweep the Chevy. Dump the contents in a sieve. Nothing but forty years' dust. Dried mud and cowshit from boots. Lint from my mother's dresses. Strewn in the California breeze. They move on to the bus.

Huddle around the sieve. The big cop comes to the car door, opens it. Forty-four Magnum in one hand. "Yep. You're in a heap a trouble."

Pinched between stubby thumb and forefinger. Nicotine amber. Dirty, chewed ragged fingernail. A hangnail. A marijuana seed.

Honest John seems to have experience in such matters and starts wolfing. All the way downtown to police headquarters. I'm not so confident myself. The sheriffs back home just sit around the recreation hall playing pitch and drinking beer. I'm not used to having rights read, pictures taken, fingers printed, questions by big burly strangers. Milling around in godawful green cinderblock rooms with ever manner of hippie freak derelict bank robbers and the like. Phones ringing, folks screaming out from down dank hallways. Black eyes, bloody noses. The smell of some very dangerous excitement in the sweat of some of these fellows tossed in and doing the tossing. In short, I'm scared shitless. I mean the next step is the lockup. These people aren't thinking about letting us out.

We've been here twenty-thirty minutes seems like, even though the clock says three hours, and Honest John is still wolfing. Carrying on about a phone call to his lawyer, his rights, starts hassling about the tagging of personal property with the man behind a steel-caged counter. "Hey, man. Get that all right. Don't be stealing any of that money. You think we don't know how much was in those hats? Huh?" Face pushed right up in the screen. Taking it all in.

"Cool it, buddy. Where you're going, you ain't gonna be needing no money."

"You haven't got a chance. You've already violated so many rights even a crooked judge would have to throw the case out." I'm wishing he would cool it myself.

"You hide and watch, buddy. And move back from the counter. You stink. You're getting cooties all over the place. No telling what you got living in that tangled mess on your head. You allergic to water, or what?"

"You know. You sure are an original fellow. That's one thing I've noticed about you pigs." *Cool it.*

"Yeah. Well."

The phone rings behind him, he turns. Honest John pulls me over whispering. "Your arms are longer. Get it."

"Get what?"

"The seed, asshole, the seed. There, on the countertop."

"But I . . ."

"But nothing. What the hell you worried about, getting in trouble? We are in trouble, man. Now get that seed, you dumb Okie."

I see his point, the worst that could happen. I cram my arm under the bottom of the screen through the space for sliding things, jam, peeling skin off the shoulder, stretch, just can reach with the tip of the middle finger, press hard, and it sticks, pull it back, into the mouth, crunch, swallow, just as the cop turns from the phone. I pace back nonchalant. Knees about to buckle. Honest John jumps back on the case. "When are you going to let us out of here? I'm talking to my lawyer, you think we're going to let you get away with this? You don't even have any evidence. Where's your evidence?"

"You still here, buddy? I thought you'd given up by now."

"Where's the evidence?"

"You want evi—"

Eyes glue to the spot where he thought. Dart back and forth across the counter, up at Honest John, down along the floor. He turns to the phone. A couple of minutes later a conference of police and men from the D.A.'s office gather. They mumble awhile, leave. Honest John sits down beside me on the bench. "It's time to shut up now, Oke."

We sit for another hour or so. I've forgotten what I'm doing here. Just watching people in and out. Starving. Finally a sergeant comes up to us, grunts, motions us to the counter. "Here are your things, you're being released."

Honest John smiles to the man behind the counter. "You know, it's a pleasure to find an honest cop. Hang in there, buddy."

Looking angrily at us. "You'd better not let us catch your asses in town again."

We pick up our vehicles at the police garage. The Chevy's in bad shape. Door panels still piled in the back, mattress in cockeyed. Underwear, socks, pants, shirts, aftershave, mutilated toothpaste, road maps, flashlight, notebooks spread everywhere. She sure feels good though, pulling out onto the street.

And we don't stop except for gas until we're across the desert into Nevada.

Heading back to the shortgrass country.

Like I was saying, I just had to see Isadora Faire again. And I had a plan. I start letting my beard grow, dye my hair dark brown, get some Roman sandals, bellbottoms, I mean elephant bells, bright blue green yellow red paisley shirt, strung with cowry shell and sharktooth beads, large leather hat with ostrich feather, Foster Grant shades, fake tattoos, *Born To Lose* with a crucifix in the middle on my right shoulder, *Fuck War* on the other, borrow Honest John's VW bus with a passel of necklaces, rings, bobbles and bangles, and headed for the farm.

At first I was just going to drive right in the drive like a traveling salesman. Coming in from the west, over the bridge, slowed down, about to break out crying. Blue sky, red dirt. And the buffalo grass along the bank. The creek where the corral, the sod house. Had to admit it was looking good, like someone lived here, no question. Rumbled across the bridge. The fence rows, the fields and trees. Sun shining brilliant, the road, sunflowers, jimsonweed, bluestem, poppies. Faint red wake behind. Up the hill, grasshoppers butterflies locusts crows flying out across the trees along the creek. The house and granary, mulberries come into view. Down the hill. Disappearing. Two vultures rising from the edge of the road. Climbing slowly in second. A snake wriggling across. Up the hill, the house and barn and trees coming back into view. I'm starting to sweat, hollow stomach, turn north along the mulberry trees, toward the west drive. I can't, what am I doing. Marcus. Isadora Faire. Don't even know what she looks like. Grotesque, distorted. Crazy. Slow almost to a stop. The house. Windows open. Curtains stirring in slow shifting air. The chicken houses. Machine shed. I can't do it. Accelerate past the drive down the bois d'arc windbreakers, the north ponds and pasture. Look out over the rising land to the top of the hill east. At the elms and cedar planted along the horizon, I see the pickup. Marcus, tall as the trees, and Mackey waddling a rocking walk behind him. Why. Why, Marcus.

I speed up to the next section line and head east into town.

The place is changed. I stop on the rise west of town just to look. Spread out, over across, northeast. The old school building and several prefab annexes. Across the county road a trailer savings bank on the building site. Tumbling across the valley, voices babble of children on the playing fields around the school. Little League. The tree-lined road north of Main Street. The old brick houses, small now beside the bare-lot low-line modern new buildings. I get back in the bus, drive the half-mile south to Main, turn east. The Methodist Church's building a brick addition. A new façade along the north side of the main business block. The Bar and Grill now the Town n Country Lounge, station wagons and recreational vehicles parked in front. The old barbershop—His and Hers Stylists. A Quik Shop where the Mercantile used to be. Women in shorts and haircurlers scurrying in and out.

I cruise the length of the street, turn around and park at the vacant lot where the cream shed, now torn down, had stood. I don't know why I'm going through with it now, all energy drained, but here I am, so I set up my table and spread the black cloth and lay out the merchandise. Not really knowing what to expect. Angry, confused, lovesick and horny all at the same time. I wait.

Pretty soon a few people carefully approach to check me out, snickering now and then behind the backs of their hands. Every now and then I notice someone I know, Simpson and then Irene, who pay no attention to me, to anything. A few high school girls, junior high, and their mothers. Coming over from the Quik Shop with orange slushes. Before you know it I'm carrying on as if the reason I came was to sell jewelry. Like a barker at the county fair, hooting and hollering, singing. The throat getting sore from the fake voice I'm using. One or two men, women, children, dogs, engineers in Oklahoma City, schoolteachers, a couple of quarter-horsemen's wives. Newly come to town to live, to get away from urban blight, excited by the hippie craftsman signaling suburban charm.

Then I saw it.

The pickup rolling into town from the west. To the Quik Shop across the street. It was her. I choke, flush, grow weak, fall silent. Watch her out of the cab. Isadora Faire. The people around the table seem to part to give me a view. She stops. Looks over. A long time it seems, eyes deep, mouth gone soft. Turns into the store.

A few mumbles around the table. People gradually drift away. I stand alone where the cream shed used to be. Evening stretching shadows on the sidewalk. Waiting. Wondering what I'm gong to do when she comes out.

Carrying a bag of groceries. My voice cracks. "Isadora." She stops. Moves on to the pickup. "Isadora!"

Looks over at me. Puts the bag in the cab. Walks across the street to the table, looks at a couple of the rings. I can't speak again. Finally looks up at me. "Who. Are you?" I hold out my hand, the green jasper ring. She laughs or cries. I don't know what to do. "What are you doing here? Dressed up like. Like this?"

"I came to see you."

"You crazy, crazy."

"Fool."

"We can't."

"Isadora, I."

"I know, it's."

356

"Yeah. I've."

"Me too. Sorry."

"I know it's."

"But."

"At the swimming hole."

"We both know."

"Tonight."

"And besides."

"Meet me there."

"No. The fantasy's over."

"No. It isn't. Not for me. Come with me, Isadora, I need you. What does it matter. The town is gone, and Marcus is part of this, his progress he's so proud of."

"Sorry, I know he, but . . ."

"Isadora. Listen. The water table of western Kansas dropped a hundred feet in the last ten years because of the high-pressure deep-well irrigation. They're dumping a billion pounds of DDT, chlordane, aldrin, dieldrin, heptachlor to kill the tent caterpillars, bollworms, cutworms, webworms, hoppers, miners, loopers, beetles and weevils, but haven't killed off one of them in the history of the world, immune to all the poisons we can throw."

"What does that have to do with—"

"I've traveled around, talked to people. The corporate farms grow for the franchises. If the onions are too big for the bun, throw the fuckers away, if the potatoes are knobby, throw the fuckers away, people don't like knobby spuds, peaches too big for the can, throw them away! Cut down the hedgerows, strip-mine Wyoming, oil truck and drilling rig dust so thick in eastern Montana the ranchers moving out, the Californication of the West! Lake Tahoe, Vail, Colorado, condominiums from the town to the continental divide! Isadora, I know why the aspens are quaking!"

"Sorry. What in the hell are you babbling about?"

He stops. Wipes a hand across his nose. "Goddammit, Isadora. I love you. Come with me."

A woman with two kids comes out of the Quik Shop. Watch at a distance.

"No, Sorry."

Look at each other. Sorry shrugs, looks aimlessly over the left shoulder. Isadora reaches out to touch, doesn't, brings back her hand to her hair, the fingertips along her ear. "Sorry. I said it wouldn't be easy. And it hasn't been. Anyone born in a house made out of dirt and grass can't be easy. Can't have an unchanging view of things. It's been a long history of crude and difficult change. What's big and lasting is the resolve. And a hard determination to cope. You've got to look it in the face. And grin."

Both look at the red dirt in the rough oil and gravel road. She looks back up. "And, Sorry."

"What."

"I'm. Marcus and I. We're pregnant."

He looks at her. Slowly takes off the shades, the leather hat. Wipes his eyes with thumb and middle finger. "That's. Don't that beat all."

And packs away his wares. Isadora Faire watching. He gets into the bus, starts the engine. They look, can't speak, he puts it in gear, can only wave. She raises a hand. And he pulls away from where the slanty cream shed used to stand.

Where Isadora Faire.

Isadora Whitehands
Meets a Man

ISADORA Whitehands drives through the blackjack hills in the old Ford loaded down with hay on her way back to the ranch. Dull mottled asphalt narrow, breaking up at the edges, but a groove through the curves. The V-8, the sway of the load. New-mown, new-baled hay. Backing off into the corner, accelerating out, around the bluff, anticipating every rise, bend, bump, bridge, culvert, descending fence row, cockeyed telephone pole, shiver vibration through the wheels, the rods, steering column. Overcast warm. Autumn. Mind, body, truck, road. Isadora Whitehands absorbed, cresting the ridge, the valley below, quilted gridwork windrows and moldboard furrows. Maize overlying the contour terraced watershed creekbed course into haze.

She begins to sing. A green corn song. The mind finding focus, precipitating. The dam. The lake. Then a sudden heaviness in the forearms, wrists, the steering wheel pulling against her shoulders. Vague sinking. Damn! A flat tire pulling hard left, sweat breaking out, palms and armpits. She brakes slowly, struggling against the drag, to the right shoulder. Stops. Sits for a while. The lack of movement. The silence. And hissing from the punctured tire.

Opens the door. Jumps to the ground as an old black car rounds the downhill curve, swerving slightly when it perceives her, braking on up the hill past. Reverse around perpendicular to the road, turning downhill, reverse uphill, then pulls down behind.

A man, blue Sears shirt, stetson hat cocked to one side, long blond hair and sad eyes gets out. "Need some help?"

"No, I can." Pause. Looking at. "Well. Yes."

Looking at the tire. "That's no problem atall. Unless you don't have a spare."

"Luckily, we do have a spare left."

Looking at her, at the truck, rubs his hands along the thighs of his Levi's. "Well. We'd better get this wheel off so we can get on down the road. Where's the lug wrench and jack?"

"Right here." Takes out the scissorjack from behind the seat, hands him the wrench, unfolds the crank handle, hooks it to the jack, slides it under the front axle, starts cranking it up. Watching him spin the lug nuts. "My name's Isadora."

Starts. Puts down the lug wrench. Looks at her closely. "I'm Sorry."

"What for?"

"That's my name, Sorry."

They look at each other. Laugh. He picks up the lug wrench, she starts cranking up the jack again. "Where you headed?"

Removes a lug nut. "Passing through."

"Just passing through, huh?"

"Yep."

He removes another lug nut, goes on to the next. She watches. Cranks the jack. "What do you do for a living?"

Stops. Looks at her. "You sure ask a lot of questions."

"But you don't give many answers."

"That's right." Removes the last lug nut, puts it in the hub cap. "I'm a stranger here. Wandering through helping out damsels in distress. Looking for better times."

"Is that right."

"Yep."

He takes off the wheel, rolls it to the rear, leans it against the truck bed, crawls under for the spare. She inspects the load, squats down to look at him. "I don't know about better times, but I've got a proposition for you."

"Is that right."

"Yep."

Slides the spare out, stands, dusts off. Looks at her again. "What you have in mind?"

"How'd you like to buck bales for a day or two with me and my brother?"

"Your brother?"

"He's back at the ranch."

The Ford rolled into the barnyard, backed up to the door. Sorry parked the '31 Chevy by the gate, got out. A herd of horses frisked and ran across the pasture. A few brahma bulls brooded in pens beside the barn. Gordon Starvingdog came from the large sliding doors to greet his sister, knocked the dust from his paisley pearl-button shirt and jeans, wiped the pointed toes of his hand-tooled leather walking-heeled boots on the backs of his calves, big-tooth smile, got the word from Isadora Whitehands and looked over at Sorry standing at the fence, doffed his hat. "Hey, just what we need, a hippie to help with the hay. Glad to meet you! Come on down, don't have time to stand around jawing, too bad, but we're running pretty late. Put your things in the summer kitchen and get you a hay hook and let's get on with it. Although I don't for the life of me know what would make a man want to work this ranch. Course I suppose you're not doing it for posterity. This time next year, like as not, we'll be standing in thirty foot of water. All we got is hickory nut and hominy soup. And a wet future. Yep. So now's your last chance to back out."

Sorry picks up a hay hook. "Well. I guess a man that's spent most of his life out in the wheat fields can stand some hickory nuts and hominy. But what about all this water?"

"The Army Corps of Engineers is planning on flooding us out. Wants to build a lake on top of us. But let's get this hay in, then we can go into town for a beer and get to talking about forked tongues and the like."

Isadora Whitehands, watching the two from inside the barn, grabs her hay hook and laughs.

The tavern is large. Wood floors, molded panel walls and high pressed tin ceiling, four broad-bladed wooden fans turning. The bar the length of the place, a mirror behind. Racks of potato chips, cornchips, peanuts, sunflower seeds, beernuts, beer sausages, jerky. Gallon jars of pickles, boiled eggs. Three men and a woman sit on high metal stools talking with the woman behind. A worn pool table in the back by the toilets, three hooded lights hanging over. Two young kids, one in a T-shirt, the other shirtless, shoot a silent game of eight-ball. Round metal tables, round metal chairs. A man with one arm, an army shirt and green beret playing cribbage with an old man in bib overalls and a Ditch Witch hat. A game of dominoes. And pitch. Three pictures on the wall opposite the bar. *Chief Ross. Will Rogers. Custer's Last Stand.* Low conversations punctuated soft easy laughter. Everyone greeted as Gordon, Isadora Whitehands and Sorry enter.

Gordon went up to the bar for the beer. Isadora Whitehands took the silver pipe from her leather bag, stuffed it carefully. Lit it, blew smoke in four directions, handed the pipe to Sorry. He didn't know what to do, started to decline, looked at her, she nodded, he took a puff, coughed. Rough tobacco. Gordon returned with a tray of Miller's. Sorry handed him the pipe, he slowly drew in smoke, rolled it around the tongue. Let it slip from the mouth. Sorry glances at Isadora Whitehands. She smiles. They all drink a silent toast. Gordon looks from his sister to Sorry, lifts his glass again, they drink. Sorry smiles a toast again.

A middle-aged man, stocky, paunchy, long black braided hair head-bound, pulls up a chair and sits. The pipe is passed. Conversation. The haying season. Cattle prices. Rainfall. A woman enters the tavern, joins them at the table. "You hear about Wesley Alcorn's boy? Just got the telegram this morning. Killed. Stepped on a booby trap in the Central Highlands."

Silence. They gather around the table to listen. Remember. The time he won the stalk shoot at Redbird Smith's birthday. He saved the game, state baseball finals last of the ninth against Tahlequah, jumped clean over the six-foot centerfield fence to backhand the ball, landed in the bullpen on the other side. Best hunter in these parts next to Richard Chewey. Seems like they always take the best. The funeral Wednesday. And fell silent again.

Sorry looks at his hands. Isadora Whitehands watches him take nervous swallows of beer, blue eyes, long lashes. Watches him get up, T-shirt tight on his shoulders, the muscles of his arms, worn blue jeans, uncertain swagger across the floor to the toilet. She smiles. One of the old men leans back in his chair, folds his arms across his chest. "What are you gonna do about the dam project, Gordon?"

Gordon leans over on the table, forearms flat, holding the beer glass in both hands. Looks at Sorry returning, his sister, at the old man. "Guess we're gonna fight them."

"What good will that do? They got eminent domain."

"I reckon it won't do any good. But that's never stopped us from fighting them."

"I hear Wendall Sorethumb wants to sell quick."

Isadora Whitehands pounds her glass on the table. "There's always some Indian wants to sell."

Take. In the eyes. "Um. Wendall Sorethumb says if you fight, you will hurt everybody involved. They'll win and take the land at a lower price than they're offering now. Punishment for defying them."

"They'll win for sure if we don't all stick together. Like they always have."

She finishes her beer in several rapid gulps, and looks everyone the table round, in the eye, except Sorry. All silent. The pool game the only sound, the balls, the ceiling fans batting at the air. Everyone around the table thinking. Long. A long time. In the blood. It's led to this.

The Green Corn Busk

SORRY lay in the summer kitchen. Wood plank walls. Dark varnish. A window and door in the front, a window on the side. Open joist pitched roof ceiling, starling and sparrow nests. Sagging plank floor. Potbelly at the far wall. An old enamel-topped table, a kerosene lantern, two chairs in the middle. An iron cot along each side wall.

He looked at rough-hewn wood. Smelled the must. Dust. Muscles aching. Been awhile. Soft living. Lay and looked, thinking. In a summer kitchen, northeastern Oklahoma, Isadora Whitehands and Gordon Starvingdog's ranch, land the government, land. The Cherokee Nation. West. And before that. Change. Lay in the bed, the empty cot, stale aroma of how many others. Initials carved. Worn wood floorboard. Chipped coffee mug. Stiff leather glove hanging on a nail. Yellow newspaper turning to dust.

He got up. Walked to the window. Wood rotting around the pane. Glass cracked, reflected, deeper lined, eyes more distant looking out across the yard, the '31 Chevy, a house among the older trees. Looking out across.

Till the white light begins to expand, extend, the kerosene lantern sputter and die, the face flicker and gone. The summer kitchen dark, the earth brown, purple cloud covering, white south wind. The east turning red.

And he sees her white shift, walk into the canopy of the yard. She stops, looks over at him, the silver pipe, four puffs of white smoke drifting toward the summer kitchen. The white eyes meet. Can't turn back. White light. She walks across the middle of the yard.

Isadora.

Not really knowing who he meant.

The green corn busk started at dawn at the Redbird Smith place. They pulled in between a beat-up pickup and a brand-new Lincoln Continental parked along the road. Gordon disappeared on up the trail, Sorry hoisted the Coleman cooler up on a shoulder, Isadora Whitehands carried the blankets alongside. "What a morning. How does it feel to be mixing among the people?"

"You sure palefaces are allowed?"

"As long as you don't get drunk and vulgar."

"Not me."

"Good. I'd hate to see you vulgar." Looking out the corner of the eyes, bumping slightly hip to hip on the uneven path. "This sure is a beautiful spot. The good earth *Asga-ya-galun-lati* made."

"Who?"

"The Great Spirit. You know originally there was only water, and *Asga-ya-galun-lati* didn't like that, so he ordered the lesser spirits to form the earth, the barred owl, diamondback rattler, the fishing hawk. They all tried and failed. Just couldn't think how to do it. Finally the Great Spirit, who was getting tired of all the bungling, told the earthworm to dive into the water, clear to the bottom, and swallow all the mud he could. He stuffed himself, could scarcely make it back to the top, and when he did, he spit the mud out onto the water, and that made the earth. Flat at first, then thunder sent wind and rain to make the hills and valleys and rivers. That's all."

"That's how it happened, huh?"

"Well, some claim it wasn't earthworm, it was the water beetle that dove down to swallow up the mud."

"Makes more sense. I mean, where did earthworm come from if there was no earth."

"I can see you're a cynic. Probably like anthropology too."

"Just an idea."

"Well, if you really want to know the truth. It actually happened like this. I'm surprised you didn't wonder about it. How did the earth stay on the surface of the water?"

"Now that you mention it."

"Look. There was a huge turtle swimming in the area when earthworm. Or water beetle. Came to the surface with all the mud. And he spit it all over the turtle's shell. And that's how it happened."

"How did man get here?"

"You mean the Cherokee. The Great Spirit gave us the land."

"Right here?"

"No. A lesser spirit gave us this land. Much lesser. I mean Georgia, North Carolina. The southern Alleghenies."

"But where did the Cherokee come from?"

"The Great Spirit made us."

"And the white man?"

"Now that's a question been troubling folks for centuries." Walking on up the path, grinning semisecret grins, to the sloped clearing.

The seven clans gathered. Seven large circles of fires. Pigs on spits, ribs. And piles of corn. Women in the center, rattles on their ankles, tortoiseshells, pebble-filled condensed milk cans, slow beating drums, singing, begin to dance. Seven songs, dancing the gathering of the wood. Men join in, the drums fall silent. Rattles and gourds. Singing seven songs dancing the harvest of the green corn. Dust, smoke, barbecue fires, bells, gourds, rattles, singing jovial now, song after song.

Isadora Whitehands comes for Sorry. "Come on. You got to do the friendship dance. Come on."

"Ah, no. I don't think I. I mean, I don't know the steps. I'll."

"I'll teach you. Come on. If you come to the stomp dance, you've got to stomp."

Drags him by the hand, instructing, shouting, laugh. Until he self-consciously gets in step and they dance. Until it's almost time.

People gathering around the fires. Salivating, growing silent, festive. The preachers, the conjurers, speak blessings, offering around the medicine prepared, everyone takes a Dixie cup portion, silent. Smoke, fire spitting dripping fat, conjurer standing arms crossed across the chest. *Gha!* Consoling, praising, takes up an ear of green corn, roasted, barbecue wispy drifting among the clans gathered again to raise the cups, the medicine and drink, the conjurer dedicate consecrate, offering corn onto the fire.

And everybody eats.

Then the stalk-shoot. Set up the bound corn stalks, shocks, lined up at 150 feet. Bows and arrows brought up from the trunks of cars, homemade, storebought, lemon wood, metal, double pully championship models, lined up to shoot the stalks.

Sorry and Gordon watch. You get points for every stalk you pierce with your arrow. After several rounds Wendall Sorethumb is far ahead. Gordon walks up and congratulates him. Wendall looks at Gordon, then to Sorry, standing a little behind, and grunts. Gordon turns to Sorry. "That boy never was too friendly. Come on. The fun is about to begin."

They walk back to the blankets. Lots of people standing around, in shorts and tennis shoes, the men carrying two-foot sticks with animal skin netting, the women, rattles on their ankles, carrying gourds. Gordon picks up a tom-tom. "Come on, Sorry, you're on the team."

"What we playing?"

"Ball play. Here's your stick, here's the ball."

Examining the deerskin ball, two inches in diameter, the stick. "Like lacrosse?"

"You've got it backward, man. Lacrosse is like ball play."

"Oh." Throws the ball up, catches it in the netting of the stick. "Nothing to it. Here you go."

Slings the ball with the stick to Gordon, good shot, passes it on to another, a circle for warm-up tosses, around, back and forth, behind the back, leaping catches, spiraling, throwing before hitting the ground. Sorry catching on, getting the hang. "All right. Send me in, coach."

"Not yet. You got to dance first." Gives him a drinking gourd. "This'll assure victory."

Points over across the clearing. Wendall Sorethumb's team already dancing. The tom-tom begins, the team starts singing, dancing. Sorry glances over at Isadora Whitehands, tentatively joins in the dance, humming, mumbling along. Not too bad. Once you catch on. Beats the pep rallies back in high school.

After four songs and dances Gordon sits down with the tom-tom facing where Sorethumb is. Isadora Whitehands lines up with six women behind. He begins singing, beating the drum, the women dance forward and back. After the first song he says something in Cherokee, laughter ripples, one of the women says something, more laughter. Insulting clansmen on Sorethumb's team. Your mama eats kitty litter, stuff like that. Gordon begins drumming, singing, the women join in singing, but do not move. After each song insults across the field. Sorethumb, his brother, the team, a drummer, the line of seven women facing this way. Hurling insults. The thirteenth song, the women dance forward and back again. The team gathers around a washtub of water. Gordon chanting the whole time, caught up in the excitement. Strip off the shirts. Throw water over face shoulder and back. Smear grease over back and chest, arms and legs.

Sorry looks at Isadora Whitehands rubbing grease on his chest. "What's that for?"

"Ritual cleansing, ritual ointment. Make you harder to hold onto. This is a rough game."

Looks him in the eye. Gordon passes around chewing tobacco remade for victory. Hooting and shouts, deep knee-bends, stretching wind sprints. Isadora Whitehands ties a red bandana around Sorry's forehead. Sorethumb's team headband a sinister purple and yellow, take the field crowded around yelling jumping up and down, Sorry about to vomit, almost smell musty stale dank lockerroom fungus, nervous sweat. The game about to begin. Two drivers in shorts, black and white striped referee shirts. Big muscular full bloods. Gordon and Sorethumb consult with the drivers, Gordon trots back, yelling instructions. Sorry calls over. "Hey, coach. I think I better hang back on defense until I understand the flow of the game a little better."

"Okay."

Jogged back toward the goal posts, shouting, sun hot September on the skin of his back, glistening grease. Whipped his stick a few strokes through the air, weak in the knees, bounced up and down. A roar went up, a tangle of bodies in the middle of the field, dust, sun, drivers wading in throwing folk out, the ball flies out to a man yellow-purple snagging it midair sprinting down the side right at Sorry. Wendall Sorethumb. Get position, back pedal. Sorethumb fakes right, fakes left, stick and ball held away, stay, turn with him.

Sorethumb lowers his head shoulders Sorry in the stomach flat on his ass, fending off sneakers, tromping over to score.

Sorry struggles for air to his feet, Gordon slaps him on the rear. "Understand the flow now?"

"Yeah. I think. I got it."

Jogs in place to forget the pain. The scrimmage trample toward the other goal, crowd screaming. Sorry focuses back on the action. Stands on the left side of the field. Gordon goes up for a pass, cut off at the knees flipped over, the ball flying into the netting Sorethumb's brother sprinting down the right sideline. Gordon back on his feet, Sorry fighting the tendency to abandon his position, can't yet, other yellow-purples charging down left side three on one, come on. Gordon catches the brother, hacking at the ball with his stick. Sorry moves toward the middle to cut off the passing lane. His teammate takes the third man out of the play with what would be a personal foul in most games, attracts most of the players on the field. Sorethumb's brother whacks Gordon over the shoulder losing the grip on his stick, the ball bouncing on the ground. Gordon blocks, jabs him in the side lifting him off his feet shouting pain. Sorethumb out of the melee on the right side of the field.

Sorry moves laterally to cut Sorethumb off face to face. Hunched forward dancing, holding him off with the stick in both hands. Sorethumb chops it in half with his left, lashes Sorry across the shins with the right, down again. Sorry bounces up stick broken whops Sorethumb on the shoulder going past, and sees the high looping pass from Gordon over Sorethumb's head. Sorry leaps and catches it in the netting of the broken stick, sprints for the opposite goal. Open field, crowd cheering, glances over his shoulder goddam Sorethumb gaining on him. Gordon running down the right sideline. Sorry flips a pass just as he's hit from behind, crashing dust dirt blood grass spit. Cheers from their side of the field. The score one-one.

Limping back toward the goal Sorry sees Isadora Whitehands, goes over to rinse out his mouth.

369

"Is the game always this rough?"

"Especially against Sorethumb's team."

"Why's that?"

"You forgot the government dam project. Sorethumb hasn't."

"Oh."

And a sudden roar called him back on the field.

The game ended a five-four victory for Gordon's team. Sorry amazed no one killed or maimed, caught up in the movement, the group, side-aching raw lung physical effort. Together. Slapping hugs, jumping off the field, faces, voices, sweat and blood. To the shade, cool still afternoon air. A towel. A beer laughing. Kisses. Isadora Whitehands. Touches the back, hand along the arm. Group gone, ringed clearing. On the blanket. Quietly finish the beer together. Passing the can from hand to hand. Talking. Looking. Lying on their backs side by side staring up through moving branches into sleep. And afternoon passes into evening.

More dancing, stalk-shoots, grapevine tug-of-war, men against the women, *chinkge*. Children roaming, running. Flights of birds across the sky settle in a shagbark hickory, calling. Light yellow, orange, purple, red, blue to gray dusk to darkness. Moon. Venus. Fire light rippling. Voices flux and scatter. Fractured across, beside, behind. A tom-tom sings.

Sorry looks at Isadora Whitehands. Smoke. Light in the treetops. Black sleek hair to the shoulder, the narrow face, pointed chin, firm mouth, long straight nose. High cheekbones, brows, broad forehead and large deep dark eyes. Rattlesnake gorget at the throat. She looks at Sorry. He looks down at his boots, back at her. She leans over him reaching for the beer, the shoulders touch. She smiles. Finishes off the beer. And laughs. Sorry takes the can, the fingers touch. "What's the matter?"

She laughs again. Takes his hand. "Come on. I want to show you something."

They skirt the clearing, from the lower edge to the high ground, enter the forest on a close narrow overboughed path. Walk slowly along the dark. Voices sifting down and firelight. Approached a small clearing. Forty or fifty people. She stopped. Speaking whispers. "A Keetoowah conjurer, keeper of the sacred Wampum Belt. A ritual purification. Of body and spirit. Come on."

Sorry hesitates. She pulls him into the sphere of light, centered by the fire, seven woods, seven clans. The conjurer, white beard, large wrinkled nose, bib overalls, maroon corduroy long-sleeve shirt. Chanting over a galvanized half-bushel bucket, a gourd dipper. Sorry and Isadora Whitehands. Where is she? Chanting. Conspicuous. Too much beginning to swirl around, movement light voices, song, crickets, smoke, Keetoowah full-blood, deep furrowed fire red purple blue, sweating, moving among the people. Sorry's hot wet hand loose. Alone. The conjurer moving about the circle chanting flat, tense pulsing long tones descend cascading intervals chorus drones sustain the pitch. He stops in front. Sorry suddenly standing alone before the proffered drinking gourd. Smooth yellow tapering from the steady conjurer hand. Gentle swelling body, a smooth rounded teardrop of medicine. His furrowed face impassive into Sorry's. "Drink."

Sorry looks for Isadora Whitehands. Broad shifting shadows, light. Takes the gourd, looks around again, faces flame shadows tumble trees. Lifts it slowly to his mouth. Looks into the conjurer's eyes. Swallows hot sweet cold first across the tongue cringing teeth, stomach, somewhere, everywhere exploding chill convulses his body trembling panic! nausea spinning! The conjurer calmly takes his hand to the clearing edge. Sorry pushes through crashing into dark branches snagging underbrush vine leaves damp moss. Heaves retching vomit to his knees. Aching again and again.

Finally falls back against a moldy stump. Shivering weak. Deep slow breathing. Warm. Beady sweat. Chanting song through tree trunks. Calm.

Isadora Whitehands kneels beside him, dank, smell bile, acid. He watches light glistening moving over her wet chin. Serene. "You should have warned me."

"How do you feel?"

"Cleansed of impurities, no question about it."

"Let's go eat."

Midnight. The corn dances begin. The planting of the corn, four songs, gourds and rattles. The medicine dances. Drums. Gordon Starvingdog laughs and hugs Sorry around the shoulders. "Come on, man. These dances are to renew health. And friendship, men and women. You know what I mean. *Gha!* I've seen you two putting white eyes into each other's body all day and night. Can't fool your brother."

They stomp through the four songs.

Fire glimmering down last embers, the east above the trees growing light, white, red rising morning. Gordon takes up the drum, women begin the four round dances. The busk rising to a close. Night hanging, dissolves on trees, seven fires, stars veiled dust from dancers feet and singing. A form. A body. Moving unison rhythmic ritual. Sorry recedes into shadow. Eyes, ears, air pulsing against the forehead. He drifts. The corn busk drifts. Red, white. From what is. Fragments. Becomes a continuum. Unbroken, organic, reaching. Red. And old.

Isadora Whitehands
Wonders What She's Doing

I guess I should have known it wasn't a good idea. But hell. I was tired of moving around. Me and her and Gordon seemed to get along. It just seemed like a good idea to settle down. A physical sense of place, that's all.

I guess I should have known I was, we all were in for trouble.

Should have known walking down into the bushes to take a leak. After the first corn busk. Feeling, I don't know. Calm. Caught up in a particular world that seemed to expand and last. And here come Sorethumb and his brother up to me on horseback. I try to be nonchalant, I mean, standing there with dick in hand between big muscular roans, full of themselves, snorting and prancing. I say morning. Sorethumb and his brother just stare down at me, one on each side, shanks quivering, steaming cool sun-up air. I say nice ball play, really enjoyed playing with you fellers, nice game. They don't say a thing. Then Wendall reaches into the pocket of his khaki jacket and pulls something out. "Give this to Starving-dog."

Threw it to me, spun the horse, squeezing me between shoulder and buttocks, and they galloped off. I look at a black bead necklace in my hand.

Sorry made his way back to me. "What's this all about?"

I look at the black bead necklace and don't know what to say. Treachery in the blood.

It wasn't until a month or two later Gordon told him it was a declaration of war.

It was a war on two fronts. One with Sorethumb and his brother, and a bureaucratic one with the government and its agencies. We'd write letters to state senators and congressmen, the Bureau of Indian Affairs. Go to the county seat to testify at hearings, before committees. Sorry would come along for the ride. We'd drive around the settlements to talk to the elders. He'd sit back in the corner of the council houses, like he's trying to be inconspicuous. Or we'd be out on a ridge above the water all night long. Use tobacco, talk about the Prophecy and try to organize support. Sorry would want to stay home sometimes, said he felt out of place, he was hurting us by being there. But we needed his help. I wanted him around. About decided I don't care what people say or think. Told him it was more his fight than he realized. He drove when we were tired, did chores when we were gone, delivered letters to the post office. He was another body in the committee rooms. But we were being worn down.

Go into town evenings after a hard day, just looking for some relaxation, and there's Sorethumb. We would try to talk with him, convince him, and some of his friends. He had most of the other ranchers along the floodplain on his side, but we'd try to convince them to fight against the government:

"*Gha!* What will you have after you sell the land? It's been Cherokee for a hundred and fifty years." Standing, others in the tavern seated in semicircle tables, Wendall Sorethumb leaning against the bar. "Can't you see the pattern? It's what happened in Georgia and North Carolina, it's what happened during and after the Civil War, it's what's happening now. They divide us, set one against the other, exploit our differences. How can we fight them and each other at the same time?" No one looks at Sorry, listening hard. "It's how they took our land in the first place, all the Indian lands, the entire continent, and it's how they'll take our land now, some of the last still in the hands of the Cherokee. If we'd band together we could hire lawyers to fight, could make alliances with historical societies, with environmentalists, the American Civil Liberties Union and the American Indian Movement would be interested. Who knows, even antiwar groups and the Black Panthers. We could do it!"

I'd sit down. Or Gordon would sit down. Murmurs. We had people on our side. Mostly full bloods, the Keetoowahs. But Wendall Sorethumb had most of the ranch owners.

"Listen! It's not the only way they've taken land. Taken it any way they can." Looks over at Sorry. "One thing we should have learned by now. They will get the land. Sooner or later. We've got to be sensible. Even your great-great-granddad knew that. If we don't take the offer sooner, they'll take the land later, and we'll be without the land and without the money it's worth. That's all."

Usually just discussions like that. But you could tell there was bad blood between us. And getting worse.

And I really was thinking of us as us. Sorry seemed, I don't know. It seemed stupid to worry about betrayal. He got along with everybody in town. There did seem to be a standoffishness though, right when you'd expect him to, to give in to us, to me, he'd withdraw. I don't know, seemed to hold something back. I couldn't figure him out. So good-looking and I'm trying not to make it too obvious, not too sure I want it obvious at all, but. Wondered, was it because of me, or something else? Some passionate crime, what tragic love affair he was running from? Sit watching him play the steel-bodied guitar, the tendons and muscles working the back of his hand and forearm over the strings, fingers dancing on the frets, and his forehead when he looked out and sang, the voice clear like clean evening air after a thundershower.

We'd go fishing all night long down at Tenkiller Lake, drink beer and swap lies, skinny-dipping when the fish didn't bite. Became the top pool shooting team in the county. No one could beat us. "If only you could organize ranchers as good as you shoot straight-rail." Gordon would laugh and order up another round of whiskey. Kept kidding Sorry, like everybody in town, when we gonna tie the knot, what are you waiting for, stuff like that. But Sorry'd just laugh and look away. And never did anything.

We'd go to rodeos, corn busks, stomp dances. Work all day together on the ranch. Days when it rained, just hang around in the hay loft with the barn swallows and cats. And talk. It looked like Sorry was feeling right at home. But he never made the move, never said anything about who he really was.

"Tell me something, Gordon. How come you and Isadora have different names?"

"We're different people."

"I mean last names."

"People can have lots of names. Until they get one that fits them. Wasn't until I was in high school I got the name Starvingdog. A bunch of us always used to go hunting, coon in autumn, rabbits in the winter, deer all the time, even when it wasn't season. And one winter, it was one of the first times I'd ever gone out with them. They didn't really like me much, cause we lived in the big house, Dad one of those in the tribal government. Because we were supposed to be rich and think we were white. But I finally got to go out with them, mainly cause I knew Richard Chewey, and we were walking along the Grand River, colder than a witch's tit, about an inch of hard crusted snow. I had my brand-new semiautomatic Winchester .22 rifle, but had never really ever gone hunting before this. I came through a stand of cedar trees and jumped up a warren of rabbits, I mean a whole cityful of them, hundreds of them and I start shooting. I go berserk. Rabbits flying ever which a way, all around me. I blow one away and five more'd hop up, like a damn shooting gallery at Tsa La Gi. Must have kept firing for five minutes straight. My hands hurt from loading clips and pulling the trigger. And when it was over I stood there hunched against the wind gone quiet. The snow blood-splattered, twitching bodies all around me. And I was overcome. What had I done! Eighty-nine rabbits slaughtered. Everyone slowly gathered around me. Silent, surveying the carnage. Then Richard Chewey gave a low whistle. 'Goddamn, Gordon. You went after them cottontails like a starving dog!' And that's been my name ever since."

"What did you do with all those rabbits?"

"That was an important lesson for me. I was shellshocked and ashamed for killing so many. I didn't need them, I wasn't hungry. It had been a coldblooded rampage. But we gathered them all up and drove around all night giving them to people in the settlements. Not an ounce of meat or fur wasted. And I was a big man. Called Rabbitboss for a while. But the name Starvingdog stuck."

Rain running sheets over the open barn door. Isadora Whitehands has a straw hanging from the corner of her mouth. Sorry looks over at her. "What about your name?"

Long pause. Looking at him. "Richard Chewey gave me my name too. When we were little."

He looks at her. Waits for her to go on. She sits pensive in the shadows on a rafter joist high above the floor of the barn beneath the rain pounding the shingles of the roof. Leans toward him and she smiles. "What about you? Yours isn't the most common name I've ever heard."

They look at each other. His mouth twitches a smile, he looks down, gives a quiet laugh, then falls back on a broken bale of loose hay, his stetson pushed over his face, hands propped behind the head. "Well. That's an interesting story. You may of wondered what I was doing out on the highway that day I met you all."

Isadora Whitehands moves back, takes the straw from her mouth and spits. "Roads full of people on the move nowadays."

Glances at her from under the hat, then covered again. "Well, it's actually kind of a sad tale that I've got to tell. All started when my daddy was killed in the war, fighting to make the country safe for somebody or other. My mother didn't know what to do, had to try to run our big wheat farm by herself, and my uncle, my dad's older brother, who, because of connections at the county courthouse, had been exempt from the draft, weaseled his way in, friendly like, and finally tricked Mama into marrying him. Now he never did like me, used to beat me, lock me in the closet, and eventually succeeded in ruining my mother's health. She died a broken woman when I was just six years old. My uncle had no use for me, hired me out as a barn boy to a local dairy farmer. He was kind to me, but went bankrupt in the recession of '54, and instead of going back to my cruel uncle, I ran away. Been on the road ever since."

"But what about your name?"

"Oh yeah. Well, I went in for a chauffeur's license when I was sixteen trying to get a job driving for a circus, and the man asked me if I had a birth certificate confirming who I was and was I old enough to handle a truck. I said I'm sorry, I didn't. He looked at me over the counter and said, 'You were born sorry.' And I realized he was right."

Gordon Starvingdog laughed. "Born sorry, huh. Let's go get something to eat."

I watched Gordon and Sorry climb down the ladder from the loft, laugh and splash out into the rain headed for the house. Woman. What are you doing? Blond-haired stranger. A lonely man. And me. Treachery in the blood. Bullroar. We're both born in Oklahoma, here together. The same land and the same struggle, and neither of our ancestors came from here. Both of us, the same sun and wind, circle with the redtail hawk, roil and tumble with the clouds, the call of the crow. I've got as much white man as he's got Cherokee, culture, heritage, history, blood. And we're both responsible for the rest. If the people moving out throw a drunken party the night before you move into a place, you're the one has to clean it up or try to, cause they sure aren't. And it's not made any easier when some of the hungover sons of bitches are still sleeping in the bathtub and refuse to leave, demand a little hair of the dog. We've all been in this together since about 1540.

And besides. I like the way he moves.

Why the hell isn't he moving my way?

Sorry Has to Face It

I was tired of moving. But I should have known the day Gordon told me about the black beads. I was in the wrong place again. I didn't want to go, had nowhere to go to. Living and working now like it made sense, for the first time in a long time. Since before Marcus. And Isadora Faire.

But what was I doing here? Trying to forget? And Isadora Whitehands right across the yard. I just couldn't bring myself to make the effort, the whole damn town making comments, Isadora Faire and Marcus probably had a couple of kids by now. And me hanging around the summer kitchen alone, Isadora Whitehands, all this time I've been here. What the hell am I waiting for? The wrong damn place again.

And then one day. The first snow of must-have-been-my-second winter there had fallen two days before, fitful, covering the brittle grasstops, dry brown scrub oak leaves and branches. Melted off by noon of the next day, and the third day was warm again.

Clean and still. I was sitting on the porch of the summer kitchen, in the sun, playing the old steel-bodied guitar, and saw Isadora Whitehands carry a wooden bushel peach basket of laundry on her hip from the house. Short loose sleeveless dress hanging from the shoulders, bare throat and clavicle backlit to the clothesline. Sharp, angular. Hanging slips and underthings to dry, slowly moving, stretching along the line. I break out singing. She turns and looks at me. A long time. Then laughs and goes back in the house. I drop the guitar against the wall. Rough gray board porch. Creaking as I finally move off to the Chevy, got to get out of here awhile, and head into town.

Not really knowing what I'm up to, until I get there, got to do something, it can't go on like this, and I pull into the butcher shop. Pass the time of day with Guymon Tallchief, the butcher who'd helped bring in the hay.

"Guymon, what you been up to?"

"Not too much. How bout yourself?"

"I don't know."

"You don't know?"

"Nope." Look around the shop. "Tell me something, Guymon. What do you. I mean. How long you known Gordon? And Isadora Whitehands?"

"Since high school. Gordon anyway, used to hunt together. Didn't really get to know Isadora until she come back to the ranch."

"Doesn't she. I've never seen her with anybody."

Guymon puts down the hamburger he's grinding. Looks at me and laughs. "You been hanging around Isadora Whitehands all this time, and you still don't know?"

"Well. I have been wondering."

"What's there to wonder about?"

"Well. I don't know . . ."

"You don't know. Ever body in town can see it but you, and you're too busy with making white eyes. I'll tell you what you do. Get her a little gift. I got some first-rate pork here."

"No lie."

"There she hangs."

"Looking good, I must admit. But it's not exactly—"

"What you should do is buy some, mighty good price, for Isadora Whitehands."

"Yeah well okay, I'll think about it—"

"Buy some."

I laugh. Why not. "You think I ought to buy her some pork, huh?"

"As a gift."

So I do. The hindquarter right there on the spot, and pack it back to the ranch. Toss it over my shoulder, walk into the house, Isadora Whitehands standing in the middle of the middle room like she's waiting, and I give it to her. "Brought you something from town."

She looks at the ham, back at me, "Now I know. We'll have pork for supper."

And we did.

Greens, yams, rice, hickory nuts and hominy. I'm lying back thinking in the summer kitchen on my bunk. Full. Pork fat still on the lips. The aroma. Belching mighty tasty gases. Thinking. The knock, the door opening before I say. Isadora Whitehands. Standing there. Red kerosene light. White eyes. Blue. Dress. I sit up.

"Evening."

"I've come."

"Good. To see you. Sit down and make yourself to home."

"I will. You're my husband now."

"What say?"

Sits at the foot of the bunk, starts unbuttoning the dress over the shoulder, around the back. "According to custom."

"Whose custom?"

Pulls the dress over her head shifting kerosene light and shadow in its wake, sits there, satin sheen slip "Cherokee."

"But I'm not Cherokee."

Moves closer. "You're a human being, aren't you?"

"More or less."

"That makes you Cherokee then. If we stretch the point."

Long pause. I slowly rise. Look. Get slowly up on my knees. Touch the shoulder strap. "What custom?"

"You brought the pork. I cooked. I came. A Cherokee woman, or man just comes. I came to you."

"That Guymon thinks he's slick." Push the strap till it drops over the shoulder. "What if I don't want. Don't. You know. Accept?"

"Put me out."

"Oh."

Look at each other awhile.

"Well?"

"What about the white man's. Customs."

"This is Indian Territory."

Look a little longer. Lantern flicker wood, satin, shoulder and arm. We laugh.

I lift my hand. Reach up to touch her face, the cheekbone, my hand fingertip. The jasper ring. Isadora Faire. Reach up to touch, to pull her down warm black hair shoulders damn breathing over.

"Sorry. You're . . ."

I want her. Pulling at my shirt, the slip, tangling sheets, blanket, damn hand to touch green jasper—!

"Isadora."

Isadora Faire. The green jasper ring on my hand to touch, pull. The ring from. Damn. She's here, Isadora Whitehands, here, her hands, her mouth, my hand green jasper, pull the ring she's here. "Sorry, I'm here."

She's here kicking pillow from the feet, goddam iron cot, crashing collapse. Bunk hot, sweating, come on goddam she's here. Won't. Twist the ring.

"Isadora."

From the finger, won't can't, her hands along my leg, loin tangle flaccid limp. Goddamn. Here. Isadora Faire still here— pound the wall with a violent fist "shit!"

She recoils startled.

Silence. The light dims. She looks. He looks away. The green jasper ring on the floor. Cot twisted slant to the stead. The kerosene lamp. Red. Dress blue. White eyes. A minute. Another. Silence.

"It's all right, Sorry."

Looking away. "I." The ring. "But . . ."

"I said it's all right, no worry about it. Is there?"

"I. Well . . ."

"Is there. I mean I didn't. Did I . . ."

"No. It's."

"You just need time." Isadora Whitehands, rises, face flushed. "To get used to Cherokee ways."

"It's more than that."

"What is?"

"That's not it."

"What do you mean?"

"Who knows."

Pause. "I don't."

"I don't either." *Isadora* "You see. Right after I left high school, thinking I knew everything, I found out I didn't know anything."

"Nothing unusual about that. And what does that have to do with . . ."

"I mean who my dad and mother were."

"What are you talking about? I thought your dad died in the war."

"Oh." Long pause. "No. He didn't. My dad." Starts to slip the ring back on the little finger. Doesn't. "My uncle. It's all got something to do with land. I think. Nothing seems right, seems mine. You and Gordon being flooded out. And I . . ." Rolls the ring with his thumb and fingers. "I feel like. You see, I never knew . . ."

Isadora Whitehands pulls him back to the slumped mattress, gentle laugh. "You white men are all alike. Always looking for lost innocence. You were never innocent. No one is."

Silence. Sorry turns. Long black hair, lifts the face and looks, kisses the eyes. She wipes tears with her nose and cheeks.

"Don't worry, Sorry. It's all right."

And I knew it wasn't.

First bits of sleet and frozen rain bluster through town, shaking trees and metal Quaker State signs. Gorden and I pull into the filling station on our way back to the ranch from the city. I stay huddled in the cab, mighty cold, the heater doesn't work, and Gordon hops out to fill her up. Pretty quiet the whole trip, I'm wondering just what the hell is happening, is going to happen tonight, want her to, but, I know she'll come again. What if. Damn jasper ring. Deep in my sheepskin coat. I'm trying to disappear in the corner warmth, consolation, hissing freezing rain across the hood and windshield, thinking all along the day was up to no good. I'm sitting there trying to keep it all out, the sleet, the wind, the memory, the angry voices.

Angry voices?

Goddamn! Wendall Sorethumb and his brother hassling Gordon in the sideview mirror. Wham! Got him up against the side of the pickup, up to no good, waving a pistol in his face.

Shit. I leap from the cab, cold, goddamn, not a good day, on a better day would of had him, headgear right in the old, but make a weak, cold arm tackle, scuffling, ice in my face, pistol, Gordon on the brother now, station owner ducking for cover, I got a wrist, forearm up down. Crack. Poke in the thigh, kicking out from what? I'm face down on cold concrete.

Boots stomp past. Swirling frozen rain, acrid smell gasoline. I jump back up. Warm flow down the leg, burnt hole in my jeans. Powder burn. "Gordon! The fucker shot me. Let's get on back. We got enough gas?"

"Gas? We better get a doctor!"

"Naw. I got medicine in the blood. It's just a scratch."

"Got to get the bullet out."

"The bullet's in my boot."

"You sure?"

"Is this what we came to town for?"

You give me fever boom. Boom. Boom. Boomboom. Fever in the morning, fever all through the night. Little Willie John.

"What is it?"

"Burning up. Like a potbelly stove. Feel his forehead."

Fever all through the night hand is cold.

"Is the doc coming?"

"Not in this blizzard. There's a drift four feet deep across the road in front of the house."

In front of the keep hot water coming house. Isadora. Purple red what? That's me. Boom. Boom. Boomboom. Hot water soaking. In the room gray dim rattle banging storm windows. Fever. Water. Isadora over me cold back of the hand on forehead ice cold ice storm. Isadora Whitehands, Isadora Faire—blond hair, why did you? Marcus. Flowing rolling prairie sod houses, roads angling muddy red, snaking across over hollows, taking on shale, blacktop, concrete. Wooden housese brick highway buildings grow expanding decay. Marcus. Blanchefleur. Lyons. Hot water flowing. Isadora Faire, Isadora Whitehands. Gordon.

"Some water, Gordon. Water."

"How's it going, man?"

"Medicine in the . . ."

Isadora Whitehands, black night into the red. In the blood. Kerosene lamp in the bed, warm hot. Couldn't Isadora Whitehands—it's all right. Understand? Isadora! Here all alone you're not all alone here but what? From what it was Isadora! To what it'll be and never is, Isadora! Isadora Faire. Fever all through the night. You are Isadora—white dress white hair bound up, smell Lysol, smell black in the night, fever all through the. Red purple need you lonely golden cup. Die. What if I die and never see her. Need Isadora Faire. Gordon. Come to soothe. White dress to soothe to. Gordon!

"What?"

"Gordon! Go get her. Isadora Faire. I need her. Need her, will you get her, Gordon, go get her, you understand. Ball play together, bucking bales. Not a cause. Effect. Go get her—Isadora!"

"Take it easy, brother."

"What? Gordon."

"You've been talking out of your head, man, feverish."

"What was I saying?"

"All sorts of crazy shit, man. Saying Isadora was fair."

"Oh." I'm hot, sweating, miserable chill, leg swollen aching. Look up at Gordon Starvingdog. My brother. Why not my brother. "You have to help me, Gordon."

"We're doing the best we can. No way the doctor can get here now in this blizzard. Should have gone when we were in town. You're gonna be all right."

"I don't mean that." Tears welling, blurring fever, sweat in the eyes. "I love Isadora."

"That's good. She . . ."

Teeth chattering. "Isadora Faire. I love Isadora Faire. Too. Still."

"Who. What do you mean?"

"There are two Isadoras." Limbs trembling. "I've got to settle with Isadora Faire."

"You're babbling, brother."

"No. Listen. I'm cursed. My uncle's wife, Isadora Faire, we're cursed."

"You'd better try to get some sleep."

"No. I see it now. I tried to start over, like Isadora said. But you can't jump over your own shadow, man. It won't, you're never free. I've got to see her, talk to her now, you've got to go get her. Here, take this ring, she'll know. She'll have to come. Take the Chevy."

"Hold it. You're serious?" Looks down at me. I nod. "Since you're feverish. And since you're generally a lovable cuss. And since you caught a bullet meant for me, I'm going to listen. Which means you're going to explain what the hell you're talking about."

He wipes tears, the sweat from my eyes. I start explaining. Marcus. The farm. Lyons Blanchefleur Keeper. Isadora Faire. And it comes clear to me.

Isadora Whitehands from beyond the wall. Gordon leaning over. Listening. She comes to pour hot water. Stands there in the room, blurred. Listens. Sharp. Deep black burning eyes staring down at me shimmering distorted in the steam, in the dark, in the storm. Pours hot water in the bed, goes back from the room angry. It's clear. I've got to face it down, some scores to settle.

I finish the story. Confused now. It was so clear. Feebly hand Gordon the ring. He looks at it turning it in his fingertips. Slowly sets it on the table by the bed, by the lithograph of the black-braided woman in a canoe, buckskin, moon scattered over water, bow and arrow poised for fish. Sets the ring down on the table and wipes the tears from my eyes, wipes the sweat. "That's one you're going to have to handle, brother. All by yourself. Nobody can help you. Even if there weren't no snow."

And leaves the room. And me. And Isadora Whitehands silent in the door. Feverish clear again. Effect not cause. Howling. Wind. Curling snow across windows, plumes, streams. She will not come, will not. The wind. Black. And calm. Will not come.

And there is no place to run.

Isadora Whitehands wakes. Dresses in the dark. Almost midnight. Looks in the room to see Sorry glazed eyes, sweat matted hair, red face. Staring out of dark hollows. She pulls on boots, her great coat. Angry. Hurt. Betrayed. *Nicotiana rustica* in the left hand, silver pipe in the right. To discomfit. And to kill. Steps out on the icy porch, makes way through sharp honed snow drifting the yard. The field. To the creek. Singing billowing frozen vapor. Three times.

The red snapping turtle has come now to perform.
She has come now to rest on the other side of the Nightland.
She has come now to rot!
You two dwarves are great wizards.
You two fail in nothing.
Quick I have come now to chant you two wizards the word.
Quick I have come now to put Sorry the red knife in your right
*   hand!*
Quick I have come now to put Sorry the red stick in your left
*   hand!*

Down the snow-blown drop to the creek. The sky turning blue black. Ice crystals drifting from the trees calm backwind beneath the bank. Water ice-choked gurgling over sandstone. She finds dry tinder below the ridge away from the driven snow. Midnight. Has the fire, the pipe lit, to sing again, to blow the smoke to the east, to the north, to the west, to the south. To return to the house. To the middle of the middle room. Blow smoke into the room. Where Sorry lies. Spread the ashes. To sit. And does not eat.

"Where's Gordon?"

"Gone. She will not come."

And will not eat.

Isadora Whitehands in the middle of the middle room. Staring black. Marcus has beaten me again. Has Isadora Faire, to take Isadora Whitehands away. Face it. All these years trying to find out who you are, attaching to someone else. It's not enough. History and how you fit. Not even Isadora Faire can help you now. Unhindered. Flowing. Can't go back. Can't stay here now. Can see the patterns. Make patterns. Something new flowing from what it was. And one with me just like my very hair.

Sorry, o buddy. Whatcha gonna do now?

Landscape.

Summer hot night prairie, vast rolling grass. White yellow slow coursing broad current shifting, silent air. A road. Through the hills. Fence posts barbed wire highwires. Across the plains. Distant. Low. Channels air constant, flat, undulate. The town another huddled in draws along the creeks wandering cottonwood, native elm, cedar trees, inchoate gridwork bois d'arc section line.

All whispering too.

Slow windflow through the leaves.

The sky. Tall, black blue iridescent icy green, is filled. Tumbles heavy clouds slow thunder, hear it? Beneath the sighing of the wires, the hissing of the leaves of trees.

Then the sighing stops the hissing, stops the air, has stopped.

Listen!

Deep resonant prairie. More than sound, a presence now, feel it? The absence of the air flashes, there it is! The funnel vortex! Horizon white gray, depending violet green meandering land, the sky close vibration, rumble roaring dust debris, twisted up to substance toward the town. Exploding. Houses explode one by one, churning boards brick glass wire tin popping electric arc white blue, sucking up coruscating glower into spinning mass.

Inexorable. Stark.

You cannot move.

In awe.

Open up the eyes.

In a room that is never mine.

Let's Shoot Snooker

THE smell of bacon frying. The old man slowly moving among the cases of empty beer bottles to turn it with a fork. Poured another cup of coffee from the chipped gray porcelain pot and replaced it on the back burner of the gas stove in the back-room corner by the barrel of red sawdust and push brooms, the boxes of paper towels and toilet paper. Took the toast, only done on one side, from the toaster, stooped into the old GE icebox for the butter. Took the bacon from the skillet onto a folded newspaper, drained some of the grease into a red Hills Brothers coffee can on top of the stove, back to the icebox for the eggs. Cracked two on the iron edge, stood over absently splashing grease on the yolks with the spatula. Scoops them onto a plate, picks up the bacon strips, carries the plate and the coffee cup to a table with a Silvertone clock radio. Turns it on. The news. And begins to chop away at the eggs with the edge of the fork. Listening. Body counts. Kill ratio. Ever since his youngest missing over Khe Sanh he hasn't had much of an appetite.

Scraped what was left into a gray tin trash basket lined with a grocery sack, poured more coffee and walked into the pool room. Pulled the shade up on the front door, unlocked it. The old post office building the Pizza Hut opposite bright warm early spring sun. The street crisp. Began removing covers from the snooker tables, turning on the table lights, brushing down the felt. Filled the talc dispensers by the cue racks on the wall, erased the blackboards, straightened the dominoes, the decks of cards. Went behind the bar, corrected the pendulum clock. Opened the safe, took out, counted change for the cash register. Checked the glass case, went to the back room for a couple more boxes of Mississippi Crooks. Got rag and Windex and started to clean the mirror when the door glass rattled and banged with the door. In the reflection he saw the silhouette standing beyond the first snooker table.

"Sapulpa Slim."

"That's me."

"I got something for you." Lays three bills on the rail. Two hundreds and a fifty. "I owe it to you."

"I can't rightly say I know who you are, son. Step into the light so's I can get a better look."

Limps around the table. "I couldn't finish a game up in Buffalo Gap a few years back, something came up."

"Is that a fact." Rubs his eyes with thumb and forefinger.

"Yep. But I didn't want you to think I'd run out on you."

Slow smile. "I'd never think such a thing, Butch. Never think such a thing.

Stand looking at each other. Sorry sets the leather case he's carrying on the bar. "You interested in a friendly game?"

Pendulum clock ticking. Sapulpa Slim starts grinning. Leans down beneath the bar to get his cue.

"Let's shoot snooker."